CONALL

Praise for
RALPH PETERS

"An excellent novelist."

Los Angeles Daily News

"Peters has breathed life into the kinds of soldiers
and officers that all of us have known . . .
He has captured the essence of Men at War."

James C. McBride, Colonel, Armor (Ret.)

"Ralph Peters performs with great literary skill."

Richmond News Leader

"Peters is unsurpassed . . .
in the depth and richness of his characters."

Flint Journal

"Ralph Peters is the Tolstoy of the genre . . . You'll
end up reading [his novels] again and again."

Army Times

GUCKin

PRAISE FOR
THE WAR IN 2020

"Mr. Peters, who proved himself a master storyteller in his previous books, is better than ever in this one. The plot of *The War in 2020* is as sweeping as the steppes of Central Asia . . . and its characters . . . are people Mr. Peters makes us care about, not just human props for the stunning technology that rips through these pages from beginning to end."
Washington Times

"*The War in 2020* is extremely well executed. It's big, it's textured, yet it manages to be fast, a rare and winning combination. It has numerous extended action sequences [that are] gripping and relentless . . . Surprisingly rich in characterization."
Washington Post Book World

"*The War in 2020* is several cuts above average . . . It is, in fact, of considerable literary merit. Ralph Peters is an excellent novelist with an extremely clear and readable style . . . Intimate knowledge of the military shows in every line."
Los Angeles Daily News

"*The War in 2020* is an exciting, shoot-em-up war story . . . The United States responds with its most technically sophisticated cavalry regiment, peopled by those colorful, three-dimensional military men whom Peters crafts so well."
Los Angeles Times

Other Books by
Ralph Peters

THE PERFECT SOLDIER
FLAMES OF HEAVEN
THE WAR IN 2020
RED ARMY
BRAVO ROMEO

RALPH PETERS

TWILIGHT OF HEROES

AVON BOOKS  NEW YORK

TWILIGHT OF HEROES is an original publication of Avon Books. This work has never before appeared in book form. Any similarity to actual persons or events is purely coincidental. The views expressed in this book are those of the author and do not reflect the official policy of the Department of the Army, the Department of Defense, or the U.S. Government.

AVON BOOKS
A division of
The Hearst Corporation
1350 Avenue of the Americas
New York, New York 10019

First Avon Books Printing: January 1997

AVON TRADEMARK REG. U.S. PAT. OFF. AND IN OTHER COUNTRIES, MARCA REGISTRADA, HECHO EN U.S.A.

Printed in the U.S.A.

RA   10 9 8 7 6 5 4 3 2 1

PARA MI ESPOSA Y COMPAÑERA,
KAT, "LA PASIONARIA"

"WHO DARES TO CALL THE CHILD
BY ITS TRUE NAME?"

—GOETHE, *Faust*

THEY SLEPT IN a barn in the low ground, near the rawness of the clinic they had been sent to build. A lone sergeant walked the night, weaponless and wary of snakes. The Indians swore the snakes grew to a length of thirty meters over in the Beni, although no one believed that. Anyway, snakes were like men—it was usually the small ones you had to worry about.

The sergeant—a master sergeant with a life like a battered old car—was not so much worried as exhausted. The work schedule that had been imposed upon his team was unrealistic and mean, a consequence of diplomacy, of host-government sensitivities, of ignorance. Get in, do the job, and get out. The sergeant moved with the heaviness of a man at the end of a long march. Planting one boot in front of the other was the only way to stay awake. His soldiers were so worn down he and the captain had put them on a stretched guard rotation, walking for just one hour at a time, one man at a time, to maximize rest. Under other conditions, the team would have posted at least two guards and these would not have moved at all. They would have manned concealed posts, waiting to surprise any intruders. But all the rules were different here, and few of the decisions that affected the team's members were their own. The team was not allowed to carry arms. That, too, was a diplomatic matter. So the team took a makeshift approach, each lone sen-

tinel patrolling as visibly as possible in the meaty, tropical night, hoping to deter any troublemakers. Thus far,
the only problem they had encountered was pilferage.

When his path brought the sergeant close to the barn,
he heard the sounds men make when they are weary to
the point of emptiness and their sleep is iron. He knew
the individual sounds of his soldiers the way a parent
might know them. He knew which of them had night-
mares. Picturing the other men collapsed under their
mosquito netting, with their faces spattered and fingers
swollen to bursting, he felt a kindliness that briefly
calmed the sickness biting at his gut.

They were twelve in all. Bound to one another by
routine deprivation and occasional danger, they were of
a kind the privileged back home no longer understood.
They believed that some things remained worth dying
for. They would have died for each other, although each
man much preferred staying alive. Some had children
who called every adult ''Sir,'' or ''Ma'am,'' and wives
unfathomable to those brilliant women who write books
skeptical of happiness. Others had failed at every relationship into which they had ever blundered. Some collected women or weapons, while others immersed
themselves in foreign languages and tithed to their
church. One wrote poetry, another drank savagely when
he was stateside and bored. Two were marathon runners,
and one soldier, who could ski and shoot with inhuman
energy and precision, had represented his country in the
Winter Olympics. Somewhere in his rucksack each man
carried a crushed green beret.

The team was one of the many small tools used to
sculpt the foreign policy of the United States. Each man
had at least a vague sense of this most of the time, but
for now they were too tired to think beyond working,
eating, and sleeping. They had deployed to build a clinic
for the poor of a town on the banks of a big river. Mendoza already had one clinic for its poor, but it was too
small and even poverty had a hierarchy. The existing

clinic was for the established, connected poor. The new clinic would serve the truly poor, those who had recently wandered in from the bush, imagining a better life where a road went through.

The soldiers, at the instigation of a doctor with electricity in her eyes and hands, and with the blessing of the town's noisily progressive mayor, had sited the new clinic outside of the town proper, on a bump of dirt down in the flood plain, where the shanties kept the rain out and the diseases in, and where the faces were flat and brown and no one had a trace of Spanish blood. The doctor stopped by intermittently, looking worn and hungry and determined not to be pretty in her stained T-shirt and too-big khakis. The sergeant felt drawn to her, as did everyone, but he determinedly wrote her off as one of those saint types who get everybody around them into trouble. The sound, then the sight of her dust-painted jeep always made him edgy, and he was glad she did not have the time to visit more often. The mayor, on the other hand, came down the cratered dirt road at least once a day, in his Mercedes, to inspect the soldiers' accomplishment.

The soldiers hated the sight of the mayor's car. It meant lost time. When every minute mattered. They had been given thirty days to build the clinic. It was only a matter of a small waiting room, a doctor's office, a storage room, and a primitive surgery, but thirty days was ridiculous. Although experienced in odd jobs around the world, the team's members were soldiers, not professional builders. And the estimate of time required for the project had been forty-five days, minimum. But the U.S. ambassador had decreed a shorter deployment at the last minute. His cable, an information copy of which had filtered down to group headquarters at Bragg, said there were already too many U.S. military personnel running around Bolivia "out of control." And the clinic had not been the ambassador's initiative. The commander of the Milgroup up in La Paz had been forced to compromise, since he was anxious, for his own reasons, to see the clinic built. It was, in the sergeant's view, a typical clusterfuck of the sort that occurred whenever State meddled with the military.

And the promised building materials rarely arrived on time. Or they were of inferior quality. A detail of soldiers from the local garrison had been assigned to help, but they only worked when their officers were about, which was a rare thing. Hardly more than children, the Bolivian conscripts did almost as much harm as good. They were small, mostly illiterate boys who had inherited a rich legacy of avoidance techniques. But the Bolivians had to participate visibly in order to demonstrate the cooperative nature of the project to the locals and the press. An important collateral goal of the project, so the team had been told, was to build trust between the population and the Bolivian military, whose behavior had been erratic in the past. So everything was cooperative, at least until things took a serious turn. On the thirtieth day, the president of the republic and the United States ambassador would fly down from the highland capital for a dedication ceremony. The event would have great importance for the mayor, for various other politicians and officials, and, perhaps, even for the local poor.

The ceremony, with full press attendance, would also demonstrate the positive nature of Washington's commitment to a democratic Bolivia. Off the record, an embassy officer had told the team that the U.S. ambassador hoped the new Bolivian president would stop pussyfooting and eradicate the coca crop raised by the peasants in the Andean foothills, as he and his advisers had damned well agreed to do before the election. Crop eradication in South America, the State rep continued in his terrier voice, was the key to solving the drug problem in the United States. The ambassador was convinced of it.

The sergeant had been there before, in Peru. Coca

eradication was the most enduring of a long series of promising solutions, none of which had worked. This time, of course, everything would be different, the embassy rep had assured them. He was typical State, with skin like wet plaster and eyeglass frames as wide as his shoulders. The sergeant, whose career had focused mostly on Latin America and who had been through plenty of downrange, off-line deployments, knew the eradication math did not tally and that it would have been political suicide for the Bolivian president to attempt a serious coca eradication program. But the cookie-pushers didn't think like that. Crop eradication was quantifiable and photogenic, and you could get promoted because of it. The sergeant had worked counter-drug ops in Colombia, Peru, Ecuador, and Venezuela, and he could have told the pencil-necks up in D.C. that eradication was horseshit. But no one asked him. So he went where they sent him, did pretty much as he was told, and had begun thinking seriously about retirement.

Each day, the Special Forces team worked from first light until the heavy river darkness doused them. Every man lost weight, some from sickness. They had come to the town armed only with building tools. *Narcotraficantes* controlled entire provinces, but Bolivia was a big country and the town was not in drug territory. You could tell by the poverty and unpaved streets. In any case, the ambassador's standing policy ruled that none of the U.S. service members who deployed to train or build or vaccinate would carry weapons in ''his'' country. Carrying weapons was a provocative, political act. And the consensus was that the narcos did not want to harm Americans. American deaths would only mean trouble.

So the team had deployed to the town, which was right at the end of the world and just across the river from Brazil, to conjure a clinic where the poorest poor could go for salve or pills or to have surface tumors cut away. There was intermittent cholera and meningitis out in the bush, dengue fever, and, sometimes, plague, and most of the population had parasites. No one really knew the infant mortality rate because no one really knew the birth rate. Statistics were a miracle that happened in the capital city. In a moment of bitterness, a sergeant first class had described building the clinic as "putting a Band-Aid on a hemorrhage." But he, too, was a man who had spent most of his adult life doing just that and he was short-tempered with exhaustion when he made the remark.

Now the clinic was three-quarters finished. The team would need only average luck and a few more rainless days in order to complete the mission on time.

The sergeant on guard walked slowly, thinking about his world. The night was black to the point of brutality: no moon, no stars, with vast clouds witching down from the Amazon. On better nights, the huge river, tributary of a tributary, silvered the treetops with reflected moonlight and the animals spoke. Tonight the world seemed dead. The last lights had gone off in the town up on the high ground, and the shacks close by never had any lights. A man who had not experienced a great deal of darkness would not have been able to move at all.

The sergeant moved through the human pall near where the team had dug its latrine, fighting a groundwater problem. He had a Panamanian wife, a Toyota pickup with a camper shell, and a tract home in Fayetteville, North Carolina. Even now, worn out and intermittently pierced down deep with a persistent illness, he walked erectly, his posture a souvenir of a training jump on a windy day. He had broken his back on landing, after which his parachute had dragged his ruined body across the drop zone, and the specialists had wondered aloud if he would ever walk again. Since that accident he had made seventy-four additional parachute jumps and had run eleven marathons.

Walking through the brittle grass, he thought of the newest, youngest member of the team. The kid had just received a piss-off-and-die letter from a wife to whom he had become a stranger. The sergeant knew what that was like. In the sweat-soaked daylight, the kid had made a joke of it. Now, hidden in the darkness, he would be crying his eyes out. The sergeant knew what that was like, too. Then he asked himself, for the ten thousandth time in his career, why on earth any man would willingly put himself in the middle of crap like this when he could be back in the Land of the Big PX, pulling a nine-to-five, and sleeping with Mama every night.

The sergeant laughed contentedly at the fool he found himself to be, and his boots powdered a patch of dry soil.

Then he stopped.

Heard something.

Close.

Shit.

Please, God, not a goddamned snake.

He hated snakes on the best of days, although he would never have let any of his fellow team members know. That would have invited nightmarish pranks.

Dear God, he prayed with the shamelessness of a child, just don't let it be a goddamned snake. Not one of the bad ones.

He listened.

And heard a final sound of human breath.

2

TWELVE METAL COFFINS waited beside the runway. It was not much of a runway, just packed red earth and gravel, and when the rainy season came, it would be unusable for months. The mayor of Mendoza had wanted the Americans to pave the runway for him, since he had read an article about ecotourism and dreamed of luring dollars into the local bush, but Church had pushed the more affordable and realistic clinic project on him. For Eva's sake. Now the clinic lay unfinished, the runway was unpaved, and twelve soldiers were dead.

The mayor had apologized profusely upon Church's arrival the afternoon before, insisting that the U.S. Army colonel—as an old friend—ride with him in his Mercedes from the ramshackle building with the ''international airport'' sign to the basement that passed for a morgue then out to the site of the murders and the unfinished clinic, where the policeman posted as a guard showed more interest in his cigarette than in protecting the bloody, picked-over property of the dead. The mayor was an ambitious man, and he sensed losses far more important than a handful of gringo lives. The president of the republic would not visit now. Any dramatic expansion of the local tourist industry would have to wait. The mayor did all that he could to persuade Church that, given the enthusiastic friendship the people of his town felt deep in their hearts for *norteamericanos,* the horrible event that had temporarily obscured this warmth was an aberration of the sort that only happens once in a millennium. The man's fly gapped, his old polyester trousers a counterpoint to the gold Rolex on his wrist, and sweat mapped the obesity under his shirt. He did everything but invite Church to spend the night in his home, consigning the colonel to the town's vivid lone hotel, where distended native women missing teeth woke visitors after midnight to see if they had grown less discriminating.

Church understood that the mayor did not want him to see how well an enterprising *alcalde* could live amid the poverty of his electorate. But Church already knew how the mayor lived. Church knew a great deal about a great many things. He knew, for instance, that he, Colonel John Church, Bolivia's senior gringo in uniform, was responsible for the deaths of twelve of his comrades and countrymen, no matter who had wielded the guns and knives that had killed them.

It was morning and the mayor was gone now. His fine car had left a veil of red dust over the smoothness of the coffins as it raced away from the airstrip, away from all the bad luck. Church squatted down, alone, idly tracing lines in the dust on the top of the nearest coffin as a child might have done. Usually when he came to visit the town, the locals surrounded him, begging for free hops on the C-130 he controlled. The cargo plane had Bolivian markings and a Bolivian crew, but the United States had provided it, trained the crew, and maintained it. The aircraft was intended exclusively for support of counterdrug operations, but this was a restriction Church interpreted broadly. The people in this town and in others on the military circuit knew that if the plane was not overloaded—and it normally was not—a daughter could buckle safely into a web seat for the flight to La Paz and the university, or a farmer with a sick relative over in Riberalta could sit on top of a cargo pallet, if the plane was going his way. Priests hungover with liberation theology swallowed their principles for an hour or two of flight time, and nuns who wanted to fly were ubiquitous. The families of the military and federal police had first call on free space, and Church was always amused at how many people claimed such affiliations. He let the anxious and luggage-laden fool him, because helping them cost nothing and because he believed it did more for his country's image with the Bolivians than most of the formal aid programs designed by bureaucrats who never left Washington. As any of the locals could tell you, he only drew the line at hauling farm animals, primarily because the Bolivian crew objected to the mess.

Today, the citizens milling about the combination waiting hall, customs office, and control tower kept their distance, now and then crossing themselves if Church incidentally caught their eyes. When he visited the fetid latrine around the side, just past the sidewalk on which the Indian women pounded out dough for the lunches they would sell to passengers waiting for the backcountry flight to Brazil, the people he encountered made way for him quickly and silently, as though Church must be out for vengeance.

But Church was not out for vengeance. Not yet, anyway. He just felt soul-sick. The job as Milgroup commander had been planned to be his last assignment, his retirement job. But he had not expected to end twenty-six years of military service like this. With the blood of twelve good men on his hands.

He was brokenhearted, and he was ashamed. His wife had always been proud of him, and he knew Ruth would try to be proud of him now. But she was a terribly honest woman, with herself and with him. She would know that he was responsible for this. She knew everything that mattered about him, as, he believed, he knew everything of consequence about her. They had loved each other since college, and had loved no others in that time, and she had followed him to the places where the roads stopped, ever with a good heart. After his initial tour in

Vietnam as a lieutenant, his career had focused increasingly on the southern half of his own hemisphere, a "backwater" region shunned by more ambitious officers, and his wife and his growing family had followed him when and where they could. He and Ruth had backpacked their children to Mayan ruins in Yucatán and Belize, and with the kids growing relentlessly, they camped by Jesuit ruins in Paraguay and skied so high in the Andes that Carla had come down with severe altitude sickness. Up-country in Panama, Ricky had picked up a parasite that had taken a year to kill. Through it all, they had been exactly the family he had wanted, better than any man deserved. Now the kids, relying on videos and magazines from *el Norte* for their definitions of cool, were doing well at the American school in La Paz, where they studied beside the spoiled children of Bolivia's first families. Church was not worried about Ricky and Carla. They would not condemn him. They did not understand things like this yet, did not care about things that really mattered. But Ruth would know. For the rest of their lives together, she would carry the knowledge that he had failed and failed badly, that his incompetence had killed innocent men. He feared that.

He was ashamed, too, of his selfishness. Again and again, he caught himself dwelling on the personal penalties. Even after he had seen the bodies. Under the rawest electric light on earth. Men he had visited repeatedly to spur them on, trying to put a good face on the unfairness of their situation. The last time he had stopped in the town, the team's members had looked as though they were literally working themselves to death. And now they were dead. Hacked up so badly that, at first, the doctor had not realized they had been shot as well.

He had helped the doctor, a woman whom he respected endlessly and of whom he was fond, as she and her assistants lifted the disfigured bodies into the metal coffins he had brought down with him. They were poor-quality coffins, for which he had paid too much, and they were not good enough for U.S. soldiers. But there had not been much time, and these coffins only had to carry the remains up to La Paz, where a C-141 was due in from SOUTHCOM with proper containers. In La Paz, the bodies would be laid out properly, by experts flown in, before resuming their journey home. The Bolivians would provide an honor guard at the airport, and the president of the republic would likely come to pay his respects to these soldiers after all. The U.S. ambassador, for whom soldiers were, at best, an annoyance, would show the flag and say things he did not mean. Then the dead would fly to Panama, where the first full solemnity of the U.S. military would be waiting for them. The Commander-in-Chief, U.S. Southern Command would come out to salute the men who had died on his watch. Then the dead would fly on to Delaware, and then down to Andrews Air Force Base, just outside the Beltway, where the Old Guard would have a detachment standing at stoney attention and the Army Band would play slowly and heartbreakingly while widows and children rushed up from Bragg would try to make their husbands and fathers proud. The dead would go on to Arlington, or to the small-town cemeteries preferred by some families. At Arlington, the Chief of Staff of the Army, or maybe even the President, would salute his casualties. The bugler would play and another detachment from the Old Guard would fire blank rounds into the sky, their actions crisp as the autumn air. For the dead who went home to rural areas, men from the local chapter of the American Legion would fire less precise salutes, uniforms strained at the waist and tears in their eyes, making a brief little spectacle stray urban reporters would find maudlin. The earth would cover the dead, and life would go on, and, slowly, even their families would forget them. But Church would not forget them. Their blood was under his fingernails, and it would never wash away.

He heard a vehicle coming up behind him and turned to see a white four-wheel-drive with a red cross painted on the visible door. The driver, a woman all energy and bones, parked beside a derelict plane at the edge of the apron and got out as though she had no time to waste. She was small and too thin for her khaki trousers. Her reddish hair had been cut short with resolute practicality and it just fringed her jaw. Her features were European, but not markedly Spanish. Church always thought of her as a woman who had chosen not to be beautiful. She had, he knew, made many difficult choices.

She wiped her wrist across her forehead, bothered by sweat and dust, and the slenderness of her forearm appeared far too delicate for the rough work she did. She smiled, as always when she approached him, then she remembered the occasion.

"Good morning, Eva," Church said in English. The doctor always felt the need to practice her English on him, even though she spoke the language with greater art than most of the embassy gringos.

"John," she said. Extending her hand. He took it, feeling the rough strength of her small fingers. Her hands were her worst feature, misshapen, too active, tormented-looking, the skin raw. As though she had been tortured. But it was only her disregard of such things and the price of her work. She was a woman no man dared touch unbidden. Thanks to her father's power.

"Thanks for coming by." He smiled faintly, looking briefly up through the haze that hid the sky. The big rains were coming in a week or so. "You know, this is one of those times when you think you ought to be alone but you'd be glad if even a mangy old dog came up to keep you company."

She smiled again, touching at her hair in self-mockery. "So I'm a 'mangy old dog'? I knew I needed some work, but I didn't know I was that far gone."

"Eva, you're the queen of all Bolivia, as far as I'm concerned."

She turned serious again. "If I were the queen of Bolivia, I would change a great many things." Then she refused to think too much. She had come for his sake, a good doctor. "Ruth's well?"

"Yes."

"You're a fortunate man, John. You'll never be alone."

He shrugged. She was not helping much.

"And your children?" she went on. They had not really talked the day before. At the morgue. Silenced by the filth of death.

"Smarter than me. And better looking. Eva . . . who did this?" He looked at her with all the earnestness his soul could muster. "And why, for God's sake? They weren't hurting anybody. It wasn't a counterdrug op. And the locals knew it. Who did this?"

She took the question seriously. With brown eyes made foreign by a strain of green. Born and raised in Bolivia, she looked more like a woman from northern France. That was her father's blood. Although her father was not French in the least, as Church knew.

"I wish I could tell you," she said. "I wish I could punish whoever has done this. And not just because our clinic won't be finished."

"Who on earth would have done this?"

She shook her head. Unknowing. Tired.

"This isn't even drug country," Church continued. "The local violence is all cockfights and jealous husbands, isn't it? With maybe some nickel-and-dime smuggling. Am I missing something, Eva?"

She shrugged again, and he sensed that she was uncomfortable, unsatisfied. As disturbed by events as he was. It dawned on him, belatedly, that she, too, would feel responsible for the deaths. She had asked him, some months before, if he could build a clinic for her poorest patients, after hearing about one another team had built over in the Beni.

"The *traficantes* are everywhere," she said. "But

there's not so much of it here. It's still mostly up in the Chaparé and places like that. Maybe there's a little more traffic going across the border into Brazil these days, but they just pass through. If there had been a major change, I'd know about it.''

Church folded his arms. Standing close to the woman made him feel like a bear. With his big, encompassing hands. ''If not the narcos, then who? The guerrillas are finished.''

She looked down the line of coffins. ''I don't know.'' Then, abruptly, as she might have handled a rough patient, she said, ''There are going to be more deaths around here. Not this kind. But I've got two cases of cholera. Right here in town. And now I've got an emergency call from down-country. All garbled. Something out in one of the settlements near Pezas. Sounds like it could be cholera, too. I'm heading down to have a look.'' She glanced up at the dreary sky. ''God, it never ends.''

''I suppose the clinic would have been a help.''

The doctor shrugged. ''Not so much, in this case.'' She was a thoughtlessly honest woman. All of his favorite women seemed to be like that. ''They always wait too long. By the time they get to me, most of them just need a place to die. Nothing much I can do. Water, salt, and sugar. And hope for the best.'' She made a lost face that only lasted for a second. ''La Paz doesn't know we exist. Except when there's an election.''

''Eva? I want to ask you a favor.''

She looked at him. Wary despite herself. An attractive woman, or at least a woman who could be attractive, alone in the middle of a very male continent.

''Yes?''

''Could you talk to your father? See if he knows anything at all about this?''

She pulled away from him. It was only a matter of an inch, perhaps even less, but she had withdrawn. ''I don't speak to my father. I've told you that.''

''I know. I understand. It's just that—''

"And why should *he* know? He's in Santa Cruz. This is a local matter."

He could not let her go yet. "Eva, you and I both know that when somebody decides to kill twelve U.S. soldiers, it isn't likely to be a local matter. This isn't Colombia. Death still matters here. And your father knows more about what goes on in this country than anybody else on the continent."

"You give him too much credit," she said, as though talking to a stranger or even to an enemy.

Unexpectedly, he felt anger toward her. Her father could have built her an entire hospital. Ten of them. But she was so damned proud. He almost told her what he was thinking, but then he saw her again, a slight, prematurely aging woman who could have had any life she chose and who had chosen to spend her life among a thousand miserable varieties of death.

"Forget it," Church said. He turned away slightly. "Let it go."

She moved toward him again. "I'll ask around. I'll find out everything I can. I want to know, too."

He nodded.

Her expression changed, and she crossed a forearm between her small breasts, as if she were about to scratch her shoulder. "John?" She changed her stance so that he could not see her eyes at all. "Something's wrong. I mean, obviously there's a great deal wrong. But there's something about the deaths . . . the way they died . . . I don't know."

He looked at her with renewed interest. "Such as?"

She shook her head, and limp hair brushed the line of her chin. "I can't say. It's as though a voice is calling to me, but it's faint and I can't make out the words. Something's nagging me—is that the correct usage? 'Nagging?' "

"Eva, you speak better English than the United States ambassador."

She curled one side of her mouth, looked around. "I

worry that I'll forget it here.'' She looked around at the scrub jungle sneaking over abandoned fuselages. ''Sometimes I think I'll forget everything.''

''So what's nagging you?''

A forlorn dog nosed out of the brush just beyond the federal police guard post and wandered onto the runway.

''Look,'' the doctor said. ''There's your mangy doggie.''

Church had to smile. ''I guess a mangy old dog isn't such an attractive proposition, after all.''

''So I'm at least preferable to this individual dog?''

''Eva, if I weren't married—'' He stopped himself. It was an idiotic, ill-mannered sort of thing to say.

They watched the dog lope off into the brush again.

In her abrupt manner, the doctor said, ''Well, I'm sorry. For everything.'' She looked up at him as if questioning a patient, with no question off limits. ''Will this be bad for you, personally?''

He snorted. He did not even see her standing in front of him now. ''Not bad enough. Not as bad as I deserve.'' He looked up at the sky, searching the haze for his C-130. ''I suspect they'll just retire me on schedule. We were going home on terminal leave for Christmas.'' He thought about it. ''Of course, they might keep me on active duty a little longer, until all of the inquiries are wrapped up. I'll get spanked. But the no-weapons policy was the ambassador's pet pig, and an ambassador cannot be wrong. Certainly not a well-connected ambassador like Ethan Rice Plymouth.'' He raised his right hand in mock blessing. ''When the dust settles, everybody will write this off as the cost of doing business.''

She lowered her eyebrows. ''They won't try to find the killers?''

''Oh, they'll try, all right. Not just the military. We'll have the DEA and CIA and every Bolivian we've ever bought calling in the chips on this. Henry Vasquez is going to make life hell for every two-bit narco between here and Paraguay. And we might actually find the killers. And, if we find them, there's a slight chance we might even be able to punish them. But—'' He stopped short. Wary of the sin of despair.

''You were going to say . . . it won't bring these men back.''

''Yes. That's what I was going to say. More or less. But it's the sort of thing that's been said too many times.''

''Still . . . 'when all of the dust settles' . . . you intend go back home and be a teacher?''

''If they'll have me.''

''You'll be a fine teacher, I think. Your students will respect you. You'll be a success.''

''Hard to see the proper qualities in myself this morning.''

''I wish you could be a teacher here.''

Church snorted. ''Down here I'm the student. And it looks like I've been a slow learner.''

The two friends looked out across the runway, into the bad-tempered scrub that came before the true jungle.

''John? Will you be coming back here?''

''Probably. I'll probably have to lead every visiting VIP on a pilgrimage to the murder site until I'm wheels-up for the States.''

She moved a damp strand of hair from one side of her forehead to the other. ''So we'll see each other again? When you bring your VIPs?''

''I suppose so. Some of them will want to talk to you. To hear your professional description of the murder scene. Anyway, I know they'd rather talk to you than to our illustrious friend, the mayor.'' He remembered something else. ''By the way—are you going to be back in town tonight, or will you still be down-country?''

She looked at him in surprise. ''You're not going back today?''

He nodded toward the coffins. ''They are. I've got to begin my penance. The C-130 went back to La Paz to pick up one Lieutenant Colonel Kurt Sieger of the

United States Army. He is the personal representative of the Chief of Staff of the United States Army. One of the chief's inner circle of whiz kids, a fair-haired, blue-eyed boy. Or so I've been told. I have never met Lieutenant Colonel Sieger, but I can tell you that he will be young-ish for his rank, probably handsome in a rugged kind of way, divorced at least once because he put his career above all else, and he will be certain that he outranks me, since I am discredited and he works directly for the Chief of Staff. He will be very bright and energetic, physically fit and capable of leading men into battle, and he will know a lot about football and enough about mil-itary history to carry on a discussion with his subordi-nates. He'll become a general, as long as he doesn't do anything foolish.'' Church suddenly realized how bitter and self-pitying he sounded. It was not his style, and he wrapped things up by saying simply, ''The chief wants his own man to find out what happened. Sieger will want to talk to you. If you're available.''

She shrugged. ''I have to drive down to Pezas. To see about the cholera problem. Or whatever it is. But I should be back by eight or so. We could meet at Enri-que's. The food's better than at the hotel.'' She smiled brutally. ''And maybe slightly more sanitary, although you're still taking your life into your own hands.''

''You'll be tired. We could just swing by your place.''

She looked at him. ''John, this is a backwater of a backwater. And, liberated U.S.-educated woman that I am, I still know in my heart of hearts that if I am going to meet two gringos in this town after five or six in the afternoon, it has got to be in a well-lighted public place.'' She smiled.

For the first time in the two years he had known and admired her, Church suspected the doctor was telling him a sort of lie. And he knew enough about people to recognize someone who was frightened.

*   *   *

DOCTOR EVA MARÍA von Reinsee Gutiérrez drove fast. She never had time to spare, and she was in the habit of hurling her jeep down the region's trails, slowing only where she knew there was a wash up ahead or on the blind curves near settlements. But today she drove even more harshly than usual, spine jouncing and the meat of her small haunches bruising between bone and the no-nonsense seat. Something had happened. Two afternoons before. And the doctor who thought nothing of operating without anesthetic or of confronting the ugliest of mankind's ailments found that she, too, could experience fear.

She drove southeast from Mendoza, in the opposite direction from the route she had followed on the bad day, rushing through country that was closer to chaco than to the scrub jungle that began northwest of the town. Parched trees and thorn bushes waited for the rains and, now and again, the skeleton of a steer lay off in a clearing where it had fallen victim to a poisonous snake or to itinerant peasants. She had no reason, yet, to be afraid down here, but every time she had to slow and scrape through a defile hacked out for oxcarts she felt a foreign coldness on her skin.

On the bad day, on the day she would think of as "the bad day" until the end of her life, she had been on her way to a string of remote farming settlements on the Bolivian side of the river. Where half of a peasant's work was beating back the jungle every day. A young man had flagged her down along the dirt track that passed for a road. Nothing struck her as unusual, since everybody knew her vehicle and the Indians would often walk overland to the nearest road, camping and waiting glumly for her to appear so she could open one of her medical bags and drain a suppurating tumor or give a boost of antibiotics to a child near-blind from conjunctivitis.

When she stopped, overtaken by her own dust cloud, she expected the young man's family to appear out of the shade. Instead, she found her vehicle surrounded by half a dozen men with automatic weapons. Bandannas covered the lower halves of their faces.

"Get out, bitch."

Yes. She got out. The young man who had hailed her stabbed a pistol into her breastbone. His eyes had the animal look she knew only from the very sick. He laughed, but his eyes did not change.

"No meat on this pussy," he said.

The other men laughed with him. Slowly, he drew his gun down over her stomach, her belly. The muzzle stopped only when it found bone. He nudged her. Once. Twice.

"None of us ever fucked a doctor," he said. "Where we come from, the doctors do the fucking." He turned his head, his eyes. "Anybody want to fuck this one?"

No one answered. It was a one-man show.

The young man thrust the pistol into her bone one last time, then stepped back. "Bitch, if I didn't have respect for your father, I'd feed your pussy to the vultures." He looked at her with the grimmest expression she had ever seen. "Next time you see him, you thank your daddy for saving your life."

Eva did not move.

The young man closed in on her again, but he did not bother with any more *pistolero* theatrics. "Listen. The people up here don't need you anymore. We're taking care of them now. You ever come down this road again and we're going to lock you up like an animal, turn every syphilitic *indio* we can find loose on you, then, when we're in the mood, we'll kill you so slow you'll think you're in hell." His eyes hunted into hers. She had never before encountered eyes that could make her feel so penetrated and dirty. "You understand?"

She did not answer, could not answer. She heard the insects back in the bush, imagined that she could hear the heat itself.

Still holding the pistol, the young man grabbed her T-shirt with both hands, lifted her up, and slammed her against the side of her jeep.

"You under*stand* me, you fucking gringo whore?"

She groaned, trying to speak, to nod, to do anything to show her acquiesence, her subservience. She realized she was crying.

He smashed her against the metal again, then did it a third time.

"Under*stand* me?"

"Yes." It was a broken shout. Then her voice came again, much more weakly. "Yes."

The young man released her and she crumpled into the dust, clutching herself, weeping.

"Do what I told you," the young man told his companions.

The other men entered her vehicle through the back hatch and the side doors, pulling out her medical kit and anything else that was not firmly attached to the frame. They emptied the bags in the middle of the dirt track, tramping on vials and syringes, bandages and implements. A tube of salve erupted near her foot, its contents coming at her like a snake.

At the end of it, the young man spit on her and said: "Get out of here."

Then he and the others disappeared into the undergrowth. Some time later, Eva heard an engine starting, followed by the sound of a vehicle moving up through its gears, fading away to the north. She wanted to get up and go, but found she could not move. She could not move and she could not stop crying. She had encountered a new self, after thirty-five years. Her father had nicknamed her his *Landsknecht* when she was eight, and she had charged through life, not ever afraid. Now she sat curled in the dust, crying and sick.

Sick. She rolled to the side and vomited meagerly against a front tire, shivering as though she had been thrust into the Antarctic. As soon as she imagined herself capable of driving, she tried to get up and vomited again, a thin off-hue broth. Finally, dutifully, she crawled toward the precious waste left on the trail, determined to salvage what she could. But she could not even do that much. She felt as though she were being watched, even though she knew the men were gone. She wiped her mouth with her T-shirt, realizing she had soiled herself in other ways, too.

On the long drive back to town, it shocked her to recognize how incapable she had become. The only thing she recalled clearly was the look in her tormentor's eyes. She could not remember anything distinct about any of the others for a long time. They were a blurred mass, a swarm of insects. Who were they?

Mixed-bloods, she decided after she had calmed a little. Yes. Not Indians. Eyes, hair, skin tone. Movements too sharp, if nothing else. Narcos, not guerrillas. Their clothing was not backcountry, and she was certain that the young man who had confronted her did not have an ideological bone in his body. She had encountered the guerrillas a few times, in her first years in the town, when they needed medical help and their cause had already faded. They had seemed unfocused and a little lost, and now they were gone. Very much unlike her ambushers. She thought again of the one who had threatened her, hurt her. Not very tall. But with a mean strength. He had spoken Spanish easily, but not with the local accent. Beyond that there was nothing else. Except her fear.

She already knew she would not go to the police. At most, they would drive up, look around halfheartedly for a few hours, then come back. The police were ever less effective the farther they moved from the town and their *cuartel*. Nor would she speak to the mayor. Because she did not trust him at all. And because, in the end, she wanted no more part of this. She would do what the young man had ordered. She would abandon the settlements along the northwestern road. For a few moments, she was able to console herself that she had plenty of work to do elsewhere. But she could not lie to herself for long. She recognized cowardice when she saw it.

She had come home and washed, unable to eat. Then she had been called for: a cholera patient. Withering, discolored skin. Rice-pudding vomit. And seeping shit. Eva isolated the woman in the shed behind the clinic and set up an intravenous bag with saline solution, following the first bag with another. The woman's eyes had already quit this world. Stupidly, infuriatingly, unforgivably, after a delay of several hours, the man who had delivered the patient mentioned that his daughter was sick, too. As if he had only just remembered. Eva found the girl smeared with her own waste, listlessly holding a homemade doll. Dying. Only after midnight had Eva been able to collapse onto her own bed.

Her maid woke her very early in the morning. The mayor himself was waiting for her. To tell her about the Americans and to ask for her help. The horrors had begun to cascade.

Eva had never seen such absolute butchery. Neither of men nor even of animals. The corpses lay on or near their bunks, except for one out in the field whose throat had been slit. He was the least disfigured, as though he had been only an obstacle in the way, not a target. The others had been hacked unnecessarily, as though the murderers had enjoyed the work and had not wanted to stop. The faces wore masks of flies.

She had smiled. A little mad. Lunatic. Her wish had come true. She had wanted the outside world to discover the town.

The mayor, too, wanted bolder type on the map. If for different reasons. He was not the absolute worst of men as provincial mayors went, and he had already brought the town a Japanese-financed nut-processing factory. Surrounded by the dead Americans, he looked utterly lost, and for a moment, she forgave his routine corruption and his bullying of the local girls, several of whom had needed to come to her, discreetly, for help.

She had wanted money for clinics and clean water.

Now there would be guns.

When she realized that Church was coming down from La Paz, she was glad of it. She knew he had nothing to offer her now, but he had become her last link with all that she had given up, with the naive, well-scrubbed earnestness of North America, with the conviction that virtue was more than fooling your priest and your spouse. For her, John Church embodied all that was good about the United States, the dream homeland she had almost adopted. Maybe he even embodied all that was good about the male of her species. As good as it was rare. Eva was truly sorry at the thought of lying to him.

She quickly made a deal with herself. She would not tell Church anything about her encounter on the road. Because it was none of his business, and because she did not want a drug war here. The narcos wanted to be left alone, she knew, and she was willing to make that compromise. But she would tell him all she could discover about the murder of the soldiers. Because that belonged to him, and she owed him that much. She knew she had failed to draw clear lines, because the chances were very good that the two events were related. But, for now, she would try to keep them separate.

Eva was good at keeping things separate.

Thinking about blood and fear and cholera, and about Church, who had looked old and absolutely shattered, Eva bounced through a dry wash and downshifted to ram the jeep up the far, crumbling bank. The vehicle grunted and climbed, then shot out onto the flat, sending a wild pig scurrying into a thicket. Roads. Someone had told her that, wherever the narcos moved, they improved the roads and brought relative prosperity. It was a world without clear lines.

She approached the first settlement at which she had planned to stop, and just short of the cluster of mud and thatch shacks, a boy waved his arms from the side of the road. As if imitating a bird. Remembering the incident of two days before, Eva almost stepped on the gas. Then she caught herself. This was a child. With a sober Indian face and ragged trousers.

She pulled off and parked by a corral woven from strands of thorn bush. The boy ran after her vehicle, stopping at a respectful distance. But no sooner had she shut down the engine and stepped into the heat than he lunged for her, grabbing her forearm with both hands.

She revolted. Instinctively. Shocked with unreasonable, unaccustomed fear. But the boy would not release her. He was remarkably strong. Everybody, it seemed, was stronger than she could ever be.

He spoke hurriedly, in an Indian dialect, and the only word she could get was "Mother." The boy tugged her toward the hut.

"Stop it," she commanded in Spanish. "I'm coming, damn it."

He released her. Leading the way, he looked back again and again to be certain she had not attempted to flee. She followed him through a desolate courtyard haunted by balding chickens. A sugarcane press stood in the center of the murdered space like a tall grave marker. Its long handle drooped.

The local huts were windowless and the interior she entered was dark brown, almost black, except where the doorlight fell. After the bright ambience outside, Eva felt blind. She oriented herself by the smell of sickness and the sound of pained breathing.

"Over here," the boy said, impatient, speaking fractured Spanish this time. He touched her wrist, guiding her toward a mound of rags that concealed a human being. A woman, Eva sensed.

She still could not see properly and touched her way until she found the woman's forehead. It felt as though someone had just splashed her with hot, slimy water. The skin felt wrinkled under the wet, the hair wiry and ancient, but Eva knew the woman was probably no older than she was herself.

"She's dying," a male voice said.

Eva jumped as though she had felt a creature at her ankle.

"She's dying. Isn't she, *señora*?" The voice was heavy, its Spanish that of the bush.

Eva turned, trying to find the speaker in the gloom.

"You," she said to the man's deep shadow. "Come here and help me. We're going to take her outside where I can examine her."

The child moved against her flank, afraid.

Eva bent over the sick woman again, searching under the rags for a pulse. The woman's hand and wrist, too, were soaking. Her odor was ferocious. Cholera? she thought doubtfully. Her senses had gone on alert.

A man who smelled of work and piss and stables edged up to the bed. The child pressed more closely against Eva.

"Take her under the shoulders," Eva commanded. "I'll get her legs. You," she told the boy, "help me, too."

Clumsily, they found places to grasp the woman and lifted her from the bed, shedding fouled cloth. The job was a terrible strain on Eva, but she often had to strain. The man of the house led the way, a dark silhouette against the ferocious brightness of the doorway.

The glare blinded Eva anew as she laid the woman down on the earth by the doorway. A moment later, as her eyes focused, she screamed.

The woman had not been sweating. She had been bleeding. There was blood all over her face, in her hair, on her hands and legs. Her skin was erupting with gore, pulsing crimson.

Eva had blood all over her hands and arms, soaking her clothes. She wanted to run, to scream again. All of it was suddenly too much. She wanted someone else, anyone else, to take charge so she could run away and hide.

She bent down over the old woman for a closer look, giving her muscles savage commands, heart rigid, intolerant of the coward she had discovered in herself.

This was not cholera. It was something she did not recognize. Something horribly worse.

She looked up at the man's stiff Indian face. "Is anyone else sick like this?"

He looked down at her. Any emotion he felt he kept inside.

"Everybody," he said.

SIEGER PACED THE barn in disgust. Blood and flies, flies and blood. The over-the-hill colonel responsible for the mess hung in the background, near the door, as if he wanted to run away. The national police captain who had driven them to the site had already gone back outside into the fresh air. Disinterested. Like the whole godforsaken country, as near as Sieger could tell.

"Reminds me of Rwanda," he said, thinking out loud. "Smells like it, anyway."

"You were in Rwanda?" the colonel's deep, soft voice asked. Church. That was his name. Church looked like the photograph of Ernest Hemingway you saw on the paperbacks. The one with the mustache and the typewriter. Sieger figured that about summed the guy up. Church belonged behind a typewriter. Typing away with his great big fingers, writing reports nobody would bother to read. Not down here in bandit country killing his own soldiers.

"Yeah. With Jim McDonough," Sieger said offhandedly, still prowling. "Just got back. Barely had time to unload my ruck."

"How was it over there?" the colonel asked.

Sieger liked Hemingway. At least the military parts. And the hunting descriptions. But he did not like this soft-voiced colonel who looked like Papa's poor relation.

"Bloody, brutal, and hopeless. Getting out quick was the smartest thing we did since Inchon." He stopped. "*Je*sus Christ."

"What's wrong?" The colonel moved in closer.

Sieger stared at the ground. Then he dropped onto his haunches to be certain of what he saw. He rose again, just slightly, and drew his handkerchief from a hip pocket of his field uniform.

"What is it?" the colonel asked.

Sieger rose to his feet, holding out the shred of flesh on a white field. "Somebody's fucking ear." He felt the rage coming up in him again, bile climbing his throat. It was best, he knew, to remain professional, controlled. But the colonel, with his graying hair and his prissy mustache and his goddamned beagle eyes, was somehow too much to take.

"For God's sake. Couldn't you at least have rounded up all the body parts before we sent them home?"

"I'm sorry," the colonel said slowly. "It got overlooked."

Sieger shook his head. "Overlooked. A guy's ear."

"It's my fault."

Yes, Sieger thought. Damned right, it's your fault. He looked at the older man again. Amber light of the barn. Twilight of this old bugger's career. The colonel looked like a bear dressed up in a uniform for a circus. Sieger had heard that Church had gone native, but nothing about him looked Latino. Instead, the colonel looked as though he should have been on a campus in New England, wearing brown corduroys and a shetland sweater, sucking on a pipe.

"Here," Sieger said, thrusting the handkerchief and the ear toward the older man. "You can take care of it. Sir."

The colonel accepted the task with an air of penitence, carefully folding the handkerchief around the discolored flesh, then placing the object in the map pouch he carried slung over one shoulder. Sieger kicked at a bloodstained cot. Everything that was left had been rummaged through: the bare-bones personal effects, the transparent plastic bags of garbage with the remains of field rations and paper waste. All of it sauced with blood. Even the earthen floor was stained black, a feast for lethargic flies. To Sieger, it stank of incompetence as sharply as it smelled of death. Lives wasted. To help people who didn't want to be helped. Worthless bastards who stole from the dead.

"So who did it?" he asked. "In your opinion, Colonel?"

Church had positioned himself by the open doorway again, arms folded. He took time to formulate an answer.

"I don't know. There are a lot of possibilities. It doesn't fit any pattern."

Sieger lofted a fallen mosquito net. Cut through a dozen times. "Your pal Vasquez says it was Colombians. Expanding their turf down here."

"You talked to Henry Vasquez?"

"He talked to me," Sieger said. "Met me at the airport. In La Paz. He's pretty energized about all this."

The colonel nodded. A slow man. Part of his environment. "Henry Vasquez . . . prefers hip shoots to preplanned fires."

Sieger dropped the mosquito net and moved on. "Tells me he's got eight years in-country. Colombia before that. Senior Drug Enforcement Agency man in the Andean Ridge. Doesn't that give him some credibility?"

The colonel twisted his lips as though slowly tasting a thought. "Henry's got credibility with just about everybody. Except the Bolivians."

"And you?"

The colonel shrugged. "Henry and I have different personalities."

Sieger stalked the back of the barn, fussing with the plastic bags of garbage. He did not know what he was looking for. But he had not been looking for a man's ear. And he had found one. Someone had discarded catalogs from Victoria's Secret and a mail-order electronics firm amid brown plastic ration pouches.

"Did Vasquez ever lose twelve men in a single operation?" Sieger asked.

SIEGER WALKED OUTSIDE, with Church following in silence. The younger man breathed as deeply as he could, trying to clean his lungs. The rot-tinged tropic air tasted delicious after the brimstone in the barn. He headed for the shell of the unfinished clinic, shaking his head again. Amazed at the great big mess of things.

"So you don't think it was the Colombians?" he asked Church again. Pushing.

From behind Sieger's shoulder, the colonel said, "I just don't know yet. Good chance it was the Colombians. Although I don't know why they'd want trouble with us down here. Plenty of crazies on the circuit, of course. I'm just reserving judgment." His voice became more matter-of-fact, less cautious. "Probably wasn't Bolivians, to tell you the truth. Not their style. At least not all the hatchet work. The Bols tend to take an indirect approach to things. They're not particularly anxious to kill anybody. Especially not gringos—we're more trouble than we're worth."

Sieger led the way into the clinic through an open door frame. Wires hung from the unfinished ceiling. The team had begun tiling one corner of the floor before they were murdered.

"Your Bolivian friends may not be violent," Sieger said. "But they export one hell of a lot of cocaine."

"That's business. The cocaine industry is probably the greatest positive wealth transfer in the history of South America. Take a look around you, man." The colonel gestured toward a spotted wall and the hungry world beyond. "If you were a Bolivian, you might think the coke trade was a pretty good deal yourself."

Sieger considered the man again. He was exactly as

Vasquez, the DEA man, had warned: soft on the locals, not a fighter. An old soldier who had stacked arms.

"So you think narco-trafficking's all right?" Sieger asked.

For the first time, anger spiced the colonel's voice. "I didn't *say* that. Personally, I think cocaine—especially crack—is an invasion we don't have the guts to fight. And that makes me sick. Knowing what crack has done to my country on my watch . . . is horrible to me." His eyes had come back to life. "If I ran the world, I'd put a lid on narco-trafficking in short order. By cutting the big boys down. And I mean *killing* them. No mercy." He raised a fist to waist level. "Sieger, to us the drug-lords look like the filthiest men on earth. But down here . . . pal, they're heroes to the folks they feed. And I don't much like avoiding the real problem and beating up on the little guy and pretending it makes a difference. That's not what being an American soldier's about." He shook his head, smacked on a nerve. "Damn it, man, I'm just trying to tell you how things look from *their* side."

Sieger brushed the back of his hand along a window frame. He liked to touch things. It made the world real, helped him understand. Out beyond the open rectangle a dirt road led between marsh grasses and low-lying fields to a row of thatch houses that looked like a display from a natural history museum. Beyond the houses, an anemic jungle began. It was a hopeless place.

"So . . . it wasn't the Bolivians," Sieger said. "But you aren't convinced it was the Colombians, either."

"I just don't think we should jump to conclusions." The colonel snorted. As if a fly had gone up his nose. "Henry Vasquez is a gutsy guy. And he's been around. Mr. DEA. But nobody knows what really happened down here yet."

Sieger watched a brown child in bright skivvies back down a ladder from the door of one of the huts. "Really does remind me of Rwanda," he said, speaking more to himself again, dismissive of the older man beside him. "Absolutely hopeless."

Almost a full minute later the old colonel said:

"You're wrong. These people are only beginning to hope."

Sieger let it pass, already bored with the colonel's predictability. Gone native, all right. Exactly the kind of man you did not want to have representing the United States in any foreign place that mattered. If this place mattered. Sieger stepped back outside and considered the national police captain lolling by his Japanese four-wheel-drive. The captain looked thin and incapable and disinterested. On the way in from the airport, he had apologized gushingly for the tragic events as they jolted past hovels with TV antennae and chubby girls wearing jeans that pushed their bulk upward and outward. Sieger sensed that if the town had a motto it would be "We're shit and we know it."

He turned to face the unfinished clinic and the pathetic old colonel who had screwed up so irredeemably. Trying to save the world instead of taking care of business. Sieger shook his head in a disgust that went all the way down to his bowels.

"It just pisses me off no end," he said, "that twelve American soldiers died for this."

IN A SHANTYTOWN on the outskirts of Cali, Colombia, an eighteen-year-old boy climbed a path between the shacks that vined the hillside. Some of the dwellings were raw, with a tentative, temporary look, while others had good walls and second or third rooms attached over the years. Electric lines hung lazily and half-clothed children played in the dirt. Older children greeted the boy with a mixture of surprise and hope, although their mothers pretended they did not see him.

The boy wore man's clothing, a short leather jacket open over a well-pressed purple shirt with thin gold stripes. The jacket obscured but did not fully hide a bulge at the waist of the boy's tight black trousers. Three men with carefully expressionless faces followed the boy up the rutted way, balancing large cardboard boxes on their shoulders. The boxes bore logos in English and in oriental characters.

"Hey, Angel," a girl with olive skin and hair dyed metallic gold called from a doorway, "what you got there?"

A smile spread over the boy's face like a stain. "That's a computer."

After a moment's thought, the girl laughed. "You can't work no computer, Angel. You can't even read."

The boy's smile contracted as a snake coils. "You're the stupid one," he said. "And you look like a whore."

"Hey, Carmelita," the girl called back into a room made of cinder blocks. "Angel got a computer."

But the boy had moved on, followed dutifully by his bearers. He finally stopped before a home that had been recently painted and that had a carved wooden door, the finest, by far, in the neighborhood.

"Wait here," he told the men with the boxes.

When he opened the door, his mother was already rising at the echo of his voice. She was short and thick, wearing a broadly patterned skirt and a Miami Dolphins sweatshirt.

"Angelito," she cried. "My Angelito."

He could not find good words, and he let her hug him. Soft familiar feel, familiar smell. Her weight pressed the pistol into the flesh of his stomach. She never said anything about the gun anymore, ignoring it.

"Where's Rosa?" he asked, looking around. Oily print of Christ with His heart revealed. Tacked-up magazine pictures of film stars and singers. A green velour sofa and chair other men had carried up the hillside as gifts for his mother. A net bag of foodstuffs hung from the ceiling, tantalizing the rats.

His mother shook her head. As though the end of the

world were five minutes away. "That girl. I don't know where that girl is half the time. You should stay home and look after your sister."

"Mama, I *do* look after her. You think anybody's going to mess with Rosa when they know who she got for a brother? I'm a respected man, Mama."

"She don't stay home. Because she sees her brother don't stay home."

"Listen. You know what I got? I got Rosa a computer. Rosa's going to learn how to work a computer. Nobody else here got a computer. Rosa's going to learn. She's going to get out of here, and you're going to go, too. We're all going to go. Nobody else on this hill got a computer. And this is one of the best."

He stepped back to the front door and snapped a command. The men hurried the boxes inside.

"Listen, Mama. They're even going to fix the electric lines so it'll work okay."

The old woman shook her head. "Rosa don't need a computer. She needs a good example."

Angel nodded. "Sure, Mama. I know. But she's got a computer now."

"Father Jaime asked about you. He worries about you. He prays for you."

"Yeah. Yeah, Father Jaime. You know what he wants, Mama? Money. Same as everybody else."

The old woman crossed herself. Fully recovered from her joy, she went on the attack. "And where you been, Angel? How I worry. A month. My boy is gone a month. More than a month. And I don't know where his sister is any day. My boy could be dead and buried. And now you talk bad about a priest, that's bad luck."

"Put it over there," Angel told the delivery crew. "On the table. Be careful with it. Mama, listen. You don't have to worry about me. I'm a man of the world. I travel. People respect me. I have talents like you don't know. I'm the best. And they all know it. Know where I been? You know where I been, Mama?" He paused, looking into the old woman's doubtful eyes.

"Someplace bad," she said. "You think I don't know."

He looked at her with boyish pride. "I been to Bo*liv*ia, Mama. On an airplane. On an airplane they sent special for me."

CHURCH AND SIEGER sat at a sidewalk table in front of a bar on the town square. Neither man would have patronized such a place in the United States, if they could have found such a place in the United States, but Enrique's was the most orderly bar in Mendoza. The tables and chairs were old without charm, and the bar itself resembled an unclean cave, but the Paceña beer was cold and it was the best place in town to sit and let the heat weaken with the light.

The two men had declared a brief, conditionless truce. Sieger had forgiven the older man nothing, Church realized. But, for this awkward evening, they shared a sense of being fellow Army officers in a bad place far from home.

"So this is the Amazon," Sieger said. He looked tired now. Travel, stress, blood. Sieger did, indeed, have fair hair and blue eyes, but he was shorter than Church had expected and not as handsome. Lean, he projected the sort of energy that has too many nerves in it, all caffeine and ambition, and his movements possessed none of the beauty prized in the mannerisms of Latin men. Sieger did not, Church judged, think much about how he did things. He just got them done. The gringo archetype.

"Yes and no," Church said. "The Pando's on the edge of the Greater Amazon Basin. But the big river's nearly a thousand kilometers away. The river you saw when you flew in is just an upstream creek."

"Looked like the Mississippi Delta to me." Sieger drank his beer from the bottle.

"Different world down here," Church said. "Different scale."

Elbow on the table, Sieger held his bottle poised in the heavy air. "And this place." He glanced toward the square, the palms, the humpbacked building with the cross. "Colonial town?"

Church shook his head and drank his own beer. Beer always tasted silver to him, he could not say why. "No. Not even the Jesuits came up here. Mendoza was founded at the turn of the century, during the rubber boom."

Sieger looked around. "Doesn't look like it was much of a boom."

Church followed the younger man's eyes. "It wasn't. Not around here. Not like it was up in Manaus or Iquitos. This was the end of the road." He smiled. "Not that there really was a road. Figure of speech."

"I guess it still is."

"What?"

"The end of the road."

Church shrugged, drank. "Well, they do some cross-border business with the Brazilians. Unimaginative smuggling. Cigarettes. Appliances. Booze."

"Cocaine?"

"Sure," Church said. "More and more. When the government clamps down in one area, the narcos move to another. They're not moving real bulk around here yet, near as I can tell. But it's starting to become a problem." He thought for a moment. "The locals don't get much of a cut. Mostly, they just look the other way. The cops for sure don't want to tangle with the Brazilians. The Colombians are bad enough, but the Brazilians are crazy. Gun crazy. Mean as water snakes, when you get them riled up."

Birds rose from the hidden river, climbing darkly and neatly into the fading light.

"So it could have been Brazilians who did the killings?" Sieger asked. "You want another beer?" He signaled to the waiter, who responded languidly.

"It's possible. Although the problem with that is that I can't think of any reason why the Brazilians would want to attract attention to this neck of the woods. They have it good the way it is. It's quiet. Nobody bothers anybody."

"Somebody bothered twelve American soldiers."

Yes, Church thought. I know.

The waiter came up and stood over them, noncommital, newly wary of their uniforms.

"Two more beers, please, Francisco. Cold ones."

"My pleasure, my colonel." And he faded.

"So it wasn't the Brazilians," Sieger said. "In your view. Or the Colombians. Or the Bolivians."

Church grimaced. "All I'm saying is that the jury's still out. *I* don't know who killed them. And I don't believe any other gringo knows. Ever worked in an embassy, Kurt?"

"No."

"Well," Church said, "I've worked in three. And every embassy has its own personality. La Paz is a shoot-first-ask-questions-later embassy—you haven't met the ambassador yet?"

"Only Vasquez. He came up to the airport to meet me."

"Well, you *will* meet the ambassador. I guarantee you. Because he's going to want to be absolutely certain you smell okay. When that C-130 comes back for us tomorrow morning, you won't just be on your way to La Paz, you'll be on the direct route to Ambassador Plymouth's office. In most embassies, the DCM runs the counterdrug show. But not in Bolivia. Ethan Rice Plymouth doesn't share his toys." Church smiled one of his minor smiles. "You might like him. He's a take-charge kind of guy, which can be very appealing to a military man like you."

The waiter delivered fresh beers with a mumbled courtesy. As darkness fell, the town's residents came out to stroll, to flirt, to sit on the benches in the square and wait for the future.

"But not," Sieger said, "to a military man like yourself."

Gently, Church waved an open hand. "The ambassador and Vasquez are birds of a feather. They get things done. I just happen to think they get the wrong things done. From my perspective, which currently may not matter very much, they generate a lot of activity without making any real contribution."

"Ambassador Plymouth gets good press. He's one of the few ambassadors anywhere I can name."

Church nodded. "He does the kind of things that get good press. And he's very well connected. He just doesn't make a positive difference."

"He's on the cutting edge of our counterdrug strategy. According to the *Washington Post*."

Church smiled. "We don't *have* a counterdrug strategy, my friend. Just a collection of uncoordinated programs allowing every U.S. agency that's ever shown an interest to undercut the work of every other agency. So everybody can compete for a share of the budget pie." He waved his hand more broadly this time. "Anyway, how many reporters from the *Post* do you see here tonight? Things look different in La Paz than they do here. And they look very different back inside the Beltway than they do in La Paz."

An old man, led by a boy, came along the sidewalk, strumming a guitar and singing in a tormented voice. The boy halted him two tables away.

"I thought," Sieger said, "we were winning the drug fight in the Andean Ridge."

Church smiled, friendly, calm. "We're not even making a dent. We're a fly on the back of an elephant."

"Isn't Bolivia eradicating coca?"

Church chuckled. "Sure. When the ambassador threatens them with eternal diplomatic damnation, they find some peasants who'll sign up to have their fields cleared for a fee paid out of a fund we've established. The actual farmers rarely see the money, of course. And for every hectare of coca cleared, the *cocaleros* plant two or ten or twenty more. The Bolivian government can't afford the political cost of a serious eradication effort. They'd have a full-blown insurrection on their hands in no time. And the *indios* may be slow to get going, but when you finally piss them off they can be mean as bankers. Hung one president from a lamppost a little while back." Church leaned back in his chair, drinking the freshening air. "Lot of history down here, Kurt. More civil wars and revolutions and coups than New York City has lawsuits. Anyway, the Bolivians try to root up enough coca to give the ambassador good press back home." He smiled again. "Suppose you were the president of Bolivia. Here's the deal. You've got a country poor as a piss-pot that barely connects to the outside world, and coca is your number one export earner. By far. And, as long as you're exporting it, your electorate is reasonably content, the rich are getting richer, and the gringos pay you big bucks in aid dollars and development programs because they're so concerned. On the other hand, if you eradicate your coca, you stop earning the export dollars, the natives get restless, and the good old U.S. of A. cuts off the aid with which it was trying to bribe you to wipe out coca. From the Bolivian perspective, eradication is a lose-lose situation. They know we wouldn't give a damn about them if it weren't for coca. It's their one ticket to stardom."

Sieger looked at him with hard eyes. "So you think we should just pack it in and let the narcos have free rein."

"I didn't *say* that. I've told you that before. Stop putting words in my mouth."

The singer, who had eyes white as hard-boiled eggs, let his child guide tug him toward the officers' table.

"What song you want to hear, mister?" the boy asked.

"What's he saying?" Sieger asked.

"He wants to know if you have a special request."

"Anything from a distance."

Church drew a fat roll of filthy currency from his pocket and chose a few of the notes for the boy. "On a night like this," he told the singer and his young manager, "music should be for those in love. Serenade that couple over on the bench across the street."

"With much pleasure, mister."

Church watched them go. The soiled white cloth on the old man's haunches. The boy's hair thick as molasses.

"So," Sieger said, "if everybody else is a member of the gang that can't shoot straight, what would you do to beat the narcos, Colonel?"

"I don't know," Church answered, taking the question seriously. "How about setting a good example? How about development aid that looks at the problem before it decides on a solution? How about teaching the military that the Army is not the ultimate electoral college? How about supporting democracy where it actually seems to be working? And how about facing the fact that, as long as North Americans are willing to spend a couple of hundred billion a year on illegal drugs, people so poor they don't have clean water are going to be glad to grow those drugs for them?"

Sieger opened his mouth to reply, then changed his mind and took another drink of beer instead. He watched two young women trail by. They glowed in the fresh darkness, with wonderful futures in their imaginations.

Finally, Sieger said, "Sir, I've got to tell you. Sometimes, the way you talk, I don't know whether you're Army green or Greenpeace."

Church let it go. He looked at his watch. Almost nine. And still no sign of Eva.

He turned to the younger man, "Dr. von Reinsee must've gotten stuck somewhere down-country. You hungry, Kurt?"

Sieger looked at him doubtfully. "You really think it's okay to eat here?"

Church grinned. "Well, it's that or go hungry. This is where the elite meet to greet in Mendoza." He mastered his face, then lost control again. "You might get the trots. But you'll probably live." He called to the waiter in quick Spanish. The waiter replied, and Church nodded in agreement, holding up two fingers. "We're having chicken stew," he said. "Limited menu, I'm afraid."

"So . . . what's the story with this doctor? A woman, right?"

"Right. Dr. Eva María von Reinsee Gutiérrez. The name's another story. For another time. She's a crackerjack doc and a fine woman and probably a saint, except I don't think she's terribly religious. She was also one of the first people called to the scene after . . . the murders. She can tell you what the whole mess looked like before anybody touched it. In case you can't imagine it for yourself." Church took a quick hit of beer. "I thought you might like to hear what she has to say."

"If she shows."

"If Eva misses an appointment, it's for a good reason."

"She have anything to do with building this clinic?"

"Yes," Church said flatly. "I was having it built for her."

"For her?"

"For the people. The poor. For whomever. Because the one clinic they've got isn't big enough and won't take just anybody, and because I'm a burned-out case who has a soft spot for anybody who gives up a chance to be a star heart surgeon in the United States to single-handedly take on the mess down here. Which you aptly described as hopeless. And she does it with outdated, cast-off medicines and the nickels she can beg from La Paz, and for all I know, she probably takes donations from the narcos now and then. But, unlike most of us, she makes a difference. So I figured, as part of a training deployment, the United States government could build her a clinic. It's a pretty routine operation, you know. We've done it before.''

The waiter came toward them carrying steaming tin bowls. The handles of two big spoons thrust skyward.

''Have realistic expectations,'' Church said.

The waiter set down the bowls. Gray liquid jutted bones. The waiter promised to return with bread just as a white jeep turned the corner, driving too fast. A phantom behind the wheel tortured the brakes and the vehicle halted just across the street from the sidewalk restaurant. The driver's door showed a dusty red cross.

''That's Eva.'' Church rose to his feet.

The engine died and the doctor dismounted with a jump.

''Christ.'' Even in the bad light Church could see that her clothing was a mess. He left the table and stepped into the street. Several of the strollers had noticed her as well.

''Stay back,'' she told the curious in a voice struggling to be calm. ''I'm very dirty. Stay back.''

Church approached her. He sensed Sieger just behind him.

''You, too, John,'' she said in English. ''Don't come any closer. I may be infectious.''

''What's wrong? What's happened?'' He knew her well enough to recognize that she was badly upset, which was a rare thing, indeed. She was trying to mask her distress as best she could.

''John, I'm going to lower my voice. Some of these people speak English. If you can't hear me, stop me. But keep your distance.''

Church nodded.

''John, I've got an epidemic on my hands. It's overrun at least one village about an hour and a half from here. Some kind of hemorrhagic fever. Maybe it's *machupo*. Or something even worse. I need help.''

"Eva . . ."

"John, *help* me. Please. Can you get one of those mobile medical teams of yours to come in? Like last year for the vaccinations? Please. La Paz will be too slow."

Sieger stepped up and spoke up. "Doctor, let me spare you any false hope. After what's happened in this town, there isn't going to be another U.S. service member passing through for a long, long time. It wouldn't matter if you had the second coming of the Black Death."

She looked at Church. Imploring.

"Eva . . . I'll ask. I'll try. But Lieutenant Colonel Sieger has a point."

"John, this is the worst thing I've ever seen."

"Worse than twelve Americans butchered in their sleep?" Sieger asked.

Church wheeled on him. "*You*," he said. "You go back and sit down. That's an order. I still outrank you, boy."

"John . . . don't . . ." Eva said.

"I said, sit down." Church repeated. "Sit down and eat your soup. Before it gets cold." He turned back to the doctor and stepped in closer to her. She made a gesture for him to keep his distance, but she was not one of the things he feared. "I'll see what I can do," he said, close enough to see the weariness in her eyes, the loss of elasticity in her skin. Close enough to smell the rancid human spillage soaked through her clothing. "I can't promise anything. That lieutenant colonel's probably dead right. But I'll do what I can, Eva."

"Thank you, John." She looked as though she was going to cry. "God bless you." He had never seen her like this. He had always believed she was indestructible.

"Go home and wash. Go somewhere and wash. Sleep. Shouldn't you take some antibiotics or something?" He did not want anything to happen to this woman. On a different continent, he would have put his arm around her.

"I'm sorry," she said. "John, I'm sorry for everything."

He nodded. This was how things ended. Badly.

She got back into her jeep and drove off before anyone else could see her weakness.

BUT THINGS HAD not ended. As he lay trying to sleep on a broken bed, someone knocked at his hotel room door.

"Go away," he called in Spanish. "I'm not interested."

Then he heard an unexpected voice. "John? It's me. Please."

He clicked on the bedside lamp and pulled on his trousers, trying to hurry. But he was stiff. Aging. Worn out.

She stood in the harsh light of the hallway, clean now, but aged with exhaustion.

"You should be sleeping," he said. "You need your rest."

"I need to talk to you. Just for a minute."

Across the hall a human cry punctuated someone else's history.

"You shouldn't be here." Church looked at her endlessly lonely face, then added, "Come on in. At least let's get you out of sight."

"Maybe it won't matter anymore. Everything's such a mess."

"You need to sleep, Eva. You'll feel better after you've slept."

She sat down on the bed, narrow shoulders turned inward on her breast. Her eyes were just about the only fully living part of her. Her eyes and her inexhaustible, ruined hands.

"I told you something was nagging at me," she said. "You remember?"

"Yes. Something about the murdered soldiers."

She nodded. Then smiled as though she had seen far too much too young. "Odd how the mind works. I was showering. Trying to wash every part of me clean. Even though I know, as a doctor, there are some things you can't wash off or wash out. I couldn't stop thinking about today, in that settlement. John, it was unbelievable. Horrible. Like something from the Middle Ages. Then, all of a sudden, my mind shot off in a totally different direction, and there it was."

"What?" He stood before her, unsure what to do with his hands. She made him feel so large. Clumsy and huge.

"The bodies." She looked into the lamp as though its shade were a window into a hidden dimension. "I've seen a lot of wounds around here. Machete wounds like that. And there's a pattern."

He leaned back against the cool wall, felt an insect mount him, and stood straight again, brushing his shoulder with a slow hand.

"John, when you're a doctor, you learn to see in patterns. Maybe that's the most important thing of all. And the pattern just wasn't right." She turned from the lamp, looking up into his eyes. "I wish the bodies were still here. So I could show you. So I could look again myself."

"Show me what? You're sounding pretty morbid, Eva."

"The wounds. The pattern. John, when somebody is attacked with a big knife, or a club for that matter, it's always the same: wounds all over the forearms and hands. They try to shield their heads, their bodies." She swallowed. "But . . . your soldiers . . . they weren't like that. When I think back, I don't remember any concentration of wounds on the forearms. Maybe a few, I don't know. But the wounds I saw were on their backs, their chests. Buttocks. Heads. Extremities hacked off." She shuddered. "The wounds I remember seeing on their arms were up high, around the biceps and shoulders."

He was tired. Slow. "Eva? What are you trying to tell me?"

She lifted one shoulder, then another, as if fighting off a chill, and put on an unsure expression. "I think your soldiers were already dead when the business with the knives started. I think they were already dead, but dead wasn't enough. Somebody wanted to make things uglier than death." She looked up at him. "Do you think that means anything?"

ON THE LAST leg of the flight into La Paz, Church stood behind the pilot and copilot, sipping from a plastic bottle of mineral water. Beyond the cockpit windows, the Andes jutted gray and white and shining, with a few breathy clouds below the peaks and a hard blue sky above. Familiar crags flanked the aircraft, a small, growling container of human beings penetrating a forbidden world. This flight path had always made Church feel exhilarated and fortunate in his chosen profession, and it moved him now, despite all that had passed.

But he did not, could not, forget his dead: the men who had preceded him on this route the day before, unseeing, forever unaware. He wondered if the big C-141 would still be on the apron when they got to La Paz, or if it had already left for Panama. His first priority on the ground would be to get to one of the embassy's secure phones, to call Quarry Heights and beg SOUTHCOM to conduct full autopsies before relaying the bodies northward. Perhaps his efforts would be unnecessary, perhaps such autopsies were part of the routine. He did not know. For him, these events were unprecedented. But he wanted to know if Eva's suspicion was correct, if the men had been shot to death before the hacking had begun. It seemed important, although he could not say exactly why. Maybe it would help in the effort to figure out what the killings meant. Maybe he could identify the human beasts who had done this thing.

And maybe the Andes would melt, Church thought, abruptly limiting his fantasies of self-redemption.

Popping the plastic cap, he took another drink of water. Preparing for the dehydrating altitude of La Paz. After even a few days down in the lowlands you had to reacclimatize. Beautiful city, La Paz. If you liked ghosts. But a bitch of a place for flesh-and-blood human beings. With its high, stingy, searing air, and the horrible water, its smell of black secrets. His wanderer's heart quickened at the thought of the place.

Church knew he had a flawed sensibility. He had never gotten Jackson Pollock or Andy Warhol or performance art. He assessed himself as unprepared for modernity, and he suspected that was one of the reasons he had fallen in love with this continent. His soul had been able to relax here, at least part of the time. And he and Ruth had reveled in the sheer unfashionable beauty of the landscapes and the people.

A peak loomed left, close enough to worry an inexperienced passenger. Church wondered how many more times he would make this flight, how much longer he would be privileged to see this world, his adopted world, from the perspective of a little god. To his front, the Bolivian pilots flipped switches and prodded controls with a professionalism indistinguishable from that of their U.S. counterparts, proud of what they had learned, of all they could do. He had given them that. And the U.S.-surplus flight suits they wore, with the colorful patches grown men found so irresistible.

He had fought the hardest fight of his life convincing a succession of ambassadors and skeptical superiors up north that in order to fight the scourge of cocaine in the Andean Ridge you had to professionalize the local militaries, the national police. To give them training, uniforms, pride. To make them worthy opponents for the druglords, proud of their country, of its honor, however

tentative, and not just of their military academy class or
their rank. He had watched the Bolivian military units
he had been able to touch move from the bottom of the
heap to a fragile but wonderful professionalism that, at
its best, surpassed the skills of neighboring militaries
that had looked down on the Bolivians for centuries.

He had fought to school them in personal responsibility, in human rights and training methodology. He had
gotten the best of the young officers to the point where
they despised the corrupt old generals who concerned
themselves more with capital politics and privileges than
with the welfare of their impoverished soldiers or the
security of the state. A few months before, he had arrived unannounced at one rural *cuartel* to find a half-
Spanish, half-Lebanese captain, just returned from the
School of the Americas at Benning, teaching his brown-
faced soldiers how to read. Church knew that would not
much impress any senators or journalists back home. But
to him, it was breathtaking progress.

The engines churned to pull the thirty-year-old aircraft
over the last jaw of mountains hiding the altiplano. The
world's highest prairie, with its endless brown dust and
the long ice-blue lake to the west. Normally, Church
roused any gringo visitors he had on board to share in
the spectacle, leading them up into the cockpit with a
kid's enthusiasm. But a new awareness of his naiveté,
of the inappropriateness of such enthusiasm, immobi-
lized him now. Anyway, he had only one passenger
aboard this time. Sieger, the avenging angel from Washington. The lieutenant colonel dozed on the commander's bench at the rear of the cockpit, and Church let
him sleep.

The airplane began descending, its engines calming to
a milder drone. In the distance, Church could already
see the new suburb up on the plateau. It was becoming
a city in its own right, a collection point for hungry,
ambitious *indios*, sprawling, poor and cancerous. La Paz
proper hid down in its enormous gulch, gateway to the

old silver mines, to the ripe foothills and the grazing plains, and now to the coca plantations.

I have killed twelve men, Church thought, through my willfulness and selfishness. I killed twelve men because I refused to see risks I did not want to see, because I had come to believe my judgment infallible.

He thought of the way the Indian women made pilgrimages on their knees, offering their suffering to a religion that had enslaved those of their ancestors it did not kill. Church would have welcomed a way to crawl on his knees in atonement, but he could not think of any action that would not be inconsequential and shabbily theatrical.

With the man-made desert of the airport spreading in front of the aircraft, Church sat back down beside Sieger, who looked like a sleeping blond boy, and locked the seat belt around his waist.

THE AMBASSADOR WAS the last member of the country team to enter the bubble, leaving the city noise and prying ears of La Paz behind. He slammed the latch of the inner door shut, sealing off the room, and slowly looked around the table before moving for his seat at its head. He was too tall for the cramped secure facility and he bent and maneuvered awkwardly into his chair, letting his tie hang askew with the nonchalance of a man who knows he need not care about such things in present company. His face had a perennial sunburn from sailing on Lake Titicaca.

"Everybody here?" he asked. He knew everyone was there. The deputy chief of mission had seen to that. But, with two words, firmly and perfectly enunciated, Ethan Rice Plymouth had taken charge.

The other team members, from Church to the CIA resident, nodded, one or two mouthing an unintelligible assurance that the gathering was complete. Henry Vasquez, the senior DEA man, sat in a corner just off the table, near Lieutenant Colonel Sieger, a guest personally invited into the bubble by the ambassador after their initial meeting.

Ambassador Plymouth settled himself at a cant, too big for his big chair. His brown hair was streaked with gold, not gray, and his untrimmed eyebrows had burned blond above eyes cold as the New England sea. Church waited out the man's routine. First, the ambassador looked at his watch. Then he dressed his cuffs, shifting to settle his jacket so it would not turtle-shell away from his shirt collar. But he never bothered to straighten his tie. It hung twisted, showing a label not as good as might have been expected.

The ambassador looked from face to face one more time, skipping Church.

"I'm late," he said. "Let me tell you why. I have just taken my one thousandth congressional phone call of the week. This was a big one. Senator Helms would like to know why the Bolivians think it good entertainment to murder a dozen unarmed American soldiers who are building them a goddamned health clinic. Pardon me if I show my impatience." He finally looked at Church. With Yankee-whaler eyes. "I, too, would like to know why the Bolivians find it a worthy amusement to cut a dozen American soldiers into bits and pieces. After I have been assured that we can stop the flow of drugs with nickel-and-dime feel-good projects and intermittent cattle vaccination programs." He turned away from Church, addressing the collective again. "Senator Helms is angry, gentlemen, and I understand his anger. *I*'m angry, too." He looked back at Church. "Now, John. Can you tell me what the fuck happened down there? Who did it?"

Church sighed, embarrassing himself. He had prepared a series of responses for the questions he anticipated from the ambassador. But none of them was good enough.

Every face around the table had turned toward him. He had no friends now.

"Mr. Ambassador," Church began, "I don't know who killed them. Not yet." He looked at the stern scrimshaw face at the end of the table. Plymouth was two years his junior, but looked younger by a decade. It was the time in the bush that got you, Church decided. "I think we have to be open to a range of possibilities."

Plymouth opened his mouth slightly, and Church sensed that the man only failed to reply because he could not think of any words sufficiently dismissive.

Henry Vasquez spoke up. "Mr. Ambassador, if I may . . . let me give you the DEA perspective on this. I can sit here today and tell you categorically that this was a Colombian job."

Church turned his head sharply.

"This has Cali written all over it," the DEA agent continued. "The dirty job done elsewhere. The sheer violence of it. Even my friend Colonel Church will agree that this does not look like Bolivian handiwork. Not even the narcos go at it like that down here." Vasquez had the rugged but fading look of a retired NCO going to seed: muscles enough, but the sleek black hair was thinning and wattles of dead skin hung under weary eyes. A swollen belly marked a life's changed priorities. "Anyway, DEA doesn't talk sources. But I can tell you this much—the grapevine's buzzing. The word on the street is that this was a Colombian job. Cali boys trying to move in, stake out turf. I think my colleague from CIA will back me up on that."

The station chief, a silver-haired man with a boy's face, nodded. "Does look like a Colombian job, sir. Can't say which family, though."

"Wait a minute," Church leaned in. "Maybe it was the Colombians. I don't have your sources. But what on earth would be the point?"

"I told you," Vasquez said. "It's a turf fight."

Church shook his head. "Over what turf? The Cali

crowd and the Bolivians have been working together just fine. The pie's big enough for everybody. The Bolivians do the production, processing responsibilities are shared, then there's a handoff to the Colombians for transportation and marketing. Everybody has their role, their niche. It's been a good deal for all parties.''

Vasquez made a dismissive face. "New crowd moving in, maybe? Or the old bunch getting greedy, muscling out the Bolivians? Maybe the Bols have been getting too big for their britches. Could be some greedy sonofabitch like von Reinsee wants to run the whole show himself and pissed the Cali boys off. So they come down here to dump on him and his crowd. Any number of possible scenarios. But this stinks of Cali. And I'm—''

"Henry," the ambassador interrupted Vasquez, "I'm willing to hear you out. But I've warned you before. Mr. von Reinsee has never been charged with a single crime, and the president of this republic regards him as a personal friend. As do I. Now, we've all heard the rumors and innuendos, but I suggest to you that a great deal of that is jealousy, nothing more. Von Reinsee's clean— isn't that right?'' The ambassador looked at the CIA station chief, who nodded his agreement. "What's more, the man is at the center of the economic renaissance down in Santa Cruz. Best thing that's happened to this country in centuries, and I do think we all want to see the boom continue, don't we? So just keep Herr von Reinsee out of this.'' He raised an eyebrow, fixing his attention on Vasquez. "Unless you have concrete evidence against him. Do you have concrete evidence, Henry?''

"No, Mr. Ambassador.''

"Then let's stick to business.''

"Mr. Ambassador," Church tried again, "what about the Brazilians as a possibility? We've been seeing more and more signs of Brazilian activity. And, if you want to talk violence, the São Paulo crowd is ten times worse than the Colombians. The Colombians just gun you down. The Brazilians are a lot more creative about it.''

"Oh, for God's sake, Church," Vasquez said. "Would you stop being contrary? You remind me of my aunt Isabel. There is no *way* this was a Brazilian job. All those boys do is truck some stuff across the border. They're more interested in Peru.''

"And *where* are they trucking stuff, Henry? Where does the main road across the frontier run? Right past Mendoza. Or what if it wasn't the Brazilians *or* the Colombians. What if it was some upstart Bolivian crew?''

"All the more reason for the Brazilians—or the Bolivians—not to call attention to their backyard.'' Vasquez raised a hand as if taking an oath. "If anything, I'm concerned that the Colombians are just getting started. This could be the beginning of a campaign to drive us out of Bolivia at the same time Cali's taking control of the business down here. Look at the evidence before your eyes, man. This has 'made in Colombia' stamped on every side of the box.''

The ambassador nodded. Slowly. Thoughtfully. "Colombians. I've been warning *el presidente*. I've been telling all our Bolivian friends, 'Watch out for the Colombians.' '' He looked around the table. At everybody but Church. "So what do we do?''

Vasquez pulled his chair in closer. "Mr. Ambassador, we have to hit the Colombians as hard as we can and as fast as we can. Here in Bolivia. We've had pretty good fixes on some of their labs for months, but the Bols have been nervous about going after them head-on. I've pulled out all the stops now, called in all the favors. Knocked a few heads. I think I've got two hot labs— one down on the edge of the Chap, another just northwest of where our boys were murdered. We ought to start by taking down those labs.''

"Those the labs the Bolivians say don't exist?''

"Yes, sir. Big-time operations,'' Vasquez said. "The Bols haven't wanted any part of it. But this incident gives us leverage. The DCM's been working this one with me. If you were to get involved personally . . .''

The ambassador made a steeple with his fingers, bringing the fingertips against his mouth. The nails of his index and middle fingers were rimmed with brown stains. He sat back. "You said one lab down in the Chaparé, right?"

Vasquez nodded. "And the other up in the Pando, in Amazonas. Hop, skip, and a jump from Mendoza."

"The Chaparé's hot," Plymouth said, each word sculpted. "The *cocaleros* are organized, they've got every warmed-over Trotskyite from the National University advising them. And they get good press. Government's on the defensive. Although I must say they play it for sympathy more than becomes them." He swiveled a quarter turn to the side. "I still believe eradication is the only answer. You know that, Henry."

"If the ops against the labs go well," Vasquez said, "maybe we can get the government energized on eradication again. One thing could lead to another. No regional or national elections coming anytime soon. Great time to smack down the *cocaleros*."

"Mr. Ambassador," Church said, trying to find an acceptable tone, "taking out labs is always a good thing. And if there's a lab I didn't know about up in the Pando, I say yes. Take it out before the business takes root up there, too. I have no problem with that, as long as we do it right and mount a clean operation. But, at the end of the day, will we have identified the killers? Aren't we just lashing out? Without thinking through the consequences? Without a plan?"

The ambassador turned in his chair. Slowly. Until he faced Church. For a long moment, Plymouth did not speak, but Church could tell by the changed weight of the air that he had been written off. The ambassador could project himself, his will, with a knack Church had never acquired, and he made Church feel small.

"Ever the voice of reason," Plymouth said finally.

"Ever the voice of reason, John. But maybe it's *time* to 'lash out.' Given that we do have a gift of leverage, thanks to those men who died down there. The Bolivians don't know if we're going to nuke 'em or just cut all foreign aid forever. And Washington wants results. The Bolivians may not have elections coming up, but we do. Maybe this is our opportunity to make the drug war a real war." He smiled. He had a wonderful, confident, accomplished smile. "Within the bounds of legality and allocated funds, of course." The ambassador cocked his head, looking past Church. "What do you make of all this, Lieutenant Colonel Sieger? As an outsider? What does a military man think?"

Church turned in his chair to look at Sieger, but the younger officer avoided eye contact with him.

"Mr. Ambassador," Sieger said, "I'm a novice down here, and I know it. But when I see twelve dead soldiers, I want somebody to pay for it. If we're convinced the Colombians did it, then we should kick their asses all the way back to Bogotá." He looked over at the DEA rep. "Anyway, I don't see how going after drug labs can be a bad idea."

The ambassador smiled again. "Good. Glad to have that vote of confidence. And I'm glad you're here. Colonel Church has been through a great deal, and he needs a rest." He turned to Church. "You do have plenty of other things to do, don't you, John? I want you to take a week or two off." Without waiting for a reply, the ambassador returned his attention to Sieger. "Kurt— your given name's Kurt, isn't it? Kurt, I want you to work with Henry here on the military support we need to hit those labs. Colonel Church has built a good Milgroup team here in the embassy, and they'll be able to help you out. For my part, I'm going to shake some of the dust off our Bolivian friends. The siesta's over. I'm going to make Bolivian support for these ops a test case." He looked around the room. "Any questions?"

Church sat in silence. He did not recall any other time in his life when he had felt so broken.

"Good," the ambassador said, straightening his tie at last. "You all know what to do. Let's really fuck 'em."

THE OFFICE OF the Commander in Chief, United States Southern Command, sits on the back side of Quarry Heights, on the edge of Panama City. Quarry Heights is a military reservation that commands both the city and the great bridge spanning the Pacific entrance to the canal. Like the other forts and air bases in Panama from which the U.S. military is ebbing, Quarry Heights is a wonderful relic of the days when the United States did not have to give a damn about anybody else's opinions, and it has many ghosts, some of them in weathered campaign hats, others in white linen dresses, and darker-complected wraiths with tragic eyes.

The administrative buildings, shaded by enormous trees, and the fine old officers' quarters designed to withstand heavy rains and sneaking jungle have been left to decay gently, since the United States presence will be gone by the turn of the century and there seems no point in major investments in maintenance. There are wonderful birds, sometimes monkeys, and, occasionally, startling reptiles in the backyards, and some of the views away across the canal to the jungled mountains make old soldiers stop and wonder at the enormity and achievement in which they have played their small, twilight parts. A huge Panamanian flag flies atop the hill now, symbol of the sort of progress championed by men and women back in Washington whose opinions have never been tainted by experience.

The CINC's office is on the second floor of a building just across the street from a maze of bunkered tunnels. To get to it, visitors must pass a succession of guards, outer-office staffers, secretaries, and, finally, the general's executive officer. The Commander-in-Chief, U.S.

Southern Command has ever fewer troops and a shrinking budget. He is constrained by legislation, interagency squabbles, and the labyrinth of Latin American politics. For all that, he remains the single most powerful man south of the Rio Grande, and the only one able to reach across borders, mountains, and rivers to influence an entire continent. He is chosen with great care.

The current CINC, General "Black Jack" Parnell, decorated his own office. Each photograph or historical picture, each book and every souvenir has been selected and positioned for its effect upon the visitor. Any visitor important enough to enter the CINC's office learns from the visible evidence that the CINC shakes hands with presidents and loves his family, that he is abreast of the current literature important to his region or to Washington, which is usually not the same thing, and that he is proud of the military tradition he serves.

The CINC himself never surprises his visitors, because he looks exactly as they secretly believe a four-star general should look. Handsome, with a face carved from Irish-American granite, he looks smart, serious, and capable. Few guests ever realize that his left arm is crippled. He is a survivor, capable of fighting as savagely and cleverly in Washington offices as he fought in Vietnam and during Operation Desert Storm.

There is a high price that goes with his title, however. His time is never his own. He is often away, gone south or gone north, and when he sits at his desk in Panama, his staff fights a constant holding action to keep him on schedule. Five minutes of his time can decide what happens in an allied country for the next year, and an hour can, without fanfare, shift the foreign policy of the United States. He resembles nothing so much as one of the great consuls from the apogee of Rome's empire.

THE WINDOWS OF the CINC's office had gone dark under the afternoon rain clouds, and down on the walkways and in the parking lot officers and civilian employees hurried to beat the inevitable late-September downpour. A delegation of Panamanian businessmen had just left, after asking if the general did not think there might not be some clever way of maintaining a U.S. military presence in Panama, despite the canal treaty. The general had been generous with his time, warm with his words, and utterly noncommital. He had his views, and his strategic goals were not dissimilar to those of the Panamanian businessmen, but their rationales were utterly different. The businessmen, the CINC knew, wanted the U.S. to stay because they had belatedly realized how important the troop presence was to the local economy and, even more important, because a stabilizing U.S. presence made the country safe for the international banks sprouting downtown and along the waterfront to launder the hundreds of billions of drug dollars that flew across the hemisphere.

The CINC hated drugs and anyone who touched them. But, although the decision was almost final to move his headquarters to Miami, he would have preferred to keep it right where it was. He was a soldier with experience on five continents, and he knew that you could not feel the pulse of Latin America from the continental United States any more than you could get a feel for Africa from Alabama. To make a difference, soldiers had to be out in the world and part of it. And he understood that the U.S. stake in Latin America was growing just when Washington's means of influencing Latin America were withering away. As a second lieutenant, he had chased snipers through the back streets of Santo Domingo, and he knew that diplomacy was nothing but a night on the town as far as the Spanish-speaking world went—you felt great while it lasted, but woke up with a headache and empty pockets. Only two sources of power made a lasting difference down here: money and military contacts. It wasn't only the French who voted their pocketbooks. And politicians came and went, but the colonels stayed forever. Especially in this newly democratized, merrily truculent Latin America, the local militaries were the greatest source of continuity.

With his visitors gone, the CINC briefly massaged one of his thighs with his good hand. He had taken a hit above the knee during his first tour in Vietnam. That one hadn't been a showstopper like his shot-up arm, but just before the rain came, the ghost of the old wound woke down deep. He called on the intercom for his aide to bring in the cable book.

Instead of his aide, the XO showed up in the doorway.

The CINC looked up. He did not say anything. He did not need to say anything.

"Sir," the XO, a conscientious, overworked colonel, said, "I just got a call on the STU from John Church. He wanted to talk to you personally, but I told him you were busy."

The CINC shook his head, absently rubbing his thigh again, unable to touch the deep hurt. "And?"

"Sir, he wants you to hold the bodies from that A-team massacre here for autopsies. To find out exactly what killed them. Apparently, they only had the time and facilities to do a half-baked job on the site and he suspects something."

The CINC sat back. With a sharp, slapping sound, the rain came. Dense as oil. Beyond the windows the sky had entered a false night.

"He's probably clutching at straws," the CINC said. "And, if I were in his shoes, I would be, too."

"Sir, for whatever reason, Church thinks the men were killed first, then hacked up just to make a show. He thinks there's something really wrong with this."

The CINC's hand stopped along his trouser leg. He did not say anything for a moment, and his XO, who had survived longer than any of the CINC's previous XOs, knew he was supposed to wait and not interrupt the general's thoughts.

"Interesting," the CINC said. He smiled. He had two

smiles, one small and wintry, the other big and Irish. This smile was the January variant. He had met Church a few times and had his own opinion of the man, but he asked the XO, "You know Church?"

"Sir, I've met him. But I don't know him."

The CINC swallowed the smile. "Never thought much of his programs down there. No real results, nothing tangible." The smile crept back. "But you know something, Tim? I *trust* that sonofabitch. As a man. He's the only one in that ego-ridden embassy who knows a damned thing about the country he's in. Now . . . what if . . . just what if old John Church is onto something?" The CINC snapped right to business. "C-141 still on the ground?"

"Yes, sir. Medical clearance, quarantine exemption and all that. Takes a few hours. You want me to hold the plane?"

The CINC pushed a button on his desk, summoning his sedan. Then he told the intercom, "Get the head of the hospital on the phone. Tell him I'm coming down the hill to talk to him. Privately. No straphangers." He looked back at his XO. "Get Jim Mackesey and tell him that airplane has a safety problem he hasn't found yet and it isn't going anywhere until tomorrow morning." The CINC thought. "Then call Bill Black up in Crystal City. Tell him that plane's going to be a day late and that he should start dancing. By the time the questions filter back down here, it'll be tomorrow morning."

"How much do you want me to tell Bill, sir?"

"Nothing. Just that the plane's going to be late. The less he knows, the better. For his sake. This is going to throw off a lot of schedules. Everybody's going to want to know what's going on, including the press. And, if there's anything to this, they don't need to know about it. And the Hill doesn't need to know, either. Not yet."

"Sir, are you sure the autopsies can be done by tomorrow morning?"

The CINC looked up icily. "They'll be done. Or

there's going to be one unhappy head surgeon in Old Panama.''

"Got it, sir,'' the XO said.

The CINC stood up, and thunder boomed out over the canal. He leaned over the intercom box again, pressing down with one finger. ''Reschedule anything I've got that can wait for another day, and push the rest of it back to sixteen hundred.'' Then he smiled at his XO. This time it was the big Irish smile.

"Knowledge is power,'' the CINC said.

ANGEL WALKED INTO the computer store with a very different attitude. The morning before, he had entered nervously, unsure of his place in this forbidding world of machines that could do anything. He had not even been certain he belonged in the increasingly wealthy shopping streets of his own city, despite his bravado. He had been cautious, patient, uncharacteristically humble. He had allowed the salesmen to take advantage of him, and he had paid cash, without bargaining. His attitude was very different today.

It was business now, and he had not been in the bright new shop five seconds before he knew that three of the five people present worked there and the other two were customers. He knew exactly where they stood, and he could sense which way they would move next, where they would be in ten seconds or in thirty. He did not intend to stay long.

The manager recognized him, smiled in welcome, and hurried toward Angel, strutting forward between the aisles of screens and boxes and keyboards.

Angel moved steadily forward as well.

The manager stopped in front of him, his smile suddenly more tentative.

"What can I do for you today, Mr. Domínguez?''

"I was Mr. Domínguez yesterday,'' Angel said. "Today I'm somebody else.''

The manager's smile disappeared. A second employee came up from the side.

"You sold me shit," Angel said. "My sister can't make it work the way you showed me."

"Does your sister understand computers?" the manager asked.

"Maybe you didn't buy all the programs," the clerk said.

"Or it could be an installation problem," the manager went on. "The Compaq 650 is a tremendous machine, the best, just like you asked for."

"You fucked me," Angel said. He moved far more quickly than the manager or clerk could have suspected, accustomed as they were to the slovenliness of petty thieves. Angel shot each of them once, perfectly, in the middle of their faces. Then he shot the other three people before they could react in any way, grateful that they were all male. He did not like the idea of hurting women. Each target received one bullet in the head.

Angel did not bother to check his work. He was a confident young man, on his own ground again.

Before leaving, he took one last dismissive glance around the shop.

"Computers," he said, and spit.

"IT'S A HEMORRHAGIC fever of some sort," Eva told the mayor. They sat in the man's home office, where he preferred to spend the hot afternoons when he did not feel the urge to be with a woman. Eva gulped the coffee a servant had delivered, energizing herself with the near-scalding liquid. "A very bad sort."

She had been on the phone to La Paz most of the morning, battling bad connections, absent officials, and sheer bureaucratic inertia. When she had gone to school in the United States, she had often heard the people complain about their bureaucracy, but they had no idea, really. Here, one official out of three was off with his

mistress, a second was tending to private business, and
the third was very sorry, but nothing could be done.
Maybe a fourth promised that something would be done
just to get off the phone. Everything had to be bargained
out face to face, and even that was no guarantee. And
she had no time to travel to La Paz.

The mayor's jowls sunk even lower than usual, and
the liveliness of fear woke in his eyes.

"*Machupo?*" he asked, voice just above a whisper.

"Maybe a mutant strain," Eva said. "I can't tell. A
virus, though. That's almost certain. It's got that kind of
speed and lethality. It looks even worse than machupo
to me. Kills faster. Kills more. There's hemorrhaging
right through the skin."

"Could you be infected? Should you be here?"

"If we're really lucky, it'll just burn itself out. It's
pretty inefficient, from the point of view of a virus. It
appears to have a short incubation period, then the victim can die within twenty-four hours of onset. A smarter
virus would keep its host alive longer." She remembered to whom she was speaking. "Anyway, we can't
count on luck. This is ugly, and bad, and if it spreads
to town, you won't have any tourists for a long time.
And the nuts from the factory might be quarantined."

"They can't do that," the mayor said, voice rising.
"Nuts don't have anything to do with it."

"And they'd have to close the airfield. Except for
military flights."

"That's impossible." The mayor's breasts jiggled like
those of a thickset old woman. "But this thing might
just go away?"

Eva nodded. "Or it could sweep right over us all. The
Indians come into town all the time to buy things they
need."

The mayor's coffee cup shivered in his hand. "We
can set up roadblocks. Keep the Indians out."

"A lot of them just walk in through the bush."

"We'll forbid them."

"The disease could already be here. Incubating."

"Listen, my friend. My esteemed Dr. von Reinsee. We have to control this thing."

Eva leaned forward. She had slept a little, eaten. Then she had gone to the established clinic to talk to the town's other doctor, a highlander who had gotten into serious trouble at a hospital in La Paz and had come to the town unexpectedly. The locals who had any money welcomed him, certain that a male doctor, even one with a troubled past, must be better at his trade than a woman. She had described the situation in the villages to Dr. Mandia and arranged for him to handle her cases while she was gone during the day, although she knew he would neglect those who could not pay. For his part, he was glad to leave the epidemic to her and he assured Eva that he would move heaven and earth so that she would have no additional demands on her time.

"What I ask you to do," she told the mayor, "is to call everybody you can think of in La Paz. Beg them. Threaten them, if you can. But get medical personnel and medical supplies down here quickly. We need a lot of antibiotics. Just about anything is better than nothing, since we have no idea what might work. And you need to have full authority to order the federal police to set up quarantine lines, if and when we have to. The military might have to help bury the dead. Or burn them. I'll work that out." She looked at the older man, whose sun-darkened face was missing its usual confidence. "We may have to burn out some of the settlements. There may be nothing else we can do."

"But . . . then they'll know. Can't we keep this quiet? Until we see where it's going?"

Eva started to lecture him, then caught herself. Instead, she simply said, "I've already informed La Paz, the people I know. You can't keep a thing like this a secret."

"You *told* them?"

"People are dying. I only got to three settlements, and

they were all infected. One is nearly wiped out. A disease like this could kill half the people in this town. More than half.''

"So La Paz already knows." He lowered his eyes. "That's bad."

"Mr. Mayor, I need your help. This town needs your help."

Their empty coffee cups rested on the table between them.

"Yes," he said resignedly. "I'll do what I can, of course."

THE MAYOR WATCHED the doctor drive off, cursing her to himself. He needed time to think, time to make a plan. But some things, of course, would not wait.

"Fortunata," he called in a loud voice. Then, without giving his wife time to respond, he shouted as loudly as he could. "Fortun*ata*."

His wife appeared in the doorway, willing to come no closer unbidden, long familiar with her husband's anger.

"Fortunata, my love, my wife," he said in an unexpected voice. "You're going on vacation. With the children."

His wife looked at him in surprise. "But when?"

"Today. Now."

"But Miguelito . . . the school . . . and—"

"Damn you to hell, bitch," he shrieked. "You do what I say. Now you pack. And get the children ready."

She began to cry. "But where will we go?"

He walked toward her. She recoiled. But he had changed yet again. He took her in his arms with a tenderness she had nearly forgotten. "You can go anywhere you want, my beloved. And it's not what you think. I know what you're thinking, and it's not that. But you and the children have to be on the flight to Santa Cruz this afternoon; you'll have to hurry. Maybe you can visit your sister in Sucre."

"But *why*?" she asked, simply not understanding him.

He patted her shoulder, remembering all they had shared. He could be a very sentimental man, and he knew he had not always been a perfect husband.

"Because the world is as it is, my life. Now go pack."

After a last, furtive hug, she pulled away and hastened to do as she had been told, already wondering how much money she would be allowed and if she could not, perhaps, bargain a shopping trip to Buenos Aires out of the situation. She had not been there in . . . in almost five years.

The mayor watched her go a few steps, then turned back to his office to deal with men's work. He noticed the two empty coffee cups still on the table.

"Fortunata," he called after his wife.

She stopped at the foot of the stairs, looking back at him.

"Have María come in here and take away these coffee cups. Then I want her to clean my office. To give it a thorough cleaning."

His wife smiled, already moving. "I'll take the cups," she said.

The mayor stiffened. "No," he said. "Have María do it. And she isn't to wash the cups. I want them destroyed."

CHURCH DECIDED TO leave a bit early and walk home from the embassy. He liked to walk. It gave him time apart, time to think. But first he took care of the chores waiting on his desk. They were small matters in the great scheme of things, but each was important to one or another of his subordinates. He proofread and signed an efficiency report on a warrant officer, approved a temporary-duty travel claim, signed a requisition for toner for the copier, and returned two phone calls before changing, heavily and sadly, into the civilian clothes he kept in his office.

The word was out on the ambassador's meeting. Church's staff, uncertain how to act around the fallen warrior, sought ways to avoid his eyes as he was leaving. The officers and secretaries bent low over papers or plunged into officious conversations in side offices. Only Captain Darling, his aviation expert, risked an attempt at solidarity. Darling followed Church out into the hallway. The younger man's elegant brown face grew unstable with emotion as he told his boss, "Sir . . . I just wanted to say . . . that you're the best damned officer I've ever served under." It was awkward, if well-meant, and Church thanked him and told him to take good care of Sieger.

He went downstairs and out through the warren of hallways, waving casually to the Marine sergeant manning the guard post. The embassy was housed in the upper floors of an ailing commercial building across from the La Paz city hall, a reminder of the days when events in Bolivia did not resound in Washington. A splendid new embassy was scheduled to open soon.

The street was bright and pungent with the weekday flow of small businessmen, money changers, vaguely employed women in European-style clothes, and the shuffling Indian women—walking Christmas trees of petticoats, topped with derbies, lugging children or goods on their backs. The Indian women seemed to live in a different mental dimension, asymmetrical to progress, and they moved as though they saw neither buildings nor buses nor anyone not part of their world. Picturesque from a middle distance, up close they offered a lesson in how negligible a difference the centuries of government rhetoric and decades of aid programs had made in the lot of the native population.

Church wondered if he had made any difference at all.

Turning onto the Avenida Mariscal Santa Cruz, he walked downhill past the traffic-island mounuments to failed heroes and neglected art nouveau facades, past cafés advertising German pastries and high-rise buildings housing foreign companies on tax vacations or hotels whose names changed every few years. It always struck him as odd that you could feel real affection for a city, and especially for one such as this, with its wretched sanitation and disregard of old beauties, with its passion for all the wrong ideas and its creative feudalism. Yet he adored this city of hidden churches, poisoned drainage, and pouting women, seduced by its alternating bouts of manic activity and sloth. Perhaps, he thought, he loved it because he and Ruth had been so happy here.

Until now.

He had not lost much of his acclimatization in the lowlands this time and he walked well. Striding down through the exhaust fumes, their stench especially sharp in the high, thin air. He stopped for a beer in a snack bar across from the university, his favorite people-watching spot, and took a seat by the window next to a longhaired, travel-crusted couple who wore dirty, disparate bits of native weaving and spoke something Scandinavian. The male looked as though he intended to save the rain forests by becoming one, and he and his broad-faced companion appeared stoned and unaware and very far from home.

He had walked so that he could try to think clearly, so that he could be alone for a bit before he had to face Ruth with his failure, but he was not quite ready to think yet and he gave himself over to the bite of the beer on his dry tongue and the look of the world beyond the windows. The grubby national university across the street was so crowded you expected students to spill out of the upper windows. The`students were all Indians or mixed-bloods. The white elites would not have dreamed of sending their children here. The old Spanish families, or the more recently arrived Germans and Middle Easterners whose energy had demanded an accommodation with the traditional ruling class, sent their children to Stanford or Yale or, if they were not terribly bright, to some minor U.S. college that needed the money. You had to have a gringo education to go anywhere. Or even to marry decently.

The students across the street from Church and his beer were brown-faced, hope-faced, dull-faced, love-faced, milling and merging like students everywhere. A few drooping banners hung from the main building, leftovers from a *cocalero* march on the capital. The peasant leaders, rarely peasants themselves, had accused the government of caving in to the Yankees and destroying the livelihoods of its own poor farmers through the on-again, off-again coca eradication program, and they had bought themselves another respite. The situation was not entirely clear-cut, though, and the quality of the march-ers' banners had been too professional for student work. It looked as though the big cocaine interests had financed them. But the coca-growing peasants had been more right than wrong. Church had surveyed the demonstration in the company of a Bolivian officer. When the long march climaxed peacefully in front of the marvelous mixed-message facade of the Church of San Francisco, the Bolivian, a man of the old school and of moderately good family, said dismissively, "Coca has done nothing for them. At most, they have a radio now." And Church had thought, yes, that seems like nothing to a man who has always had a radio.

Well, his contribution to Bolivia was over now. For what little it was worth. He finished his beer and went out past a khaki-uniformed policeman flirting with the cashier. The policeman was blessedly oblivious to the leftover hippies, who were dancing on the edge of a cliff in a foreign place they clearly did not understand. Church silently wished all of them well. The single beer calmed him, even gave a tiny hint of pleasure, and he only smiled, bemused, as he walked past a red scrawl of graffiti: *¡Fuera yanquis del Chaparé!*

Yes, Church thought, why not. Because, *mis amigos*, the global village has a drug problem, and you are the only part of it they can see or hurt with any regularity. Because everybody's right and everybody's wrong and I'm too tired to sort it out now. He wondered if Ruth had remembered to pay the gardener.

It was a long way down the valley to his house, to the wonderful house he and Ruth had decided to rent, even though the cost exceeded his allowances. He lived down in the unfilthed valleys, where the the only Indians were servants or gardeners. Because, he and Ruth had reasoned, life in La Paz would be hard enough. When the truth was that they were just tired of the hard edges of their itinerant lives and wanted something approximating the safety and comfort of home. Someplace clean. The years were beginning to tell.

He walked down past the new luxury hotel, past mini-slums clinging to steep embankments, waiting for a hard rain to sweep them into the ravines, past small cemeteries and parks and shoe-repair shops, past neighborhood bars and grocers, then past walled-off estates and, far along, he marked the handsome tower of the new USAID building in the background, a structure that the agency's senior resident, a master of creative accounting, told visitors "did not cost a single U.S. tax dollar." It was the sort of self-delusion Church had always mocked, and of which he now found himself guilty. The millions that had bounced back and forth between government accounts to build this monument to the U.S. government's good intentions were nothing compared to the lives his own two-bit attempts at saving the world had cost.

Rocky hills and mesas framed the lower valleys. Church had climbed some of them on weekends, fighting the thin air. Ruth found that sort of going too rough these days, and Ricky and Carla had better things to do, so he usually went alone up into the hills, watching the sky for storms and going carefully on the scree.

His daughter called the ridges "stoney-boney," and they formed a stark background for the grand homes the country's new money, drug dollars, and drug trade trickle-down built on their slopes. It was a country of mutant delectations. Church turned from the road and began the switchback climb up cobbled streets to his home. The effort literally took his breath away, and it was not just altitude now. The old soldier was getting older. He pushed on, though, unwilling to baby himself. Sweating in the mountain cool, he came to the rear garden of his house.

His dog, a black Lab his son had named Ninja, trotted down the walk and thrust his nose out through the grille of the gate in the high white wall. Church patted the wet muzzle, saying, "Good boy, good boy," then let himself inside.

The light was going, but it was still lovely in his little oasis, with the terraced gardens and the roses Ruth tended herself when she wasn't working as a dispensary volunteer. He paused for a moment before going inside, with the dog glad to stand by him and the good view over the valley. They had been so happy here. The children, of course, were more than ready to go home, anxious to immerse themselves in the garish teenness of North America. And he and Ruth had aging families back home, and good friends, and other plans, too. But they had been happy here, as they had been happy in so many places, as long as they were together, and Church knew that he would think of this place, this house, this world, longingly, with a love as unreasonable as that between a man and a woman.

"Come on, boy," he said. He wondered why Ruth had not come out, thinking she must not have heard him. The kids would wait for him to come in, but Ruth always came out to meet him. Of course, usually there was the sound of the embassy vehicle dropping him off. He let himself into the house, his ache to see his wife more powerful now than his dread of her diminished opinion.

The first face he saw was that of María, their Aymara maid, a swollen, exaggeratedly petticoated woman with long clean braids, whom they had paid to bring down from a hopeless village. She smiled and rubbed her hands dry before her starched white apron, kitchen aromas trailing her like the aura of a saint.

Welcome.

"Where's Ruth?" he asked in Spanish.

His daughter came lackadaisically around the corner from the sitting room, where she did her homework before dinner.

"Mom's at the warehouse. The food shipment came in."

Yes. He had forgotten. There had been a flight scheduled in with the pallets of food ordered by the embassy staff. Everyone got together and agreed to split cases of this, cartons of that, and when the goods arrived, every family had to send a respresentative to help break down the shipment. Although the embassy had a small commissary, it was overpriced and unlikely to carry a favorite cereal or the chocolate chip cookies that were part of a child's life-support system far from home.

"Give your dad a welcome-home hug, huh?"

Carla loped over to him, awkward-aged on her way to her mother's warm loveliness. "Dad, it's only like two days. It's not like you've been gone forever or something." But she hugged him. At first it was perfunctory, then the embrace lazily grew genuine.

"Dads just like hugs. It's a known dad weakness. Where's your brother?"

She withdrew, shifted, all legs and shoulders waiting to find an adult shape. "He's upstairs. He doesn't want anybody to bother him. He just got some videos in the mail from Micky Donegan. Like anybody else in the world wants to see them. Daddy, why does he have to be such a nerd all the time?"

Church smiled. "It's a law of physics. The Law of Brother and Sister Relations. Didn't they teach you that at school?"

"I hate physics."

Church nodded. "So did your mom."

A car pulled in. Everyone looked toward the door, although there was still nothing to see.

"That's Mom," Carla said. "She pulls in faster than you."

"She's a reckless woman," Church said happily, unaware of his happiness and briefly free of guilt. He switched back to Spanish. "María, whatever you're cooking smells great."

The woman, who always seemed happy in her general silence, said:

"It is the soup of the vegetables. But your wife, Mrs. Ruth, has made it. For you."

"I'll go out and help your mom," Church told his daughter. "You finish your homework."

And he went out. Alone. Ruth was just locking the drive-in gate behind the family Jeep Cherokee.

She looked up in surprise.

"I stopped by the embassy," she said, "to see if you needed a ride. No one knew where you were."

He put his hands in his pockets, a boy. Ambling toward her. Over the years, her waist had thickened a bit with the children, and gray streaks warned through her hair. But she had never really changed at all to him.

"I walked. Let me help you with that."

Together, they opened the hatchback, revealing cardboard boxes full of home.

Before they began to unload the vehicle, she put a hand on his wrist.

"I've heard it was pretty bad," she said, her voice exactly right.

"Yes."

SIEGER FAILED. HE had to stop, gasping for air, bending over with his hands braced just above his knees. Church had warned him about the altitude, and he had felt a shortness of breath just walking the few blocks from the embassy up to his hotel. But Sieger ran at least four miles a day, more when his schedule permitted. Every day. In any kind of weather. And that was that. He had been certain he could run in La Paz, too, as long as he did not push the pace. So he had done sixty-four push-ups in his hotel room, irritated that he could not do his daily one hundred, and had gone, light-headed, out into the narrow street after handing in his key at the hotel desk. He started off uphill, fast.

For a block, he felt good. By the end of the second block, he already felt the strain, gulping down backstreet air stained with garbage. After four blocks, his lungs burned and howled, and his legs could only stagger. By the time he reached the compact square with the cathedral and the candyland government buildings, his body refused to take any further orders and stopped on its own, sweating as if in sickness, despite the cooling air. Worried that he was going to faint, he stood, hunched over, embarrassed, furious, as a couple of guards in *Nutcracker* soldier outfits watched from down the block.

Sieger was not accustomed to failure. Fond of saying that there was no shortage of talent in the world, only a shortage of determination, he was accustomed to being the first across the finish line. His marriage had failed, but he figured that marriages were becoming temporary arrangements in contemporary society, and he frankly did not miss his wife, with her endless demands for attention. There were women enough.

He held a job other officers envied, working for the Chief of Staff on whatever special projects arose from the Chief's intellectual grazing. Sieger had worked on the Revolution in Military Affairs, on Bosnia, and on a series of African crises, and simultaneously on a related project to refashion expeditionary force packages. Sometimes he accompanied the chief on his international journeys or travels to stateside training sites. Sieger's view of the Army, and of Washington and the world, was privileged, and it promised more privileges in the future. After the holidays, he would begin preparing to take command of a battalion in the Eighty-second. He was confident he would have a successful command, exhilarated at the thought of leading troops again. Getting himself ready to lead by example, he made time each day when he was in D.C. to run from the Pentagon Athletic Club across the bridge and up along the mall, at least to the Washington Monument, but going the full eight-mile loop around the Capitol whenever the workload allowed. He ran hard.

And now he found he could hardly trot half a dozen blocks without wheezing like an asthmatic grandfather. It bothered him to an extent it would not have bothered a more reasonable man, nearly enraging him. Behind his back, a deluge of women in somber skirts and hard white blouses poured down the steps from the cathedral. Still dizzy, Sieger crossed the street into the monument-burdened park. To sit down.

He was angry, too, because he felt things slipping out of his control. This was an unknown world to him. He had never remotely touched counterdrug ops. Never wanted to. Everybody knew the counterdrug mission was a loser, a career-killer. The ambassador had bush-whacked him. Putting him in charge of supporting the DEA rep's operations, whatever they turned out to be, and pushing Church aside, essentially letting the old colonel off the hook. Sieger knew that he was facing a minefield, and he had no illusions as to who would get the blame if something else went wrong.

He could have begged off, since his mission from the chief had been clear: come down and find out what happened with the A-team that had been hacked to bits. But Sieger never begged off anything. In his view, officers took the initiative, did their duty, disdained excuses. He was ready to do his duty now, a human swirl of vanity and courage. Only he did not know where to start.

Henry Vasquez, the DEA man, had been helpful. The guy had been around forever and knew what he needed. And Church's staff in the Milgroup office had turned out to be far more professional than Sieger had expected. They, too, were ready to help. Good sports, good troops. And knockout local-hire secretaries. But Sieger feared he was in danger of becoming nothing more than a human switchboard through which the other players passed their messages, a puppet for more experienced hands. And that was not his style. If he was going to be responsible for something, he damned well wanted to be in charge.

An ancient street vendor trudged up to Sieger's bench and demonstrated a walking paper bird with long, weighted legs and a bobbing head at the end of nearly invisible strings. The vendor smiled, gap-toothed, and said something Sieger could not understand.

He could not even speak the local language beyond getting a beer. How the hell was he supposed to keep from getting blindsided?

Shaking his head at the vendor, Sieger said, "No. *Gracias*. I don't want any, buddy."

The man bent closer, black gums and a morgue smell, and made the bird walk more exaggeratedly.

"Para los niños," the vendor said.

"I don't want any," Sieger repeated irritably. He stood up, chilled by the darkening air, and walked away. A trio of young girls giggled at his running outfit.

He walked back down the steep streets, hoping he had the right fix on his hotel. Thinking again that the whole country was a godforsaken hole.

The last shopkeepers were closing, drawing steel accordion screens across the fronts of their establishments, and the thinning streets gave off the feel of a whole city hurrying home for dinner. Sieger decided, first of all, that he was not going to write any blank checks. Whatever support Vasquez or even the ambassador wanted from the military would have to be justified. Sieger knew how to stand up to people. He intended to eat, get a good night's sleep, and show up at the Milgroup office early so he could start studying up on his new mission. He figured it would last a couple of weeks, no more. The Chief had other things for him to do up north. In the meantime, Sieger resolutely intended to avoid doing anything stupid.

Men lie to themselves with wonderful ease. Despite his strict-minded assessment of the situation, by the time he approached his hotel, Lieutenant Colonel Kurt Sieger, Regular Army of the United States, had begun to imagine cavalry-style helicopter raids on rural drug labs and victorious gun battles with murderous *narcotraficantes*.

*   *   *

"HEY, ANGEL. ANGELITO. Show me your gun."

Angel shifted farther away from the young woman. They sat on a sofa that was covered with a ragged blanket, drinking beer from bottles. A table lamp, rummaged from a dump, sat on the floor, lighting the room weakly through a homemade shade of rose paper. The young woman had dropped straw mats over the windows, shutting out uninvited eyes but not the night air, and her smile had changed for him.

"Mind your own business," Angel said. He sipped his beer.

The young woman laughed. As if she were more grown-up than him. As if she were the master of the situation.

"So, hey, you really think I look like a whore?" She was smiling. He did not understand why she was always smiling. He would have liked her better if she did not smile all the time.

"You look all right."

"I'd look better," she said, "if I had a new dress."

"Your dress is all right."

"It's too small for me. Look." She thrust out her chest to show the strain on the buttons.

"You got other dresses. I seen you."

She placed her bottle on the floor and took his hand, bringing it to her breast.

"Feel," she said.

He closed his grip slightly. Wanting to feel. Wanting to feel, but not wanting to give her a chance to embarrass him.

"It's too tight here, too," she said.

"You want a new dress," he said flatly.

"You got your sister a computer and it doesn't even work."

He kept his hand on her, half hoping she would not notice. "It's going to work. It takes time."

"Maybe you got a computer that works down here," she said. "Or a gun."

''You don't got to talk like a whore,'' Angel said.

She led him into the second room, the bedroom, saying, ''Mama won't be back. It's all right.''

''I'll get you a new dress,'' he said, but she did not even acknowledge the comment now. It was dark, but he had good eyes for the darkness, and he watched the outline of her body as it emerged from her clothing. She folded her dress neatly and laid it by the side of the bed.

''Angelito,'' she said softly, and drew him to her.

He let her lead, unsure of this murderous other world, of this level of being that felt so much more dangerous than any of the things he did for money. She laughed a little, now and then, but kissed him in between and helped him with his clothing. She touched him and the way she did it let him know that she had done it before.

He tried to take over, to take charge, but everything seemed to be slipping away, and after he fumbled about, she giggled and helped him find the right place. Then something very powerful took over his body, and suddenly, unexpectedly, everything came to an end.

He lay on top of her, glad it was dark, warming the side of his face on her breasts. He could tell she was unhappy, but he was not prepared for the tone of her voice when she just said, ''Get off me.''

He felt ashamed and for an instant he thought about giving her a bullet. But he didn't hurt women. It was one of his rules, part of his code. A man had nothing if he didn't have his honor.

GENERAL PARNELL SAT in a circle of lamplight in Quarters One on Quarry Heights, reading a journalist's recently published book on Desert Storm. The journalist had sent him an autographed copy with a scribbled, overwrought dedication. The CINC found the book instructive. Soon, he realized, even the participants would forget the reality of the war and begin to believe the published accounts. That was how history happened.

Outside, the rain had stopped and the moonlight worked down through the haze, turning the foliage into old Spanish silverwork. Birds commented on the night, and out beyond the dressed lawns, a monkey on a visit to his suburban relatives cleared a path with screeches. To Parnell, it was all evidence of the empire his nation had loaned him, and he found Panama's sharp-edged nature soothing, so long as it remained outside of the house.

He had calmed down considerably since he had learned, late in the afternoon, that the Army Chief of Staff had sent down one of his whiz kids to sniff over the Bolivian mess without even a perfunctory nod toward asking for theater clearance or letting anyone—anyone being Parnell—know that there was a lieutenant colonel loose in the backyard.

Parnell had called the Chief, and in their usual bantering manner, he let the Chief know he was furious enough to start a shooting war over the matter. The Chief, who was a good man if a poor bureaucratic infighter, realized his staff had not done all that they should have done and that, in fact, he himself should have phoned the CINC, and the two men made things good in a few minutes. Lieutenant Colonel Sieger, whom the Chief described as "a fire-eater looking for a fire," would be in and out of Parnell's AO as soon as they all figured out "who shot John." The Chief had sent his own man down in anticipation of congressional wrath and White House fears, to show alacrity and concern. With that matter closed, the two men had laughed about the deserved comeuppance the Air Force Chief of Staff had gotten during a Senate hearing and commiserated about the shortage of training dollars. "You're not going to be able to do as much of that touchy-feely stuff," the Chief said. And that was that.

The journalist's account of the Twenty-fourth Mech Division's charge across the desert brought a smile of satisfaction to Parnell's face and he interrupted his reading only for an occasional sip of his Diet Coke. In the background, his wife made house noises, and Parnell savored the very rare opportunity to relax between official functions and the requirement to make decisions when there were no good options, a penalty of the military's recent poverty and a changed international landscape. He pushed his staff hard, but at the end of the day—on those occasions when there actually was a clear end to the day—the CINC's hours were longer than those of any of his subordinates, and the real difference was that he was never allowed to complain or appear tired or to put off anything until tomorrow. Still, he loved his job with a love woven of habit and an addiction to making things happen. He had soldiered so long it was like breathing.

A phone rang—one of his military lines, the nonsecure. He could tell by the distinctive ring.

He rose and went into his home office, finger stuck in his book. An old dark-wood table held a battalion of multicolored, multishaped telephones, as well as other more-arcane communications devices. He picked up the receiver from the console with the blinking light.

"General Parnell."

"Sir, this is Dr. Metzger. Down at the surgery. Sorry to bother you at home, sir, but Colonel Vishinski said you had a personal interest in this and—"

"Whatcha got?" the CINC said.

"Sir. The bodies. Those bodies. The ones from Bolivia? Sir, we've looked at almost all of them now, we've really been crashing, and two things jump out at you."

"Give it to me."

"First, there's no question about it. They were shot to death before anybody started hacking on them. Except one whose throat was cut. Somebody was having a real party with them."

"What's the other thing?"

"Sir . . . this doesn't look like a fight. It looks like an

execution. Everybody but the one with his throat cut? Same thing. Killed with one bullet. Point of entry almost identical on each body. Now, I'm certainly not a ballistics guy, but you get the feeling it might have been all the same guy and the same gun. If that makes any sense.''

"*Wait* a minute. You're telling me you think one lone killer might have taken out all twelve members of a Special Forces A-team?"

The voice hesitated, and Parnell imagined the man's worry. His tone had been hard, annoyed, self-indulgent. But the notion of a single killer seemed beyond all possibility.

And yet . . .

Parnell calibrated his voice down to a business-as-usual tone. "Anything else?"

"No, sir. Nothing. Not yet. We're still working, though."

"Good. Good work. See if you can verify what you just told me. About the single gun business." Jesus, Parnell thought, wouldn't that play great on the Hill. And in the press. Make us look like incompetent asses. "Then wrap it up and get those men back home."

The general hung up. With a very cold feeling down deep.

It was going to take skill. And luck. And more than a few headlocks and twisted arms. But nobody and nothing short of God Almighty was going to stand between Jack Parnell and whoever had pulled the trigger on those soldiers. Certainly not the sugar-plum fairies from the Department of State. He was going to track down whoever was responsible if he had to pick South America up by its tail and shake down the whole damned continent.

Parnell sat down at the table with the rank of phones, abandoning the book he had been reading. You did not execute U.S. service members. You just did not do it, no matter who you were. Not to his men. You didn't do it. Period.

His seething gradually eased into a slow, steady anger, and he thought of John Church and about instincts. Funny guy, Church. Different kind of soldier. Foreign Area Officer, one of the gifted loners who made a career out of following the bear over the unmapped mountain. To see what he could see. Strategic scouts, linguists, gypsies with jobs, FAOs tended to be bright, curious as kids, and often damned brave, and they brought home the goods for their country. But none of them fell in the center of the normal-guy bell curve, and promotion boards were allergic to them. Parnell had heard foreign area officers described as America's "thin green line," deployed at the edge of darkness. He found that a bit romantic and overdrawn, but his FAOs were, man for man, the best soldiers he had in his command. Just didn't have enough of them, and he was losing more with each force reduction board.

Yeah, Church. The guy knew his turf, and he had good instincts. But given the bloodbath down in Mendoza, the colonel seemed to have run out of luck. And luck mattered. Parnell told himself, for the thousandth time in his career, that the two things you could not train into an officer who did not have them were good instincts and good luck, and you needed both. Nothing, not even honor, was more important to success.

CHURCH HAD EATEN his dinner with enthusiasm. Even when his world was coming apart at the seams, he never lost his appetite. The stew his wife offered him was a brief reprieve from the sentence he had imposed upon himself.

After dinner, he inspected his daughter's homework, then his son's. He made the boy do one of the math problems over. Then he sat down in the living room with a last beer, surrounded by the familiar. Books, novels and histories, poets, in English and Spanish. And the artifacts and carefully chosen souvenirs of lives spent as military gypsies, roaming a hemisphere. He had a collection of fine replicas of pre-Columbian art that fooled his guests until he told them the truth and of native pottery that had wandered in from the jungles or down from Andean valleys that had no claim on tourism. Ruth jokingly, happily referred to their home as the "Museum of Us," and it was just that, a chronicle of lives he had always considered well spent.

Ruth made a fire and they sat before it, Ruth reading something by Doris Lessing and Church drinking his beer and trying to read the flames. Some Indian tribe believed you could read the future in a fire—where had that been? Costa Rica? No. It irritated him that he could not remember and he almost interrupted his wife's reading, then thought better of it. Anyway, all he could see in the fire was fire. Burning and more burning.

He got up to poke the thinning logs. "Eva von Reinsee says hello. She looks like she needs a vacation. Afraid she's got the start of an epidemic on her hands, maybe something bad." He could not bring himself to speak yet about his dead and the matter of the clinic. Or his decision.

"I've always liked Eva," Ruth said absently, sunk in the middle of a paragraph. "I wish we saw more of her."

"She's a saint."

Ruth raised an eyebrow at that. "Well, she's a tough one. But I like that side of her. The toughness. Such a delicate-looking woman. She fools you." Ruth eased back down toward her book. "I wish I had her bone structure. You think she'll ever marry, John?"

Church shrugged. He walked over to the broad window at the end of the house and looked out on the sparkling valley and the high black mountain walls climbing the horizon. Standing there, murders and sputtering epidemics seemed immeasurably far away, and he felt safe and wished one last time that he could just walk away from all of it.

He walked away from the window and said:

"I'm going up to bed."

His wife glanced up over her reading glasses. "I'll be up in a minute."

She was as good as her word, as always. She held him from behind, asked once if he wanted to talk, and let it go when he told her, "Not yet." But he could not sleep. He could always eat, but sleep was where he paid when things went wrong. After perhaps an hour, he slipped from under his wife's arm, pulled on his robe, and went downstairs again.

He stood before the big window. There were far fewer lights in the valley now, and up above the rock rims he saw the familiar southern stars he could read from a jungle clearing or in the middle of grasslands. He figured it all came down to this: his country had trusted him with the lives of its soldiers, and he had risked them without properly considering the consequences. In pursuit of his personal agenda—and it did not matter the intent of that agenda—he had sent men to unnecessary deaths. And he could not make it pretty.

He heard bare feet on the stairs. His wife. He knew the tread, could sense her across a continent, an ocean. He did not turn around.

"You need sleep," she said, coming up behind him, putting her arms around his waist.

"You know how I am. Why don't you go back to bed."

She did not answer in words, but held him a degree more tightly, his warm love.

"John," she said after a bit, "whatever you have done in your life, you have done because you believed it was right. *I* know that."

It was his turn to pause and shape words. So hard to do. He rested a hand on the hands she had clasped in front of him.

"They say anything while you were sorting the shipment?"

She rested her head on his back. "No. Just quieter than usual. You know how they are."

"Yes."

Ruth talked on, gentle-voiced, about nothing. Lulling a grown-up child. "Anne Plymouth says hello. You know, there's something about Anne I just can't help liking. Plymouth doesn't deserve her. She was funny today, though. In a hurry about something. Left a maid to sort out Ethan's damned Oreos. That didn't go over well with the other wives, let me tell you."

"I've tried blaming Plymouth," Church said suddenly. "For that stupid no-weapons policy. But the truth is that I caved. As long as he let me run my little programs, I was willing to let him make the rules. And they were bad rules, and I knew it. It was selfish and idiotic."

"And done is done. El Sal was bad, too."

Church looked out at the lights, saw another die. "Different kind of bad," he said. "Not my fault, and I knew it." He shifted slightly. "Ruth, I want to do something. Maybe you'll think I'm nuts, but I feel like I have to do it. And I *want* to do it."

She tensed. Just enough for a husband and lover to mark. "What is it?"

He felt embarrassed. Not wanting his woman to laugh at him. Because he knew that the thing he wanted to do, that he *had* to do, had no weight in the great scale of events. It was not going to make a difference. It, too, was ultimately selfish. A gesture to calm his own demons.

"I'm going to go back down there," he said slowly. "Myself. Just me." He wrinkled his mouth in a hurt smile his wife could not see. "I figure I'm still the ranking military officer in this country and I can sign my own leave papers." He stroked the back of one of her hands without realizing it. "Ruth, I'm going to take the leave I've got saved up and a little money from our

account, and I'm going to finish that clinic. Myself. I
don't think it'll be dangerous now, and it looks like
they've got even more health problems down there. And,
damn it, somebody ought to finish what those men
started.'' He pictured the bodies in the basement
morgue, the carnage left behind in the barn. ''Don't
laugh at me.''

She did not laugh. She did not say anything for a time
and he was so self-absorbed that he lost his sense of
what she might be feeling until he heard her sobbing.
He began to turn, to embrace her, but she tightened her
grip on him from behind, holding him prisoner.

''I'm not laughing,'' she said. ''Damn it, John, you're
the only man who could ever make me cry.''

WHEN CHRISTIAN RITTER von Reinsee was ten years old, his world came to an end. His family had been expecting it for years, although they did not know the precise form their Armageddon would assume. For some of his relatives, the end had begun in the long summer of 1914, when the hooves of the family regiment of *Uhlanen* clopped through the streets of Gumbinnen on their way to a last great victory. Others would have dated the beginning of the end from the hunger winter of 1918, or from the massacre of fortunes that followed Versailles. His father had believed, although the belief had come late, that the real end began in 1933, when a malodorous man with the table manners of a peasant became chancellor of Germany.

For his mother, with her ivory arms and her immeasurable reserves of strength, the end only really began in June 1944, when her officer-husband stole a few days to visit his family as Berlin shifted him from the swamps of White Russia to Normandy. Emaciated, he could no longer speak properly and he had the eyes of a sick animal waiting to die. She told her daughter and son that their father would be all right when the war was over. Then she received word that he had fallen, for the *Reich* he had regarded first as an annoyance then as a mortal embarrassment, when allied warplanes bombed his headquarters outside of Falaise. A family friend told her, dur-

ing a brief encounter at a railway station in Breslau, that
her husband's division had been accustomed to Russia
and had set up in an open field where prowling American aircraft soon found them. It had been, the friend
said, a waste.

There had been plenty of waste. Von Reinsee knew
that now. But during the war, he had lived protected
until the very end, and he and his elder sister had ridden
across the fields on good horses, racing around the little
lake from which he imagined the family name had been
taken, and he had enjoyed the soldier play and the made-
up uniforms and radio songs, although he sensed that his
mother tolerated the whole business grudgingly and his
father, during a leave in the early days when things were
still going well, had declared that he was the last von
Reinsee who would have a military career. He had been
right, of course.

Drums, songs, and torchlight ceremonies. Secret oaths
and playing soldier or Old Shatterhand in the endless
golden fields that stretched away toward the Baltic Sea.
His family had been there forever and ever, and the
manor house, while not nearly so grand as those of their
western relatives in Baden or Saxony, was a glorious
place to be a child, with its smoky paintings of ancestors
in pale blue uniforms with red ribbons around their
necks and the little library for the bad weather days
when their mother would take them over lessons different from those they received in the school, saying, "You
must not tell any of your friends, but you must remember: there was another, better Germany. . . ."

But how could he imagine a better Germany than this,
where his horse was the envy of everyone that counted
in his world and the Polish-speaking farmhands regarded
him with respect, even with fear, and on Saturdays, the
traveling projectionist would come to the school hall in
the village and show short subjects about German tri-
umphs in places unimaginably distant, followed by movies that made you laugh till you were tired and sleepy

and you woke to find the film done and the women and the old men who remained in the village dabbed their eyes, leaving the clean-scrubbed hall with the inevitable comment that, *"Der Jannings war doch besser. . . ."*

First they took his horse. For the war effort. His horse, and all of the other horses, save those so pathetic they were still not worthy of the *Wehrmacht* that, the film shows and radio broadcasts assured everyone, was only adjusting its lines before resuming the offensive. Then Aunt Lily came to visit with her children and she was terribly sad, and it emerged only slowly that her husband had shot himself over a thing he had witnessed at some sort of camp south of Krakau. At a family dinner not nearly so abundant as it would have been a year before, the servants were sent out and the small circle of guests began talking about the Jews, whom Christian had been taught at school to picture as dark and very cruel. But the family members did not seem to think it was quite so simple, and his mother said, in the direct, hard tone women of her family used notoriously, that the shame of this, if it were true, would haunt Germany until the end of time. Turning to Aunt Lily, who was blond and really did smell of flowers, an elderly uncle who had commanded a corps in Galicia during the last war and who held the *Ritterkreuz* remarked that to choose an honorable, officer's death under such circumstances had been the only acceptable course. Lily slammed down her silver and said in a stablehand's voice:

"Suicide is for bachelors. He left me two children."

Then his father came home, briefly, a ghost, and wanted to do nothing but walk in his fields, as if trying to take it all in one last time, or to sit silently in the library with his wife without even listening to the phonograph he had loved so much before he went away. He tried to spend time with Christian and his sister, but it never went well, and Christian remembered overhearing the man who did not even smell like his father anymore telling his mother, "It'll be better now in the Normandy. The British and Americans are civilized."

Then he was gone, and he died, but he had grown so distant that Christian did not feel it much. In August, in that last unsmiling August, two black sedans pulled into the *Hof* in front of the manor house and men in unneccesary raincoats leapt out and came up the steps as though they had not an instant to spare. They questioned his mother about his father's friends in the military, about family connections, about her personal feelings toward the *Reich* and the *Führer*. Christian, who had been sent out of the sitting room, discovered one of the visitors nosing about in the library. Had the government not taken his horse, he might have told the man how his mother had hidden several boxes of books and phonograph discs in the barn the day before. In the textbooks at school good children always told such secrets to Germany's protectors.

The visitors left and did not return, and it was only long after the war, when Christian was already a successful rancher in Bolivia with children of his own, that he learned that the Gestapo had beaten to death the elderly uncle who had clung to his officer's honor to the end, unwilling to tell them anything about his relations with the von Stauffenberg family, even though those relations had been completely unrelated to the events of that terrible, golden summer.

The Russians came in the winter, after the last disappointing holidays. Afraid of the allied bombing to the west, his mother had delayed the family's departure too long, and in the end, she had to harness a sickly plow horse to a cart with the family's essential possessions in order to join the endless trek of refugees headed for the bridges across the Oder River.

Russian planes soared and dipped, now and then shooting at one of the vehicles trapped in the column, but most of the time they seemed merely en route to destinations farther west. Along the roadsides, aban-

doned equipment, suitcases, and occasional bodies darkened the snow. At a crossroads, the family passed a tree
dangling two teenaged boys in uniforms too big for
them, with signs hung around their broken necks declaring them to be deserters and traitors to the German
people. An officer in a leather coat and a pair of smartly
turned-out soldiers with machine pistols stood beside a
sedan, scanning the column, and now and then singling
out a refugee to demand identification. Christian always
remembered those three well-nourished men in uniform
as his personal symbol of the end of the Third Reich.

As they marched, the afternoon twilight began and the
temperature dropped. They could hear distant thumping,
but the battle still seemed far away. Snow fell, and
Christian's mother snapped at him to keep moving. She
would not let either of the children mount the horse or
the little wagon, demanding that they keep going and
not rest. A one-armed man huddled over a blanketed
form by the roadside, crying out for a doctor and shouting in a maddened voice:

"She's having a baby, my wife's having a baby. . . ."

The Russian tanks appeared suddenly, growling up
over a slope behind snowflake camouflage. At the sight
of the first two vehicles, the refugees were unsure, since
the tanks were approaching from the southwest, and one
old man shouted that they had all been rescued, that the
Führer had not forgotten them. Then more tanks came
on, until the pale horizon darkened with them, dozens
of them, and even those who could not tell one tank
from another knew that Germany did not have so many
tanks now, and the screaming began, and the running.

The tanks overran the column but never fired, did no
intentional harm. They had another destination, and
when Christian looked up from the ditch where his
mother had sheltered him and his sister, he saw an enormous dark machine roll past, with soldiers in thick padded jackets and helmets covered with snow clinging to

the turret and the back deck of the vehicle, their faces exotic and disinterested in the twilight.

When the huge sound of the tanks had passed on, their mother dragged them back to their feet, dusting off the snow, promising they could sleep later. She began to cry when she saw their old horse and the wagon intact by the roadside, the old nag too tired to run even from an armored assault.

"It's a good sign," she told them. "It's a good sign."

The refugees reassembled, fewer now, and trudged on. They had encountered the Russians and it seemed that the horror stories were untrue, just more of the propaganda that had turned the world on end. And the snow stopped. Everything was going to be all right. Somehow.

It must have been near midnight, at the entrance to a village lit by spotty fires, when the Russian support troops swept over the column. They shot those who tried to run. Christian's mother realized, anyway, that the children were too tired to flee further, and she simply clutched them to her, by the cart. Then the soldiers came, grabbing, shouting unintelligibly, and everything happened very fast.

"Take me," his mother cried. "For the love of God, she's only a child. *Take me.*"

The soldiers tore at his mother's clothing, with his sister already down on the ground, everything but her thin white legs covered by a soldier in a greatcoat. Christian was exhausted, more tired than he had ever been, but he ran toward the men who had surrounded his mother. A man with a strange, bronze face swept him away, knocking him down hard, and said:

"*Vot. Veliki nemyetski geroy.*"

And the soldiers laughed.

Another man lay down on top of his sister. His mother stopped pleading now and erupted in physical fury. For one last moment, she freed herself from their hands, shrieking, "Pigs. She's a *child. An*imals."

One of the Russians shot her twice with a pistol.

When they were finished, a young soldier lingered a moment longer than his comrades, looking at Christian and the half-naked, bleeding girl in the roadway. He fished a tin out of one of his pockets and put it in Christian's hands, but Christian could not hold it, his fingers would not close. He looked down at his sister, white skin, unexpected dark hair, blood.

The Russian soldier, who was not much more than a boy himself, picked up the little tin and set it beside the girl. He looked at Christian and raised his fingers to his mouth in a gesture of eating.

"Pokushitye," he said, and left.

Christian knew his mother was dead. He knew about death from films. He struggled to remove her big overcoat, careless and heartless in his handling of the woman; then he wrapped his sister in the garment. She did not cry exactly. She wimpered. She could not speak, her eyes did not see him. And she would not stop bleeding. He tried to dress her, to make her walk, but she could not rise. The blood soaked through everything.

There had been clean clothes on the wagon, but the wagon was gone now. Uncaring, he drew more of the clothing from his mother's body, pressing a balled-up sweater against his sister's bleeding, trying to make it stop. She was sticky, horrible.

"Help me," he shouted. To anyone. But the dark forms that hurried past had troubles of their own. "Help me, help me, help me."

It was the last time in his life he ever asked anyone for help.

Toward morning, his sister stopped breathing. He sat on a little longer, cold, unsure of what was right. His mother had always told him that he must behave honorably, that he must never forget that he was a von Reinsee. But how did you behave honorably in a world where this could happen? Why did men do such things? Because they were Russians? And because his sister was a German?

Finally, he dragged the bodies of his mother and sister a little farther from the side of the road and covered them with snow. In later years, he could not remember whether or not he had cried, but he distinctly recalled the tin left by the young Russian in the bloody slush. He picked it up, wiped it clean, and read:

SPAM. *Product of the United States of America.*

"I'VE ALWAYS BEEN fond of the Americans, you know," von Reinsee told his guest. It was just after two in the morning, the peak of von Reinsee's workday. With age, his eyes had weakened so that he could not bear the harsh southern sunlight. So he slept when the sun was high, and when the world had business with him, the world had to adapt to his schedule. He had grown sufficiently important that much of the world was glad to lose sleep for an audience with him.

"Gringos," the guest said noncommittally. He was a spectacular man in his early thirties, handsome, well-mannered, educated at Boston University, then Georgetown. His clothing rested upon him as clothing only does when made by a tailor who served first the father then the son. A nephew, he had become almost a son to von Reinsee, after the elder man's wife and male heir had died in the crash of the family's private plane in Paraguay some years before. His name was Rafael Gutiérrez Raimond, and he was as close to an aristocrat as the old families of Bolivia could produce. Trained in international business and business law, he was a great help to the family establishment, and had von Reinsee not found the notion of marriages between first cousins rather too Latin, Rafael would have been the elder man's ideal of a son-in-law. Of course, Rafael had another love interest at the moment.

"I am speaking with great sincereity," von Reinsee said, with a slight tone of admonishment. "The Americans were very good to me. I also have, as you know,

my boy, a weak spot for the Jews, but that may be something of a family failing.'' He paraded his manicured
fingers. ''As a ten-year-old boy, I walked across Germany, from what is now Poland—I shall never forget
the sight of Dresden that spring. I worked my way from
one seat of the family to another, but they were all gone,
all swept away. I ended up in Frankfurt, living in the
ruins with everyone else and begging what I could not
steal. The Americans were wonderful, really. I knew
how to get round the military police and the soldiers
would always give you something you could eat or sell.
When they learned I could speak English, they all
wanted to know if I had a sister.'' Von Reinsee smiled.
''They were innocents, of course. Far more innocent
than I. By the time I was eleven, I had acquired a number of sisters, repeatedly virginal young women attuned
to the wealth of the United States. Some of them even
married soldiers and went to Cleveland or Milwaukee or
wherever war brides went. But, as for the Americans
themselves, I cherished their naivete, for I certainly had
none left of my own.'' He leaned forward and rang a
small silver bell. ''What you must understand about the
Americans, my boy, is that they really just want to be
liked.''

A male servant appeared. Short, Indian, he looked
choked by the strict, perfect European costume that had
been provided him, the sort of formal attire worn by the
lead servants of the best German houses before the war.

''Another bottle of the Ebersbacher, Carlos.''

The servant bowed and withdrew from the room that
had been furnished from memories of summers as long
as adult decades and winters spent struggling to outskate
a graceful, long-legged sister in a lost world.

''Well,'' von Reinsee said, ''I'm glad it all went
well.'' He rose, athletic for his age, still a horseman in
those dawn hours when the light was weak and bearable.
He crossed the room to a deeply carved library table
dressed with old books and religious statuary both finer

and less florid than that the Spanish had left behind.
Picking up a cigarette box, heavy, sleek, Viennese Se-
cession, he brought it to his guest.

The younger man declined. ''Your Americans
wouldn't approve,'' he said. ''They're far more serious
about restricting tobacco smoking than they are about
cocaine.''

Von Reinsee replaced the box, took a cigarette for
himself, and lit it with an antique lighter of the sort once
used by German cavalry officers. ''Well, they're a curious folk. But, if it wasn't for their Red Cross, I would
never have been 'discovered' by my Uncle Willy.'' Von
Reinsee smiled. Charmingly, as if there were invisible
women in the room. ''Odd fellow. Don't think you
would have known him. No, you would have been too
young. And there was no relation between our families
at that time. Black sheep of the family, Uncle Willy.
Didn't want any part of the '*Herr Rittmeister*' business.
No soldier, he. Took off for Argentina in twenty-eight,
found the best seats booked, and wandered up to Bolivia.
One of the first Germans here, you know. Before the
Jewish wave in the thirties. And long before the postwar
scum drifted in. In those days, Santa Cruz Department
was nothing but mud and cholera. Uncle Willy was
probably braver than the rest of the men in the family,
just didn't see why he should spend his life trying to get
killed when there was plenty else to keep a man occupied. Uncle Willy saved me.''

Rafael shook his head. ''Uncle Christian, you would
have been a success, whether you came to Bolivia or
stayed in Germany. Germany's a rich country now. You
would have been just as rich. Perhaps richer.''

They're not true aristrocrats, von Reinsee thought.
Can't stop bringing money into the conversation. At the
wrong times.

''Contemporary Germany,'' von Reinsee began, ''is
a nation of whores pretending to be nuns. I'll look my
sins straight in the eyes, thank you. I have never regret-

ted leaving *that* Germany behind.'' He sat back below
an oil landscape of windswept meadows. A line of
straining birches suggested a road into the village in the
painting's middle distance, where a brick Lutheran steeple dominated low, tidy houses.

The servant touched at the door, a token gesture, then
entered with the wine. Slender brown bottle with a black
geometric eagle on a stark label. The servant uncorked
the wine swiftly and exactly, poured half glasses, then
left with another bow.

Von Reinsee regarded the label for a moment. ''I
think . . . I believe I only drink this out of a sort of filial
devotion. This was a favored wine of my father's, although the vineyard had a more graceful label in those
days. Really, I should drink the Chileans. They're every
bit as good, if not better.'' He raised the glass. ''To our
American friends.''

Rafael held his glass ready, but paused. Evidently unsure as to the seriousness of the toast.

''Oh, come now,'' von Reinsee said with a glint of
polished silver cuff links. ''Just because you kill people
doesn't mean you can't drink their health.''

''**TO BE FRANK,**'' the elder man said after he had
drunk, ''I'm sorry they had to be killed. I take no joy
in it.'' He looked at the younger man, trying to see behind the elegant handsomeness to the core, if there was
one. ''Understand, Rafael, I do not and never have taken
death lightly. No matter what you may believe. I am
convinced that killing the Americans was the only way
to get their attention, to get them moving.'' He shook
his head. ''They're good once they're moving, but damnably hard to rouse.''

''Well, it's done,'' Rafael said.

''And done well. I appreciate your efforts. The Colombian boy sounds especially impressive. Something of

a slum boy's fantasy, I should think. I'd rather like to have a chat with him.''

Rafael looked up, doubtful. Slow-witted, for all that education.

''I don't mean it literally,'' von Reinsee assured him. ''But the boy does sound remarkable. How did you find him?''

''Trade secret.'' Rafael looked pleased.

Von Reinsee put out his reduced cigarette and folded his arms.

''The Colombians are greedy,'' Rafael said. ''They don't understand what's happening.''

''And they won't. Until it's too late. So they gave you the boy?''

''More or less. You know how they are. Subordinates always jockeying to take the boss's place. They'll sell you anything.''

Von Reinsee looked at the younger man with renewed closeness. Then he smiled and crossed his legs. ''I have never thought much of the Colombians. I find them arrogant and crude. All of them. Even the society crowd of Bogotá. The Colombians have overstayed their welcome in Bolivia. Our new friends are more civilized.''

Rafael sat up. ''Mother of God. The Brazilians are the bloodiest crowd on earth.''

He never got it, von Reinsee decided, the boy never got it at all. But he was good enough, in his way. And he had his uses. Especially with the women. With one woman.

''They're ten times worse than the Colombians. I'll tell you right out, Uncle Christian, I still have my reservations. I certainly wouldn't call them 'civilized.' ''

Von Reinsee smiled, tasting the gray wine, the Riesling steely like the flash of his father's ceremonial sword.

''Civilization,'' von Reinsee said, ''is relative.'' He rose again and crossed the room to where a portrait of a seated woman in the high fashion of the Weimar Republic hung over a dead fireplace. "Isn't it remarkable," he asked the younger man, "how much Eva resembles her grandmother. Positively uncanny. Blood will tell."

"Your mother was a very beautiful woman," Rafael said, helping himself to more wine. For all his social fluidity, the young man's etiquette was never exact.

"Yes. Remarkably beautiful. Eva could be, too, of course. If she'd just get over her rather extended period of rebellion."

"Eva," Rafael said, "is hard as stone."

Von Reinsee cocked an eyebrow at the bluntness, then smiled. "Rafael, you've just never met a woman like that. Not the Bolivian sort—they can be mean as scorpions, but Bolivian women are never hard the way you mean." His eyes left for a brief memory. "If anything, Eva's grandmother was the harder of the two. Incredibly strong woman. I never realized until much later, of course. I suspect she was far stronger than my father."

Von Reinsee smiled, strolling his domain and allowing his thoughts and words to ramble just a bit in this comfortable hour. "The portrait's just a copy. I had it done from a photograph in Uncle Willy's family album. One of those Peruvian artists who specialize in forging colonial masterpieces painted it. Fine work, I think. I really do remember my mother that way." He looked up at the portrait from across the room now. "The women in her family were famous for their hardheadedness. The von Glasenek girls. Silesian. Which meant a bit more Polish than anybody was willing to admit in my mother's day. So Eva's all right?"

Rafael turned in his seat, ready to assure the older man. "I'm sure she's frightened. But she's all right. I gave very clear instructions. They reported back to me afterward."

"They didn't hurt her?"

"No. They threatened her, shook her up a bit. But they understood the penalty for actually doing her any harm."

"All right." Von Reinsee drew his hand along the back of a Biedermeier fainting couch. "They're Colombians as well?"

"Yes, sir. Nothing but Colombians. I mean, I've got a few Indians doing the menial labor. For authenticity. But there'll be Colombians everywhere the Yankees look. And the Colombians don't suspect a thing."

Von Reinsee leaned back against a cabinet of splendid marbled wood, twin of a piece in a Hamburg museum. "I want you to be certain that any of the Colombians who were involved in the little business with Eva are there when the Americans come. Anyone who touched her or spoke to her or even saw her humiliated like that, I want them dead. I want the jungle to lick their bones." He was no longer the old European gentleman.

"I promise."

"Good. More wine? I have a wonderful video I'm planning to watch. The Gruendgens *Faust*. You're welcome to stay if you like."

"Is that one of your operas?"

"No. Not this *Faust*. This is Goethe." The old man thought better of his offer, recognizing the folly born of his loneliness. Sometimes his discipline slipped. If rarely. "Foolish of me, Rafael. It's in German, anyway. A very German matter, all in all. You wouldn't be interested. But have a last glass of wine. They still do a decent Riesling."

"Uncle Christian?" Rafael had changed his posture, his voice, with business shut behind them now.

"What's on your mind, my boy?"

"I do my best to make sure Eva's all right. Nobody in Amazonas would lay a hand on her."

"And I appreciate that."

"But she's unmanageable."

Von Reinsee put a question on his face.

"There may be something going on up there. An epidemic. I just got a call. Something out among the Indians. Something unusual."

"Cholera? God, not machupo?"

Rafael's expression declared that he did not know. "It's a recent development. Maybe nothing. But Eva showed up in the middle of the town square last night—the night before last—absolutely covered in blood. She met two American officers."

"Church?"

"Yes. And somebody new."

"Watch Church. He's the only one with half a brain."

"We're watching all of them."

"And what happened? When she met Church and his friend? Did she tell them about her experience along the road?"

"I don't know. It doesn't sound like it. It was somewhat public."

Von Reinsee bore down. "She'll tell Church. Give her time. She trusts him. It's very important that she tell him what happened."

"I've fed the location of the lab to the gringos already."

The older man shook his head. "The Americans like two sources of information. Two is confirmation. Then they move."

"The DEA will move on its own. Vasquez has the ambassador's ear."

"Even so. Even if they do," von Reinsee said. "I want it all to seem very clear and straightforward. No questions. No doubt in any North American minds. I want that ass Plymouth to believe he's struck gold. Now, tell me about Eva."

"She seemed afraid. Absolutely covered in blood. She asked for help with this epidemic. My source couldn't hear all of the details. The new American said they wouldn't help anymore and Church made him sit down."

Von Reinsee laughed. "You know, I think Colonel Church is a little bit in love with our Eva. Only he can't face it, and she's oblivious to it. The plot's right out of Fontane. Anyway, go on."

"The point is . . . I can protect her from a lot of things. But if this disease is so bad . . . well, I don't see what I can do to protect her from that. Unless you want me to have her kidnapped for a while."

"No. Don't bother her anymore. For now."

"But she went right back out into the bush the next day. After calling La Paz for help and begging the mayor to get involved. She's out there by herself now."

"The mayor's worthless. She must realize that. Eva's a clever girl."

"My source said she seemed desperate."

"Well, the mayor's day will come. First things first."

"She's your only child now. This disease—"

Von Reinsee laughed. "There isn't a microbe on earth that could kill Eva. You don't know the women in our family. She'll be the last one standing. I worry more about her falling in love with the wrong man."

EVA SLEPT IN her jeep and woke to find a horse nosing at her window. The unexpectedness of it startled her. Then she recovered and shooed the animal away and went into the bushes for a minute. When she returned, she cleaned herself again with a bit of her dwindling supply of alcohol and walked back into the settlement to see who else had died during the night.

As best she could tell, her efforts had not made a bit of difference. None of the antibiotics or serums she had rummaged from the town clinic seemed to help, and when she tried to rehydrate victims intravenously she just created more blood flow. It appeared that the disease disintegrated the blood vessels.

She was convinced that the disease was something new. At least it was something new to her. The proper people for this work were not even the national health staff from La Paz but the doctor-detectives from the

Centers for Disease Control in Atlanta, with their world-wide network and database. A true professional, she knew, would be taking notes all the while, keeping a record for the specialists to help them trace the epidemic and find its pattern of contagion, its vector. But she had no time.

She gave herself one more day. If no help appeared by evening, she would have to drive back into town and try to make clear what was happening out here. The potential for a broader epidemic was very high. The disease killed quickly, often within twenty-four hours of the appearance of the full suite of symptoms, and so far she had not identified a single survivor. Both factors actually mitigated against the spread of the disease over a wide geographic area. But in the three settlements where she had found the sickness, most of the residents had already fled, God knew where, possibly taking the disease with them. And a lot of the rural people supplemented their bare incomes by a smuggling trade with Brazil across the river.

In the first house she visited, three children had died since evening and the mother had taken sick. The father was nowhere to be found, unusual with this group of Indians and perhaps an indication of the disease's ability to induce terror. In the next hut, a sick old man who should have died, given the virulence and pattern of the disease, held on to his life with a vivid hunger to feel and see one more day. She gave him a syringe cocktail of antibiotics and vitamins, all she had left.

There was so much she should be doing, she knew. The investigators who would come, who would have to come, would need blood samples from the earliest identifiable victims. They would need family networks and contact charts. Questions needed to be asked of the dying to discover what they might have eaten in common, or where they might have congregated. But there was no time, no time, no time. . . .

Within an hour, she had visited each of the dozen or

so scattered houses that composed the bush settlement
and she realized, belatedly, that everyone still healthy
enough to walk had fled. Only the dead and the dying
remained.

Alone, Eva dragged the dead by the ankles from any
of the houses where the sick still clung to life, straining
herself, wishing she were stronger. The pulpy bodies left
trails of blood, perhaps spreading the infection into the
dust, but she did not know what else to do. As she
dragged them, resting when she had to, which was more
and more frequently as the sun climbed, she could not
help looking at what remained of their humanity: faces
pulped and blackened with dried blood until even the
children looked as though they had been dead and bak-
ing in the sun for months, clotted rags of clothing over
bodies turned to putty. As long as they were alive, she
could feel for them, avoid the paralysis of repulsion. But
the corpses made her sick and it was just as well that
she had run out of food the day before.

She gathered the bodies in a central shack, then
brought in straw from an outbuilding. When she went
into the storage areas, mice fled, and she wondered if
that meant she could eliminate one possible vector, since
the animals were still alive. Finally, she set the building
with the dead on fire, aware that her effort was inadequate, that the sickness was already beyond this stage of
containment. But she could frankly think of nothing else
to do and the burning at least gave her a feeling of fighting back.

She went through the other houses one last time. The
old man had died. He was alone in his house and she
set that afire, too. Then she made a halfhearted effort to
clean herself and drove to the next settlement.

She knew there was only one person she could turn
to now, and she hated the thought. It was her final surrender. Of course, her father would do everything to help
her, give her anything she wanted, twist arms until they
broke, buy her a planeload of experts in isolation suits

with portable laboratories. He would ask for nothing in return, content that he had proved his point, that the dividing line between good and evil was not so clear as she would have it.

But there *was* good and evil in the world. When she had learned, at a fantastically advanced age and already a resident physician in a superb North American clinic, that her father was in the cocaine business along with everything else he grew, built, bought, and sold, her life had shattered. She wondered how much her mother had known and if her brother had already been part of the business when the family plane went down.

No one had ever dared tell her, not even her friends. Although everyone back home in Bolivia apparently knew. She could not believe how she had been fooled.

And when she confronted him, her father did not even try to deny his trade. He said he had too much respect for her intelligence. He tried to convince her that he was nothing but a businessman, doing good business, selling people what they wanted.

Eva, who had studied and worked in the United States for the better part of a decade, had a very different view of illegal drugs.

"What do you think paid for your education?" her father asked. "Bananas?"

She swore at him, a thing she had never done, but he only smiled. And she asked him, seriously wanting to know, why he felt he had to do such a thing when he was already rich beyond the needs of any man, any family.

"To be strong," he had said, in a matter-of-fact voice. "For me. For you. You don't know what it's like to be powerless, Evita. At the mercy of the human monster. A man can never be too strong." Then he smiled. "Besides, I could never resist a challenge. Narcotics are the business of the future. At least as far as South America is concerned. Cocaine is our microchip."

When she told him what she had seen his business do

in the streets of North America, he only asked:

"Do you really think the Yankees care what happens to their negroes?"

He had been boundlessly, publicly proud of her, the brilliant young heart surgeon, his genius of a daughter. Working in one of the finest heart clinics in the United States. So she took that away from him, coming back to Bolivia to work in the bush, wishing she had trained in tropical medicine instead of something as irrelevant to her world as open heart surgery. She taught herself on the job, ignoring her father's pleas to be reasonable, not to throw away her life. She avoided speaking to him, seeing him only at those weddings and funerals she could not avoid, asking no one about him, yet listening greedily to any conversation about him overheard by chance.

Everything she had been taught about her family, its tradition of service, the code of honor. All of it was a bucket of shit. Her father had given her all of that then he had taken it away.

Perhaps, she thought, if she had never gotten away from Bolivia, it would not have mattered so much. But she *knew* there was honesty and honor and selflessness in the world. She had seen it in the United States, a country that, for all its flaws, made her ashamed of her own.

Now she had paid her debt to the United States by selfishly asking them for more, more, more, until twelve of their boys paid with their lives. John Church was right. Her father could have built the clinic. He could have built her an entire hospital. Whatever she wanted. And why not? Why not put the money he gleaned from death to good use?

She knew why not. Because she was too proud. And because, even now, in the midst of a plague at the back end of creation, she still believed that there was an irreconcilable difference between good and evil, and that honor mattered. She had even begun to believe in God, although it was very hard.

Eva drove into the next infected settlement, where she was greeted by a body lying in the open.

AMBASSADOR PLYMOUTH WENT to his embassy even earlier than usual and called Washington on his secure line. He bypassed Latin American Affairs and went right to the number two man in State, an old friend who was also a friend of the president.

"Drew? Morning. Ethan here. How's the view from up there?"

"Save the good cheer, Ethan. It's tears-of-contrition time for you. What's on your mind?"

"I'm going to come down hard on our little Bolivian brothers. Fair warning."

"You've got a fuck-all mess on your hands."

"Trust the military. But I'm looking at this as an opportunity, Drew. One of those once-in-a-tour shots."

There was a pause, then the ambassador's old friend said, "Tell me."

"We're going to go after some labs. Big ones. My DEA man, at least, has his head screwed on right, and now we've got a hammer we can hold over the Bols. They'll play. Looks like Cali did the dirty deed, and in the end, there's not much love lost between those people and La Paz. The drug alliance is strictly a business relationship. And *señor presidente* knows I can withhold his allowance, so I'm expecting full cooperation. Should get good press coverage up your way. In fact, I'll make sure of it. In plenty of time for the midterm elections, I might add."

"What about all that eradication business? You promised the Hill, Ethan, and I was sitting beside you. You're going to have to deliver something. Law and order is the big issue for November, and those who matter want to see visible progress on the drug front."

"Then why are they cutting counterdrug allocations?"

"Everybody's being cut, Ethan. At least State'll be writing the checks from now on. We've got the purse strings, and Defense can play Oliver Twist for a while. Anyway, the president's into the rehabilitation mode. He needs the watermelon caucus, and rehab means money for their districts. Shame it doesn't work. But that's not your problem. Your problem is body bags coming back from Mr. Plymouth's neighborhood."

"You'll get eradication. Fields of coca, cut and burning. Bring your wide-angle lens. But first, we bust the labs. Get the Bols out of denial. We take out a couple of major labs and then I make the point to *señor presidente* that they weren't running on alpaca. And the Bols signed the treaties. They're fucked."

"So we get eradication by November?"

"I'm swinging my biggest bat, Drew."

"Well, you need to hit a home run. I've got to tell you as a friend—your stock isn't terribly high at the moment. Looks like you're responsible for the only war we've got, and nobody up here even knew there *was* a war. The sec's dizzy from getting hit on the side of the head by the media and the vultures on the Hill. Somalia, Rwanda, Bosnia. Take your pick. And I've got subcommittee know-it-alls second-guessing my Russia policy." Plymouth's old friend retreated into his own concerns for a moment, then said, "And another thing. You'd better watch that sonofabitch Parnell. That black-Irish bastard's up to something in Panama. The good general held those bodies up for a day and said the dog ate his homework."

"What?"

"Does Parnell know something we don't?"

"Not that I know of," Plymouth said honestly, trying to think.

"Well, watch him. The military can do stupid things, but they are not, in fact, all that dumb. Ask the president.

They handed him his ass on the fags-in-the-force business.''

''All right, Drew. Got it. Just wanted you to know the game plan. We're really going to hurt those Colombian bastards.''

''You're absolutely certain the Colombians did it?''

''The Bols are too weak-kneed for a number like that.''

''All right. Anything else?''

Plymouth remembered. Yes. One more little thing. Something Church had raised the day before in a hallway. ''Drew, one of my people thinks we may have another of those periodic epidemics kicking off down here. Maybe something nasty.''

''In La Paz?''

''No. Down in the boondocks. On the Brazilian border. Should we take a closer look at it, you think?''

''Their government ask for our help?''

''No. Not yet. I'm not sure they even know about it. It's in a pretty remote area, out near where we lost those soldiers. And news doesn't exactly go CNN around here. If the world ended, La Paz wouldn't know about it for at least a week. I mean, sometimes I feel like I'm playing the Jetsons meet the Flintstones down here.''

''Well, let them ask. The last thing we want to do is send the Bolivians Christmas presents after they shit under the tree. I can tell you, even out of the half dozen people on the Hill who know where Bolivia is on the map, you won't find much of a constituency for sending flowers at the moment. Your bad luck those killings took place during a week when nothing much else was going on. Have you seen the pictures?''

''What pictures?''

''The bodies. Green Berets in various shades of red. Some local freelancer took them. They broke in Brazil, now Gannett's got them in living color. Ugly stuff to face over your Starbucks in the morning. Whoever did it was mean, Ethan. And, by the way, I *do* have something else for you, amigo. Do you know somebody down there named von Reinsee? *Newsweek* just fingered the guy as one of the top ten drug kingpins in the Andean Ridge—and the only one in your sandbox.''

"They need to go back to Journalism 101,'' Plymouth said after a brief pause. ''Von Reinsee's a pillar of Bolivian society.''

"THE WHEELS ARE turning," Henry Vasquez said, "and you either get on board or get run over." He looked at the brigadier general in the national police uniform. The style of dress had not changed since the days when the men in epaulets made all of South America's decisions. "I'm telling you this as a friend, Luis. If your boys don't come out of the *cuartel* and help us on this one, we're going to have to go to your military. And the dollars go where the action is."

"The timing is bad," the general said. He was balding and he grew his remaining reserves of hair long, maneuvering pomaded strands across the battlefield of his scalp. "It could not be worse."

Vasquez snorted. A good mimic, he could speak the fine, time-warp Spanish of the local elites, but he could also summon at need the toughness of the Houston neighborhood where he had grown to young manhood in the days before the drug explosion and where you flexed words the way you did your biceps. "Timing wasn't so hot for those twelve soldiers."

The general held up his hands. Offering Vasquez his sympathy, his goodwill, his friendship for life. "What happened to those men was a terrible thing. When we find the guilty parties, they'll wish they had killed themselves first."

"Luis, my old friend. Let me tell you how Washington works. Because this is all about Washington. Washington is results-oriented when it comes to something like this. That doesn't mean the results have to be relevant. Not relevant as you and I might see them, as men of the law. The results just have to come quickly and be quantifiable. Photogenic results are best. Washington wants to *see* somebody punished for this. It would be a wonderful thing if we could identify the killers and bring them to justice in time for the Sunday morning talk shows and the editorial pages up in *el Norte*. But you and I know that is unlikely to happen. So we are going to go after some labs. You and me, pal. And nobody is going to stop us.''

Vasquez could tell the general would have liked to show his anger, to tie him to a chair and beat him with his fists for his effrontery. But the general knew better.

"I don't know about any laboratories," the general said. "If the national police knew where there were drug laboratories, we would have raided them long ago."

"I'm going to help you out. Just make sure I've got a company of the best you've got. Wherever I want them, whenever I want them."

"If there are drug labs, I want to know about them. They are my responsibility as general officer in charge of narcotics strategy for the national police. Where are these drug labs?"

Vasquez looked at his old friend. He knew far more about the man than the Bolivian realized. He knew, for instance, that although the general kept a young mistress for public effect, Brigadier General Luis Sandoval was impotent and had been for years. In Bolivia, that was the kind of information you held back until you needed a fifth ace.

"The first one we're going to hit is down in the Chaparé."

The general grimaced and held up his hands again. "There. You see? You know we can't go into the Chaparé. The president's only just got the *cocaleros* off his back. Nobody wants more trouble in the Chaparé.''

"That's where the coca is, Luis.''

"I'm told there are some labs maybe going up in the Beni. Maybe we could do something down there.''

Vasquez smiled. "Luis, if you got labs down in the Beni and you know about them, I'm sure you'll take care of them. But I need big ones. Not Boliviano. One hundred percent Colombian, the revenge of Juan Valdez.''

"Who?''

"That's why *you* don't have to worry. The labs we're going after are Colombian investments.''

"Colombians have Bolivian partners.''

"We're after the Colombians.''

The general shook his head. "You know,'' he said, "I'm keeping a very beautiful young woman waiting on your account. If we weren't old friends, Henry, I'd throw you out the window.''

Vasquez smiled. "If she's a real woman, she'll wait for a man like you, Luis.''

Both men smiled.

"Do yourself a favor, Luis. Play ball with me on this one. When the dust settles, my people will remember the support of the national police. And you'll be doing your country a favor. It's up to you to get your president out of the doghouse with the U.S. Congress.''

"The president does not want trouble with the *cocaleros*. Between you and me. He is very much against drugs, of course. But he doesn't want trouble.''

Vasquez nodded. "Ambassador Plymouth will help him get over that. Now, Luis. On a totally unrelated matter. ONDCP's holding an Andean Ridge counterdrug strategy conference in Washington next month. They're funding one billet for a homegrown expert from each of the regional states.'' The DEA agent offered the general another between-friends smile. "I thought you'd be the logical guy to represent Bolivia. It's a three-day conference. But I'd have to set up a few additional appointments for you. With people who could benefit from your expertise. You'd have to stay in Washington for at least a week, maybe even ten days. At our expense, of course."

The general looked at him with the eyes of a conquistador. "I would have to take a secretary," he said finally, after taking a moment to judge the offer thoroughly.

Vasquez smiled. "I know you'll have the sense to take along a secretary who's a credit to Bolivia at social functions."

The general smiled, too. "I can promise you, she'll be a walking advertisement for the wonders of Bolivia."

Vasquez stood up and extended his hand. The general rose and met the gesture. Holding the other man's hand tightly in his own, Vasquez, who was larger and stronger, said, "A company that can shoot. With good officers. Men who do what they're told."

"A platoon would be enough."

"Right. And that's probably all I'll take along. But I want to pick my platoon. And I want the rest of the company on call. A first-rate company, Luis."

The general nodded. "After an exhausting strategy session, my secretary and I will need to rest for a few days in Miami on the way home."

Vasquez smiled at the man's vanity and greed. He knew he could refuse this last concession if he chose. But he just said:

"Try not to set the place on fire. With that secretary of yours."

"WHO OR WHAT are the *Diablos Rojos*?" Sieger asked Church's secretary. She was a handsome Bolivian woman, about thirty, with the scent of a divorcée and a cold sore on her lip.

"Oh," she said, "the Red Devils? They are the helicopters. Captain Darling works with them."

"Darling?"

"The negro one. You spilled coffee on him this morning."

Sieger remembered. Not pleased that the secretary had remembered. He could see Darling's head behind a word processor in an adjoining room. He had not gotten all the names straight yet. Church had dozens of permanent and temporary-duty subordinates scattered through cubbyhole offices. Some in uniform, some in civvies. Sieger did not have their names straight, and he knew he did not have the facts straight, either. Not yet.

"What's his first name?" Sieger asked the secretary. "I can't see myself calling a guy 'Darling.' "

"His name is Luther."

Sieger strode across the office with an image of Henry Vasquez floating in his brain housing group. Vasquez had made a series of demands on the Milgroup at a morning meeting held by the ambassador. The only additional attendees had been Sieger, the DCM, the station chief, and a State narcotics man. Everyone deferred to Vasquez, and the ambassador backed the DEA man on every point.

Captain Darling, who had soap opera good looks, sat working behind a word processor while his two office mates joked about a date one of them had experienced deeply the night before. When Sieger stepped into the doorway, the banter stopped.

Yeah, I'm the angel of death, Sieger thought.

"Luther?"

The captain looked up. "Yes, sir?"

"That coffee come out of your trousers?"

"No problem, sir."

"Listen, I need some help. Could you come into Colonel Church's office with me for a few minutes?"

"Yes, sir. Just let me do a save."

Sieger led the way back through the outer office, past one night-eyed secretary after another. A slender woman in tight jeans and a baby-doll sweater cursed the copy machine.

Church knew how to pick secretaries, Sieger decided. Or somebody did. He wondered how much of a problem it had been to get clearances for them.

"Esmeralda, we're going to use the colonel's office for a few minutes," he told the woman with the cold sore. Then he led the way into Church's domain. He had not seen the colonel since the afternoon before and figured the man was laying low, licking his wounds.

"Shut the door, Luther. And have a seat."

Sieger sat down as well. Instead of the Civil War prints and congratulatory plaques that decorated the walls of most military offices, Church had hung old lithographs of South American wannabe Bonapartes and family photos taken amid jungle-suffocated ruins. A ragged peasant weaving hung behind the colonel's desk, and a newer one colored the floor. Lot of books, in English and Spanish. A little bronze cannon thrust out an engraved barrel, but Sieger could not read the tribute, only the name "Major John Church." Beyond the off-tone bulletproof windows, shabby high-rises hid the hills and sky.

"Tell me about the *Diablos Rojos*."

The captain made a face that said: sure, whatever you want. "Those are our Hueys, sir. I mean, technically speaking, we've handed them off to the Bolivians. They fly them. And they do a pretty good job. No night-vision capability to speak of, and you have to keep the ops pretty basic. But they're better than you'd expect. We still do most of the maintenance for them, although the Bols are coming along."

"Who gives them their orders?"

"We do. Although we try not to be heavy-handed about it."

"So the bottom line is that we have helicopters with Bolivian drivers. And we can do what we want with them."

The captain backed off. "Not exactly. Under the terms of the funding, they're only to be used for counterdrug support. Of course, that can mean a lot of different things."

"But, if we have an operational mission, they show up where we want them and they do what we say."

"Yes, sir. Of course, we have to give them some planning time. We've got gringos to help out with that. Contractors, retired military. But it's still slower than a U.S.-only op. And they base out of the mil airfield down in Santa Cruz. If they need to deploy forward, that takes time, too." He looked at Sieger, and Sieger sensed resentment barely held under control.

The DCM, the ambassador's hatchet man, had slashed through the office early in the morning, formally and loudly announcing that Sieger was in charge, by order of the ambassador. That was when Sieger spilled the coffee on the captain.

"If you need them to do something, sir, tell me," Darling said. "I'll make it happen."

"Well, we've got a couple of missions coming up. Henry Vasquez still owes me the details."

Darling's expression was very controlled, a mask on a face destined for success. But the captain's eyes were alert and not friendly.

"You've got something on your mind, Luther," Sieger said. "What is it?"

The captain opened his lips to speak and they had the look of sculpted muscle. Then he decided to keep the words for himself.

"Come on, Luther. Man to man. What's on your mind?"

"Sir, you need to watch Henry Vasquez. Colonel Church says . . . I mean, the feeling around the office is that Vasquez is a loose cannon."

"He seems to get things done."

"Yes, sir. But maybe they're not always the right things."

"I get the impression he and Colonel Church don't get along."

"Vasquez hates Colonel Church with a passion. The colonel's the only guy in the embassy with the rocks to stand up to him. Vasquez has been here forever, and he knows what's hidden behind all the cobwebs. He's got everybody cowed. If it's not out of line, sir, you'd better be careful with him."

No, Sieger thought. It's not out of line. I'm not even sure where the fuck I am. All honest advice welcome.

"The ambassador seems to trust him," Sieger said, testing.

"That's another story, sir."

"Sounds like you don't think much of the ambassador, either."

The captain sat up straight, going military, a subordinate's way to signal that the tap had been turned off. "Sir, Colonel Church has a policy. Nobody ever says anything bad about the ambassador. And if we have anything bad to say to each other about anything, we say it behind closed doors. Away from the Bols."

Sieger tinkered with the barrel of the souvenir cannon. Sloppy workmanship, not much of a prize. "It sounds to me," he said, "as though you think pretty highly of Colonel Church, Luther."

The captain nodded. The fine tan planes of his face spoke for him now, but he supplemented their language with words:

"Sir, Colonel Church is the finest officer I know. And I don't think I'm the only officer here who feels that way."

"And that means . . . that I am not particularly welcome."

"Sir . . ." The younger man searched for a way to express himself, and Sieger felt the captain's dilemma: how much to reveal, how to speak truly without blatant disrespect. How to get along and still maintain some dignity. Finally, the captain found his words. They were blunter and more assured than Sieger expected.

"Sir, my view is that you're a target of opportunity. The ambassador's just using you. If Henry Vasquez screws up, you're going to take the fall. You, and Colonel Church, and the whole Milgroup."

It was not particularly reassuring to Sieger to have his own thoughts spoken out loud by another. He looked at the younger man.

"Where are you from, Luther?"

"Washington, D.C., sir."

Sieger straightened his neck.

"I volunteered for this assignment, sir. I wanted to work counterdrug. I've seen what drugs do up close."

Sieger let the captain sit for a moment, then asked, "You're rotary wing, right?"

"Yes, sir. I'm rated on Hueys and Blackhawks. That's why Colonel Church put the *Rojos* on my plate."

"And you get along okay with them?"

"Yes, sir. They're pretty good guys. Sometimes one of them goes bad. The drug money can be pretty tempting. But mostly they just want to be accepted as gringo-quality chopper jockeys." The captain almost smiled. "Everybody down here wants to be a gringo, no matter how loud they yell 'Yankee go home.'" Then the smile grew genuine and Darling flicked his head back toward the closed door and the secretaries beyond it. "Or to marry one. The girls already know you're not married, by the way. That's the first thing they check out on a new arrival. Anyway, I get along with the *Rojos*. I think they find me a little less threatening than they do the anglos. I think I kind of give them hope, although they generally don't have much time for blacks. But I'm a gringo black, so I'm okay. Sort of."

"Complex world."

"Yes, sir."

"Luther, I'm going to need your help."

"Yes, sir."

"Even if you resent the hell out of me being here, keep the mission in mind."

"Yes, sir."

"I want you to tell me anytime you see me walking into a minefield. Before I get us all blown up."

The captain shook his head. Slowly. "Sir, you're already in the middle of one. The whole counterdrug thing is nothing but a minefield. It's not like the folks back home think."

Right, Sieger thought. He was building up a backlog of questions he could not fairly ask a subordinate. But there were mundane matters, too.

"You have any idea where Colonel Church is today? I haven't seen him around."

The captain looked up in surprise. "Colonel Church went on leave, sir." Then, at Sieger's expression, he added, "I figured you knew that."

"Leave?" Sieger asked. "When?"

"This morning, sir. Early. He came by to sign himself out. He was already leaving when I came in."

"He tell you where he was going? On his leave?"

The captain made a helpless face. "Sir, I didn't ask. I'm useless before I've had at least three cups of coffee."

"Shit," Sieger said.

"Sir," the major leaned forward, soldierly in his willingness to help even an unwelcome comrade, "it should be on his leave form. Esmeralda ought to have it; she takes care of all the admin."

Sieger stood up and walked directly to the door, with the captain following him.

The secretary was putting salve on her lip with the help of a compact mirror.

"Esmeralda? Do you have a copy of Colonel Church's DA-31?"

She nodded, testing her lips, not speaking. Wiping her finger on a tissue, she turned to the filing cabinet beside her desk. The suddenly exposed drawer looked disastrous, but the secretary found the document in seconds and handed it to Sieger.

He scanned down the numbered blocks, with the captain reading over his shoulder.

"What the hell?" Sieger said. "What on earth would he want to go back down there for?"

"BECAUSE SOMEONE HAS to finish this," Church said, picking his way through the shell of the clinic. Scavengers had already ripped out the wiring, and the windows he had seen on his last visit were missing. Two turds lay in a corner of the reception room.

The national police lieutenant shook his head, unsatisfied with the answer to his question. When Church had called from the airport, an unexpected late afternoon arrival on the commercial hop from Riberalta, the lieutenant promptly came out in a pickup to offer him a ride. Assuming it was an official visit. After Church explained what he intended to do, the lieutenant spent the remainder of the ten-minute drive to the building site attempting to dissuade the colonel, trying to buy time until his captain could return from the afternoon's private business. Church remained adamant, although his heart failed a little at the sight of the unfinished clinic, derelict and instantly shabby.

"But why you, *mi coronel*?" the lieutenant pressed. He was old for a lieutenant, even for a policeman in his country, and his assignment was a poor one. "This isn't a job for a colonel."

"Maybe I'm not much of a colonel. Listen, Eduardo. You know this town. Who's my best bet to buy construction material at a reasonable price?" Church felt the calculations start up in the other man as the lieutenant wondered what the profit might be for himself, and Church added, "The government's not paying. This is coming out of my own pocket."

The lieutenant's face looked shadowed by fate.

Church quite liked the solemnity that overtook Bolivians faced with even minor decisions. "Deal with señor Hagopian. He's the most honest. But, *mi coronel*, why should you be the one to do this? You don't owe these people anything. They don't even care about themselves. The *alcalde*'s a rich pig, if you will permit me to say so. He could pay to have the clinic finished and not feel it."

Yes, Church thought, the lord mayor. A truly heroic figure. "Eduardo, stop thinking so much. The world won't come to an end just because an over-the-hill colonel gets a few callouses on his hands. Are you Catholic?"

"Of course."

"Then think of this as my penance. I sent those boys down here to build this. What happened to them was my fault. On some level. The least I can do is finish what they started. It's not a big deal." He tried to kick ravaged bits of plaster into a pile, to begin cleaning up. "Could you loan me a broom from the barracks?"

"Of course. But you are not Catholic. I didn't think Protestants had penance. I thought you were like the missionaries who come through here. All clean and shining and nothing inside. If you permit me to say so."

"Sometimes I think it would be easier if I were Catholic. It's so much more systematic, you always know where you stand." Church smiled. "How about asking Mr. Hagopian to stop by to see me." He looked up at a ceiling that had been torn open for the sake of a single wire: a poor country.

"Sure. But you're not staying here? Not at night?"

Church looked at the barrenness surrounding the two of them. "I figure I'd better. If I want things to stay put."

"You could sleep with us in the *cuartel*. You'd be safe."

Church shrugged. "Thanks. I'll take my chances."

"That is foolish of you, *mi coronel*," the lieutenant

said bluntly. Church realized the man was thinking of
his own career and he wondered how much the lieutenant had already suffered because of the murders. In the
national police, a captaincy was already a sufficiently ex-
alted rank to allow an officer to deflect blame downward
except for the very worst transgressions. But lieutenants
were lieutenants everywhere. Church had begun to wa-
ver in his decision as to sleeping arrangements, out of
sympathy for the lieutenant, when he remembered how
quickly the murdered men's possessions had been looted
while under national police guard. The lieutenant's men
had not done much to protect the clinic itself, either.

When Church did not respond, the lieutenant said, "I
could place a guard here at night in your stead. There
would be no more unfortunate problems."

Church was already looking for a place to hang the
string hammock he carried rolled up in his rucksack. He
certainly was not going to sleep in the barn. It still stank,
literally, of murder. And Church had been down south
long enough to believe in ghosts. Sometimes the ghosts
of El Salvador came to visit him.

"Thanks for the offer, Eduardo. I'll be fine. But track
down Mr. Hagopian for me, please. I want to get to
work. And I need tools, material. . . ."

The lieutenant, expression dark as poetry, held out his
hands. Absolve me, I have tried to save you.

"I'll be all right," Church assured him.

And the lieutenant left. Church stacked his gear in a
corner that had not been soiled and set to work as best
he could with his bare hands, hauling the larger pieces
of plaster waste and broken wood outside.

A brown child in skivvies stopped by the side of the
road to watch. Then two more kids came up. They stood
immobile and dead-faced, fascinated, starved for any
kind of entertainment. Finally, Church set down a broken plank, smiled, and waved to them.

The children smiled brightly in return, their teeth not
yet rotted. They whispered together, giggling.

Still smiling, the tallest of the three turned his face back to Church, lifted his chin, and slowly drew a finger across his throat.

"AND THAT'S MY plan," Henry Vasquez concluded.

Appalled, Sieger looked at the other three men gathered in the ambassador's office. Hoping that at least one of the faces showed reservations. But the ambassador, who always wore an expression wary of invisible cameras, simply nodded, and the DCM followed his lead. The station chief, who should have been the most knowledgeable in such matters and the wariest, chewed on a dead pipe and smiled to himself as if daydreaming.

Sieger found the DEA agent's plan inexcusably ragged and amateurish. He had expected something much better and he spoke up, in his element now and confident, wanting to be a part of the team, to help.

"Henry, that's certainly an aggressive plan . . . but it frankly isn't good tactics. You don't land the choppers right on the objective. You can get shot to shit that way."

Vasquez gave his mouth a twist and tossed one black-and-white blowup after another across the table toward Sieger. "I showed you the layout. I explained it. There's no place else you can land up there. Just that clearing by the lab. Anyway, we want surprise. Don't want to give them time to get away."

"Well," Sieger said, reaching for words that would not come right out and say how damnably stupid he found the entire concept of the operation, "if you don't have good LZs and you want surprise, you go in overland. Hump in through the bush."

Vasquez shook his head, smiling with unmistakable condescension. It struck Sieger that the man must have been good-looking when he was younger and thinner. "Kurt, this isn't a military operation. You've got to remember that. It's law-and-order stuff. And I'm a cop. I kick in doors. And the Bolivian narco cops don't much like going cross-country. For that matter, I don't have time to go bungling through the jungle myself.''

"Maybe you should try it," Sieger said, trying to control his anger, to keep his voice at the bantering level. "Landing right on top of the target like that is a good way to get somebody killed. Maybe a whole lot of somebodies. And it's not jungle, according to the map. Look at your own photos. That's highland terrain. You can move fast over ground like that. Sleep by day, move at night. We'd be all over them before they knew it.'' He looked at the ambassador, seeking an ally, but found an opaque stare and shifted immediately back to the DEA man. "And what about rehearsals? You've got to practice an operation like this. War-game the things that could go wrong. I don't care if it's cops and robbers or World War Three, you're still talking about a helicopter assault. I may not know much about the counterdrug world, but I understand tactics.''

"I'm sure you do," the ambassador interrupted. A few dark crumbs clung to the corner of his mouth. "But Henry understands the environment down here. He's got a wealth of experience. I think we have to defer to him on this. Although we all value your input, Kurt.''

"Mr. Ambassador," Sieger began, but as he looked at the man's face he realized he had already lost the argument. So he shifted his effort. "Why go after this lab first, anyway? Why not go after the one closest to where the team was killed? It stands to reason that the guys with the blood on their hands are probably the ones closest to the scene.''

The ambassador slowly turned his gaze to Henry Vasquez.

"Tactics," Vasquez said. "Political tactics. If we hit the northern lab first, the Bolivians might figure they can close the books on this whole affair. But we've got to take advantage of the opportunity to really hurt the Colombians, to show them we're serious players down here.

So we hit the Chaparé first. Then we can still tell the
Bols that we have to take out the northern lab because
they're the likeliest perpetrators and all that. Tactics,
Kurt. *Tac*tics.''

That much, at least, made sense to Sieger. But there
were still more questions to be asked, so many he kept
losing them from the front of his mind. "What if this
raid makes the guys up north bolt? Then we lose the
guys who probably did the killings.''

Vasquez looked at him calmly. "No. We'll get them.
I've got all my lines running. We're going to take those
bastards out.''

"Henry,'' the ambassador asked, "you said our Bolivian friends are on board?''

"Yes, sir. We'll have a first-rate company supporting
the op. Good officers.''

Brushing his fingers over the corner of his mouth, the
ambassador turned to Sieger. "Kurt, I believe it's already apparent to you that we've had some difficulties
with Colonel Church. On operations just such as this.
That's why I've put you in charge. I want you to make
damned sure Henry gets all of the support he needs. And
I want you right there with him on this operation. In
case anything goes wrong that requires a military man
to put it right.''

Sieger cocked his head a quarter turn, looking at the
ambassador through ever more skeptical eyes. "Mr.
Ambassador, I thought it was illegal for U.S. military
personnel to participate in direct-action counterdrug missions.''

"That's right,'' Plymouth said. "And that's why you
won't be armed. You'll go along as an observer. To
monitor the Bolivian performance.'' The ambassador
shifted his attention to Vasquez. "So tell me, Henry,
when do you plan to stage this little operation?''

"Tomorrow.''

Sieger opened his mouth to tell the ambassador it was
impossible, that he already knew the Bolivians would

need more time than that to deploy their helicopters. But he realized that he had lost, and that he was being used, and that his only options were to go along or to bail out. He almost quit, nearly got his refusal to participate in the folly into words, when it struck him that, if the operation turned bad, he probably would be the only one involved who could make a serious attempt to set it right again. Anyway, he did not much like the idea of quitting. Quitting followed a man.

He realized that the ambassador had just spoken to him. But he had missed the words. He felt he was missing a great deal now.

"*Kurt*," the ambassador repeated, "I asked you if Church is giving you any problems."

"No," Sieger said. "No problems at all, Mr. Ambassador. He's not even here."

The ambassador's eyebrows had a grammar all their own, cold and articulate. "What do you mean, he's not here?"

"He signed himself out on leave. You told him to take some time off, sir. He went down to Mendoza. I figure he's trying to find out a little more about what happened. He probably feels—"

The ambassador rose to his feet. He was tall, and the sofa and chairs in which the others sat were low. Plymouth towered over them.

"That sonofa*bitch*. That—he's done enough damage. I want his ass right back here. No. I want that man out of this *coun*try." The ambassador turned to Vasquez. "Can you get in touch with the sonofabitch? Without getting the Bols involved? I don't want them to know there's dissension in my embassy."

Vasquez leaned forward, anxious to help. "A cop would do it through his wife. Wives always know how to get in touch with their husbands. Unless it's the marriage from hell. And Church and his wife have that whole Ozzie-and-Harriet thing. Work through Ruth Church."

Plymouth strode across the room. It was a surprisingly characterless place, furnished by the General Services Administration school of interior decorating with dull, presentable furniture. The artwork was the visual equivalent of shopping mall background music and had no connection with the continent where it hung. The ambassador picked up one of the phones from a counter behind his desk.

"Donna, get Colonel Church's wife on the phone. Yes. Ruth Church. If she's not at home, find her." He hung up and looked back across the long, soulless room. "Sieger, an embassy has to be a team. And Colonel Church is not a team player. I expect better from you." He began to walk back toward the group. But his focus remained the army officer. "Another thing. I hear you have a bright future. But let me tell you something. This continent's been a graveyard for bright futures for five hundred years. It swallows people whole. Unless they have somebody powerful to take care of them." The ambassador's sun-blonded eyebrows curled. "I take good care of my people, Kurt. Until they let me down."

"Yes, sir." He had a sense of falling, with no way of stopping himself.

One of the ambassador's phones rang. Plymouth reversed course and picked it up.

"Ambassador Plymouth. Yes. Mrs. Church. I want you to listen carefully. You are to contact your husband and tell him I've ordered him back to La Paz immediately." He paused. "Then I want the two of you and your family out of this country by the end of the week. The embassy staff will assist you with the move. To ensure there are no delays. Do you have any questions, Mrs. Church?"

The ambassador jerked the phone away from his ear as though he had heard a painfully loud noise, holding it just at the level of his shoulder. His lips parted and his eyebrows crumpled.

Finally, slowly, he put the phone back in its cradle

and turned to the empty space between his desk and the waiting men.

"I can't believe," he said in a voice of wonder, "that a woman like that . . . said a thing like that . . . to *me*."

RUTH CHURCH COULD not believe she had said such a thing to anyone, much less to the ambassador himself. She had never cared for the man, finding him pretentious, self-important and a very bad loser at tennis. Nonetheless, she had surprised herself—no, *shocked* herself—with the suddenness and depth of the anger she felt toward him.

She was terribly worried about her husband going down-country alone, given all that had happened. But she knew her response to Plymouth had not come only from nerves. She sensed that the man was attacking her husband on a fundamental level, hitting where it mattered and where John could not defend himself. It made her at least as angry as if someone had tried to harm her children.

But she was sorry now for what she had said. She sat by the great window, in her husband's favorite chair, staring off at the houses climbing the far side of the valley. She was sorry because she knew she had only made things worse and John was going to have to pay the price for her lack of discipline.

She began to cry, letting herself go. Thinking of John down there like the fool that he forever insisted on being, trying to build that damned clinic with his own hands when nobody cared about it in the least. She cried slowly, open-eyed, the way she cried occasionally when things were bad and John could not see her. She knew he was a foolish man sometimes, in his more-heart-than-brains way. But she would not have changed him. Not a bit. Not for anything the world had to offer. She knew that she had been a very fortunate woman to have lived the life she had lived with the man she had been blessed to marry by her side. Poor John. He was the best man she had ever known. And now she had done him harm.

"Señora?" It was the maid, dish towel forever in hand. "Is there something bad?"

They would have to find a good family for María, people who would treat her with respect.

"No. Nothing really."

"You should not worry about the colonel," the maid said. "God will take care of him."

"Yes."

No. Ruth decided that she was not going to just accept whatever Plymouth dumped on them. The ambassador was a jerk. A jerk's jerk. Poor Anne, married to the beast. Ethan Rice Plymouth was not going to get away with hurting John Church.

Ruth stood up, wiping her eyes, a bit embarrassed. "It's all right, María. Thank you. I've just got to make a telephone call."

She walked through the room full of travel mementoes, of a life's record, and went to the phone in the hallway, looking up a number in the little book of family friends, acquaintances, and get-things-done-before-the-apocalypse connections. With her hand on the receiver, she hesitated for a last moment, sniffing to clear her nose so that she could speak properly. Wondering if she would only make things worse. Then she decided that things could not get much worse. She dialed.

"Señor Gabriel Ortiz, please. Yes. I'll wait."

And she waited, reconsidering again. And again. She had never taken a step this big without consulting her husband. Interfering in his world, a thing she had not done since she had been a company commander's wife and dealing with the other wives and their problems had been part of her unpaid job.

Beyond the narrow hall windows with their black metal arabesques, Ruth could see green grass and roses against a white wall.

A voice came on the phone. Jarring her.

"Yes. Thank you. This is Ruth Church. Colonel John Church's wife. From the U.S. embassy. You were our guest for dinner a few months ago. You made jokes about our ambassador."

The voice on the other end of the line assured her that she was unforgettable and that the jokes had not been serious.

"I need your help," Ruth said. "My husband needs your help. You know those men who were killed? The U.S. soldiers? They were building a clinic. Yes. Well, my husband went back down there. By himself. He wants to finish that clinic. Yes. Just him. Thank you. Well, the problem is the U.S. ambassador. The one you don't like. He's trying to prevent John from finishing the clinic. Yes. John's trying to finish that clinic on his vacation time and with his own money and labor. And Ambassador Plymouth's trying to stop him. He's ordering John out of the country. I thought you might be able to help."

"Your husband," the voice said, "is a very good man." Behind the voice Ruth heard the hollow, clattering sounds of an office that had not yet entered the era of automation.

"Yes. He's a very good man. But he needs help. I thought maybe you could write a story, let people know. So that John can finish his work. That's all he wants. To finish the clinic."

"Absolutely. It's a great story. Wonderful. But I'll need to ask you a few more questions—do you have a good picture of your husband we could use, by the way?"

"Yes," Ruth said, wondering already if she was not just making things worse and worse. "I have a number of pictures. You can choose any one you like."

"That's good. Very good. By the way, did your husband mention anything to you about an epidemic down there? There's a rumor going around."

"He said something. I don't remember his exact

words. I think it was out in the Indian settlements. He didn't know much about it.''

"But he went back down there in the middle of an epidemic to finish a clinic for the poor people of Bolivia. At a time when the government of Bolivia itself is ignoring such problems."

"You could say that."

The voice laughed. But in a kindly manner. "I *will* say that. It's a great lead. But, señora Church, I have to admit something to you. I'm not accustomed to writing stories about good-guy gringos. I mean, I liked your husband from the day I met him, but this story is going to be a novelty. A gringo hero in Bolivia. I mean that in a polite way, of course."

"Yes. Of course."

"I think this will make your ambassador furious. I hear that he is always very unhappy when the newspapers fail to portray him as a great diplomat."

"Yes. I expect so. So you'll be going down to see John, to interview him?"

The voice laughed, with more edge this time. "That won't be necessary. We Bolivian journalists are extremely creative."

THE BLOOD ON her face had already dried when Eva awoke. She had no idea where she was for a long, slow time, for an age, and her return to consciousness was an instinctive struggle. She lay against the canted door of her vehicle in the darkness, head swollen under her dirty hair but no permanent harm done. Suddenly, she sat up, tried to sit up, fought to find a way of sitting that made sense.

"Oh, hell," she said.

She could not remember what had happened. But she was in her jeep. And her jeep was nosed into a gully, stalled out. Her head hurt and remembering came slowly.

Driving. Driving back to town. So tired.

Her body felt battered, and she tested limbs and fingers. All right. But her shoulder was sore. And her head throbbed. She realized that she must have fallen asleep while driving. Too weary to drive. Too far gone to be any good to anyone.

She believed now that the epidemic remained confined to a small pocket of settlements well off the main highway, and she hoped to keep it that way. But some of the inhabitants had fled. Those who had taken their animals with them would wait things out in the back country. That was all right. But she worried about those who had simply disappeared, heading for town or for the homes of relatives in other settlements, perhaps carrying the disease with them.

She needed help. She needed the military or at least the national police to close roads and trails, and she needed health teams from the capital. And she was more convinced than ever that experts had to be called in who had the wherewithal to identify the disease, even if the epidemic burned itself out like a brush fire. But driving back to town, she had felt willing to settle for a shower, a few hours of sleep, a refilled medical kit, and if she was lucky, a few pairs of hands to help her dispose of the dead. She felt small and incapable and wasted.

Finding her bearings, Eva tried to crank up the jeep, hoping to coax it back onto the road. But the battery was just one more corpse. She realized that she must have been out cold for hours, with the headlights draining the charge. There was nothing to do but get out and walk.

Although she never let another soul in on her secret, Eva was often guilty of the sin of despair. There were times when she had to bully herself through the days. Because, in the end, she could not see that she made much of a difference. And now this.

Walking down the empty blacktop, under a sky that had come clean of clouds and shone as though heaven were true and close, she thought about the twelve dead

Americans. And Church. She was sorry they had died, but now it was an especially selfish sorrow. Had they not died, Church would have been able to help her. He was a man who was born to help, and she suspected he did it better than she did, and her vanity was great enough that she would have been jealous had it been anyone but him.

She thought of him now, her bruised spine jarring with each step, imagining him with his family in La Paz. She had been a dinner guest in the Church home twice, sitting by the fire, sipping wine after civilized meals and talking with the luxurious feeling you got from a long hot bath. Soaking in the grace of it all, the full bookcases, the well-behaved children, the decency possible between human beings. She wished she could take Church away from all that, just for a little while, so that he might help her. She felt as though she had never needed help as badly as she did now.

Eva stepped awkwardly on a stone and her shoulder stung her with another deep pang. She hoped she had not done it any serious damage in the accident. She could not afford that. Not now. There was much too much to do. Exhausted, she looked up beyond the black trees and night noises. The lights of the City of God burned across the valleys of infinity. She was not afraid of the darkness or of the things that lived in it. She was only afraid of being too weak for the calling she had chosen for herself, too weak for the demands of her pride.

She thought of Church again, picturing him seated comfortably with a book in his hand and his wife quiet by his side, and then she thought back to her time in the United States, to her residency in a fine clinic and hospital tucked up in a drowsy town along the Pennsylvania–New York border, far from the famous centers of wealth and culture, a symbol of how a civilized country should be. Here, even La Paz did not have a single facility of remotely similar quality. But there, in a pocket of comparative poverty, the quality of care available to the semiliterate, to the badly dressed and ill-employed, had been jarring to her and remarkable. Talented, she had enjoyed her specialty, delving into the human heart, clinical, dispassionately controlled, and at the same time, imagining souls in her hands. It had been a wonderful, safe, clean world of machines that could do everything short of creating life, a world of complex skills taken for granted. She had left all of that and a fellow doctor who loved lovemaking, pasta, jazz, and her, to walk alone down this road.

For years, Eva had believed her choice had been taken both to spite her father, who had been unspeakably proud of her, and to teach him. But in time, she had come to see that she had been happy in the little town in the Pennsylvania hills with her work and her patient lover, and happiness was something she could never bear for long.

CHURCH LAY IN his hammock, wondering if he should be afraid. Despite all that had happened, the notion that he might be in danger had not really occurred to him until the child's gesture. He had been far more worried about the bureaucratic consequences of his actions.

He knew that every sensible man had things of which he was afraid, and he counted his fears as he swayed faintly in the darkness. He feared losing Ruth. Or the children. He wondered if that was not selfish, to fear losing them in that order. But it was true. When he imagined loss, he first imagined a world without Ruth. The children, whom he loved beyond the power of words to tell, came second. Church remembered how, as he had been leaving before dawn to go to the embassy, then the airport, his wife had answered his farewell kiss with an embrace so powerful it hurt his back a little. She didn't say anything trite or discouraging. Just "Call me when you can."

He supposed he feared pain and dying as much as the next man, but such things did not have much reality for him. Perhaps, he thought, I have a limited imagination. When U.S. troops descended to put an end to Noriega's tantrums, he had been involved in one of the downtown shoot-outs, walking forward unarmed to talk a gang of terrified Panamanian bullies into surrendering before they started getting artillery rounds through their doors and windows. It had worked, and the shooting had stopped in that part of the city, and Church had been surprised that other people insisted afterward that he had behaved bravely. At the time, it had just seemed in the order of things, like filling out a form.

The night smelled. The unfinished clinic sat on a knoll in a lowland where swamp vegetation perished and rotted and started up again, and there was a persistent background stink of dead water. But a window frame let in starlight the color of fresh milk in a last reprieve before the big rains. The starlight coated the sacks of mortar and cement he had paid for in the evening and the secondhand tools the merchant had loaned him when he finally realized that Church was honest, if a bit irrational, in his explanations. Church had quite liked the man, recognizing the type, one of the strewn Armenians who, despite lives of hard work and intermittent successes, never quite crossed the threshhold of riches familiar to their brethren who had chosen to sell different goods in other towns in better times. A gleaming shovel handle caught Church's eye. He decided he could defend himself with it if necessary.

He thought about Eva von Reinsee, hoping he would see her, wishing he could help her, wanting her to be all right but not quite trusting this world when the welfare of others was involved. He had seen no signs of epidemic or panic as he passed through town on the way from the airport. Only the usual rural teenagers with their inchoate dreams of other realities, and the workers forever hacking at brush, and other men sitting with inhuman stillness by the doors of their shacks. Women shuffled baskets from one place to another, and a Romeo buzzed along on a puny-engined motorbike. The town had been snoozing in prickly-heat normalcy. While Eva roamed the bush, guarding the population with her pills and syringes and her child's shoulders.

Thinking about Eva led him to her father. Church had met him once, at a reception at the German embassy, where von Reinsee was celebrated as a walking dramatization of all that Teutonic fortitude could achieve among Latins. The man wore a mixture of charm and death the way another man might have worn cologne. The charm came from a combination of manners, instinct, and a look at once virile and pale, Herbert von Karajan meets the lord of the vampires. The death part came from all that Church knew about von Reinsee's central business endeavor, a matter absent legal proof despite substance perceptible to all. Watching the older man work the room, Church had suspected that von Reinsee played in the drug world the way another rich man might have played high-stakes poker—challenging fate because men were not challenging enough. When Church asked him bluntly how the cocaine business was going, von Reinsee smiled gorgeously, white hair gleaming under a chandelier, and said:

"Splendidly, Colonel, it's going splendidly. Best thing that ever happened to Bolivia. Wish I had a piece of it. And thanks so much for looking after Eva. She's a pistol, but she means well." And he turned, with a hint of a bow, to the Russian ambassador's wife, who was eating passionately.

Von Reinsee had left Church feeling petulant and inadequate, as though he would be forever unfit for the world into which the German had been born.

Floating in his hammock, Church did not imagine that von Reinsee had anything to do with the deaths of his

soldiers, because the man seemed so far above that kind
of thing. Von Reinsee dealt at the levels of hundreds of
millions of dollars, perhaps of billions. Church understood that the German could simply ignore the ram-
bunctious nonsense generated by the U.S. embassy in its
counterdrug crusade. Perhaps the German was even
amused by it.

An ugly-voiced bird called. Unanswered, it called
again. The bird was likely one of the luridly feathered
creatures tourists longed to smuggle home, but Church
could not help picturing it as a vulture.

He very much wanted to put the counterdrug stuff
behind him when he retired. He knew it was important,
a matter of genuine national security interest. But the
men responsible for national security at Washington's
highest level were not really interested, and if the big
boys didn't care, nothing decisive would ever happen.
Church even suspected that he had a richer appreciation
of the importance of the counterdrug issue than anyone
else in the embassy. Except for Darling, who had grown
up closer to it than any of them. Certainly closer than
the ambassador, whom Church found typical in his ignorance of the day-to-day concerns of his fellow citizens. Even Henry Vasquez, Mr. Death-On-Drugs,
somehow lacked seriousness, for all his spectacular lab
raids and photogenic bonfires. For that matter, there was
something just a bit off about Henry, although Church
could never quite figure out what it was. Maybe the
DEA man was just too much of a hot dog for his tastes.
Or perhaps it was his own insulted pride, given how
noisily Vasquez disdained him.

It was hard to endure being condemned to failure,
especially if you had worn a uniform for more than two
decades of your life only to see the parade end badly.
Church knew that nothing his country was doing in Bolivia or anywhere else south of Panama made a damned
bit of difference in the end. In one country they sprayed
a few fields, in another they uprooted a few hectares of

coca leaf and burned their inconsequential booty. With
dignitaries, officials, and everybody but the family dog
in attendance for the photo op. But it was never enough
to do more than piss off a few unlucky locals. Arrests,
when they came, meant nothing. A few illiterate stooges
went to prison, but anyone with influence, anyone who
mattered, went free on some invented technicality. Even
the occasional successful raid on a drug lab did not do
very much, because there were hundreds of labs out
there, maybe thousands, more of them all the time, just
as there were ever more creatively criminal organiza-
tions that outmaneuvered or simply ignored the arthritic
local governments Washington blessed as model democ-
racies. Slumped in a hammock at the end of the world,
Church felt as though he had a front-row seat on the
future, watching invisible new-model empires metas-
tasize across borders the comfortable world of governments and treaties still pretended were inviolable.
Reality no longer matched the diplomat's maps.

He thought again of Henry Vasquez, all energy and
noise. Henry got results, all right. But the results did not
matter. And as Church knew from his Bolivian connections, the drug bosses just laughed. Sometimes, Church
had heard, they even threw DEA a bone to keep the
gringos happy for a bit. For Church, who had gone
through a mandatory youthful zen and martial arts period, all of Vasquez's sound and fury was exactly the
trap of which the *roshis* warned: activity was intoxicating and could easily be mistaken for achievement.

Then again, Church reminded himself, Henry Vasquez
had never killed twelve of his own. It all just seemed so
damned unfair. Church looked out through the glassless
window and the harsh-throated bird back in the trees
called again.

When he had finally let himself collapse dirty-pawed
into the hammock, Church had believed he would fall
asleep instantly, worn out by the day. But his body's
weariness had been a trick, and sleep was terribly far

away, and his thoughts were despairing. He remembered old things, lost things, and scraped his soul on hopeless problems until, at last, he slipped out of the hammock, barefooted and careless in the moonlight, and worked a hand down into his rucksack until he felt the cool plastic case of his radio.

It was a compact shortwave set, an old friend and routine indulgence on deployments. He drew out the antenna and flopped back into the hammock, fooling with the dial. Festive music, probably from Brazil across the river. A voice in a distant Slavic language, then French with the dreamy, sorrowful accent of West Africa, French like heated syrup, and a sound of bells amid static. He tilted the antenna toward the window.

Suddenly, with wonderful timing, he heard the first long rising notes of *Parsifal*. He centered the tuning and upped the volume a touch, resting the set near his ear, grateful for the tiny, distant sound.

He listened truly then, lulled and drowsing but not quite sleeping, until Good triumphed over Evil.

CHRISTIAN RITTER VON Reinsee sat in a worn armchair he could not bear to discard, listening to a broadcast of *Parsifal* from home. He still thought of Germany as home, although he had no desire to return for more than his annual vacation or the intermittent business transaction. Even his last trip had not swayed him, although he had been able to cross into Poland to visit his family estate after five decades, returning to the painful daylight world for the sake of memory.

The automobile ride, with its border crossing and bad lunch, had climaxed with the sort of disappointment that drew a smile of self-knowledge. The tree-lined roads had been the same, and the villages were instantly familiar, if dowdier than he remembered them, beyond his driver's shoulder. The manor house still stood at the end of a dappled lane. But it was only a Polish farmhouse now, *verkommen*, gone to seed, its size not half so grand as nostalgia promised. The coat of arms remained above the door, its bleached stone contours softened over centuries, and the woman of the house recognized his name with a start, staring into his thick sunglasses with a fear sprung from her genes. She spoke no German, but he dredged up enough of the childhood Polish he had used with the farm workers to realize that she was afraid he had come to claim his patrimony. But the land was Polish now, he accepted that as others less successful and less removed could not, and he had no wish to return there just to die. His home in Santa Cruz was far grander and more comfortable, and Bolivia was the world of his adult life.

Given his words of reassurance, the Polish woman, who clearly had been the *Dorfschönheit* before years of childbearing and poor diet disfigured her, was first relieved, then oddly disappointed, asking if, after all, he might not be interested in buying the place at a fair price. She offered to let him come in, but he feared that a bit, and he only smiled and asked if he might walk in the grounds, at least as far as the clear lake of his youth that revealed itself as a clogged green pond now, past the bracken that once had been a celebrated rose plantation and along the edges of worked fields that once had pastured his father's horses.

Where the pond still breathed, a farm boy fished in dumb bliss. Von Reinsee surrendered to the measured warmth of the sun, a sun deeply remembered, so much gentler than in his adopted land. His soul enlivened at the unchanged sound of the bees, at the indestructible scent of August. His mother's fragrance remained, too, the minor aristocrat's admixture of sweat and second-quality perfume, a ghost that would not go, and even the stench off the stables that held only ill-tended draft animals now called his sister from across the dell. She rode toward him with an energy that only lacked time to become a woman's grace. His sister, making girl faces at the sight of his boy face. She would forever lack time. And yet she lived, here and now, in well-worn summer. . . .

The events that filled the day had been smaller and drabber than he had anticipated, and he knew they held no real meaning. Yet a crippling beauty remained. The home of his childhood was like a life's great love lost only to be encountered again in the misfortune of age, repellent to the senses, yet indispensible to the memory.

He found *Parsifal* beautiful, too, its best passages as slow as those boyhood summers, although far more knowing, shadowed. Innocence recollected rather than directly experienced. Von Reinsee could not abide the common Wagner of the *Ring*, impatient with horned helmets and tin brassieres, all that cheap, false Germanness. But *Parsifal* reached him effortlessly. As did *Tristan*. *Der fliegende Holländer* was, of course, something of a personal tale. Despite all the stomping. Wagner was the archetypal German composer: contradictory, self-dramatizing, not a little self-loathing, easily seduced by lunatic notions masquerading as ideas . . . and capable of unexpected, confounding beauty.

Sitting erectly, as he had sat since childhood, the aging, flawlessly dressed German touched the air with his right hand, joining the music, caressing it, helping it along. The broadcast was of a recording almost as old as he was, made falsely young by technology. Hans Knappertsbusch conducting. Von Reinsee remembered the man's dashing forelock, his scarlet cheeks and poet's eyes. He had been introduced to him once, during the war, at his aunt Cecilie's in Dresden, before the blackouts, before that world ended, too. He remembered the in-town house with its Persian carpets rose and blue, and the big mirror in the entranceway crowned by a winged, smooth-breasted woman in bronze, and the colored glass in the staircase window. His widowed aunt Cecilie, once the family beauty, dark and intense as the air in her salon, a woman who had forgotten the sun—perhaps, he thought, that, too, runs in the family—with her directing hand upon his shoulder, introduced him to a silver-haired man in a white dinner jacket. Knappertsbusch had been distinctly out of favor with Goebbels and that lot, thanks to his slow humor and slower cadences, and that made Aunt Cecilie value her friendship with the man all the more.

He remembered. He remembered it all so well. He was cursed with the power of memory. *Parsifal* was splendid, music that poured into the ear like dark honey, but it was more, too. It was the echo of a lost world. With his glass of wine forgotten on the table next to his chair, von Reinsee wondered if anyone else listened and felt the music as he felt it. Surely someone somewhere valued this. Or they would not trouble themselves to play it. Someone somewhere shared this cheap, trite, unbearable, glorious yearning. But not here, in this still-savage place where the women thought sophistication was a matter of sewn-in labels.

How could that other world be lost? How could it be gone forever? When this music still sounded in the night? When his aunt Cecilie still absently touched her pearls and stared at a guest's retreating shoulders? Memory was the cruelest drug of all.

He had gone back to Dresden, too, to the perfectly rebuilt Semper Opera. But the city outside had been so heartbreaking that he heard little of the performance. A huge, scabrous apartment building rose where his aunt Cecilie's precise, unwasteful elegance had been at home, and the faces in the street were brute and worn. As soon as he could raise his driver, he fled the city to drive on through the newly Russian-free countryside.

He always grew impatient with the second act, where Wagner risked being Wagnerian, and this time his mind traveled to his daughter. As far from the second act's Kundry as a woman could be. Eva. At times, he despaired of her. He wanted grandchildren. To carry on the blood, of course. But he also wanted to tell them

what he had seen and known, to pass on that which
should not be forgotten, to give his lost world some
shred of immortality. Eva was thirty-five, and she would
be thirty-six in November. How many more years did
she have before it would be too late?

He had fully expected her to come around, to tire of
all the rural nonsense. But she had proven the stubbor-
nest of a stubborn line of women, with nothing of her
Bolivian mother at all. He smiled to himself, thinking,
The German boot has crushed the Spanish flower. But
it could not be passed off so lightly. He sensed that Eva
was nearly lost to him, and that time ran ever faster. If
he could have had one wish now it would have been for
her to turn back six or seven years, marry her North
American doctor beau, and accept happiness. She was
an impossible woman, a terrible daughter, and as he saw
with helpless pride, the stuff of heroes. But his family
had produced heroes and heroines enough, and all of that
had ended badly, naked in the snow, with a can of processed meat for a memorial.

The music reached toward a particular crescendo that
always offended von Reinsee and he thought briefly
about business. He had spent the evening closing a deal
to increase his Chilean holdings. Chile was going to be
the key to the legal markets of North America, given
the trade agreements that were in the wind, and he quite
liked the Chileans, anyway, if only for their devoted attempts to be as German as Latins could make themselves. Chile had a future.

And what was Eva's future? He could not get away
from the question. Now the business with this epidemic,
if there really was one. He had brushed off the danger
when his nephew raised it, but he worried secretly. His
anger rose with the music. La Paz had infuriated him,
and they were going to feel it. He had phoned personally
in an effort to move the medical relief system, to send
Eva a bit of help. But they were so incompetent they
did not know where to begin, could not say who could

authorize what. The state was a pitiful, arthritic thing, hardly worth killing.

And his daughter was squandering her life on these people. Perhaps that was Bolivia's revenge on him. He wished her safe and far away, wanting her near him at the same time. Really, a husband from the U.S. would have been ideal. In virtually every way. He could not wish a Bolivian husband on her, knowing the man would ultimately squander her fortune on mistresses and suits no real gentleman would wear. Smiling with lips thin as pencil lines, von Reinsee remembered the file he had examined on the latest U.S. officer to come to Bolivia. Kurt Sieger. The man even had a German name. In the photo that accompanied the text, he looked like the blond fantasies Hollywood liked to dress up in German uniforms, a caricature of the real thing. Under other circumstances, he would have been ideal for Eva, with her discipline and her elective loneliness. They might have had splendid children.

Von Reinsee moved from thoughts of one North American to thoughts of others. The United States was going to be his ally, his benefactor, and Washington would never know it. The might of the United States was going to take care of the Colombians for him. The Colombians were yesterday's bargain, increasingly bad partners. It was time to move on to bigger, more forward-looking things. Before he was done with them, the gringos were going to be so outraged with the Colombians they would drive them out of Bolivia, even if it took a war.

Eva got on well with the North Americans, of course. They were her types, the gringos. Puritanical. Crusaders. And endlessly naive. Von Reinsee was an economy-minded man and he had staged the threatening scene with his daughter to send a credible message to the Yankees, certain she would break down and tell Church, at least. But there had been a second purpose, too. He had hoped he might frighten some sense into her, to make her grow up and begin her proper life before it was too late. As a minimum, he wanted her out of the border area. It was only a matter of time until the Pando became hell on earth.

After a high-German pause for program notes, the final act began its passage from turmoil to the soul's triumph. Von Reinsee turned his attention back to the music.

WHEN THE WAY became too rough and steep for the taxi, Angel paid the driver and got out with his package, a gift box wrapped in silver paper and decorated with gold bows and plastic bells. The box was light, and he felt lighter himself carrying it under his arm, and his heart transformed the broken trail that climbed the hillside in place of a street into a path to happiness.

"Angel," a young man called in a respectful tone, "Angel, you need anybody to do some work for you?"

Angel smiled his safety-razor smile, briefly, and made a slight gesture of greeting with his free hand. He said nothing.

"Carry that box for you, man," the job-seeker tried. "Anything you want, Angel."

Angel kept going uphill, thigh muscles tightening as he turned into a switchback. He felt good, master of his world. He had slept deeply, with his night cramps on holiday, and he had risen to action before the world around him began to wake and throw its scent. He had walked all the way into the city in the morning cool, walking because he chose to walk, confident that he could have waved down any of the passing cars and bought them. He still did not know what he would do with all the money his last job had brought him.

Down in the heart of the city, though, he had collapsed into his usual awkwardness. Something about the way the people walked and talked and bought things so casually seemed done on purpose to remind him that he was just a kid who had scratched his way up from the city dump and who did not know all the secret codes other people, the lucky ones, shared among themselves. This expedition had been especially difficult and painful. Vexed by saleswomen who acted like rich men's wives and ignored him, Angel had finally slammed down a fistful of bills. After that, the women were friendly as whores.

Now he was home again. Where he knew all the secret codes.

A small child for whom walking was still a novelty crossed Angel's path with choppy sailor steps, heading for an embankment that dropped off sharply above shacks pressed into the lower hillside. In a fragment of time sliced off a second, Angel looked around, saw he was alone with the kid, and jumped to grab one waving arm.

"You shouldn't do that," he said, as if to an equal. "Get your mama all upset and stuff."

The child grinned, pink gums, pink tongue.

"She don't even wash you right," Angel said in marble disapproval. Reducing his stride, he led the child to a house that was a disgrace to the neighborhood, where most of the inhabitants did what little they could to live decently. He stood in the doorway, grimacing, and looked down at his new companion. "Stinks," he confided. "How you going to live like that?" Then he called:

"*Madona*. Get off your lazy back. Come get your kid." His tone might have made an educated listener think of cruel viceroys and inquisitors.

After a few moments—too long a time for Angel—a woman in a decomposing robe appeared from the interior shadows, driving back sleeper's hair with one hand.

"Yeah," she said.

"Your kid was ready to go off the bank over there.

What kind of mother are you? And you ought to be dressed, for God's sake.''

''It ain't any of your business, Angel. You're not like the mayor or nothing.''

Angel would not budge, physically or in any other way. ''You want to have a kid, you got to take care of it. Look at that. Bugs in his hair.''

''Fuck off. Like you're a saint or something.'' She grasped the child's wrist and pulled it after her into the noontime darkness.

Angel shook his head. He liked children, felt comfortable around them. He could never understand how kids could turn into such worthless adults, people without a code. You couldn't make anything of yourself without a code. You had to honor yourself. Angel looked around the blue, spoiled day, sensing that great things were going wrong with the world, that the age was a bad one.

He turned the next switchback and saw his sister with a crowd of the kind of neighborhood kids who were impatient to go bad. Standing like a bunch of do-nothing bums on a flat space carved out for a basketball court.

''Rosa,'' he yelled. ''Hey. Rosalita.''

When the boys in the group saw him, they took off, one of them clutching a brown paper bag. Scrambling over humps of dirt and broken concrete, they disappeared into the maze of shacks and mud like surprised mice. Rosa remained, flanked by two other girls in their early teens. Angel strode up to them, waving his free arm dismissively.

''You bums get out of here. Go on. And you stay away from my sister.''

One of the girls hissed something Angel could not hear and they laughed with mean, explosive sounds that wanted to be grown-up. Rosa laughed, too. But the other two girls slunk off.

''So what's in the box?'' Rosa asked, spite-voiced. ''Another computer?''

"None of your business. And you're going to learn to work the computer you got. You know how much money that cost?"

Her eyes were dark and burning, already much too knowing. "Not going to learn no computer," she said. "I can't do that. What's in your head, huh?"

"You can learn computers. I seen bums do it. You're my sister. You're smart."

She looked at him. "Like you?"

He straightened. "I'm smart enough. Not like that trash standing here."

"They're my friends."

"Yeah. Glue-sniffers. You want to go nuts like that whore Madona?"

"And who are you? The president?"

"I don't want you hanging around with them. They're bums."

She looked at him with the inexhaustible sullenness of a girl who was almost not thirteen anymore. "What are you going to do? Kill them or something? You think you can just kill everybody in the world?"

"Don't talk like that. Who you been talking to?"

"Everybody knows about you. You want them to. You want everybody to think you're so tough."

"I'm a respected man. Who's been talking to you?"

Rosa laughed, and two black birds chased beneath an unshielded power line. "You're respected. Make me laugh."

"I get a lot of respect," Angel said. "A *lot*. People know you don't mess with me. And you don't mess with my sister, either. You don't even know how much respect I get. And not just here, in this hole. They respect me in places you never heard of."

"People laugh at you," Rosa said flatly.

He almost struck her. Raising his free hand as though it were the hand of God. But he braked himself. He never hurt women. And certainly not family. You had to take care of your family. That was all part of the code.

"Who laughs at me?" he said in the inquisitor's shrunken voice. *"Who laughs?"* Quick as doom, he grabbed her by the forearm. "You . . . tell . . . me . . . who . . . laughs."

Rosa giggled, a child who had managed to provoke, blithely immune to mortality. "Everybody's laughing at you," she said merrily. "Carmelita told everybody."

Angel looked at her with his killer's eyes. But she did not seem to see the change. She giggled again.

"What?" he demanded. "What's she been saying?"

Rosa giggled. "Let go of my arm. You're a jerk."

"What did that bitch say?" he demanded, not letting go, unwilling to ever let go.

His sister's face turned into that of the eternal female opponent of the male. "She told everybody how you can't even do it like a normal guy, how you can't please a woman."

Angel looked at his sister in horror.

"She calls you the Three-Second Volcano."

Angel released his sister's arm. He struck her on the side of the face, a thing he had never done. Somehow it did not surprise her. Only later, when he had had too much time to think, did he get the bitter meaning of her lack of emotion.

His sister reacted physically, though. She leapt backward and turned, crouching defensively, practiced. She took another step backward, then another, holding the side of her mouth. Angel saw blood. And hating eyes.

"Carmelita says you only have a little tiny thing," she said. Then she turned and ran.

Angel was breathing as though he had run all the way from the center of the city. It was the way he breathed after a job was over and he was gone from the place where he had done it. Mechanically, he walked back across the roadway to a lip of rock that jutted out above a clutter of shattered junk and animal carcasses. The drop was enough to break bones, maybe to kill a man who was unlucky.

Angel let the gift box fall.

*   *   *

GENERAL PARNELL'S MORNING had been devoured by a series of budget planning briefings, each more disheartening than the last. Everyone wanted results, but no one was willing to pay for them. In the next fiscal year, deployments would be down, training would be down, flying hours would be down, troop strength would be down. Parnell had spent much of his career in Europe, preparing to fight an enemy that finally defeated itself, and now he had come to believe that Latin America was the place that mattered for the future. It was painful to watch his country disengaging at a time when the region presented opportunities and dangers on an unprecedented, heroic scale.

It was hard, too, to reach four-star rank only to preside over decline. And then the distant men with the power and the purse strings told you to make war on drugs while observing peacetime laws, thanks. So good men died for nothing. The Bolivian affair rankled him without cease. The implications of the autopsies made it sound as if Superman had done it. One pistol, twelve dead soldiers. So much for teamwork. He had hammered his J-2 to get information any way he could, to find the killer no matter what it took. The intelligence one-star had stared at him, mouth open, terrorized at the prospect of trying to identify and locate a lone gunman who had an entire continent for a hideout. When he found his voice, the J-2 pleaded that the intelligence system wasn't structured for that kind of mission. Parnell had been merciless with the man.

The general sat behind his desk in the scant minutes left to him before a scheduled lunchtime speech to the Panama City Rotary Club. He signed his correspondence, then tried to read through the file of key messages his subordinates prepared for him each day, but he kept thinking of how much the world had changed since he had served as a company commander tramping the woodlines east of Fulda. Was it a better world now?

His XO appeared in the doorway with a bit of paper, knocking cautiously for attention.

"What is it?"

The colonel strode forward to the big desk. "Sir, we just got a fax in from La Paz. One of Colonel Church's subordinates sent it. Captain Darling, his aviation planner. It's pretty interesting. Thought you might want to take a look." The XO extended the papers.

There were two fax sheets and you had to lay them side by side to get the effect. It was a newspaper article. In Spanish. The print was fine and light, and Parnell had to get out his reading glasses, which he did not much like, since they marked his age. He bent over the pages, reading slowly, translating each word as he went. Finally, he looked up.

"My Spanish isn't all that it should be. Am I getting this right?"

The XO nodded. "Yes, sir. Old John Church is the flavor of the month down there."

"What's this all about? Is Church grandstanding?"

The XO shrugged. "Whether he is or not, it's the first time in living memory the U.S. military's gotten good press in Bolivia. The journalists down there are the world's last Bolsheviks."

Parnell stared down at the piece, thinking hard.

"Old John Church sounds like Francis of Assisi," the XO added.

The general snorted. "Doesn't make our friend the ambassador sound all that pretty."

The colonel knew the limits allowed him and made no comment on the ambassador.

Parnell let out a single sound that meant a laugh. "Plymouth's an ass. The guy's a walking catalog of everything that's wrong with the Department of State." The general looked up over his reading glasses. "All that Foggy Bottom self-righteousness. But I'll tell you something, Tim. Ethan Rice Plymouth has a price tag on his ass, too. He wants one of the big embassies. And tomorrow, the world.''

''Sir, you want me to do anything with this?''

Parnell stared at the colonel, who was loyal, smart, and a proven soldier. ''Tell me one more time, Tim. What's your impression of John Church? Your unvarnished personal impression?''

The XO made a thinking face. ''Only met him once, really. At your last conference for the DATTs and the Milgroup commanders.'' The XO looked down at the plush blue carpet, then met Parnell's gaze again. ''Seemed balanced. Sound. Knows Latam inside out. And he gives good cable. If the chips were down, I think I'd trust him, sir.''

Parnell stared through the colonel's torso and across half a continent. ''But what exactly would you trust him to do? The right thing, as *he* sees it? What if that's not the right thing for everybody else?'' The general looked back down at the article, adjusting his glasses, searching. Finally, he smiled. Almost guiltily. ''This gentleman from the press calls Ambassador Plymouth a 'fascist bully and fool with no understanding of humanity'—I translate that right?''

''Yes, sir. Except the word they used for 'fool' is a lot stronger in Spanish.''

''God love 'em. Journalists are getting better all the time. You know, Plymouth thinks I'm soft on drugs. So does his buddy Drew MacCauley, Savior of Muscovy and Arkansas traveler. Because I won't give them title and deed to every airplane the Air Force loans me. And so on. Never met a diplomat who didn't secretly want to be a general. At least not down here. You think I'm soft on drugs, Tim?''

The XO waited a beat, then said, ''Sir, I think you have a number of different missions to address. . . .''

''Diplomatic answer. Which means even you think I'm not really engaged. Well, let me tell you something, Colonel. Something for you to remember if you ever become a CINC. There are no halfway military solutions. If you want to use the military, you declare war.'' Parnell made a bitter, almost laughing sound. '' 'War on Drugs' my Irish ass. If those heroes with weather vanes for peckers inside the Beltway really wanted a war on drugs, they'd change the rules. *Make* it a war. A real one. Stop pretending Andy and Barney can bust the Cali cartel and every corrupt politician from Laredo to La Paz before Aunt Bea gets lunch on the table. Then maybe you could make a difference. But I refuse to squander the lives of men and women in uniform just so some candy-ass cookie-pusher like Plymouth can get his picture in the *Post* and a promotion to an embassy with more perks and better water.'' The general sat back. But his anger did not fade. ''I *hate* drugs. Hate drugs and the sonsofbitches who sell them. But I refuse to pretend we're making a difference when all we're doing is rearranging the deckchairs on the *Titanic*.''

The XO stood quietly, waiting. Parnell let him wait. Thinking. Drumming his fingertips against one another. Then he said:

''Three things. First, I want the J-3 to identify and prep for deployment the best damned combat engineer platoon he can reach out and touch on short notice. Get me good builders. Second, have him put together a crackerjack medical team, with a good bug doctor and some touchie-feelie types to give out shots and lollipops. A high-octane MEDRETE. Third, I want a C-130 ready to go, if and when I say. Make that two aircraft. Get overflight clearances so they can land right on top of brother Church without touching down in La Paz. And then just hold in place. Until we figure out what's really going on down there.''

''Yes, sir. Sir, do you want me to coordinate this with the Milgroup folks in the embassy?''

''No, damn it. You're not *lis*tening. *If* we go in on this—and that is not yet a foregone conclusion—we're not going to have anything to do with La Paz beyond the absolute minimum required. And we're going to cut some corners on that. We're going to make money for SOUTHCOM, mom, and apple pie, not for the guys in the ties. We'll bail our friend the ambassador out on paper, but that's it. Let him find out what the real world looks like outside his office.'' Parnell remembered something else. ''What about those ballistic tests? We ever find out for sure if the same weapon fired all of the shots that took out that A-team?''

''Not conclusively, sir. The lab's still working on it. But it looks—''

''Well, light a fire under them.'' The general looked back down at the fax. ''A saint in Army green, an ambassador who wants little children to suffer, and an epidemic at the gates. With cocaine and narco-dollars all over the place.'' He smiled the small hard smile he had worn when he drove his division through an Iraqi corps without losing a single one of his soldiers. ''I wonder what the hell's actually going on down there.''

9

THE LEAD HELICOPTER flew the trace of an un-
named tributary that wandered into an unpronounceable
river. Sieger sat just off to the side of the door gunner,
a compact, helmeted boy braced behind a clean M-60
machine gun. Beyond the open door frame, three other
helicopters followed perfectly, echelon left, their shadows smoothing over the sand flats one hundred feet below. Animals appeared along the water or back in the
suntanned bush, three cows marking the presence of
man, an explosion of deerlike animals ignited by the
throb of the aircraft, a white, swaybacked horse. The
landscape trimming against the horizon reminded Sieger
of East Africa, but without the starvation and massacre.

Long fields opened up and hurried toward the aircraft.
Some of them had a recently harvested look, while others had gone fallow. Sieger wondered if any of the fields
were coca plantations. He thought he recalled Henry
Vasquez saying coca grew higher up, in the hills where
they were headed. Or maybe the DEA man had said that
the *good* coca came from the highlands. Sieger could
not remember exactly.

He had seen enough of Bolivia to wonder how it
could be a single country. Up in the fringes of the Amazon region, where the soldiers had been killed, it was
poor man's jungle, green and stinking in the lowlands,
its humanity mildewed, yet the neighboring earth crack-

led south across endless prairies, dying for rain. In the west, abrupt mountains walled off an utterly different world, permanently brown, ice glassing the air, the high plains dotted dirty-pastel with indigenous folk. La Paz was an old whore. And here the country was a sea of dying grass, with islands of wind-shaped, runty trees, and low hills looming ahead with a promise of first roads and buildings. Bolivia was a place where the First World met the Last World, a true frontier, and Sieger would have been much more interested by it if he had not had to worry about becoming its victim.

Vasquez sat at a ninety-degree angle from him, readjusting his headset, talking to the pilots in a voice Sieger could not hear over the enormous grumping of the rotors. The DEA man sat facing forward, seat belt undone, rising now and then to peer at the approaching hills. He wore aviator sunglasses, a half-opened red shirt bright as a pimp's convertible, and jeans cut off close to the crotch and worn too tight, highlighting thick, white, tufted thighs and creating an even bigger surge of belly than Vasquez normally showed. Combat boots with socks turned down over their laces, a laden pistol belt, and a little black carbine completed the agent's outfit. Unarmed in his neatly pressed battle dress uniform, Sieger could not have felt more repelled.

He had begun to despise Vasquez, who had initially attracted him with his aggressive posturing. The agent was consistently unwilling to listen to advice, dismissing everything with the observation that he, Henry Vasquez, knew Bolivia and the Bolivians. Now they were flying helicopters nursed beyond the end of their projected service lives to their maximum range, instead of staging properly. En route, they had picked up their national police contingent, a silent little platoon cut from the assembled company like cattle at an auction. Vasquez had herded them onto the helicopters without giving them even a perfunctory briefing on the operation. All of it was exactly the opposite of what the manuals and common sense required.

The DEA man turned to him, cradling the carbine, and formed an inaudibule word. He pointed forward toward the hills and nodded.

Sieger understood. Target coming up.

He did not feel fear, only the silver thrill that comes over some men before action. But he felt plenty of anger. He understood that there was some indeterminate chance that he could die in a mess not of his own making, which made him want to hit somebody, and he knew that, if things went belly up, he was going to take a healthy share of the blame. Maybe all of it. With every hour, he gained a greater, if grudging, regard for Church, and he frankly wished he had the vanquished colonel on board now. Sieger suspected that Church had ways of handling Vasquez.

The helicopters dropped down. Fifty feet AGL. One of the trail birds had a U.S. contract flight instructor in the copilot's seat, a legal way of controlling things, but the Bolivian military boys knew how to fly on their own. The national police raiding force, on the other hand, just made Sieger nervous. They looked as though they were playing dress-up for the day, and they handled their weapons as though uncertain of their purpose. Their ill-fitting helmets looked borrowed, and nobody had bothered to bring along a medic. Yet the policemen did not look as though they expected a holiday, either. They looked wary, unhappy, and profoundly undependable.

The engines gunned and the helicopters sailed up over the first slope, lulled into a stream-greened valley, then climbed again. An empty dirt road sliced into a hillside and a wooden cross memorialized some local tragedy. Beside Sieger, the door gunner primed his weapon and glanced forward, trying to see beyond the aircraft's frame and the pilots.

They rose and dropped across a series of hills, each time rising a bit higher, never descending quite as low again. The vegetation darkened and climbed farther from the drainage lines, and intermittent shacks marked subsistence farms.

Sieger twisted in his seat, staring ahead. Vasquez stood just behind the pilot and copilot, bracing himself with one hand, holding his carbine in the other. Had it gone off, it would have shot the pilot in the ass.

Under his mustache, Vasquez made words into the mouthpiece of his headset. A moment later, the pilots canted the bird and they began to follow a gentle valley.

Vasquez had not listened to Sieger's advice. The plan remained the same—land right on top of the objective, in a field between the suspected lab and the low barns, adjacent to the huts where the workers sheltered. If anyone had been forewarned, or if anyone so much as had a single automatic weapon handy, the helicopters and their crews would be the targets of a lifetime.

Vasquez slipped, righted himself, and pointed through the Plexiglas with his carbine. The pilots stayed low, trying for whatever surprise they could get, their efforts crippled by the huge sound of their machines. Even good soldiers could not do much with a bad plan.

Trees blurred beneath the aircraft's skids. The doorgunner waved at a comrade echeloned back, and a flock of birds erupted, fleeing. It was real now. Sieger felt the closeness of the target, and the sweat came, starting under his arms, between his shoulder blades, in the folds of his palms. He wanted a weapon. Even if this was not his fight, even if it would do no good at all. He wanted a weapon, and he wondered now how those twelve soldiers had felt, and he began to hate men he barely knew, men who had power over his life and so much more.

He heard a shout. Vasquez. Loud enough to blur in the ear despite the sound of the rotors lacerating the sky. Up there. Yes. Sieger recognized the layout from the photographs. That was it.

Going in.

The helicopters headed for the clutter of buildings and

a field that looked not much bigger than a basketball court. Much too tight for four helicopters to put down safely.

Sieger saw small figures erupting from doorways, three, four, half a dozen men running. Racing for the tree line beyond the field, trying to beat the helicopters. None of them appeared to carry weapons, although it was difficult to tell for certain. At least none of them paused to turn and fire.

Sieger heard Vasquez screaming unintelligibly. The door gunner had gone into a crouch, visor lifted to reveal a face that had fought the Spanish guns with stones.

The lead bird headed straight in, slowing only enough to maintain the absolutely essential level of control. Sieger saw a crumbling barn or stable, low and old, and a series of tin-roofed, open-sided shelters that looked like they were set up for vocational training. A few wooden hovels drowsed, their windows and doorways empty and dark. The running men disappeared into the scrub and Sieger saw no further signs of life.

Hovering just off the ground, the lead helicopter swung around so that the door-gunner could cover the barn's decayed masonry, a rustic fortress. Sieger snapped open his safety belt so he could jump, if necessary. The second aircraft tucked in closer to the dormitory shacks and angled so its machine gun could sweep those buildings.

It was time to dismount, to move, to make things happen. But when Sieger looked back to the DEA agent, Vasquez was bent over the pilot's shoulder, gesturing upward. A moment later, the helicopter began to rise, engines straining.

What the fuck? Sieger wondered.

They rose and hovered just at the tree line, as if determined to remain vulnerable for as long as possible. Then, slowly, the lead helicopter began to make a circuit of the area, staying low, remaining in sight of the compound. To Sieger, it was lunatic, purposeless.

The two trailing birds peeled away and began a wider circuit. If Vasquez was trying to catch the runaways, Sieger knew it was a sloppy way to do it. And it was already a closer business with the fuel than any U.S. flight safety officer would have permitted. It was a long walk back from Indian country.

Vasquez turned around, caught Sieger's eye, shook his head. He spoke into the mouthpiece again and the helicopter grunted and slipped to the side, turning back toward the drug lab. This time the aircraft settled down onto the earth, rocking, followed by its mate.

Vasquez jumped out into the sunlight, boots, hairy legs, gut. The DEA man had drawn a crumpled bush hat from his kit and he settled it over his bald spot as he strode forward, holding the carbine at his side like a big pistol. A national police officer trotted up from the second bird to confer with Vasquez, and Sieger, forgetting his weaponless state, followed them, ready and curious. More of the policemen appeared, bunching up around the authority figures and clutching their rifles like the safety bars on a roller coaster.

The DEA agent led the way toward the lab shelters. Under one of the roofs, the earth was steaming.

Vasquez turned back to Sieger, grinning, and said:

"Got 'em with their shorts around their ankles."

Then he spoke in Spanish to the officer beside him and the officer relayed the order. The policemen split into smaller clusters, fanning out toward the various structures, jogging at first, but quickly settling back into their loping, unfocused strides. Behind them, the aircraft engines idled low, conserving fuel.

It was as unlike a military operation as anything Sieger had experienced. Except for the door gunners, who remained alert, no one seemed concerned about security. The police troops wandered as much as they searched, and when a shot briefly electrified the air, it turned out that one of the policemen had gunned down a dog.

The machines, drums, and pits under the tin awnings

meant nothing to Sieger. But Vasquez was grinning and the Bolivian officer beside him became extremely animated. The agent kicked over a receptacle and a table; then he pulled a small camera from his day pack.

For five minutes, the agent took photographs of the site. Then he looked at Sieger.

"Want your picture taken? Great souvenir."

Sieger shook his head. No, thanks.

"Well," the agent said, "you mind taking mine? For the record?"

Sieger took the picture, then snapped three more as the agent posed against different backdrops. To Sieger, the man looked an utter fool, with his furry legs and jump boots, his gut straining the red shirt, and the self-consciously brandished weapon.

As Sieger handed back the camera, a muddle of shouts sounded from the barn.

Dropping the camera into his pack, Vasquez trotted toward the excitement. A moment later, one of the policemen burst from a cattle door, followed by two Indians in jeans who moved bent-shouldered in the timeless stance of prisoners. Three more national policemen followed the two captives, their weapons exaggeratedly ready.

"What have we got here?" Vasquez asked the day.

The DEA man straightened his back and reset the waistline of his cutoffs. Then he went in close, towering over the prisoners and shouting questions. Sieger watched from a distance, not liking any of this, but wondering, finally, if he wasn't just being an asshole about things. Maybe his rules truly did not apply down here.

"Kurt?" the agent asked, turning and lowering his voice. "Would you do me a favor and go over and see what the hell the boys are up to in those shacks over there?"

"My Spanish isn't worth a shit."

"Doesn't matter. Just go see what they're doing. Make sure they're not getting into any trouble."

Sieger shrugged and went. On the other side of the helicopters, with their rotors turning like slow ceiling fans, the remaining police had disappeared into the dormitory buildings. No one had gone to establish a perimeter or posted a single guard. Sieger decided that, even if Vasquez could get results like this, it was still bad medicine. If anything went wrong, the little force would never recover. And the two reinforcing helicopters were nowhere to be seen.

He found the police troops churning the interiors of the huts, helping themselves to the few items of relative value they turned up. A cheap radio, a pair of plastic sunglasses out of an Italian movie from the sixties, some toiletries, a ragged UCLA T-shirt. The cocaine business did not look very lucrative at this end.

Had they been Sieger's own troops, the careers of everyone in the chain of command would have ended prematurely. But they were not his troops, and they paid him no attention, not even bothering to retrieve their rifles from the corners where they had left them. Sieger realized that he was just a hard-luck tourist in the wrong theme park and he went back outside. The temperature in the hills was pleasant, at least, and the air was fine. It did not appear that anything much was going to happen.

Walking into the sun, Sieger dropped his eyes and saw metal glinting in a tuft of grass. He bent to see more clearly and found a shell casing. He assumed it was from the policeman who had shot the dog. But then he found two more casings within a few strides. A dozen more lay scattered as they would have fallen upon ejection from an automatic weapon.

He did not bother to pick up all of them. The three in his palm were enough. He quick-jogged back past the lab shelters, heading for the barn.

The two prisoners squatted against the wall, hands bound behind their backs, faces bloodied. Two policemen stood over them and Sieger sensed a change in the atmosphere, the way the first spilled blood brings out an appetite for more. The prisoners glanced up at him briefly then carefully lowered their stares to the ground.

There was a commotion in the barn. Sieger stepped inside, briefly encompassed by darkness. Then his eyes began to adjust. Several figures stood toward the rear. Vasquez was easily recognizable, red shirt vivid even in the false twilight.

"You. Sieger," the agent called. "Want to see something that'll make your trip worthwhile?"

Sieger approached the little group. They stood at the lip of a cavity sunk into the floor of the barn. The policemen had shifted some straw, lifted a few planks, and uncovered what looked like a healthy truckload of bricks wrapped in dark plastic. Vasquez held one of the bricks in his hand, its top end askew. The agent shook it, admonishing Sieger.

"You know what this is?"

"Cocaine?"

"You bet your booty." Vasquez gestured at the pit. "These guys aren't just into base or paste. This is Pennsylvania Department of Agriculture–certified, money-back-guaranteed cocaine." He paused, considering the treasure. "Enough to make somebody very rich." Turning his eyes back to Sieger, he concluded, "That's a lot of dope, pal."

"Those Indians told you where it was?"

"Would've found it anyway."

"Then why beat them up?"

Vasquez was unfazed. "Not my doing. The Bols like a little rough stuff. Makes them feel in control. No harm done."

"Well, maybe your Bolivian buds ought to put out a little security instead of beating up prisoners and doing their Christmas shopping." He opened his palm, revealing the three shell casings.

The agent looked down at the bits of brass. His expression did not change, and when he looked up, he just asked:

"And?"

"Henry, come on. Three casings. Not even dirty or weathered. And I saw at least a dozen more of them. Somebody on this reservation has a smoke pole. And where there's one . . ."

Vasquez tossed the brick of cocaine back onto the sunken stack. "Everybody's got firearms. But not everybody's got the guts to use them. You hear any shooting out there?"

Sieger crossed his arms over his chest. "Henry, this is an accident waiting to happen."

Suddenly, the agent grasped him by the upper arm, pulling him. "You come outside, you fucking Pentagon smart-ass. And if you don't want to walk back to La Paz, you better listen to what I say."

Sieger almost struck him. But he kept his self-control, a soldier, after all. He wrenched his arm free but followed Vasquez outside into the dazzle, then around the side of the building, into a space churned up by heavy tires.

Vasquez waved his arms in the shadow of a dead tree. "Fuck me. Goddamn it. You sound like John goddamned Church, you know that? Want to talk about one worthless motherfucker—you know what we got here, Sieger? This is a serious lab, boy. *Ser*ious. These guys aren't just middlemen. They're making that good stuff right here in the backyard. Juan Valdez is expanding." The agent pointed to the barn. "That pile of drugs in there happens to be a mountain of cocaine by Bolivian standards. Hell, by any standards. This is a major haul. We have broken the paradigm. And you're worried about a couple of bloody noses and some shit you found in the grass. Get real, man."

"Henry, I'm glad you hit a home run. I hope your Colombians put on their black crepe tonight. But what I'm trying to tell you is that somebody could be watching us right now, and that somebody could have at least as much firepower as we do. And we're counting on a couple of very fragile machines to get our asses home.''

The agent turned away. "We're just wasting time."

"*Hen*ry," Sieger called, loudly enough to demand attention.

The DEA man stopped and looked back, dramatizing his impatience.

"Just tell me this," Sieger said. "If this is such an important lab, and if these boys have automatic weapons, why didn't they fight for it? Why just let us stroll in here and help ourselves? Why isn't anybody minding the store but a handful of Indians who beat it into the bush? Where are all those megaviolent Colombians?" Sieger looked at the man with loaded, furious eyes. "And why aren't there any vehicles? Look at the ground, Henry. You've got four-wheel-drive tracks right under your feet, but there's not so much as a spare tire to be found. What's going on?"

Vasquez looked at him. The DEA man was no longer theatrically angry, nor was he the vivid crusader of embassy staff meetings. His face held very still.

As he turned his back again, the agent just said:

"You're out of your league, Sieger."

VASQUEZ TOOK MORE photographs, then he organized the destruction of the site. The police troops responded with the enthusiasm of children on a wrecking spree, and barrels of chemicals splashed over the earth and the huts were set afire. All that was breakable was broken, and a row of drums of kerosene migrated into the barn, where Vasquez first soaked the cocaine in the pit, then arranged the barrels around the cavity's edge as a petrochemical Stonehenge.

"Shame to just burn it," the agent told Sieger in a great-white-hunter's voice, their argument set aside for the present. "Not even a thorough way to do it. But we can't leave it here. Wouldn't want to try to guard it overnight. And we can't carry it with us.'' He shook his head. ''I would've liked to weigh it. Just for the record.''

The police loaded the two prisoners onto the trail helicopter. The two stray birds reappeared above the treeline, making it a foursome again, edging away from the smoke off the shacks and shelters. With the engines of the helicopters that had put down gaining torque, Vasquez personally set fire to a fuse trail leading to the barn and ran for the command ship, where Sieger had resumed his seat by the door gunner.

The barn's roof lifted like a man kicked hard, and the force of the first explosion passed through the helicopter with dangerous power. Vasquez struggled with his headset, shouting, *''Go, go, go.''* Then they were airborne, turning out of the smoke, rising. A succession of explosions roiled the helicopters, chasing the machines. When the lead bird turned again, Sieger saw a tempest of fire and smoke, the lab site nearly invisible under the maelstrom.

The pilots went for altitude, no longer worried about danger from the ground or gaining surprise, released back to the mundane concerns of fuel gauges and oil pressure indicators. To the last, Vasquez strained out of the cargo door, bracing himself with one hand and taking photographs with the other.

RUTH CHURCH GOT lost in the box of photographs. She was very glad of the way the newspaper piece had turned out, and other journalists had phoned throughout the day, and she hoped it would gain John the time he needed to make peace with himself. But she knew that the family would be moving, very soon, no matter what else happened, and John would count on her to be prepared. She had begun their ritual of ''sorting the sacred,'' sifting the house for items such as family photographs and little gifts made to one another over the years that were to be packed in personal luggage and safeguarded en route to their next home. A wooden box of old photographs, mostly of John in uniform or in mufti, had stopped her, seducing her with memories, until she forgot the purpose of the day.

One photograph showed a second lieutenant so green he looked like he had just been picked from the tree. Ruth smiled, wondering if she had ever managed to love him enough. With the stubby gold bars on his shoulders, John looked like a boy, not a leader of men. And she had been a girl, and it had been two and a half decades now, and it had been only yesterday.

There was a picture of him at Fort Polk, as a company commander. They had lost their first child there, and Polk had been a sour, heartless place, and they had come closer to marital crisis than ever before or ever again. From the same years, she found a picture of the two of them posed artificially for a hack photographer hired to cover some battalion dining-out or brigade Christmas ball. John in his dress blues, erect and self-conscious. And her face drawn, still sick, and uncharacteristically lonely.

Panama, during their first, better tour. A monkey on John's shoulder, a toddler in his free hand. To be honest, Carla had been an unattractive baby and it was a miracle to see the young woman she was becoming, legs still too thin but destined to flesh out, a torso just blossoming, a face waiting for the first imprint of adulthood, of the first awareness of loss. Photographs from Kansas City and red-brick-green-grass Fort Leavenworth, with Carla Appalachian-thin and little Ricky runty and inquisitive. Snaps from vacations in Oaxaca and Yucatán, from Belize and Costa Rica, and then, terribly, from John in El Sal. She had aged in that year of unadmitted war, a year in which she had seen him for a total of less than four weeks. She never let him know, not then and not now, how much she worried about him, selfishly desolate at the imagined prospect of his loss. When she dressed to meet the plane bringing him back finally, alive and whole, the mirror had terrorized her with the middle-aged woman she had become, and she had imagined John tanned dark as a native and forever young. She remembered that day with startling, random clarity, her near panic during the drive to the airport, and the children difficult, boorish, and loud, with the plane delayed out of Miami. And John had held her too briefly, turning too soon to the children, picking them up, fooling with them, and she had hated him for it. Then, suddenly, spiting the rest of the world, he clutched her to him in the middle of the airport and kissed her like a half-drunk teenage boy in the backseat of a car, wetting her and saying, "Get rid of the kids for tonight."

She had always wished she could be more beautiful for him, thinner, and smarter, more sophisticated and less selfish. And the years had gone by and they had stopped being two separate people, and it was lovely and comfortable until you stopped to think about it, and then it was terrifying. She genuinely did not know what she would do without him, and could not imagine a world in which he would never reappear in the doorway, with the naive smile he had preserved from his days as a lieutenant, with his big kind hands. When he had to travel, she slept with his dirty undershirts for the smell of him, the way a dog or cat might do.

At the sound of a car horn down the street, she reawoke to the task before her. It was not the first time she had packed alone. The life of the Army wife. A good life. With a good man. She felt as if she could tear the ambassador's throat out with her fingernails. Bastard, bastard, bastard . . .

María, the maid, appeared in the doorway.

"Yes?"

"The colonel will eat family dinner?"

The maid lived in a world of her own, and outwardly at least, it was a genial one. But she missed a lot of social detail.

"No," Ruth said, in a controlled, heroic voice. "Not tonight."

"NOW," ANNE SAID. "Fill me up. . . . Fill me *up*."

Obediently, her lover pushed against her, pulsing within her, impeccable but for one brief cry. He was a wonderful lover, the best she had ever had, and there had been more than a few. He collapsed on her, the lightness of engaged muscle suddenly transformed into dead meat. But she liked that. The weight. She liked the covering, the near suffocation of it. For about ten minutes. Then she wanted the male animal off.

But for now, it was warm and rich and her groin radiated. Her lover smelled of expensive cologne and of fresh, golden sweat, and she liked all of it. She tightened her legs, wanting him to stay inside a while longer. He panted, a finished athlete, head upon her shoulder. She looked at the white ceiling, cool and endless in a room shuttered against the day.

"You make me crazy," her lover said in sex-flavored English, exhaustion audible between each word. Dressed, he spoke beautifully, his English perfect as only a foreigner's can be, but good, furious sex rubbed down his vocabulary and grammar until most of the polish was gone.

She wondered if all the claptrap about Latin lovers might not be true. Or perhaps it was just this one man. Anne suspected that each race had more than a fair share of inept males. At least that had been her experience.

Her lover turned his head, scrubbing his half day of beard across the flesh stretched over her collarbone, coming at her neck with his lips, briefly letting her feel the hardness of his teeth. His eyes were closed, she could just see that, but he said:

"You are very beautiful."

He slipped out of her, diminished, trivial, and she felt her habitual sense of loss at the sudden emptiness.

"No," she said firmly. "I'm not beautiful. I'm presentable." She considered the matter, running through an abbreviated chronicle of her past. "Desirable, when I get it right."

"You always get it right."

She did not reply. Silence was better. Even the best men spoke too much at the wrong times. It baffled her still, the swiftness of the male's spiritual disengagement. Physical, too, of course. But you came to expect that.

Anne slid her arm over her lover's shoulder, pulling him close, making him be quiet. He was growing too heavy now, but she could tolerate it a bit longer, and this peace for which her language had no word was more important than comfort. She did not want to have to think.

But the thinking was there, mean, pernicious. He had spoiled it. With words. Magnificent lover, though. She wished she had a girlfriend she could tell. But that would have taken an international phone call, and the lines were not safe from hungry ears.

The white ceiling. And just behind Anne's forehead, in foreshortened darkness, a grimed old painting of Virgin and Child watched over the bed, a good work from better times, when this part of the world was on top, not on the bottom. Across the room hung two first-rate oils of saints, Michael—Miguel, patron of a squalid continent—and George. Her lover had described the paintings to her as representative of the School of Potosí. He said they had been in his family for over three centuries. All the same, she thought it bad form to hang the holies in the fuck room. It did not really bother her, since she was not religious. But she would not have done it.

"Have I made it good for you?" her lover asked.

She pushed at him a little and they had been lovers long enough for him to understand the gesture. He shifted from atop her to her side, embracing her, giving her his scent again.

"Rafael, for the love of Christ. You know you're a

good lover. Don't be such a guy.'' But she kissed him a little to reassure him. Men were such predictable, childlike, crushable things. Even the best of them. In fact, the best were the most vulnerable. The worst of them were simply oblivious. Like Ethan.

''I want to be the best for you.''

Anne sighed and faced the reality of the male. ''You *are* the best. Bar none. Cross my heart and hope to die. Now be quiet and hold me.''

He pulled her against him. He was just in his thirties, almost a decade younger than she, and she loved that about him. The billboard muscles, the beachboy flesh not yet corrupted by fate. He enclosed her, pulling her wetness against his, shifting himself with his hand, locking her against his meat, his smell. He was better than a fantasy. And when his clothes were on, you could talk to him. It was, in fact, far better to talk to him when his clothes were on. He was sophisticated the way the word had once meant, not the way it meant back in Washington, where sophistication had been reduced to the right restaurants and smart-ass conversation. Washington was a drab, unsexed city, full of small-towners playing at worldliness. The men, and, increasingly, the women, who shaped global events, Anne knew, had been unpopular in high school without being particularly keen. They screwed, of course, and produced children to prove it. But Anne imagined their sex lives as horribly dingy. Not unlike her own, if you only counted the marital part.

She had married Ethan because he seemed appropriate, a sustainer of the right things in life, and because her friends envied her the opportunity. He had seemed tolerable back then, and he could make her come as long as she told him what she needed and didn't let him weasel out of it. It had not taken long for the marriage to go to shit. But she had been too vain to admit it. And they had Robin, her own mother's namesake, who was now, blessedly, off at a good school and probably doing dreadful things. Ethan quickly proved to be the kind of man who, in the resentful, admiring phrase of his peers, lived for his work. She knew, of course, that the work was only a tool to higher positions. Prestige mattered far more to her husband than did real achievement. Ethan wanted, as a minimum, to hold the sort of major ambassadorship his father had occupied, and he confided in her that he believed he had a shot at becoming SecState one day. Anne did not believe that. She knew her husband did not have that sort of quality or appeal, that she had married an also-ran. But there was no point in telling him.

Odd, how life dragged on, how it simply got away from you. You woke up one day surrounded by nothing.

"Can I speak now?" her lover asked.

"Yes."

"Anne . . . I believe that you are beautiful. I'm not just making compliments. You're a very beautiful woman in the kind of way smart men see but other men miss."

"That's a nice way of putting it, anyway."

"But you're very hard. You don't need to be so hard with me."

Anne smiled. "Beneath this armored exterior beats a heart of steel."

"I stopped telling you that I love you. Do you know why?" He rose slightly so that he could see her and she him. He was laughably handsome, dark hair askew, noble-eyed. "It is unbearable for a man to tell a woman he loves her only to have the woman laugh."

She tried not to be too mean. She valued him, after all. "You don't love me, Rafael. You like to fuck me. For now. And I'm a significant conquest. You're like the knight who seduces the queen. Not that I'm much of a queen. But that's a large part of the allure. I'm a trophy. You could just about cut off my head and hang it on the wall. Between your saints."

He pulled her up to him with just the slightest hint of

brutality, wonderful at nuances. Speaking close to her mouth, he said:

"I wouldn't hang up your *head*." Then he kissed her, his mouth tasting dark, dark. When the kiss lay done between them, he propped himself up on his elbow, looking at her with black eyes that made her wonder if there had not been a deft insertion of Indian blood somewhere back among his insufferable Spanish forebears.

"I'm a bit of a monster, you know," she said.

"Yes. My monster. You are my love monster."

Anne laughed. "Yes. Certainly that. Could you move just a bit? Thanks."

"You do not think your husband knows anything?" her lover asked abruptly.

That was a broad and rich question. "No. I'm discreet." She looked up at his fine, shadowed face. "I have always been discreet. And my husband is a very self-immersed man."

"The way you speak of him I do not think he is a man at all. How could he be married to you and not want you all the time?"

"Oh," Anne said, amused, "it happens."

"I would never let you rest."

"Prove it," she said, and laughed. But it was a happy little-girl laugh.

He kissed her, touched her, always serious in response to her words. Ethan, on the other hand, never even listened anymore. She was grateful for this man's hours. She felt the years running away and Rafael had the ability to put on the brakes for an hour or two.

Soon, Anne thought, I will not be able to attract such a lover. Not even in my trophy mode.

He paused, not quite ready to begin again. Stroking her flesh as though it were young and perfect. At times, she believed that no one in her past had made her feel the way this one did, but she realized that it might be only a trick of immediacy versus memory. Who could even remember a kiss with any accuracy? You remembered the action, the ghost of the experience, but not the experience itself.

"So what is your husband doing now? While you are here with me?"

Anne shrugged. A naked, flat-on-her-back shrug. Not wanting to think about Ethan. "Oh, he's probably berating some bored official. Or chatting with one of his pals back in Washington on his precious direct line. Or granting an audience. The sort of things United States ambassadors do in countries that can't stand up to them."

"But what are his interests now? I only read about him in the newspapers, and they make him sound very bad. Or I see him at parties. He is always so confident."

Anne closed her eyes. Dreaming away. "Yes. Ethan is certainly confident. And he's not very bad. He's only a little bad. Ethan is not 'very' anything."

"Everyone says he is on a crusade against cocaine."

Anne touched her lover lightly, trying to interest him again. "Ethan's not a crusader by nature. It's a career move. Ethan just wants to make his mark. Couldn't we talk about something more cheerful? Like cholera?"

"But, you see, for Bolivia the question of coca and cocaine is a very complex one. We have traditions, economic problems. . . ."

"Rafael, is this going to turn into a political science seminar? I get enough of this at home."

"I am sorry." He moved toward her, back atop her, a glorious predator.

"Anyway," she said to please him and close the conversation, "Ethan's all preoccupied with the Colombians these days. He wants to liberate Bolivia from the cruel yoke of Colombian drug traffickers. Especially after that mess with the massacred soldiers."

He roiled their bodies together, warming the sweat and sex-trace that still wet them, and touched her exactly. Anne moaned.

"That's good to hear," he whispered.

*   *   *

AMBASSADOR ETHAN RICE Plymouth was elated, despite the nonsense with Church in the press. He sat tall, arms outstretched and fists on his desk as if seizing an empire. Henry Vasquez had just phoned him from Cochabamba, where you could get back into the cellular net, with a report on the lab raid. Vasquez had not been able to discuss everything, of course, since it was not a secure connection, but the bottom line was that things had gone better than expected, better than hoped for, and in the DEA man's words, there were "Colombian fingerprints all over the place."

That was good. For two reasons. First, it gave him more leverage with the Bolivians to get them moving against the Cali crowd. Second, Washington would love it. And Giles Manschette would be angry as hell. That was a third plus. Plymouth smiled. Here he was, down in godforsaken La Paz, operating more effectively against the Colombians than Giles could manage up in Bogotá. A little professional lesson for Giles, whose ego was insufferable.

Vasquez and Sieger, the new Mil man, were flying up as soon as they could turn around an aircraft, and Plymouth was anxious to debrief them. Vasquez had photographs, too, although they would have to be developed. But the political section could have a cable drafted for release first thing in the morning. And the staffers would have to prepare a good press release. The embassy was going to have a late night. For a good cause.

Plymouth tried to ring Anne at the residence, to tell her he would have to beg off on the dinner party, but the help said she had not been home all afternoon. Anne and her charities. And the like. Good ambassador's wife, Anne. Excellent. Flawless taste. Always knew what to do and what not to do. And presentable, as she liked to say. His little Annie. Grateful for her good fortune. Plymouth shifted a stack of correspondence from one side of his desk to the other. Anne had her faults, of course. A bit too much energy, among other things. But nobody was perfect.

Even the thought of his wife could not spoil the ambassador's good mood.

IT WAS A joke. Rafael Gutiérrez Raimond watched the woman as she took her nakedness away from him. She was very businesslike about it. Stepping into her briefs with one hand on an antique chest for balance, an endlessly brazen woman flanked for the moment, as she had suggested, between two saints. She was wonderful in the shutter-harnessed light, her body better than that of far younger women, and he briefly pictured her doing her aerobics as she had described them, fierce in her battle with the thin air of the mountains. She handled her bra as roughly as a workman tying rope, doing the clasps, then rotating it around and driving her arms through the straps, covering herself from his eyes. She had brown, no-nonsense hair that fit her face like a tight, well-chosen frame and precise features that reminded him a bit of his cousin Eva. But where poor, foolish Eva looked haggard and half-starved, this woman looked sleek and groomed and thoroughbred.

"Anne," he said.

She looked up, eyes ever alert.

"Nothing," he said. "I only wanted you to look at me."

She continued with the chore of dressing, already closing herself off. In sex, she was challenging, uncompromising. Furious. Of course, that was part of her appeal. She was probably right. She was not beautiful. Not if you took her features apart, one by one. But she had something burning in her, something more than just the animal part of her he treasured. Anne, his unquenchable love. He was experienced enough to know that, for her, much of the sexual rage was revenge for a missed life.

He had set out to seduce her as he might have hunted a rare animal, cynically aware of the value of the information she would bring to his pillow. And his success had been rapid, and she had been useful, as expected. He knew more about her husband than any other man in Bolivia, and his uncle was grateful for the essentials he passed along. Anne was a good, vibrant lover, and no trouble, and a wonderful source of intelligence on his enemies.

The joke was that he really did love her.

CHURCH HEARD A vehicle approach and he lowered his trowel. Grateful for the interruption. His arms
and back ached, and he felt his years. Postmilitary career
options would not include construction work. Glancing
through an unfinished window, he made out Eva's jeep
in the fading light and his heart quickened. He had been
hoping to see her, curious about her bush epidemic, curious about her.

He wiped his hands on his ruined jeans and stepped
out into the twilight. The front end of the jeep was disfigured, one headlamp missing entirely, a gouged eye.
Fragile against the tough machine, Eva hurried toward
him. Eva always hurried.

As she closed the distance, he saw that her face was
swollen on one side.

"What happened to you?" he asked.

She smiled. "Accident. Nothing significant. John,
what are you doing here? I couldn't believe it when I
heard it."

They stood a few feet apart on earth spongy with
groundwater. Church gestured toward the clinic. "I'm
going to finish it."

"You can't do that by yourself."

He grinned, showing his hands. "I'm beginning to
wonder. Never was much of a handyman."

"It's too much. And it could be dangerous for you."

He shrugged. "Doesn't bear talking about. I've decided to do it, and I'm going to give it my best shot. But tell me about you. What's happening out in the bush?" He gestured toward the shell of the clinic, which looked no different for his long day's effort. "Care to join me in my parlor?"

They walked toward the structure, shoulder to shoulder.

"I've come to you for help." She held out one of her ruined hands, a blind person feeling her way. It was an odd gesture, at once mysterious and devoid of conscious meaning. Church wondered if it could be a sign of physical breakdown, of a body pushed to the limit.

He looked at the churned earth near the entrance, half seeing the litter of bent nails and slivers of trimmed wood, of cement crusts. "I'm afraid I'm on the outs with the embassy, Eva. I can't get you any of that kind of help." He turned, looking down at the woman. She had aged ferociously in days. "Bad out there?"

She went into the shelter and sat down on a bag of cement mix. For a long moment, she could not find the words.

"*Eva?* Are you all right?"

"Oh, God," she said, waking to him again. "Sorry. I'm so tired." The eyes were vivid in her starved face. "Nobody's willing to help. Not La Paz. Not the mayor. Not the police. I've gone to them all." Her lips twisted bitterly. "The only result is a roadblock a few miles down south. To keep the Indians out of town. At the mayor's orders." She smiled, a ghost amused at the world's unreformability. "I fell asleep on the road last night. I had to walk the last fifteen or so kilometers. Then the police didn't want to let me through their barricade. They were terrified. I had blood all over me and they thought I was going to infect them. They'd heard wild rumors." She looked up and her face showed a bitterness of which she would not have been capable even a week before. "Of course, the rumors fell a bit

short of the reality." A windswept pond, her face
changed expressions yet again. Now she looked earnest
and weary and beautiful in a fashion that was painfully
human, ethereal as slow jazz. "John, I really might be
contagious. I still have no idea what I'm dealing with."

"You're one of the most contagious women I've ever
met. So what happened?"

She smiled. "I bullied them. The police. It's pathetic,
really. Most of them are local boys, one generation out
of the bush. You can still pull white-skin rank on them.
But they were frightened. Nobody in town will come
near me. Of course, that might be for the best. But I had
a devil of a time getting my jeep towed out of the ditch.
And it needed some repairs. Took most of the day." She
looked away, reviewing recent memories. "A day gone
to waste."

"What's going to happen? With this epidemic? I can't
believe you're still working on this alone."

She ran a hand back through hair that had been
washed but not properly combed. "I don't know. I suppose the mayor and those bastards up in La Paz are just
hoping it'll go away." She stared at him, a helpless
truth-teller. "I suppose I'm hoping for the same thing.
So far, it's only hit four small settlements, as best I can
tell. And they're remote, well away from the town's water sources." Her forehead lined as if God had done
some rapid pencil work. "This disease, whatever it is,
has a lethality rate that's just astonishing. And it's mean
as rabies. I haven't a clue as to the vector. Or anything
else. I mean . . ." Suddenly, she began to shake. Crying
without tears. Her voice rose in unheralded panic, as if
her emotional muscles had all given way at once. "I'm
waiting for the symptoms to come over *me*. I've never
been afraid like this. I've never been so afraid."

Church moved toward her, but she recoiled. "*No*.
Don't touch me. Please, John. You'll get sick."

Ignoring her, he sat down on the dusty bag beside her
and put an arm around her shoulders.

"It's going to be all right," he said without conviction.

She gave up and rested her face against the slope of his chest. She felt tiny, her bones nothing but splinters, and she reeked of disinfectant.

"I don't know," she said. "I just don't know."

"Just rest."

"I can't. There's too much to do." But she rested.

"I contacted Panama. Before I left the embassy. I asked for help, for a MEDRETE team or anything else they could send. But I'm not optimistic. My stock's pretty low."

"Maybe it really will just go away. Diseases like this are strange. Sometimes they flare up, then just disappear. They burn so hot they consume themselves. It's just that it's all so wrong. I can't even pay anyone to help me with the physical side of things. They're afraid."

"I'll help you."

She raised her face to him. Her slightness made him feel enormous, a bear.

"It would be too dangerous. You have a family."

"I'll help you. I'll be all right. The clinic can wait a day or two."

"John, you have to really think about it. You could die. You might never see Ruth again."

"I'll help you."

"I need help with the ugly things. Disposing of the bodies. Burning them. Burying what's left. I just can't do it myself."

"I'll help you, Eva. It's all right."

She shifted, moving closer against him. A woman packaged as a child.

"Well, I'm going back out in the morning. I can't do anything else tonight. I mean . . . I don't know. Maybe I can't face it again just yet." She rested her hand upon him. "I'm going to call my father. To ask him for help."

Church nodded. "Sounds like a good idea. Whatever

else your father may or may not be, he's probably the most efficient man in Bolivia.''

"It's hateful to me.''

"You're a proud woman.''

"I'm too proud.''

Church remembered a line that had struck him and stayed with him. "You know what T. S. Eliot said?''

"I've never read Eliot. Poetry is still hard for me in English. Poetry is the hardest thing of all.''

"Eliot thought so, too. But that's by the by. He wrote that 'humility is endless.' In the sense of boundless, liberating. Eternal. I've always thought he was right, but I didn't know how to get there.''

"You're a humble man,'' the frightened little girl said. "Too humble.''

He realigned his spine, with darkness falling. "Only my achievements, such as they are, are humble. I am consumed by vanity. As we all are.''

"No. You're not.''

"I even like the ribbons on my uniform. Wish I had more of them.''

"You're a good man. You are a good, good man.''

Church snorted. "Eva, why don't you go home and get some sleep. You look like the S-3 at the end of an ARTEP.''

"What's that?''

"An S-3 is a man who is professionally unhappy, but ambitious. An ARTEP is a form of ritual torture used to select future kings. But this torture has many names.''

"Oh.''

"It's all very arcane and unimportant. You need to sleep.'' He looked around at his shabby collection of tools and building materials, wondering how many of them would disappear in his absence. "Tomorrow morning, I'll go out with you. Come by and pick me up.''

"John?'' She pulled away from him just a bit. Reluctantly.

"Yes, Doctor?''

"You deserve better."

He smiled. "I've been trying to convince the Army of that for a quarter of a century."

"I mean from me."

"And how could such a thing be?"

"I lied to you."

He bent forward, toward her, almost imperceptibly. "About what?"

"I didn't lie, exactly. But there was something that happened. Something I didn't tell you."

He said nothing. Listening. Waiting.

"A few days ago—I've lost track of the days—but before your soldiers were killed . . . I was making my rounds up north. And men stopped me. They threatened me, told me never to come back. They had those little machine guns. And they weren't Bolivians. They were the mean kind, the kind you don't want to ever get near again. They knew about my father, but they didn't care. They weren't afraid."

"Bad sign if they're not afraid of your old man. I'd be afraid of him. And I probably don't know the half of it."

"I'm sure they're drug people. Maybe Colombians, I think. But they didn't have that high-flown Bogotá accent."

"Up from the slums, probably. Not every Colombian speaks like a Bogotá hostess."

"Maybe . . ." she said very slowly, "these are the men who killed your soldiers. I didn't tell you . . . because I didn't want fighting here, in my town. See how selfish we become? *My* town. I didn't want a lot of American guns and killing and trouble."

"I can understand that."

"You don't trust me anymore. Do you?"

"Don't be silly."

"Can you ever forgive me? For lying?"

"Water under the bridge. Anyway, it wasn't a lie. Not

technically, I don't think. You'd have to ask a priest or somebody like that.''

"And now I've told you. And you'll tell the embassy."

"I think Henry Vasquez already knows. A couple of things he said make sense to me now."

"And now they'll come with guns."

Church nodded. Slowly, looking into the fresh darkness, into the future. Almost absentmindedly, he said:

"It's the only way we know how to settle things."

THE PHONE RANG before Anne could take off her jacket and hand it to the maid.

"One moment, please," she told the caller in her formal, careful voice. She slipped her arms out of the sleeves and extended the garment. "Thank you, Magdalena."

When the maid's footsteps had gone sufficiently distant, Anne said:

"Are you crazy?"

"I had to talk to you. I'm sorry."

"It hasn't been half an hour."

"I know. I understand. But I had to talk to you. Please. I want you to do something for me."

"What?"

"I want you to come down to Santa Cruz."

"When?"

"Tomorrow."

"Oh, for God's sake, Rafael. I can't just drop everything like that. I have responsibilities. Tomorrow, I'm supposed to visit a—"

"Do they matter? These responsibilities."

"They keep me sane."

"You're not sane, Anne. You're crazy. Like me. But you won't admit it. You are a stubborn woman."

"I can't just leave on such short notice." Her voice changed, seeking distance. "This is childish."

He laughed. "And when I say that I am childish, you correct me. You say, 'Rafael, you may be childlike, but never childish.'"

"Well, you're being childish now."

"Come to Santa Cruz, Anne. Please. You can stay at *Los Tajibos*. It's very nice."

"I know. I've stayed there. It's lovely."

"It will seem proper that way. Please, Anne. Perhaps this is nothing to you, but it means very much to me. I *love* you, Anne. Even if you don't believe it."

Damn you, Anne thought. I wish it were nothing to me. She decided she would have to put a stop to things, once and for all. Knowing that she would not do so. He'll make a terrible fool out of me, she warned an unlistening self.

"I can't."

"You *can*. Only two nights. Give me one full day. Fly down tomorrow. Please. I have never begged a woman for anything. I want to wake up next to you in the morning."

She almost laughed out loud at his earnestness. It was positively adolescent. Then she thought, Oh, yes. Let him wake up next to me. In the morning. Let him have a look without the makeup, before I've had time to begin the long coffee-driven process of becoming who he thinks I am. Let him have a good look. Then see if he still wants to talk about love.

EVA SET HER alarm for midnight and telephoned her father when she knew he would be at his best. When he finally came on the line, he sounded exuberant. They had not spoken for three years.

"Evita, *mein Engelchen*. How are you? How can I help you?"

It was too quick, too direct. She needed time. "I'm fine," she lied. "How are you, Father?"

"Fine, fine. Strong as a peasant. But isn't this late for you?"

"Not for you."

"Eva, you could call me anytime. Wake me up. I don't mind."

"Father . . ."

"You know what I was just doing? Listening to Brahms. The Violin Sonata in G major. It used to be one of your favorites, remember? We used to listen together. Your grandmother loved that piece, you know."

"Yes. You told me." The delight in her father's voice startled Eva. She wondered, again, if she had not been too hard on him, too hard on everyone but herself.

"It's wonderful, you know. What they can do with these compact discs. Digital technology. Why, yesterday I got a birthday present in the mail from your aunt Amalie. A Lotte Lehmann collection. Clear as a bell. As if it had just been recorded. Can you believe it? Your grandfather adored Lotte Lehmann, but Mama couldn't abide her. Mama said Lehmann sang like a trollop. I remember that. '*Die Lehmann singt wie eine Dirne.*'" Eva's father chuckled.

"Your grandmother liked to keep up appearances," he continued. "In the moral sense. I suspect she was a bit of a volcano, actually. She had a deep voice that made men listen. But I never saw the top button of that woman's blouse undone. Eva, she was such a wonder. She took such great care of my father's gramophone records all the while he was at the front. He loved music so much. She even hid the forbidden ones from the Gestapo. After his death. I suppose that was all she had left of him."

The old man's sentiments filled the receiver in Eva's hand, overwhelming the mediocre connection, the worn lines. Even when he paused, he gave her no real opening. It was as if he had forbidden her to speak, demanding that she listen to make up for lost time.

"Lehmann was on the proscribed list after she went

to California, of course. The later recordings must have
been smuggled in. I wonder how my father got hold of
them. Possibly gifts from our wealthier relations. They
were better connected; they could have gotten things like
that. And they were generous, very kind, and everybody
knew how much *Vati* loved his music. Truth be told, we
didn't have two copper coins to scratch together. Everybody knew that, too. Except my sister and I. The genteel
poverty of the aristocracy east of the Elbe." The old
man sighed. "Amazing, how much we can remember.
The details. Lotte Lehmann. 'Digitally remastered.' We
live in an age of miracles, Eva."

"I'm sorry, Father. I forgot it was your birthday."

"But you've called. That's enough. More than
enough. It's a wonderful present, Evita."

"I didn't call because of your birthday."

"It would be even more wonderful if you'd come see
me. We could listen to your favorite music together. Or
even better—I'm going home next month. For the autumn performances. You could give yourself a vacation
and go with me. I'm going to Dresden again, although
you know I find the place a bit depressing. I'm thinking
of investing a bit. There are some marvelous opportunities there now. And the reconstruction of the Semper
is superb, nothing short of a miracle. Not to be missed,
Eva, absolutely not to be missed. The acoustical balance
is simply remarkable. They're doing *Die Meistersinger*,
by the way. That always made you laugh. Except that
you always laughed at the wrong parts. We could go
together, you and I. Munich has a wonderful program
this year, too."

"Father . . . I need your help."

"What is it, my love?"

"There's an epidemic up here. Out in the bush. It's
something I can't handle alone. And nobody will help
me. It's criminal. The way everybody's ignoring it. It
could be a new disease. We need experts to come in,

people with knowledge and equipment. Before things get out of control.''

''What exactly do you need?''

''The people in La Paz? Who owe you favors? Could you make them do something?''

He paused and she did not understand it. When he spoke again, he just repeated:

''What do you need, Eva?''

''They need to send doctors. We need to set up isolation facilities. And we need supplies. I don't even have enough saline solution. I'm running out of everything. And labor power, maybe the army, to take care of the bodies, to disinfect the settlements. . . .''

''How soon do you need this help?''

''Yesterday. The day before yesterday.''

''All right. I'll help you. With everything. But there's one condition.''

''What?''

''You have to leave there. Before you get sick, too. That's not your place, Eva, and I don't want to lose you for . . . for the sake of these savages.''

She hung up the phone.

SHE DID NOT mind the lamplight, and he looked at her that way. Her after-sex sprawl, part sloth, part tease, had an unthinking beauty, a discount glory rummaged like a treasure found at a yard sale. She lay still molten in the broken, frozen surf of sheets, her skin almost as dark as his own, yet fatefully different. Her eyes watched him without seeing and he wondered where she had gone but did not ask, content to admire the flesh.

Stretched long, her nakedness flirted with damp bedclothes, one thigh covered, the other tapering darkly golden. The jointure of her legs showed thick with black hair, wet now, clotted low where she had not shut completely, and she jutted slightly skyward. A fine stitch of hairs climbed her belly, a seam, stopping abruptly as a man shot dead. Her stomach's flatness marked her determination not to show the least trace of childbirth, but her breasts had begun to lose their elasticity ever so slightly, pooling away from her sternum, richer than the sight of her clothed suggested. She had good shoulders, the squared-off, almost male shoulders of a model, and a long aristocratic neck, probably the legacy of a rape centuries back in her blood. Her face was heart-shaped and a bit mean when she did not know she was being observed, her single physical flaw a tendency to show cold sores on the lips now and then. She was old enough and clear enough to know and get exactly what she wanted, and physically, she was a marvelous, challenging, even unnerving lover. Luther Darling believed that they might have had a future had she not been ashamed of him.

At the office, she treated him as she treated everyone else. After work, she would not so much as walk down the street beside him. But she came to his apartment, whenever she wanted and, sometimes, when he wanted, leaving her child with her mother and sneaking stupidly and ineffectively up the stairs. He suspected that the point was not really to conceal their relationship but to pay her society the respect of demonstrating an effort at its concealment. Her world was one of surface effects, where no one pried too deeply.

Darling refused to define himself as black or African American, doggedly resistant to biological accident. Determined not to be a cliché. Aided by hopeful parents, minor bureaucrats back home in the District of Columbia, he had worked to master proper speech and to dress effectively. Hardheaded, he had been immune to the taunts of his schoolmates. As his brother had not been. In retrospect, Darling realized how incredibly lucky he had been to escape D.C. just before the crack plague, blessed to have gone to the bad-enough schools in the days when fists and a reasonable tolerance for pain could still see you through.

He had been a scholarship student, a good clarinetist, and a clever, thoughtful boxer, afraid only of failure. Far from blind to the issue of race, he had simply followed his father's example of refusing to let anyone turn the color of his skin into a weapon against him. Thinking back, reexamining his life and the lives of his peers from the perspective of his thirtieth year, Luther Darling saw that he had been blessed in many, many ways. Lucky just to have a father who worked every day and came home every night. Odd, the things you took for granted before you gained a little distance and began to think about your world.

Except for the church, there had been no special "blackness" about his family. His father was as apt to read the work of William Butler Yeats as of Langston Hughes. To his father's and his own embarrassment—and to the infinite amusement of friends and relatives—his mother had a weakness for Elvis Presley, whose indestructible wretchedness haunted their home. When Elvis died, his mother had gone wet-eyed, saying, "That poor boy. Oh, that poor, sad boy."

Many things were different now. His parent's home was different, of course. The District had gotten so bad that his mother and father had moved out to Prince George's, sorry to leave behind good friends less fortunate and the real pleasures of D.C., the pep downtown, the concerts, and the occasional special restaurant visit, in the course of which his father always insisted on ordering a wine they could not really afford. Anyway, they had needed to leave after Calvin died. After Calvin was killed. After Calvin killed himself through his unforgivable stupidity and blindness. After Calvin, not yet twenty and just paroled, died a nigger's death.

Darling doubted that he would ever return to D.C. to live. The city insisted too much on his blackness, demanding that he be black before and above anything else, defining him down to a pathetic commonality. The city government, all cynicism and rhetoric, was a shambles that shamed him, and the streets were murderous with self-hatred. The self-pity and constant blaming of anyone or anything but the individual for failure, the conviction that collective failure was inevitable and even to be sought, the hatred of anyone who refused to play the victim—all of that sickened him and just made him wonder who he was, really.

Certainly, he was an Army officer. And a pilot, as a result of a bout of unthinking, childish lust to do something dashing and exciting. If he could have begun his military career again, he would not have gone to flight school. He had been unaware, when he made his choice, that aviators were the butt of endless jokes in the officer corps. And Darling did not like being the butt of other men's jokes. Not when he took the other men seriously.

He was an Army officer, and a successful one so far. And he knew that, in this case, the color of his skin was a blessing, if not one he sought. A minority officer who could perform at all had an unlimited future, an advantage imagined to be compensatory but in fact insulting. Insulting . . . yet Darling doubted he would ever turn a promotion down. The world of Luther Darling was one in which there was little rest for the soul.

Surprisingly, the downside of his military career had been his experience of other cultures. In Korea, as a second lieutenant, he had encountered a level of racism unthinkable back in the States, something fallen from the pages of a history book. Then, during Desert Storm, which had earned him a bronze star with V-device, the Arab officers and officials often had skin much darker than his own. But his country's passing allies saw— clung to—a difference between themselves and a tawny American. Now, in Bolivia, it was laughable. Politicians who were clearly 99 percent Indian clung desperately to a single Spanish-blooded ancestor, insisting on their membership in the elite, even as they told another tale entirely when campaigning in the altiplano or down in the Beni, away from their sharp-eyed social peers. A blond child was favored massively over darker-haired siblings, and the German immigrant communities were welcomed as genetic benefactors. Despite democracy and rhetoric and laws and the endlessly trumpeted social programs of each next government, whiteness was the key to success in Bolivia, and Darling doubted it would ever really change. The handful of blacks stranded in unimaginably poor villages up along the Brazilian border were even lower than the Indians. He knew. He had gone to see them.

He sometimes wondered if Esmeralda's attraction to him was not finally a forbidden-fruit thing, a delicious debasement. Ready to shout with ecstasy in his arms, she did not even like to sit with him in the embassy cafeteria over coffee, and she would have gone into shock had she overheard the conversations about their relationship he had caught between her fellow secretaries, who seemed to consider her an absolute slut and a bit to be envied. Their speculation about his appeal to her was shockingly and humiliatingly frank. He had even considered ending the relationship over the comments, but in the end, he found himself unwilling to deprive himself of her body. He figured that they were both getting what they needed and thought amusedly of a favored saying of his father's: "First, take care of the essentials."

His parents had been faintly disappointed when he chose a military career. But Luther Darling had never yet regretted the choice. The Army was as close to color-blind as any organization could be, starved for talent and under constant stress to produce. If skin color could be an advantage, merit still mattered most. And with rare exceptions, he found himself serving among good men. Sometimes among great men. Like Church.

He wondered if he could ever be so good a man. Church said little, did a lot, and struck Darling as honest to the point of self-immolation. The colonel took joy in the fine little things others rushed past, and Church was a family man for the ages. The secretaries went vicious in their comments on his wife, Ruth, who was no longer sleek enough for their tight jeans and gaping blouses. But the office chorus girls simply seemed lost on Church, their raw delectability inadequate in his eyes. The secretaries did not like the colonel much, forever miffed at his insistence that they actually work at least part of the working day and genuinely troubled by his unwillingness to adore them. Esmeralda had asked him once if the colonel was a homosexual.

Church was one man Darling did not want to let down. He had almost given in to impulse, had nearly taken leave himself so he could go down to Mendoza and help the older man build his clinic. But Darling caught himself in time. Maybe Church did not want company. Anyway, Darling had decided there was a better way to help.

It occurred to Luther Darling that whenever some narrow-shouldered wonk on television declared that there were no heroes anymore, they needed a good dose of Colonel John Church. Darling pictured the older man at his dinner table, forever sharing his home and family life with the bachelor officers on his staff, his entire family spilling over with love and decency and shaming you with your own meanness. Church . . . who only wore the rows and rows of ribbons he had earned when protocol absolutely demanded it.

The colonel never talked much about his career, but things came out. Church had done things other officers only dreamed of doing, and he had the gift of calm when things were going to hell all around him. Once, when they had been forced to make an emergency landing in a Huey—a landing that could easily have killed them all—Church had simply stepped out of the aircraft once it settled, walked a reasonable distance away, then started wondering aloud how they could best retrieve the stricken bird from the middle of a primeval jungle.

The jungle. If anything convinced Darling that he had

lost the last ties to his African ancestors, it was his absolute terror of the jungle. He could smile about it now, safe, in bed with a drowsing beauty he had just filled with himself. But the walk out through the jungle, with Church leading, compass in hand, and the three Bolivian crew members absolutely shaking as they followed, had been one of the most horrific experiences of Darling's life. He had never been the least bit afraid during Desert Storm, soaring on adrenaline and forever short of time, but the jungle was something else. No street in D.C. could intimidate him the way the overwhelming, dense, hot, stinking, suffocating, nightmarishly alive jungle could do. Even the scrublands, the bush and chaco, were not so bad. You could see trouble coming. But the jungle constantly surprised you, and the surprises were never good ones. As far as Darling was concerned, the romance of ecotourism was the biggest scam in the universe. He saw no reason why any human being should pay to plod through nature's cesspool, where the average snake seemed longer than a helicopter and the small, half-hidden creatures were mean beyond belief. A twenty-seven-hour march through the jungle, hacking at the undergrowth and ready to hack at anything that moved, had been enough to convince Darling that he was a city dweller at heart. Remembering the jungle night was enough to make him shudder even now.

The telephone rang. It woke Esmeralda, who had been drowsing, her breasts rising and falling in peace. She sat up part way, belly flesh rippling, and her eyes betrayed the distance her thoughts had traveled away from him.

"Who calls you so late in the night?" she asked suspiciously.

Darling shrugged and reached for the phone.

"Captain Darling."

It was a college buddy. Currently employed by the *Washington Times*. Darling had stayed late at the embassy to sneak him a fax. The ambassador's inner circle had been in a huddle over the lab raid, which apparently had gone well. Sieger had come into the Milgroup office unexpectedly while Darling was still on the fax machine, and Darling had figured he was screwed, but the lieutenant colonel paid him no real attention. Sweaty, beat-looking, with a pimple on his nose, Sieger just said the raid was a success. But he did not say it with much conviction, and he clearly did not want to talk about it. The lieutenant colonel sat at Church's desk for a while, dirty and obviously exhausted, staring out of the window at the night. Then he got up and left without another word.

It had taken Darling's friend hours to respond to the fax.

"Lu . . . how you doing? How's Romeo's love life? Hey, this looks like good stuff. Great stuff. We're going to run a couple of paragraphs in a bottom-of-the-page round-up. This is *great* human interest stuff."

"The guy's going to get shit on if nobody helps him," Darling said.

"Well, *you*'re helping him, pal. The guy owes you one."

"I'm trying. Anything more I can do for you from this end?"

"Sure," the small, distance-clipped voice said. "Keep sending anything the local yokels publish on the guy. The stuff on Plymouth is good, too. He's in bed with Drew MacCauley, you know. Old school buds and all that shit. Drew's mama spilled tea on Ethan's mama. Or vice versa." The telephone gave a harsh little honk. "The ed staff here is death on MacCauley. Things ain't great at State. Makes terrific copy, though. Gang that couldn't negotiate straight. MacCauley's dead but doesn't know it yet. Time for the Rhodes scholar to hit the road. We're going to blow him out of the water over his love fest with the Russians. 'Millions for Moscow, screw the folks back home.' That sort of thing."

Darling did not care about Drew MacCauley, whom he barely sensed. His focus was far humbler.

"You're running something tomorrow, Paul?"

"Like I said. Anyway, I don't know what time it is down your way, but we're already talking about today up here."

"You're a great American," Darling said.

"Nothing too good for my bud on the front lines of freedom—you doing okay down there, Lu?"

Darling looked at the woman growing subtly restless beside him. She shaped a kiss with her mouth, a cartoon of desire.

"I'm doing okay," Darling said.

CHURCH HAD BEEN dreaming about Eva von Reinsee when a noise woke him. He jerked up onto his elbows, hammock swaying beneath him, an unsteady base for any action. Sweat erupted on his shoulders, along his spine, in the soft meat under his arms. The sound that had pierced his sleep was the rustle of dying grass against trousers.

With ballet delicacy, Church slid out from under his mosquito net and hunched on the floor. The tiles chilled his feet. Gently, he felt for his boots and drew them on, quiet as the air. Dressed in his Army-brown shorts and T-shirt, he crept across the floor to where he had propped a shovel across the open doorway. Arming himself with the tool, he edged along the wall of the next room, the someday foyer, heading for the exit, anxious to carry this battle to his enemies, unwilling to wait passively in a trap. His sweat-slimed skin caught dirt and building scraps.

Clouds that wanted to rain screened the moon, and the night waited darkly, a blanket for his pale skin. By the doorway, he stopped and waited, listening again, forcing his body to come back under control. The muscles obeyed, but his heart fought to break out of his rib cage.

He focused. Yes. Same sound. But it had moved lat-

erally. As though circling the building, making sure of
something. Church could not get the footsteps, which
meant that the intruder was either barefoot or wearing
some sort of soft mocassin. Church had plenty of respect
for any human being brave enough to go barefoot in this
poisonous darkness. He thought back to the hacked
corpses of the soldiers and imagined a very tough Indian,
closing with a machete. And if there was one, there was
a good chance there would be others.

The rustling faded around the side of the building and
Church scuttled out into the darkness, clutching the
shovel. He covered about three meters then lowered
himself to the ground, listening again.

Nothing. The intruder was probably behind the building now. Or he had stopped. Church low-crawled out
into the scrub grass, praying there would be nothing dangerous under his body. He paused again. When he still
heard nothing, he snaked through the grass to the dark
outline of a shed and rose slowly to his feet, flattening
himself against old boards and raising the shovel like a
broadsword.

He waited. Finally, he saw an orange point of light
come around the far corner of the clinic. His visitor had
lit up a cigarette.

That jarred Church. No professional assassin would
do such a thing. A skilled patroller knew you could spot
the glow of a single cigarette from a kilometer away on
a clear night. Plenty of bad soldiers had died that way.
And good soldiers had died, too, just because they had
a single poor one in their midst.

The point of light flared then diminished again as the
visitor inhaled and lowered the cigarette. It came closer.

The man's folly was a gift, and Church no longer had
to strain to hear the rustle off the man's legs. But he
still paid full attention. In case there was an accomplice.

And there was, indeed, someone else. Church spotted
a separate figure out on the dirt road, half a football field
away. The second figure had been stationary, unreadable

in the undifferentiated light, and only a sudden shadow of movement against a paler background betrayed his presence.

It made no sense. If they were a team, they needed to be closer together, able to support each other. Their actions had no logic. If these men were killers come to take care of him, then they were probably local hire doing the job for beer money.

The cigarette came around to the front of the clinic. Slowly, almost lazily. The man moved midway between the clinic and the shed where Church had gone to ground, and his shape silhouetted against a pale, unfinished wall.

Short, a bit stocky. With an ax handle or some sort of club over one shoulder. Church sensed that he could take him and, if he got it right, do it quietly enough to prevent the more distant figure from hearing more than a single nondescript sound. The blade of the shovel had to strike directly at the base of the skull.

Absolutely drenched now, his bare legs bitten by the nightlife, Church began to stalk his stalker. He had maneuvered his bulk through plenty of tight places in the course of an eventful life and he was quick on his feet, just as he was a startlingly graceful dancer. Quickly and silently, he moved in on the walking shadow, angling just off to the figure's left rear, judging the length of the shovel and the distance he would need for his swing.

The intruder stopped.

Church feared the man had heard his approach. But the figure only dropped the stub of his cigarette and, with great care, ground it out.

Church had him. He took the last step and angled the shovel back against the sky. On impulse, somehow unable to make his kill without verifying the target, he whispered:

"Don't move."

The shadow jerked, dropping the club from its shoulder, crying:

"Madre de Dios."

Church made an instinctive decision. Instead of bringing down the shovel on the man's neck, he leapt forward, hooping the handle over the man from the rear and drawing it back hard against the man's neck. He had a prisoner now. And if the man tried to make a fight of it, he could kill him in seconds.

Church made the pressure of the wooden handle hurt. Holding it tightly enough so that the man could not speak or even breathe properly. In hissing Spanish, he said:

"Move and I'll kill you."

His prisoner gasped.

"Put your hands all the way into your pockets."

The man obeyed. He smelled of work sweat and bad diet.

"I'm going to let you breathe. If you raise your voice or try to call for help, you're dead." Church relaxed the handle very slightly. "Now tell me who you are and what you want."

The man choked, glutting himself on the heavy night air.

"Talk to me, friend," Church whispered savagely.

"Please," the captive begged. "Please, my colonel. Please don't hurt me."

The man knew who he was. Church pulled the wood back against his captive's Adam's apple as a threat, then lessened the pressure again.

"What are you doing here?"

"Please. My colonel. We don't mean no harm." The man certainly did not have a killer's voice.

"What are you doing here?"

"Guarding you," the man said sheepishly.

"What?"

"Guarding you, my colonel. Maybe we don't do it so good, I guess. But the cops, they don't do it at all, cause they're no good for nothing." The man swallowed, obviously trying to soothe his hurt neck. "We all know what you're trying to do for us, my colonel. You come back here even after what happened to the other gringos. You're a *hombre magnífico*. Like one of them holy martyrs.'' Church's captive gasped again. It occurred to Church that he did not much want to end up like any of the holy martyrs who leapt to mind. ''We're sorry for those boys of yours,'' Church's hapless protector went on. ''Truly. And we don't want nothing to happen to you.''

Church let the handle of the shovel slide down over the man's chest. Then he released the smaller man entirely. The man slumped, and it took him a minute or so to collect himself. When the colonel's protector had gathered the shreds of his manhood back together, he made an earnest, almost desperate gesture toward the outline of the trees across the road.

''There's some real bad men out there,'' he said.

EVA WOKE IN tentative light, back aching, with the rest of the world still drugged deep around her. In a squandered night, she had lain awake thinking, shaping futures, half deciding, until she finally plummeted into a sleep fierce as vengeance, with the good hours already lost. Now she woke hard and too early, her decision made. She telephoned her father again, hoping to catch him before he went out on one of his early morning rides, driving this year's horse hard, as would a much younger man, trying to beat the glare of true day that was unbearable to him, trying to prove that he was still the invincible youth who had joined a decently prosperous uncle in a forgotten country and turned his cattle business into a web of enterprises that composed a state within the state.

He had already left for his stables on the outskirts of town, a member of the staff told her. He gave Eva her father's new cellular number. This time, her father answered for himself.

"It's Eva."

"Good morning, angel. This *is* a birthday treat. Two calls in a day."

"It's not a birthday call."

"Neither was the last one. You told me. So. Have you reconsidered my offer?"

"No. It's something else."

"Just a moment." She could hear him speaking to his driver and she pictured him leaning over, his strong, crisp profile and the crest of white hair definite against the softness of the morning. "All right."

"I have to tell you something. A few days ago some men stopped me. They threatened me. They knew I was your daughter. That's not why they threatened me. At least they didn't say so. They just wanted me to stay out of the area. They had little machine guns, not much bigger than pistols, and they said they'd kill me if I came back."

"Did they hurt you?"

"No."

"If anyone hurt you, I'd have them killed."

"Don't talk like that—don't you see why I can't talk to you?"

"Those were drug people," her father said bitterly, finally.

"Yes. I suppose so."

"They frightened you."

"No. Yes. I mean, that's not why I called. I called because they said they weren't afraid of you. And maybe they aren't. I don't know. They certainly weren't afraid of me. That's what I called to tell you. I wanted you to know. Because, if anything happened to you, anything like that, I'd have it on my conscience. If I didn't tell you."

"You're making some fine theological distinctions, my dear. It's simpler for me."

"It's always simpler for you."

"Perhaps not always. Pedro, don't pull right up to the

barn. Sorry. So. Have you told anyone else about this? About what happened?''

Eva did not answer immediately. She looked out of her window, watching the edge of the sun eat its way into the sky. It rose over an endless sea of trees, where the dead and dying waited for her.

''Yes. I told one person.''

''Who?''

''Colonel Church. From the embassy. He's come down to finish the clinic where those boys were killed. He's trying to do it all by himself. He's a good man, and I wanted him to know about the danger.''

''Yes. I've met Church. Very direct. One of the better Yankees, I think.''

Eva could read her father's voice very well, and now he sounded inexplicably pleased.

''He's not involved in any of this. In any of your drug business.''

''Eva, please. I'm on a cellular phone. Anyway, that's all nonsense.''

''Don't hurt him.''

''Wouldn't dream of it. Sounds as though you're quite fond of him, though. He didn't strike me as your type. But, then, what does a father know?''

''He's married. He has two children. There's nothing like that between us.''

''Of course not.''

''We're friends.''

''Good. I think I'd like to have more friends like that myself. Church has a reputation as a decent sort. Gets on with the locals, I hear.''

''So now you know.''

''What?''

''About the men. Who stopped me.''

''Yes. Thank you. And I hope you'll stay away from them. It's an evil world, Eva. And it's getting more evil every day. Now . . . won't you let me help you?''

''Not on your terms.''

Her father paused. She envisioned him in his Range Rover, booted and exact in a tweed jacket. With the horse sounds and smells waiting for him. She had loved the stables as a girl.

"Eva, *Engelchen*. This is an evil world," he said with a seriousness as heavy as his heritage. "In the end, we have only those of our blood."

CHRISTIAN RITTER VON Reinsee returned from his morning ride with blood on his face and his temper barely under control. He was a profoundly disciplined man, and few of the actions of other men could surprise or rile him. But he was intolerant of his own mistakes.

Eyes already strained by the strengthening light, he dismounted with the fluidity of a man much younger and handed the reins to a waiting groom.

"Melchior's been a bad boy today," von Reinsee said.

"*Jefe*, this one's a mean horse, a bad horse."

The wet-breasted stallion snorted and snapped its head in agreement. Von Reinsee patted the animal's flank. Its pelt was nearly red in the young light. The horse smelled of life.

"Weak men ride weak horses," von Reinsee said, and he turned toward the parking area where he could see his nephew waiting by a second Range Rover. Drawing a pair of dark-lensed glasses from inside his jacket, von Reinsee put them on, briefly jarred by the smell of his own hand, secondhand horse scent. The world grew instantly more comfortable, but an aching lingered at the back of his skull. He missed the light, missed the fullness of mankind. In Germany, he could remain out of doors for hours at a time in the autumn or early spring, with the paltry northern sun less vivid. Here, he had become a prisoner. But he was a prisoner in his own world. A prisoner and a king. He strode over random manure in boots that cost more than many a man's life.

"Uncle Christian, what happened?" Rafael stepped away from his vehicle, concern on his face. "You're bleeding."

Von Reinsee waved a hand, dismissing the matter as trivial. "Melchior's too damned smart. I was thinking about other things, and he knew it. He knew he had me. It's a game we play. He bolted under a thorn tree. Couldn't get rid of me, though."

His nephew folded his arms. "Everybody thinks you're crazy for riding that horse."

Von Reinsee considered the younger man. Handsome. Strong. Intelligent. Capable of sound work and fortunate with women. But, in the end, a Latin.

"Serious men ride serious horses."

Rafael smiled. "Uncle, sometimes you remind me of Eva. Or Eva reminds me of you."

Von Reinsee lifted an eyebrow, hinting at a smile of his own. "You mean we're both hardheaded to the point of folly."

"Hardheaded, anyway."

Von Reinsee drew out a handkerchief and scrubbed at his palms, unhappy with the smell of the horse today. "Eva and I come from a defiant family. Sometimes we defied emperors, and sometimes we just defy common sense. It's in the blood."

"And now you're defying the Americans."

Von Reinsee began walking toward his own vehicle. The driver stood waiting with a thermos of coffee and a fine white towel. Von Reinsee traded him the handkerchief.

"Not really," the older man said. "It's only defiance if they realize it. If we act competently, they'll never figure out what happened. Nor will our Colombian friends." He held his mug of coffee as though it were full of wine, savoring the blaze of steam before drinking. "Anyway, defiance belongs to the world of honor and elopements. This is business."

After delivering the coffee and the towel, the driver

had retreated to a discreet distance. Von Reinsee rubbed the back of his neck with the rich cloth, then took a gulp of coffee, shocking his tongue with the heat and bite. "On the subject of business," he said, "I want to see our special friend. Tonight."

"Jesus, Uncle. The guy's pretty busy. He might not be able to drop everything without more warning."

Von Reinsee looked at the younger man in a manner that stopped his nephew from further speech, shrinking him to a boy.

"I want to see him tonight," he repeated. Softly.

"Yes, Uncle."

"I find him . . . a despicable man, you know."

"Yes, Uncle."

"Despicable. But useful. I always find it . . . discouraging . . . that the world will not be moved by the hands of honorable men alone. The man's a villain. In the classical sense. A Klingsor. Not a Don Giovanni."

"Yes, Uncle."

Von Reinsee smiled and tossed the towel onto the hood of the vehicle, realizing full well that his nephew had not understood the references. "Speaking of Don Giovanni . . . how is your Yankee beloved?"

"Fine. The way she describes . . . her husband . . . everything's on its proper course."

Von Reinsee looked at the younger man with the heartlessness of a surgeon. "There's something else. What is it?"

Rafael turned his attention to the earth, blushing like a teenaged boy caught out. "Uncle Christian . . . she's coming here. Just for a day. Two nights. I'm putting her up at *Los Tajibos.*"

Von Reinsee took a slow sip of coffee, tasting brown fire. "Is that wise?"

"There won't be any difficulties."

The older man lowered his mug. "You don't know that."

"I promise you."

Von Reinsee nodded. "That's not the sort of thing a man can promise. And you know it. Listen to me, Rafael. A scandal would not only be damnably bad form, it could do serious harm. Concentrate on one thing at a time."

"Uncle Christian, I know you think I'm just a playboy."

"No. I think a playboy is one of the many things you are. And I do not object to it so long as it does not interfere with business and you don't gamble." He almost reached out and took his nephew by the arm, but did not. "Rafael, she would be a very bad woman to fall in love with. Not only because of her position."

But because, von Reinsee thought, she has been starved all her life. And if you once begin to feed her, she will devour you. He had recognized Anne Plymouth right to her soul the minute they were introduced. The hand under his lips was dangerous. He and the ambassador's wife were two of a kind.

"Maybe she's like your horse. For me. My 'seriousness.' She reminds me of the women in your operas."

Von Reinsee placed the emptied mug of coffee on the hood of his Range Rover and took his nephew by the upper arm, steering him nowhere, walking out of instinct. The fresh sun hurt his eyes even through the armor of the dark glasses, but he did not want to continue the conversation inside of a vehicle with an additional pair of ears.

"The best operas," von Reinsee said, "end tragically. And so, I'm afraid, do the best women. Oh, I don't mean the best women in any puritanical sense. On the contrary. I mean the women with any gift for life. I know of no society anywhere on this earth that is structured to accomodate those women who can scald the soul simply by taking your hand in the backseat of a cab. They consume like fire. And, like fire, they cannot control themselves once they have begun."

"You don't think I'm man enough for her?"

Von Reinsee raised both eyebrows and snorted. "Don't be absurd. That's not what I'm talking about at all."

"But you think she is Isolde."

"Rafael, I could not care less whether or not Mrs. Plymouth is Isolde in a tailored suit. I just don't want you to be Tristan."

"But you don't forbid me to bring her here."

Von Reinsee tucked the younger man's forearm over his own. "Rafael, I've lived far too long to attempt any such prohibition. You wouldn't listen, anyway. Perhaps in the letter, but not in the spirit. I would simply be forcing you to lie to me." He turned them farther from a sun that threatened to break through noncommittal clouds. "You know you've become a second son to me. Since Adam's death."

"My mother and I are both very grateful to you, Uncle."

"And your father was a splendid man, truly splendid, and I miss him. I feel I owe him much. But my point is that I don't want to lose a second son. So be careful. Try to think between your apogees of passion. Between acts, so to speak."

"I promise."

Two drab birds played love tag in an orchard just beyond the entry road. "Now. On the subject of difficult women and relatives in danger. I'm very worried about Eva. Oh, she did pass on word of her encounter to her American, to Church, by the way. So that played out. But this epidemic business. I know she's a doctor and all that. But Eva is capable of being a damned fool. That runs in the family, too. And it's going to become extremely violent up there. Soon. It may be time to remove Eva from the scene, whether she wants to go or not."

"I can have her kidnapped. Just hold her someplace till things blow over. It'll frighten her, though."

"I wish I could think of something better. Anyway,

set it up, be prepared to do it on a few hours' notice. But don't move until I say so. Let me think a bit.'' He brushed his cheek with the back of his hand. ''You know, that damned horse really did me a bad turn. My face burns like the fires of hell.''

''It looks swollen.''

''Well, I suppose I'll survive. And I want you to survive, too. In every respect. And Eva.''

''Don't worry, Uncle.''

''Old men worry. I suppose young men do, too. But about different things. You'll find, one day, that there really isn't much beyond family. People like the Lebanese and the Armenians are right about that much.'' He caught the light in the gap between his dark glasses and an eyebrow and shuddered. ''I've got to be going. It's too bright already.''

He released the younger man's arm and they stood facing one another.

''We have to look after Eva,'' von Reinsee said earnestly.

''Yes, Uncle.''

The older man smiled. ''And you. I wish you well of your beloved. Just remember—that one's not just some bureaucrat's bored wife. She's one of the dangerous ones.''

''I know.''

''Good.'' But von Reinsee did not believe that the younger man understood him at all. He turned to go and saw his driver hurry to open a door in anticipation. Then the older man remembered one last thing.

''That Colombian boy. The talented one. You'll have him ready when we need him?''

His nephew looked startlingly fine in the morning light, not just a handsome man but a beautiful human being. With a beauty that was almost tragic.

Rafael smiled. ''Have I ever let you down, Uncle?''

Von Reinsee shook his head, smiling again, his mood

bettered. Before he turned away for the last time, he said:

"That Colombian boy has a sort of genius, you know. I suspect he's very unhappy."

11

THE RATS WERE huge, easily as large as dogs, and their swollen pelts gleamed. With the grunt of a bully who had eaten far too much, one of the rats lunged toward him, and Angel stumbled backward, colliding with a huddled, fatty creature with the eyes of a woman. The beast snarled and fled as Angel hammered at its obesity with his fists. Dozens of the man-rats chattered and raced beyond his reach, maneuvering behind him, seeking any vulnerability. Angel fled from one dark room to another, skidding over floors slimed with evil. A minky rat hissed and rose like a snake, its open mouth glowing, throat on fire. The rats herded against one another, groaning and keening at the edge of human speech, too intelligent to be defeated. In the final room, a trap with no exit, a great rat waited for him, bloody-mouthed, lifting its maw from a half-devoured child.

Knocking and hissed whispers woke him. He rose from the sofa where he slept when home, shorts dangling, the elastic at the leg openings long exhausted. Remembering an agony of night cramps, he fought his eyes open, only halfway returned from rat land.

"I'm coming, man," he said as he reached for his pistol.

It was one of the policemen responsible for the neighborhood. The man smiled apologetically and said:

"Angel, let me in."

Angel shook off another layer of sleep and warily allowed the policeman to come inside. "What time is it?"

The policeman was taller than Angel and he bent his shoulders to lessen the difference. "Early, it's early. I'm sorry. It's very important."

"Yeah. What?"

The policeman looked around the room as if informers lurked everywhere. Beyond a wall, Angel's mother called out unintelligibly.

"It's nothing, Mama. Go back to sleep."

"Angel," the policeman said, "you got to get out of here. Quick. They're coming."

"Who's coming?"

"Everybody. Police. Maybe the Army. I don't know. It's going to be a big sweep. This morning. The gringos have gone crazy about something."

"They looking for me?" Angel pulled on his jeans.

"I don't know who they're looking for. Somebody killed a bunch of Yankees somewhere and now it's a big mess here. Trouble all over the place."

"Yeah. Well, fuck the Yankees."

The policeman looked at him cautiously. "That's what I say, too. But you got to get out of here."

"Yeah. Well, I was going anyway. I got business." He fetched a thick pad of currency from his neatly folded trousers and skinned off the outer bills. "You keep an eye on my mother and my sister while I'm gone."

With the policeman expelled back into the street, Angel walked to the curtain that guarded the room where his mother and sister slept.

"Mama, I got to go. And Rosa's going to be late for school."

He heard old-woman sighs over the little miseries of waking. Turning to gather his necessities, he moved with the crispness of a professional, suppressing his body's needs for the time being. He was nearly ready to go when his mother emerged.

"Who was that?" she asked.

"Nobody."

She looked him up and down, cutting deeper contours of sorrow into her cheeks. "You're leaving?"

"I got business, Mama. I'll be back."

"Where are you going?"

He smiled. "Lots of places. I'm an international businessman. I'll tell you all about it when I get back." He tightened his expression. "Where's Rosa? She has to get up."

His mother's face assumed a fearful look, as if she expected to be struck. "Rosa's not here."

He had been reaching for the loaf of bread that hung in the bag suspended from the ceiling, but he stopped. "What do you mean, she's not here?"

"She's not here. I don't know."

"She was here last night. When did she leave?"

His mother's face declared ignorance. Angel knew that he would have heard his sister leaving through the front door. That left the window in the rear room.

Angel began to curse, then restrained himself. "Mama, you got to control her. Put your foot down. She's running with a bad crowd, with bums."

"Maybe if her brother was here all the time . . ."

But there was no time for such a discussion now. Angel hustled to where his mother stood, stooped and kissed her, then gave her a hug.

"You tell her I'm going to beat her like a whore in the street if she don't behave. You tell her I'll kill those little piss ants she's hanging with."

"Angel . . . don't talk like that."

"You tell her, Mama."

"Angel?"

But there was no time. He did not feel afraid, only quickened. If the gringos were good, he would be better. He was the best.

"Mama, I might be gone a while. I got big business this time. But don't worry. I got connections. They're going to take care of me, like I take care of them.''

''Angel, I worry.''

He looked down at her, already wearing his killer's eyes.

''Worry about Rosa.''

DEPUTY SECRETARY OF State Drew MacCauley summoned the Deputy Assistant Secretary for Latin American Affairs, then finished reading the compilation of news in the *Early Bird* while he waited. That done, he turned to the *Wall Street Journal*. No matter how pressing the demands on his time became, he always blocked out an hour first thing in the morning for going through the press and the cable book, thinking and preparing himself for the day. Today, his calendar showed two meetings with foreign delegations staffed just below the head-of-state level, an independence day luncheon in a basket-case embassy, a cabinet chat he would attend in SecState's absence, two prebriefs, an award ceremony for a staffer, and an early evening meeting of the Deputies Committee to vote on oil swaps with Iran—climaxed by dinner with an old friend at Galileo. No window for squash—he would have to make up for the lack of exercise tomorrow. He gazed down the right-hand column of the *Journal*.

More absolute nonsense about threats to democracy in Russia. The press just didn't get it, hadn't done their homework. Drew MacCauley knew Russia and the Russians. The movement to democracy was irreversible. The Russians just needed judicious aid and patient encouragement. The Russians were a marvelous people, although more than a bit unlucky. Remarkably cultured, though. Fine conversationalists, quoters of poetry. Educated. You could trust them. Unlike the rubes on the Hill.

MacCauley sat in a leather chair soft as kidskin behind a desk that had once been used by Cordell Hull. Behind the desk, a portrait of Woodrow Wilson, on loan from the National Portrait Gallery, backed up the occupant's authority. The office was done in native-American walnut aged almost black and one long wall had been hung with maps. MacCauley's wife had sent in a wonderful heirloom Nain for the floor, but otherwise, the furnishings were expensively spartan, handsomely restrained except for the stacks of books on the floor where the shelves did not suffice. MacCauley allowed an assorted bouquet of telephones but refused to permit the installation of a computer in the office. While he recognized the tremendous value of automation, he considered the equipment vulgar and discordant with the image of his position. E-mail was for secretaries, and word processors were, perhaps, for memoirs.

MacCauley's secretary announced the DAS for Latam Affairs, and Tick Bennet came in, leading with his pointed mouse face and failed mustache. He was gray and thin. Respected but not adequately representational, Bennet would go no higher.

"Tick. Come on in. Seen the *Early Bird* this morning?"

The DAS shook his head. "Working breakfast with the Brazilian trade del. Raytheon's got the deal locked, by the way."

"Sit down." *Early Bird* rolled in his hand, MacCauley gestured toward a leather sofa and strode over to a nearby chair. Sitting down, he located the piece that concerned him and passed it to the DAS.

"The bit on the bottom. The little thing from the *Times*. What's that all about, Tick?"

The DAS took the handout and read for a moment. When he looked back up his face was unconcerned. "Don't know a thing about it. Not important, I don't think."

"This Army colonel. Know anything about him?"

The DAS shrugged. "Might have met him down

there. Plenty of colonels in the world. One big polyester blur."

"Makes him sound like the last of the saints. And the second para's a bit harsh on Ethan Plymouth, don't you think?"

The DAS remained unconcerned. "We get that sort of thing all the time. South American mentality, you know. Lose the lottery, blame the U.S. embassy. And, my God. Consider the source."

"I thought we'd put that business with the dead soldiers to bed. Tell me this isn't going to get any bigger."

"It's not going to get any bigger."

MacCauley sat back, pensive. "Plymouth's a friend. Of sorts. Good man. Good enough. Incautious wife. But Ethan's really all right." He looked at the DAS with narrowed eyes. "I don't particularly want to see him hurt. Certainly not unfairly. Not if he doesn't deserve it."

"Oh, Plymouth gets this sort of thing all the time. The Bolivians hate him because he won't cut them any slack on the eradication treaties. He'll weather this. Won't even feel it. Really, Drew, it's minor."

"Well," MacCauley said, "I don't like it. DOD one, State zero. Personally, I'd feel better if it was in the *Post*. I can reason with those people. But I have no leverage with the *Times*." He corrected himself. "I'm not speaking of the *New York Times*, of course. That's another thing entirely. Perfectly reasonable people, as long as you aren't cutting aid to Israel. But *these* people . . ."

"Moonies and loonies. Nobody takes them seriously."

MacCauley was not convinced. He had been battered. Publicly. The DAS, a lesser target, had not. "Well, keep an eye on it." He leaned forward. "What about the CINC down there? Parnell. Always struck me as a clever boy. For one of them. He's been rooting around in the garbage lately. What's he up to? Any chance he's trying to embarrass us?" MacCauley had already formed his views on General John Parnell, but he wanted to have the DAS on record. In case things took an unfortunate turn.

" 'Black Jack' Parnell? He's not that subtle. I mean, he's *mil*itary. He just wants to grandstand a little by finding the trigger people behind those killings. Those Special Forces people who were murdered. All that cry-baby comradeship stuff the military does. I say let him run with it. No harm to us, as long as he doesn't tramp on too many local toes. Anyway, the national press has already moved on." The DAS sniffed as though he had caught a scent and his hands lifted slightly from his thighs. Then he relaxed again. "I doubt Parnell has anything to do with this PR nonsense on the colonel. The military's not that press savvy. Really just sounds as if that colonel down there went off the deep end on his own."

"I hear rumors Parnell might be the next SACEUR. Mr. NATO. Ring any bells, Tick?"

The DAS shook his head stingily, as though gestures cost money. "Not my world. You'd know more about that than me, Drew."

"I just want your views. You've dealt with the man on the nuts-and-bolts issues. I only see him when he's up here pressing the flesh and begging for handouts on the Hill."

The DAS thought for a moment, unwilling to share anything he had not thoroughly vetted. "He'd fuck you, Drew. Your Russia policy. He's the blood-and-guts type. NATO expansion by close of business today, and you can't reason with him. Gives good testimony. Good looks. War hero and all that. I'd move heaven and earth to keep him right where he is. Or help him into retirement. But you do *not* want that man as SACEUR. He'd support every two-bit wannabe state against Moscow. Totally screw things. Bull in a china shop. We could lose Russia." The DAS suddenly drew back. "But that's your area of expertise."

"The vision thing? Can Parnell see beyond lunch?"

The DAS smiled faintly. Only those who knew him would have realized that the gesture was, in fact, an extreme display of emotion.

"Come on, Drew. Ever met a general with vision?"

PARNELL TOOK ANOTHER look at the composite image on his computer screen. Canting his head slightly toward the three officers standing on the other side of his desk, the general said:

"You're telling me this *kid*—or a kid who looks like this image—single-handedly took out a Special Forces A-team?"

The J-2 spoke up quickly. "Sir . . . the kid was armed; our soldiers weren't."

Parnell swiveled his chair about. "Still . . . one god-damned kid."

"He's got a reputation," the J-2 said, "as being the most talented *sicario* in Cali. Maybe in all Colombia. They say."

Slowly raising his face, his eyes, the general stared at the one-star. The J-2 wore a permanently startled look, and Parnell had come close to firing him several times. But the general believed that part of his mission was to work with what he had. A platoon sergeant had ingrained that in him many years before.

"If he's such a hotshot, why didn't we know anything about him before this happened? How about it, Two?"

The J-2 had a manner of stammering with his entire body. "Sir . . . we're asset poor down there. You know how it is. We . . . just don't have eyes on the ground everywhere we should. And the priorities . . ."

"Twelve dead soldiers. Figure I should write that off as an intelligence failure, Two?"

"Well . . . sir, I wouldn't say that. I mean this drug thing's so complex . . . it's hard to keep track of even the top players."

The general stared mercilessly. Looking right through the man's class-B uniform, through walls and windows and mountains, across seas and continents.

"But," Parnell said, "as soon as I light a fire under the intel community's butt, suddenly we have an ID on our hit man. Why does it take my personal attention?"

"Sir," the J-3 interjected, trying to help out a comrade, "it's the nature of the beast. The deuce is right. We're thin on the ground. But when we get a clear mission, we can move out on it. I'd say we've gotten damned impressive results on this, and quicker than we had any right to expect. We've even got the Colombians playing ball this time." The old soldier looked at the big watch on his big wrist. "They should be swarming over that kid's neighborhood right now."

But Parnell was not finished with the intelligence officer. "I want to know . . . just how we identified this kid as the hit man."

The J-2 shimmied. "Sir . . . first of all . . . like I said . . . we *think* this is the guy. I mean, the information tracks and—"

"Says who? Where's our source."

The intelligence officer glanced from one side of the room to the other. "Well, sir," he said in a lowered voice, "the resident got it. It's from the Agency."

Parnell twisted his jaw to the side as if he had just swallowed something sour and mean. "Yeah. Well, you just get Mr. CIA in here. Let him speak for himself." But Parnell could not wait. "Where'd he get it?"

"From their man in Colombia."

"Worthless. I know him. The Colombians play him like a barroom piano." Parnell braked himself and thought it over afresh. Thinking very quickly. "Of course, maybe this kid *is* the trigger man and the Colombians *want* to give him to us, get us off their backs. You think about that, Two. Get back to me with a quality answer."

"Yes, sir."

"Well, tell me."

"What, sir?"

"Where that twit in Bogotá got the info. Who fed it to him? I've been around long enough to know he didn't go out and get it." Parnell turned from the J-2 to the third officer in front of his desk, his XO. "You following this, Tim?"

"Yes, sir."

"Where did Bogotá get the info?"

"From Cali. From the narcos."

Parnell looked back at the intelligence officer. "That a fact, Two?"

The J-2 nodded.

"So now we're getting fed intelligence by the people we're supposed to be putting out of business. I find that . . . noteworthy."

"Sir," the XO said in a voice carefully modulated to be firm but respectful, "it's probably best if you wait to hear what Franchetti has to say, get the Agency's side from the horse's mouth. But I can tell you that the Cali crowd's upset as hell about something. They're worried. Something stinks down in Bolivia, and they're busting butt to let us know that they're not the ones who Little Big Horned that A-team. They fed the Agency the kid, all right. You hit the nail on the head. They *want* him taken out. It's the kind of thing we'll probably never sort out. CIA says the Cali bosses are dazed and confused."

Parnell swiveled back to the J-2. "Deuce? As I recall, Amembassy La Paz is one hundred percent certain that the Colombians did the job on that team."

"Yes, sir."

"And even the Colombians admit some Cali wunderkind pulled the trigger."

"Yes, sir."

"The Department of State is dead certain it was a Colombian play."

"That's right, sir."

"And our friend Ambassador Plymouth, the Rock of the Andes, is raiding Colombian-owned drug labs in retaliation."

"Yes, sir." The J-3, bluff and bald, spoke this time. "Yesterday's raid was a striking success. Based on the preliminary reporting. Sounds like they toasted a couple of tons of fully processed cocaine like marshmallows around a campfire. We had an eyewitness, that lieutenant colonel from Army Staff. Sieger. He's got some reservations, but I'm not sure they amount to much."

Parnell considered the J-3. Then he scoured the J-2 with steel-wool eyes. Finally, he settled his stare on his XO.

"Well, Tim. We've got a Colombian hitter, and every agency from Bolivia to the Beltway is convinced that that goddamned bloodbath was a Colombian operation. That tell you anything? Based upon historical precedence?"

"Yes, sir," the XO said calmly. "It tells me it wasn't the Colombians running the op. Even if some kid from Cali pulled the trigger."

"Bingo." Parnell pointed his index finger as though his hand were a pistol. Turning back to the intelligence officer, he asked, "See the light, Two?"

The J-2 nodded, face befuddled.

Parnell slammed his hand down on his desk, shocking his subordinates with an unusual show of emotion. Each of the officers in front of his desk recoiled from the gesture as from a blast wave.

"Now, damn it, *I want to know who killed my soldiers*. And I want to know it beyond a shadow of a doubt. And I'm not going to let the State crowd turn it into one of their mutual blow-job parties with the locals. Deuce, if you have to make a pilgrimage to Bolivia on your hands and knees, I want you to find the killers. The *real* killers. The men who gave the orders, doled out the cash. Got that?"

"Yes, sir." The intelligence officer's voice was that of a beaten child.

"Nobody kills my soldiers and gets away with it. *Nobody.*"

No one spoke for over a minute, which was a very long pause, given the press of the CINC's schedule. In less than an hour he had to be across the bridge, standing on the apron at Howard to greet a congressional delegation arriving to inspect refugee camps and to get in a little shopping. None of the subordinate officers dared speak. Beyond the windows of Parnell's office, the mundane sounds of automobiles down in the parking lot and rooftop air-conditioning units scored the passage of time.

Finally, Parnell killed the silence. His voice had dropped to a tone of energized ice.

"Two, I did not literally mean for you to go to Bolivia in person. You're a professional. You do what you've got to do. But this one's important to me." He wrinkled an arctic ghost of a smile into his wintery face. "I know you all think I'm a cross between Genghiz Khan and a hanging judge, but there are a few things that really do reach me on an emotional level. One of those things is losing soldiers. I've commanded American soldiers in battle in both hemispheres, and I've seen them die, and I know that sometimes they have to die. That's part of soldiering. But I will not tolerate a single unnecessary death."

He fixed his peat-fire eyes on the brigadier general who was responsible for SOUTHCOM's intelligence operations. "I know I get rabid about the State crowd. Not very diplomatic of me. But let me tell you why. They don't see soldiers, or sailors, or airmen, or Marines as real human beings. We're 'tools of statecraft.' Not to be squandered too liberally, of course, since we're expensive tools—and we have sharp edges that can cut a lot of different ways. But, in the end, we're just instruments of policy, figures on a page, symbols on a map. Because these days no one at State has served in the military.

Hell, we're at the point where nobody in any of their *fami*lies has served in the military. They don't even *know* anybody who's served in the military. And they will make damned sure none of their *chil*dren ever serve in the military. We're the working class in the industry of government, and they picture themselves as an intellectual elite, the managers of destiny, God help the naive sonsofbitches. And God help our country. They view those of us in uniform as expendable and replaceable. Except that they don't know a damned thing worth knowing. They don't even dress as well as their fathers did. They just sit in capital cities all around the world, fat, dumb, and happy, assuring everybody that Saddam's a fine, progressive fellow or that Somalia has a bright democratic future. Then, when it all goes to shit and Iraqi tanks are doing wheelies in the embassy driveway or a screaming mob's coming over the walls, guess who they call? Not the faculty from Georgetown or Yale.''

Parnell's secretary buzzed him. ''Sir, your car's here.''

The CINC thought for a moment. ''All right. End of one of the very rare speeches of General Jack Parnell. Back to business, and we'll make this quick.'' He looked at the operations officer, whose bald head shone with sweat despite the air-conditioning. ''Three, have you seen today's articles out of La Paz?''

''No, sir. Not yet.''

The general turned to his XO. ''Tell him about them.''

''Sir, John Church is turning into a real celebrity down there. Yesterday, one of the dailies ran a piece on how he's gone back down to Mendoza to finish that clinic the murdered team was building. Doing it on leave time and out of pocket. It's the most positive press the United States Armed Forces have ever gotten in Bolivia. Maybe the best press any part of our government's ever gotten.''

''John Church as the second Christ of the Andes,''

Parnell said. "And Ambassador Ethan Plymouth as Lucifer, who wants to yank the vaccine right out of children's arms. I might add that your fax of the *Early Bird* has a short piece from the *Washington Times* on the same topic, if a bit more sober in tone. Our Colonel Church looks like a growth industry."

The secretary buzzed again. "Sir, you wanted me to remind you on the time. For the CODEL."

"Thanks, Lucy." Parnell turned back to his XO. "So. What's the status on the MEDRETE and that combat engineer platoon I wanted standing by."

"Sir," the XO said, "the Three's got the latest."

The operations officer took half a step forward. "Sir, we've got them on green ramp, camped out in a hangar. And we have two C-130s on strip alert. Humvees, mobile med shelters on trailer packs. The overflights have been approved, except for Brazil, but we can work around that. Colonel Reidel's heading the medical team personally and—"

"No," Parnell told him. "No 0-6's. I want Church to remain the senior man on the ground. We don't want to seem to be crowding him out. We're going down there to support him."

"Sir, we do have some glitches," the XO interjected. "We notified USAMRIID up at Detrick. But their reaction folks are covering something in Africa, and they've been hit so hard on the budget there's no B-team. They say CDC's even worse off. And we're short on some of the medical gear for rapid epidemic response."

"You trying to tell me we can't do it, Tim? Or that we shouldn't?"

"No, sir. Only that it's going to be a real shoestring op."

"Get used to it," the CINC said. "That's today's U.S. military."

"So we're actually going to go?" the J-3 asked. "Sir, we still haven't got embassy clearance from La Paz. . . ."

"Boys," Parnell said, "one of the reasons I have four stars on my shoulders today is that I always reinforce success. And, based on this morning's evidence, every instinct in old Paddy's body says we should follow Church's lead on this." He looked at his watch. "Got to run. But I want you to get those troops in the air as soon as you can. I figure we've got twenty-four hours before the D.C. crowd really registers what's going on down there. And another thing. I want every last swinging Richard in that task force armed. With plenty of backup ammo."

"Sir," the operations officer said, "Ambassador Plymouth has a strict ban on U.S. military personnel carrying weapons in-country. And we don't have clearance from the embassy for this mission, anyway. With or without weapons."

Parnell grinned. It was a rare thing and it startled his three subordinates. Even the XO, who knew him best, was not certain what was coming next.

"Tell you how we do it," the CINC said, rising to leave. "Just get those boys airborne. Then have the PAO send out a press release. To everybody from the *New York Times* to the *National Enquirer*. Declaring our commitment to back a good man's initiative and to help out a poor-but-deserving allied people. Offer any media people who want to go have a look for themselves space on a resupply flight, say two days out. Give the task force time to get in place." He picked up his cap from the shelf where his computer still displayed the mosaic image of a Latin teenager. "After our guys have been in the air about an hour, contact the embassy in La Paz. Go to the DCM first. He's smarter than Plymouth and he'll read the writing on the wall. Tell him we're coming to help them out. Tell him we can see that the ambassador's taking some unfair hits and we want to help him redeem his image with the people of Bolivia. Mention the press release. Casually. And be sure to say up front that we're coming in armed and landing right down there at Mendoza, with no holdups in La Paz.'' Parnell looked at the officers assembled to do his bidding. ''Plymouth's going to shit, of course.'' He smiled. ''But we've got him by the short hairs. And what's that Dartmouth dishrag going to do about it? Order a humanitarian mission to abort when it's already approaching Bolivian airspace? There's an epidemic down there. 'Ravaging the poor.' You think brother Plymouth's going to turn around that medical aid in midair? With the media watching?''

The assembled officers thought about it. For a few golden seconds. One after the other, they smiled, too. First, the XO broke into a grin, followed by the J-3, and at last, the J-2 visibly reflected the beauty of it. Strategy. Firmly married to tactics. The fruits of the years spent at Leavenworth and Carlisle, of a military education.

''Sir?'' the XO called just as Parnell was leaving to join his aide and the waiting vehicle. ''One quick thing.''

Parnell turned from the doorway, cap folded in his hand, impatient now.

''Any special name you want assigned to the task force?''

The CINC responded swiftly and decisively. With the smile of a carnivore sensing a splendid kill.

''Call it Task Force Church.''

AFTER A GRIM, heartfelt breakfast with the family of one of his new protectors, Church went back to work on the clinic. Waiting for Eva to pick him up. He had promised to help her with the gravedigger's chores out in the stricken settlements, and knowing Eva, he had expected her to show up just after first light. During the hand-to-mouth breakfast, he had listened anxiously for her jeep. But no vehicles came down the broken road.

By midmorning, he was tangled in an effort to replace the wiring that had been pilfered after the massacre. He had trespassed beyond the limits of his skills, and improvising atop a flimsy ladder, he hoped he would not black out the entire northern third of Bolivia while turning his body into burned toast. With aggravating frequency, he had to pause to smear the sweat away from his eyes or to scratch the landscape of bites his nighttime adventure had left up and down his legs and arms.

A yell from the middle distance stopped him just short of touching a live wire with a screwdriver. Then he heard more human barking. Two unhappy voices. Church stepped down from the ladder and looked out of the doorway.

Just up the road, his breakfast host, Miguel, had come out of his field to threaten an intruder with a hoe. The interloper, a ragged discount messiah, towered over the Indian, rearranging the air with big white palms vivid at the end of long brown arms. Backpacked and ponytailed, the man looked like another member of the international college-dropout lost-souls club roaming the continent in search of cheap bunks, good highs, and New Age wisdom. Except that, even from a distance, you could tell his college days were decades behind him.

Church marched out of the building and up the road, secretly glad of an excuse to take a break from his work. The scarecrow stranger pointed toward him, and Miguel turned to look, then promptly renewed his threats at a higher volume, with the blade of the hoe whacking at heaven's belly, ready to give the wanderer a lesson in mortality.

"*Miguel,*" Church called. "Wait. It's all right." The stranger looked like a walking summary of expat counterculture experiences, but he did not look threatening.

"This bum—he says he's a *periodista,*" Miguel called back in crippled Spanish. "He's a liar. Journalists don't look like that. Do they?"

"Colonel Church, sir," the stranger yelled, "I'm here to see *you*. I'm from La Paz." The man's voice scraped and crackled like an ancient phonograph record, but the words were solidly pronounced. In the accent of home.

Church closed the distance.

"It's all right, Miguel. Thanks. I can handle him."

His protector lowered the hoe. In careful stages. Slowly, Miguel backed off and ambled bad-backed into the low field he had been working. Complaining to himself about the impropriety of the modern world.

Church sized up his visitor's finer details. If the man truly was a journalist, he probably wrote for the *Intergalactic Vegetarian Gazette*. His ponytail hung long, with white hairs crowding the brown. From the Indian amulet hung around his neck to his sandled, discolored feet, he constituted a grubby, two-legged celebration of multiculturalism. A sleeveless denim work shirt and woven Andean vest hung loosely above baggy trousers that looked like part of a harem eunuch's wardrobe. The man's face was sharp as a blade behind a drooping soupsopper mustache, and he had an amber smile. He offered Church an enormous hand.

"Colonel Church, I presume. Rick Sanders. Journalist, like the man said. Specialist in Latin American affairs." Looking closer, Church saw that the intruder's eyes had the alertness men learned the hard way and his skin declared that he had been in the tropics too long. In the flat daylight, a speckling of small, wartlike nobs trailed down from one sideburn and followed his jaw. "It's a relief to find out you really exist. The Bolivian press can be pretty inventive."

Church accepted the anxious handshake and found the other man surprisingly strong, a weight lifter from a concentration camp.

"John Church. What does the Bolivian press have to do with the price of beans?"

The stranger imprisoned Church's hand in both of his own and his eyes aimed deep. "Well, they've certainly been attentive to you. Colonel John Church, darling of the *diarios*."

Church broke his hand free. "I have no idea what you're talking about."

"The articles. The interviews."

"What interviews?"

"In the La Paz papers. About your work down here."

Church did not understand. But his guard went up fast. "I didn't give anybody any interviews."

The journalist looked at him the way prostitutes look at a man who insists he's faithful to his wife. "You're kidding."

"I didn't given any kind of interviews, and I don't know what you're talking about."

"You're shitting me."

"I've got things to do, Mr. Sanders."

"Call me Rick. You mean they just made it all up?"

"Look—either tell me what this is all about or just turn around and go back the way you came."

"You're telling me you haven't given *any* interviews? None? And you haven't seen the papers? Can I call you John?"

Church shook his head and his voice took on an impatience born of confusion. "Just tell me exactly what this is all about right now."

The journalist canted his long face, then shook his ponytail. Church half expected wildlife to emerge.

"You're the man of the hour, John. The Bolivian papers are portraying you as that rarest of beasts, a heroic gringo. Risking life and fortune to finish a clinic for Bolivia's helpless and nameless. Ring any bells?"

"Who are you? I mean, really?"

The journalist produced a poor man's wallet and drew out a business card that looked as though it had been lost and rewon in countless card games. He held it up in front of Church's face as if he could not afford to give it away. Church did not want it. He only wanted to know what was going on.

"You really work for all those papers?"

The journalist's eyes lost their directness and his leathery skin changed hue. A silver earring set with turquoise flirted with the sun. "Well . . . not consistently. I mean, I'm a stringer. Of sorts." He looked back into

Church's face but focused at mouth level. A big hand searched the air for a grip. "But they've all published my work. In some form or another."

Church had been around long enough to read a disappointed lifetime into the man's gestures, his eyes.

"Mr. Sanders—"

"Rick. Please."

"Okay. Rick. Just tell me what all this newspaper nonsense is about. And, to the extent it concerns me, tell me exactly why you're here."

"You really haven't seen the La Paz papers?"

Church let his tightened expression answer for him.

"Jesus, this is rich. Man, you are going to *love* this. I'm going to make your day, John. I've got copies of all the articles with me." He grinned, teeth coated with old molasses. "Just answer me one serious question—am I truly the first honest-to-god, flesh-and-blood reporter on the scene?"

"What scene? Listen, is this more stuff about the murders?"

The journalist looked pleasantly stunned. But Church sensed calculations going on behind the street-smart eyes.

"I'm the first guy on the scene," the journalist said. It was not a question now. It was a statement flavored with wonder. "This . . ." he said slowly, "is a gift."

"Tell me what was in the papers. *Show* me."

The journalist moved his head from side to side. Reverently. "The Latin soul is *deep*ly creative. I thought this place would be crawling with reporters. And they did it all deskside." He looked at Church with the eagerness of a boy who has caught his first big fish. "You're page *one*, John."

The journalist slid off his big backpack with exaggerated care. The pack had been loaded to Ranger tightness, and Church sensed it was carrying much, if not all, of the other man's life. The journalist squatted, removing a towel that rolled open to reveal drying undershorts torn at the waistband and fatefully discolored. Freed of its cushioning, a laptop computer emerged. His visitor noticed Church looking—the journalist had a scout's eyes—and said, ''My most precious possession. Don't know where I'd be without it.''

Finally, the man retrieved several newspaper sheets pruned of the immaterial and folded small. ''Here. Look at this one. And this. That's the one that started it all.''

Church saw a picture of himself that was at least three years old. It had been cropped, but he half remembered it as a personal shot. He considered that it could only have come from his family, but he did not pursue the thought. The text pulled him in.

In a matter of seconds, Church felt himself growing nauseous. His shoulders sagged, and he wished he could sit down. But there was only the dirt road. He stood and read. Then he went back and read the worst of the articles a second time. Had they been his own property, he would have crumpled them in his fists.

''That's not me,'' he said finally, handing back the papers with a trembling hand. ''That's not what this is about. And I am certainly not a hero.''

''Spoken like a true hero, John,'' the journalist said. ''Can I quote you on that?''

Abruptly, Church turned back toward the clinic. ''This is *not* an interview. I don't give interviews. I have nothing to give interviews about.'' He spoke as he walked, hardly caring if the journalist heard all of it. Behind his back, the man fumbled audibly with his pack, hurriedly reloading it. Moments later, footsteps jogged to catch up. Church kept his eyes on the shell of the clinic.

''John,'' the journalist cried. ''*Colonel Church. Please.* Give me a minute.''

Church walked on.

Puffing, the journalist pulled even with him, pack slung over one shoulder, tie-down straps flapping with each step.

''John, you're *news*. Whether you like it or not.

Maybe it could be a good thing for you. Think about—''

"I'm just trying to finish something I started," Church said sharply. "Something that went badly off track. It's a personal thing, all right? Nothing for CNN. Or anybody else."

Church strode away from the road, following the trail up through the marsh grass that led to the construction site. Kicking a shard of plaster out of the way, he went back inside, certain that everything was ruined now. Plymouth would be sure to pull him out, kick him out of the country as soon as he could fuel an aircraft. This was the end.

He retrieved his screwdriver and climbed back up on the ladder, no longer caring that a journalist from some sixties twilight zone had followed him inside. He looked at the coppery gorgon's head of wires he had left hanging from the ceiling, took a resolved breath, and reached into the mess.

"*Don't* do that," the journalist said. He almost shouted the words.

Church paused, looking down.

"Is the electricity on?" the man asked gravely.

Church shrugged. "I think so. I don't know how to turn it on or off."

The journalist looked at him with a curious expression. "Done much electrical work in the past?"

"No. Not a lot. Not even in a former life."

"Well, I don't think you should put that screwdriver where you were going to put it. Unless you want to be a martyr as well as a hero."

Church looked down from the ladder. In male embarrassment.

The journalist carefully placed his backpack in a corner. "I've done a little of this stuff. Electrical work, carpentry, plumbing. Sometimes journalism doesn't pay all the bills, to be honest."

"I can unblock a toilet," Church said. "That's about the extent of it."

The journalist motioned for him to come down off the ladder. "If I weren't afraid you'd laugh at me, John, I'd tell you that electrical work in particular is very Zen. Harnessing the currents of the universe. Let me up on the ladder for a minute."

Church made way. Brushing past him, the journalist gave off a scent of herbs, oils, and vinegar, the fragrance of a Greek salad. Atop the ladder, he applied himself immediately and fully to the work, not speaking except to whisper intermittently to the wires. He worked very fast, big hands unexpectedly agile, reminiscent of women Church had seen working themselves to early ruin in a Guatemalan textile mill.

Suddenly, the journalist looked down. With a thought on his lips. "John, how about a deal? I hang out and help you with this. And you give me an exclusive interview. Fair trade."

Church shook his head. Adamantly.

"I don't give interviews. I can't."

With a face that was almost frightened, the journalist lowered his hands from the cluster of wires. He stepped down the ladder again, as if recoiling from a shock in slow motion.

"John. Look. Please. We all have our pride. But I'm *begging* you. I *need* this story."

"I can't help you."

The journalist's sharp eyes blurred. A middle-aged loser with nothing much left to lose. An earring, perhaps.

"I'll level with you." His voice was raw and worried. "John, you're at least a month's rent and eats to me. Probably two. I pissed away everything I had flying down here. If you won't do an interview, just let me hang around. I'll help you out. And I'll show you anything I write. If you don't like it, you can delete it from the laptop. *Please*, man."

Church heard the sound of a vehicle. Twisting to look

outside, he saw Eva's jeep, its white paint spattered and its front end mashed.

Quickly, Church turned back to the journalist. The man had ascended the ladder again, as if ready to prove his diligence and capability.

"Let me make *you* an offer. No interviews. That's out of the question. But I'll give you twenty bucks a day and the same food I eat if you stay and help me with the work. When we're done, or when they kick me out of the country, I'll do what I can to get you a hop back to La Paz. And then you can write whatever you want. But you can't screw up what I'm doing down here by writing about it now."

The gaunt figure looked down from the ceiling, a hungry giant from a fairy tale. "John, you're headline stuff. And *some*body's going to write about it, even if I don't."

"Those are my terms," Church said, listening to the sounds of Eva parking and shutting off her vehicle. "I'm going to have to go. So decide. You want the work, you'll have to stay put right here until I get back tonight. Or whenever. I need somebody to watch the tools and the supplies."

The journalist opened his mouth to speak. But the words would not come.

"Yes or no," Church said. "One of life's simple choices." Eva's footsteps approached. A small woman, she walked with a warrior's stride.

"*Okay*," the journalist said. "You're on." He looked away from Church's face. "I'd be grateful if you could leave me something to eat."

Suddenly, Church felt ashamed of himself. And he did not know why. "I've got some MREs in my pack. Army rations. In the brown plastic wrappers. Help yourself. Tonight, we'll see about getting a decent meal."

Eva came in. Hours late. The swelling on the side of her face had gone down, leaving a pattern of discoloration, ocher and indigo. She grew thinner and more drained with each passing day. Had she even slept? He wanted to shake her, to force some common sense into her. But he sensed that she was stronger than he was, at least in that respect. Eva would go on pushing until she dropped. He had known officers like that. A long time before, he had been one of them himself.

She opened her mouth, on the edge of a greeting, then saw that Church had company.

"*Buenos días,*" the journalist said, wiping his right hand on his pant leg in anticipation of a handshake. He came down off the ladder more nimbly this time.

"Eva, this is Mr. Rick Sanders. Rick's a journalist."

"Oh?" Eva said. The single syllable had a ring that got Church's attention.

The journalist looked at her and his eyes brightened like those of a child. And with the naiveté of a child or of a man who has lived apart from good manners for a long time, his look turned into a stare.

"This is Dr. von Reinsee."

"Just Eva," she said.

"Von *Reinsee*?" The journalist's interest notched up even higher. "You aren't related to—"

"We have to go," Church said bluntly. Then an idea sparked. He wondered if it had already occurred to Eva.

"Rick . . . there's another story down here. A much bigger one. Eva's a circuit doctor. She's got an epidemic out in the bush, a real killer. And nobody in La Paz or anywhere else wants to hear about it. You could cover that, help her out."

The journalist alerted, but the interest faded quickly from his eyes.

"My shots aren't up to date," he said. With genuine regret. As though luck would never be his.

To Church's surprise, Eva laughed. It was a cold, diminished laugh.

"I don't think there *are* any shots for this one," she said.

*   *   *

BORN IN SACRAMENTO, Rick Sanders had been a child of his times. In '69 he left the University of California at Santa Cruz a year short of graduation and went south. In those days his heroes included Ho Chi Minh and César Chávez, Jimi Hendrix, and the martyred Che Guevara. He had excelled in journalism classes, his fabulous indulgences sanctioned by professors who yearned to be part of the carnival of youth erupting on campus, and he turned out to be one of the rare ones who got beyond the stoned talk and Kerouac confessionals. He actually took off with a pack on his back to change the world. Pursued by a low draft lottery number, he crossed the border at Tijuana, determined to prove that the pen was mightier than the machine gun. He never went back.

He believed in the virtue of all guerrillas and in the evil of all established governments, in the natural decency of man and in the corrupt nature of those men who did not share his outlook. He believed that illegal drugs, used properly, could be of tremendous benefit to mankind, and that music could change the world for the better. Had he possessed a decent voice or a different kind of skill in his fingers, he would have much preferred to be a musician. Instead, he took Bic pens and cheap notebooks into the jungles, where the Indians were exploited and the guerrillas struggled to avenge them.

Working for evanescent counterculture newspapers and journals, he covered liberation struggles and blood-stained coups, collective harvests, experimental peasant cooperatives, and each financial crisis that threatened to deal the deathblow to capitalism on the continent of tomorrow. Only his U.S. passport, a thing maintained from necessity, saved his life when Pinochet made his move in Chile, and he broke into the mainstream papers before being beaten, then expelled from Argentina over his reporting on the disappearance of opposition students and activists. Those were golden years for activist journalism. He covered Cuba's David-and-Goliath struggle against his own country and reported for *Rolling Stone* as American rock musicians staged a historic benefit in Havana. The high point of his life came in Managua as he stood shoulder-to-shoulder with anonymous brothers and sisters, red-scarved and drunk and singing to greet the triumph of the Sandinistas. The future was going to belong to the wretched of the earth, to the dispossessed, the virtuous and poor. . . .

A dramatic minority of loves collapse in cataclysm, going under like Atlantis or Pompeii, terrible in the experience but ultimately rewarding the memory with a sense of great, poetic loss. But most loves die slowly, their mortality unnoticed at first, then obstinately disbelieved, until the quicker of two hearts moves on, and the slower heart is left with a sense of futility and a wasted life. Rick Sanders's great love, the dream of revolution in Latin America, went the second way. The Sandinistas proved little more equitable than their predecessors, and distinctly less successful in running an economy. They bought weapons, and the people rotted. The biggest change was simply a shift in which families ran Managua. That was what the fighting really had been about. In El Salvador, the military was monstrous. But Rick Sanders, in his thirties now and reporting clandestinely from the hills, with an assortment of tropical diseases haunting him, found that the freedom fighters did not much like taking prisoners and were not above killing bewildered Indians by the dozen. He lied about that in the pieces he filed.

In Peru, his reputation as a dependable friend of the revolution brought him a unique opportunity to cover *Sendero Luminoso* from the inside. And the inside was rotten, more gruesome than the worst hell imagined by any church. For the first time in his life he was constantly frightened for his own safety. Without the benefit of the old moral exhilaration. He witnessed the slaughter of entire villages whose inhabitants had no idea why they were dying. The savagery was worse than anything he had seen in Chile, where a recent visit had shown him a flourishing economy that did not square with a single tenet of his beliefs. He felt reprieved and shriveled when the *Senderos* put him on a boat to Iquitos with the demand that he tell the world about the oppressiveness of the Peruvian state, the brutality of Lima's troops, and the inevitability of revolutionary victory.

He went north to Colombia, to tune back in to that struggle. But yesterday's freedom fighters had turned into mercenaries working for the lords of Medellín and Cali. Or they ran their own bootleg narco businesses. When he filed a report for Radio Pacifica that displeased one former Marxist, he was tortured primitively with a lighted cigarette in a way that made him fear he would never have sex again.

He had sex again. But he no longer seemed to attract the earnest young tourists of revolution and suffering from the good colleges back home. He married a Venezuelan woman on impulse, but she deserted him when she realized he was as enduringly impoverished as she was. She may have had a child by him, but he could not be sure.

He drifted, selling fewer and fewer stories as states democratized without benefit of revolution and market economies threatened to succeed where every worthwhile philosophy declared they had no chance. Ever fewer outlets bought his work, and they paid badly and irregularly. And the stories grew harder to write. In the wake of liberation ideology, he encountered cocaine and greed. The new violence was big and quick and stripped of any philosophical base. He went back to Nicaragua, but the guard had changed. In Cuba every other person he met wanted his help in getting to Miami and his old friends were tired. The great Soviet sponsor of revolution crumpled and died, its sole legacy enough weapons to do a lot of residual killing. All of the dreams that had made the deprivation and disease and the loneliness bearable disappeared down the toilet of history.

He ended up in Bolivia, where life was inexpensive, if you were not too particular, and he could pay the bills by doing odd jobs for Bolivians who liked the notion of a gringo doing manual labor for them. His life came down to a room on a back street in La Paz and one final dream.

He was writing a novel. A book that would capture the heartbreak of his adopted continent. All the ruined lives and the dreams smashed in with rifle butts. The way good men and women died for nothing. He worked on a laptop computer he had lifted from a hotel men's room while covering a trade conference down in Santa Cruz. The computer was his single valuable possession—in its own right, but also because it held his book, the chapters of which he could rarely afford to print out.

He had come a long way. And perhaps he had lost touch with some parts of reality, although certainly not with the need for shelter, food, and occasional medical care. Sometimes the need for a woman became unbearable, a barren business now.

But he believed his novel was a good one. He had discovered a knack for fiction, and he had a good story to tell. The book had quickly taken on a life of its own and it had come a long way from the polemic he had set out to write. Characters meant to be villains had become complex, troubled men halfway through, while intended heroes rebelled against virtue. The left and right had begun to share a single human face. In the revisions there were only men and women making their troubled ways as best they could, unaware that history was happening all around them. After more than two decades of trying, he had learned to write truly.

It was the last good cause.

ANNE LINGERED UNNECESSARILY in the bathroom. *Los Tajibos* offered luxuries that made her think of California, and the fixtures were considerably more up-to-date than those in the ambassador's residence, but that had nothing to do with her slowness. Nor was she avoiding her lover, who drowsed on the bed beyond the closed door. She pictured him broad-shouldered and drained, recalling the wonderful passion not half an hour exhausted, and the animal side of her wanted to rush back and curl against him, around him, to enclose him and hold him fast. But the Anne who thought too much sat on the lowered toilet lid, terrified of all that was happening inside her and wondering what on earth she was going to do with the rest of her life.

She stood and brushed her hair again, then bent closer to the mirror. The marble lip of the sink pressed coldly into her belly. Not so bad, she told herself. Wicked women age well. But she felt very much unwicked, peculiarly chaste. Her unlined face had thinned over the years, losing that faint plumpness of youth that made all pretty women look alike, mass goods priced well below the exclusive beauties. She had always liked her eyes, finding them clever and alert, but now she wondered if they had not grown a bit hard. Long accustomed to her physical self, she recently had gotten restless, wondering which features might lend themselves to improvement.

At this late date. It had been a long time since she had
wanted so badly to remain attractive to a man.

She took care of herself. Lathering on the lotions,
anointing herself—or at least her bath—with oil, and
allowing a succession of cooing stylists to conduct a
guerrilla war against the white tyrant strands that seized
her hair. She exercised. At better stations, she had been
a jogger, but in La Paz, with its brutal elevation, she had
slowed to a walk, marching fiercely up and down the
long valley with its slum gullies and side canyons, from
the city's withered colonial heart down to the fine new
suburbs everyone pretended had nothing to do with drug
money. Ethan was such an ass about that.

Sometimes on her walks she spotted John Church, the
embassy's other great walker, and passed him with a
silent wave. Her husband wrote off the colonel as a
"nonplayer," which made Anne sympathize with
Church, although, with the sophistication of the loveless,
she, too, initially had dismissed Church and his impreg-
nable family as somehow unworthy. Until one evening
at a terminally boring reception when she found herself
watching the colonel and his wife, inseparable as always,
laughing and smiling with a unity as unfashionable as it
was genuine. In that sudden, unexpected moment of seeing, Anne realized that her own life had gone rancid,
and that she felt lost and alone and increasingly afraid.

In the beginning, Rafael had been entertainment in a
dull place and he had satisfied the blunt need for sex—
a thing which had long since disappeared from her marriage. Anne and her husband slept in the same bed, out
of habit and inertia, and occasionally, he held her as a
boy might have held on to an obedient setter. But that
was it. Ethan had never been a powerfully sexual male,
although, in the first tosses of their relationship, he had
seemed adequate, capable of giving enough so that her
body would not starve. Then he sank into his work, his
ambition, and it began to seem as though she even repelled him. As he had begun to repel her, with personal

habits he no longer labored to disguise and which could not be discussed short of a shriek. And Anne did not shriek.

As far as children went, there was only Robin, a first and only fruit, bitter, and closed like her father. She responded to Anne's attempts at affection as she might have reacted to an unappealing baby-sitter. Daddy's girl. Robin was one of those rare, perverse children who actually liked boarding school, and Anne made sure her daughter attended the best. Wondering what she had done that was so terribly wrong it could make her own child unapproachable.

Still, Anne had paused for a barren decade before allowing herself a lover. Then, in the thrill of rediscovering the physical world, she had taken several in succession, almost indiscriminate if discreet, shocked back to life by the rediscovery that men found her desirable. But she had kept control, kept it all manageable. Until now.

She opened the bathroom door gently so that she would not wake her lover should he be asleep. His eyes were open, waiting for her with deep patience. A slice of light entered the room where the curtains did not quite meet and a golden slash crossed his face just below the eyes. He was beautiful in a way she had never been, would never be, and it frightened her. She had never found men of such physical perfection attractive in the past, dismissing them before they could dismiss her. But now, she knew, she was caught. He looked like an ad for an overpriced cologne, like a stupid girl's fantasy. Like fate.

"I missed you," he said, smiling just below the golden streak.

"I was trying to make myself pretty for you." And it was true.

He nudged the bedclothes, asking her to enter, to flee the arctic chill of the air-conditioning, and she ran to him like a girl and bounced clumsily on the bed, happy and more afraid than she had ever been. He smelled warm and unmistakably male.

Drawing her against him, against lean muscle and bone, he said:

"You're beautiful, Anne. Just like this."

She began to protest, again, that she was not beautiful. Then she stopped herself. Letting herself be beautiful for just this one mortal afternoon. He began to kiss her, to touch her, and she began to kiss back, then parted from him just enough to say, "I don't know if I can again."

"Just let me touch you."

Yes. Forever. She closed her eyes. He was a vigorous, untiring lover, and she was not so resilient, and she worried that, if they made love again now, she would be too sore for later on, after dinner, after wine.

None of it mattered. The world was gone. She stopped thinking. And they made love again. It was so lovely and sincerely meant that she could hardly bear it. As if she had an entirely new body with this man.

As they lay together in the artificial darkness, dreamily alert to the pulse of the ventilator and the sharp sounds from the pool and patio bar beyond the room, Anne felt as though she wanted to pray. But you weren't supposed to pray for things like this, and for as long as she could remember, God had been for other people. She felt as though she were collapsing inside, and suddenly, she hugged her lover with a ferocity she had not known burned in her.

He smiled without really opening his eyes and said, "You're going to squeeze me to death." He seemed happy at the thought and said, "I love you, Anne. Why can't you believe that?"

Yes, she thought. Why can't I believe that?

CHURCH AND EVA spent less than fifteen minutes in the first settlement. The inhabitants who had not disappeared into the bush were dead, and Eva had gathered them and burned them as best she could two days before. It only remained to check the emptied huts for any returnees who had come home to die. There were none. Only dogs nosing in the charred ruins of the shack Eva had fired. The animals were hungry and worrisome, and although Eva seemed fearless, Church was glad to get her back into her jeep.

Thinned, blackened corpses had been identifiable in the burned pest house, heaped incompetently. The sight made Church realize, as none of the day's other successive horrors could, how desperately alone Eva was, one pint-size human being fighting a rear-guard action against nature. It was unfathomable to him that his helping hands should be the first. What kind of country was this after all? How badly had he romanticized it?

In the second settlement, they put on surgical masks and gloves, token barriers against the unknown, like the bird-beak masks worn by renaissance plague doctors. Again, no humans remained alive, but here the huts had to be cleared of corpses. Church and Eva gathered the dead in one of the central buildings. This time, Eva had brought jerry cans of gasoline with her and Church soaked the pile of bodies before they set the hut on fire.

"It's the best I can do," Eva said forlornly. Then she made a mannish sound of disgust. "I suppose we should burn down all the huts. But, if it's rodent-borne, we'd just drive the vectors from one place to another."

"This is crazy," Church said. "I can't believe there isn't some kind of public health task force down here to help. . . ."

Eva gave him one of her no-nonsense looks. "Where do you think you are, John? Someplace civilized?"

Overall, they said very little. Table talk at Armageddon. They deplored the heat and joked uselessly about the journalist who had come to visit. Church labored on the edge of nausea, frightened on a primitive level by what he saw, able to continue with the work only because Eva set the example. The corpses looked as if the muscles and sinews had been melted out of them, leaving a bloody mush slowly drying in the heat. The smell was beyond the reach of language, the air viscous. A tethered, terrified goat bleated at a skulking dog.

The third and fourth settlements were the same. Dead places, waiting for nature to slither back in. Watching a hut burn, smelling human flesh at its worst, they drove the jeep half a mile upwind and stopped at a cleared field. Eva broke out cloths that resembled diapers soaked in alcohol and they cleaned their faces, forearms, and hands. Eva had brought along apples, biscuits, and plastic bottles of water, but Church could not eat. He felt as though it would be a long time before he ate again. He was grateful for the water, though.

"Rain coming," he said, looking at the sky. They sat on their rumps, shoulders against the vehicle's shady side.

Eva shook her head. "Not yet. Two or three days."

Church drank, spilling a trickle of water out of the side of his mouth. "Think the rain will help? I mean, will it spread whatever this is? Or contain it?"

Eva shrugged. "I don't know anymore. I can't think, John. I just go through the motions." She bit into an apple, the sound crisp in the dead world.

Church looked across the field into a leafless thicket. Desert jungle, if there could be such a thing. It still amazed him that men settled in places like this. And yet, he thought, I'm here. When there were so many other possibilities. He wondered what Ruth was doing at the moment.

"I want to check a few more settlements," Eva said. "To see if it's spread. I don't understand this at all."

"Eva? Why in the name of God are you and I here? I mean, why would we want to be here, to let ourselves in for this? Are we perverted or something? We could both be someplace better."

She swallowed apple pulp and said, "Mystery of the heart."

"I'm serious. What I mean is, this reminds me of combat. Sometimes you're nothing but scared. Terrified. And you can't for the life of you figure out why you made the choices that got you there. You feel incredibly stupid." He leaned his head back against the metal and watched a blackbird spread wide wings. "Then, of course, there are the times it makes you feel more alive than sex."

Eva laughed. It was a tiny sound. "Well, the practice of medicine's never been quite that good. Maybe if it was I could give you an answer. As to what we're both doing here. Or at least what I'm doing here. Sure you don't want any food?"

"No."

She edged a biscuit out of a cellophane packet, then paused before eating it. "Odd, the things you think about. The things you remember."

"Such as?"

"Oh, I just remembered something that happened to me. Something I witnessed. When I was an intern." She smiled. "In your country."

"Care to tell?"

"It's a very sad story."

Church grunted. "Worse than today?"

She thought about that. "Yes. In its own way. Today's problems are obvious. Horrible, but obvious. Maybe that's why I like medicine. It's usually a black-and-white business, all self-dramatization aside. Anyway, I was an intern. Working ungodly hours. And this was a Friday night, I think. Maybe a Saturday. It doesn't matter. But I had to go out with an ambulance. To the scene of a terrible accident. A young woman in a tiny little car had pulled out in front of a truck, one of your big American trucks with all the wheels. The car was like tin foil that had been all crumpled up, but she was still alive. Although her body was nothing but pulp." Eva smiled the empty smile of a survivor. "Maybe worse than the ones we just burned. All her bones broken. But her face had only a little blood on it, and you still could see that she was very pretty. It turned out she was the fiancée of one of the local police, and the cops recognized her. They figured she was dying, and they moved heaven and earth to find the man.''

Eva pulled her knees up toward her chest, as if she had suddenly grown cold in the drenching heat. ''Anyway, we got her out of the wreck and into the ambulance. All the way to the hospital, she was slipping in and out of consciousness, crying out a single word over and over: 'Johnny . . . Johnny . . . Johnny . . . ' It was heartbreaking to look down at this lovely young face and to hear that voice and know with a doctor's certainty that she was going to die, that she was already dead except that not all of her body had realized it. 'Johnny . . . Johnny . . . Johnny . . . ' I swear to God I will never forget that sound.'' Eva gathered her knees closer, lowering her face, forgetting the biscuit in her disinfectant-withered fingers.

''Anyway, she died between the ambulance and the emergency room. We did the standard things to try to revive her, out of duty, or maybe just habit. But she was dead. And the intercom said that her fiancé was out there waiting. Somebody had to go out and tell him. And I was young and vain and hard, so I went.'' She smiled her end-of-the-world smile again. ''He was a nice young man, with a neat, well-fitting uniform. Handsome, in your clean-slate gringo way. You could tell from his face that he was sick with love for that girl. Well. I took him into a side room and had him sit down and I told him the girl was dead. He wept. For maybe five endless minutes he didn't say a thing. Then he looked up at me and wanted to know if she'd been conscious, if she'd asked for him. And I was just on the verge of saying, Oh, yes, she'd kept on calling, 'Johnny . . . Johnny . . . Johnny . . . ' when God stopped me and changed the words in my mouth. I don't know why, really, but I asked him what his name was. He told me it was Ed.''

Eva shifted her inconsequential weight. "And I told him yes. She had asked for him. And called his name." Eva looked into the distance. "I'm not sure anymore if I did him a favor."

A stream of red ants traveled between a tuft of earth and the packet of biscuits Eva had forgotten on the ground. Church didn't move.

"I'm not afraid of death," Eva said suddenly.

"I'LL KILL THE sonofabitch," Plymouth said. "This is Church's doing."

His deputy chief of mission looked aside, as if hunting an answer. "Well, whether it is or not, Ethan, you've got to make a decision. Do we let that plane land or not?"

Plymouth looked as though he had been badly sun-burned. "This is a stunt. That's what it is. Nothing but a stunt. That bastard Parnell's way off base."

"May be. But he's got us backed into a corner. Ethan, if we turn that plane around, the world's going to paint us as the big bad wolves who ate Santa Claus."

"You mean *me*," Plymouth said. "They'll make *me* out to be the villain."

"Yes."

"God*damn* it. Where's Henry Vasquez? I need to talk to Vasquez."

The DCM shuffled in place. "I believe he's off doing some of that counterdrug snooping and pooping. Anyway, Ethan, I frankly don't see what Henry's got to do with this."

Plymouth looked up. "Two days from now we are going to hit a drug lab up above Mendoza. And I damned well do not want any military tomfoolery getting in the way, or tipping our hand and driving the narcos off. I need to talk to Vasquez."

"I'll leave a message for him. To call you the moment he gets back. But right now we've got to go on line about that plane. For or against.'' The DCM smiled tentatively and moved a step closer to the ambassador's desk. "Frankly, I don't see it as all that big a deal. Church, actively or passively, has given the military crowd a chance to polish up their image a bit. And it has been rather tarnished of late. So they come in, finish up their little clinic, give a few shots . . . and then they go home.''

"It's shameless grandstanding.''

"But . . . what's the harm? In the end?''

"If you let people screw you once, they come back for seconds. I don't want Parnell and his thugs fooling around down here. The military is not to be trusted.''

The DCM looked at his watch. "Really, Ethan. Now or never.''

Plymouth lifted his hands, a grander gesture than normal, almost Latin. "Oh, for Christ's sake. What am I supposed to do?''

"Put a good face on it. Co-opt them. Turn it into your initiative.''

"I need time to think.''

"We all need time to think. But, right now . . .''

"Oh, tell them they can land, damn it. But I want them confined to Mendoza. Not off roaming around.''

"The medical team will have to make the rounds.''

"You know what I mean.''

"Right.'' He gestured toward one of the ambassador's phones. "May I?''

Plymouth waved a hand: go ahead. The DCM punched in a code, waited, then said, "Jeff, you can tell them they're cleared into Mendoza. And inform SOUTHCOM that the ambassador is delighted at this display of solidarity and assistance. Yes. We support the mission one hundred percent. That's right. Give the message to Parnell's XO personally.'' He hung up.

"I loathe the military,'' Plymouth said.

"Yes. Well, there's one more thing, Ethan. Two, actually. Parnell is sending his people in armed.''

Plymouth rose, driving his chair rearward. "*Absolutely not.* Not in my country. Absolutely not."

"Ethan, they'll be on the ground in a couple of hours."

"*No weapons.* My policy has not changed." He dropped back toward his chair, catching its edge, almost falling. His eyes flashed an instant's bewilderment; then, with an awkward flurry of hands and arms, he recovered.

"Ethan . . . Mr. Ambassador . . . please. Just listen for a minute."

"I'm listening," he said in a sullen voice.

"I know Parnell's pulling a fast one. But look at it this way. If you forbid this bunch to carry weapons and we were to have another mess like the one with that last pack, every editorial page north of the Rio Grande would lynch you." He looked down. "As would any number of the papers south of the Rio Grande. Really, the best thing we can do is to make a demonstration of absolute cooperation with SOUTHCOM on this. Let Parnell think he's getting away with something. Then just wait until the next time they need something."

"You know," Plymouth said, "it just infuriates me to have to waste time on this. Time and energy. When we're coming off the most successful drug raid in the history of our involvement in Bolivia. When we're getting ready for something that could be even bigger. Cocaine *matters.* Everything else is a sideshow."

"And, by letting the military have their fun, we defuse the Church issue with the locals. Let the cavalry ride to the guy's rescue. Blow a trumpet or two for them. He's washed-up, anyway. Then maybe we can get some fair coverage on the next raid. Really, I see things all working out for the best."

"Best my ass," Plymouth said. "You said there were two things."

"Yes. We've got a crackerjack station chief, you know. The Agency doesn't make them any better."

Plymouth nodded in damaged kingship.

"He looks out for you," the DCM continued. "And he's come up with something interesting—like to know who's been feeding all the local press copy about Church to the media back home?"

The ambassador looked up. With an expression that left no doubt that he would like to know.

"That captain on Church's staff," the DCM told him. "Darling. The aviator."

"The black one?"

"Yes."

"Christ."

"It might not be a bad idea to clip his wings, Ethan."

"Right."

"But we'll have to be a bit careful. We don't want to appear discriminatory."

"No."

"But we have to get him out of the office, out of the embassy. Away from his fax machine. I thought maybe we could send him up to Mendoza. To help Church."

The ambassador began to nod his agreement, but stopped abruptly and said, "No. *No*, damn it. I have a better idea. And maybe we can teach that sonofabitch Parnell a lesson while we're at it—I really do need to talk to Henry Vasquez."

"Ethan, you know Henry. He might not be in until tomorrow."

"In the morning, then. Whenever. But as soon as possible." Plymouth shook his head. "I feel like somebody just shit in the middle of my desk. Anything else?"

The DCM shook his head. A moment later he had escaped past the ambassador's snake-eyed secretary, a frosty woman Plymouth had brought with him from his previous assignment and with whom unimaginative people believed the ambassador was having an affair. The DCM knew there was no truth to that, whatsoever.

But he had told a little white lie in the way he responded to Plymouth's final question. There was, indeed, something else. The CIA station chief possessed the bastardly instincts it took to get things done. And he had just shared a bit of information with the DCM that further lessened his regard for Ethan Plymouth, both as a diplomat and as a man.

The DCM, career-minded and cautious, had nonetheless always wondered what it would be like to fuck Anne Plymouth. The station chief had shared a videotape with him that filled in most of the gaps left by his imagination.

THE FIRST THING Church saw was the artificial light. Driving the jeep, with Eva shrunken into a primitive sleep beside him, he steered down the side of the bluff from town and discovered a glowing island off in the lowland. Where the clinic should have waited in darkness. For a moment, Church imagined that the journalist from planet X ray had gotten all the wiring installed and the lights turned on. But that was impossible, and anyway, the intensity of this light was greater than any bulb could project through a window frame.

He maneuvered the vehicle down the road that had been scratched into the landscape between shacks and marshes and trees grown out of proportion to their world. The night smelled of rot, of earth sweat, and the headlights stabbed through swarms of insects the size of small birds. Two Indian girls, flat-faced, drabbed through the night on bare feet. The jeep's headlights created a feline intelligence in their eyes before protective hands went up.

"Eva," Church commanded. "Wake up. Something's going on." He located a bone-thin arm without looking and shook her gently. Then he needed both hands to guide the vehicle through a small canyon gouged across the road.

"What?" Her voice reached back across galaxies.

"Something's going on. You've got to wake up."

"I'm awake," she said in an untruthful voice.

Church wondered if he should stop or even turn around. But light was rarely a signal for danger. Unless you were the fool who indulged in light at the wrong place and time.

"What is it?" Eva asked. There was a bit more awareness in her voice.

"Look. Above the trees. The glow. It's from the clinic."

"My God," she said, sitting upright so quickly it must have hurt. "Is it on fire?"

"No," he said. "Wrong kind of light."

He wrestled the steering wheel as the vehicle crept along the minimalist road. The trees broke and the view across the low fields and thirsty marshes showed spotlights rigged up on poles, lighting the clinic as though it were a tourist attraction.

"Looks like the homecoming game," Church said.

"What?"

"Nothing. I was being gringo." The jeep quivered as a pothole grabbed a tire. "Eva, those look like soldiers."

Erecting an environmental shelter that bloomed from the rump of a trailer, tightening tentage lines, lugging gear and boxes, prowling over the clinic's roof, and stringing protective wire to create a perimeter beyond grenade range. Men and at least one woman in U.S. Army battle dress uniforms. Two Humvee utility vehicles stood by the side of the road, snouts out and ready. The flank of the nearest vehicle showed a white square with a red cross.

Church broke into a grin.

"What's going on?" Eva asked, sleep-haunted and bewildered.

"The cavalry's here," Church said.

It wasn't really the cavalry, of course. It was better than that. They were combat engineers and medics. Church parked Eva's jeep and shut down the engine. A boom box played thunk drums. Amphetamine guitar competed with spurring drills, soaring over the low hum of generators. The soldiers moved purposefully, creating their own environment in an alien place.

Church and Eva got out of the vehicle. As they approached the nearest opening in the wire, a sentry challenged them. Before Church could reply, a small, cracker-thin man in a brown military T-shirt jogged up, dogtags swinging. His hair was thinning early and he combed it straight back, away from his thick, chaotic eyebrows.

"It's okay," he told the guard. Then he looked at the new arrivals. "Colonel Church?"

"That's me."

The man extended his hand. "Major Lutoslawski. Bug doc. General Parnell says you're in charge."

THE MAJOR STOPPED by the clinic, which had become a serious construction site again, to collect an engineer officer with weight-lifter's shoulders. Captain Hardy, aptly named. Then the major led the party into a GP-small tent crowded with cots and commo gear. A field desk held a laptop and a printer, and a lantern hung from the center pole, drawing fantastic insects. Even with the entrance flaps open, the night was muggier inside the tent than out under the sky.

"Welcome to headquarters," the major said, smiling. Then he focused on Eva. "You all right, ma'am?"

"It's nothing," she said. "I'm only surprised. That's all." She shut a hand over her eyes for a moment. Then, when she failed to get the tears under control, she stepped outside. Church almost followed her, but decided she probably needed a few minutes alone. Anyway, there was work to be done. Major Lutoslawski and the engineer captain had plenty of questions. And Church was developing a headache.

Eva did not remain alone for long. As he described the local situation for the two officers, Church heard the deep radio-static voice of the journalist rise in the background, speaking Spanish. Church pictured the man, pathetic in his flea-market paraphernalia. Eva's voice responded angrily to something, and Church thought at first that he had been right, that she wanted to be alone. But her complaints were not directed at the journalist. She began railing against her government, furious that it took the U.S. military to help out. She was not mad at the U.S. Army, though. She was grateful. But she had no mercy on the bureacrats in La Paz.

The journalist soothed her, almost as if she were a child. Church could only listen intermittently, but he heard the man telling Eva about a good vaccination program the Bolivians had organized up in the altiplano, and then there was something about health care for out-of-work miners and their families down in Potosí, although the responsible ministry was desperately short of funds. The journalist painted a picture of hard work and hope that would have inspired Church himself, had he not served in Latin America so long.

A few minutes later, with the major explaining the authorization to carry weapons to Church, Eva came back in. She looked subdued. And tired. The journalist followed her. Testing the waters, he took a seat on the edge of a cot near the entrance. Out of the glare of the lantern. Church caught his eye, but the man quickly looked away.

All right, Church thought. You can stay. Listen for all its worth. As long as you help Eva.

Eva and Lutoslawki plunged into doc-talk about the epidemic, giving Church a thinking space. It sounded like there was a gang war going on between Parnell and Plymouth. The bottom line seemed to be that he had gained a protector, at least for now. Eva's clinic would be completed. Church felt almost disappointed at the thought of the capable young engineers doing the work for him. A part of him, maybe the best part, had wanted to do penance. The ghosts of twelve dead men were never very far away.

He found he had trouble thinking much beyond that. His headache was becoming formidable. As if his brain were swelling out of his skull. Tired, he figured. Pushing too hard. Not as young as I used to be.

The journalist hunched over a pouch of rations, filling the tent with the odor of barbecue sauce and congealed fat. Watching the ragged man shovel up the slop with a plastic spoon, Church realized he had not eaten a thing since breakfast, and it occurred to him that perhaps that was the cause of the throbbing in his head. But the thought of eating made his stomach come alive in a bad way. The day had been too full of horrors. He expected to remember those half-melted corpses for the rest of his life.

Church wondered what the story was on the journalist. Another lost soul drifting into purgatory south of the Rio Grande? The guy had done a marvelous job talking Eva around. Seemed to be more to him than rags and hair. Maybe a lot more. But then, why the hell didn't he clean up his act? Under the costume, there was something of the slickie boy about him. Church wondered if the man hadn't played him like a fiddle earlier in the day. Or was the poor bugger just doing his best to survive in a hard land. He had—

A spike of pain struck the side of Church's skull from within, as if a small, mean animal had tried to claw its way out. It hurt so much he lowered his head for a moment and found his stomach quaking. But no one noticed.

As the pain subsided, he heard Eva's voice:

"No. It doesn't look like *machupo*. Not exactly. It's quicker. Uglier."

"Could be a mutant strain," Lutoslawski told her. "We'll find out. I'll take a team out there with you tomorrow."

"It's very bad," Eva said. "I've never seen anything quite like it. I'm very glad you're here."

The major sighed. "Well, it's a bare-bones operation.

Budget cuts hit us pretty hard. If we had to deploy a real force to an epidemic zone, we'd fall apart." Then his voice regained more of its U.S. Army standard-issue can-do tone. "But we've got some orange suits with us. And isolation stretchers. Field lab. A good basic load of supplies. There's a field isolation unit, too. That funny-looking shelter out there. But I'll be frank with you. I plan to hold that in reserve in case any of my soldiers break with the disease."

Church's headache ebbed again and he looked up, stomach still queasy.

Eva's hand pushed at the air, rejecting something. "I wouldn't want to bring any of the victims near the town. Besides, I haven't got any live patients at the moment. They're either all dead or they're hiding from me." Her face filled with sorrow. "They don't understand what's happening to them. At this point, they might even think I'm spreading the disease among them, that I'm some kind of witch."

"Well, we'll do whatever has to be done," the major said evenly. "If any more victims do turn up, we'll set up a quarantine facility out where the problem is." He smiled suddenly, looking a bit embarrassed. "I'll probably sound like a real jerk, but the truth is I'd like to see a full-blown case of whatever you've got down here. From a professional perspective."

"Will there be more doctors?" Eva asked.

The major took a moment to answer. "Not military. Maybe some personnel from CDC. But they're heavily engaged in eastern Zaire right now. It's a fun world."

The journalist drew the plastic spoon out from under his mustache. He had sucked it clean and he slipped it beneath his vest. "I know I'm not qualified to talk medicine. But this disease sounds just like something I saw up in the Amazon."

Eva and the major looked at him. The engineer captain, who had drifted out of the conversation, leaned forward again and cocked his head like a dog.

"I was just down from the highlands," the journalist went on in a voice like rough wool. "Took the river network all the way to Iquitos. Trip of a lifetime. Soon as I got off the boat, I started hearing rumors about an epidemic out in the jungle. Among the Indians. Mostly hitting the Huambisas. It sounded like something straight out of hell. Indians called it 'Sweat of the Devil.' " The journalist looked at Eva. "I thought that was a bit melodramatic. Until I went out and saw the thing for myself. I hitched rides, then hired a guide to take me in on the trails. Suddenly, I was in nightmare country. These tiny little Indians, just lying there, waiting to die. Bleeding from every hole and crack in their bodies. I swear to God, I'll never forget it. Human beings turning into bloodburgers. Guide took off." He snorted, backing away from a private thought. "By the time I got back to Iquitos, I had the runs. Scared me half to death. Thought I'd picked up the disease. But it turned out to be nothing but food poisoning."

"And what happened?" Major Lutoslawski asked. "How did they contain it?"

The journalist laughed. It sounded like the caw of a metal bird. "Contain it? The doctors were afraid to get anywhere near it. I suppose it just burned itself out back in the jungle."

"That happens," Eva said. "Sometimes these viruses go so fast they more or less commit suicide. Maybe that's what's happening down here, too. That's what I've been hoping for."

"You know," the major said, with suspicion entering his voice, "I never heard a word about any such outbreak in the Amazon." He looked at the gypsy in his tent with sudden harshness.

The journalist shrugged. "There's a lot that goes on up there that the world never hears about. I filed the story. Sent it everywhere. But there was zero interest." It was his turn to make a harsh face. "Just a bunch of Indians dying at the end of the world. Who cares?"

"Maybe it'll turn out that way here," Eva repeated. "It could just burn itself out."

"Yes. Well," the major said. "We can hope so. But everytime I hear about something like this, I wonder if this time the virus is going to hit the jackpot. Sooner or later one of these brushfire epidemics is going to break into the travel net. Then it's 'Good morning, America.' "

The journalist tore open another ration pouch and said:

"I guess they'd publish that story."

CHURCH EXCUSED HIMSELF from the meeting for a few minutes. He was afraid he was coming down with a touch of diarrhea. Should never have eaten breakfast with the locals, he thought. But how could he have said no?

The new arrivals had dug a proper latrine at the far reach of the concertina wire. A long slit trench with handrails, it had a roll of toilet paper on a stick and a shovel and a bucket of disinfectant powder or maybe just lime inside the curtain panels. Luxury was a very relative thing.

Church's head ached and his body hurt. He needed sleep. Gripping the rails, he found his arms oddly weakened.

He knew he needed to eat, needed fuel. But the nausea would not go away. If anything, it was getting worse. He smiled meanly at himself. Not quite as tough as you thought, big boy. And Eva's been out there on her own for days. Gutsy gal.

With the day's essential work done, most of the soldiers had collapsed onto their cots, sleeping under a GP-medium with the sides rolled up or inside the shell of the clinic. The floodlights had been turned to illuminate the road and the approaches to the clinic. Knowing how to look, Church soon picked out guards in the shadows, hunkered down behind earthen barricades, rifles ready.

No more surprises.

He was in charge. But he could not think what he should do. The world had grown oddly indistinct, as though he had drunk much too much hard liquor. But the pain in his head had subsided for the moment. He decided to ask the doc for something to help him sleep properly. What was the guy's name?

Back inside the headquarters tent, the meeting began to break up. From sheer exhaustion, on all sides. Eva thanked everyone again. And again. She even shook hands for a long time with the journalist. Her hand disappeared in the man's mammoth white paw. Church, his energy shot and his gut still turbulent, let the journalist walk her to her jeep. His body had gone strange. It did not want to move. Yet he felt as though something was moving inside his body.

Christ, he thought, I hope I haven't picked up another parasite. Or malaria. Didn't that start with headaches? But malaria didn't get you in the gut like this.

He decided, again, that sleep was the answer. But he made no move to go over to the clinic where he had left his gear.

"Sir," Captain Hardy said, with dark circles in an eager face, "we've got an extra cot for you. There's room in the tent, if you want to bunk with us."

Church roused himself. "Got to get my bag."

"You feeling all right, sir?"

Church grunted. "Long day."

"Yes, sir. Sounds like it."

With a soldier's determination, Church got to his feet. He began to walk. And it wasn't so bad. In fact, he felt better as soon as he got outside of the tent again. The night air was fresher now, with the clouds blowing up. Rain for sure. What had Eva said? Two days? Three?

The journalist startled him. Laying a big hand on his shoulder from behind.

"John? Could we talk?"

"I'm pretty beat," Church said, turning. "How about in the morning?"

"Just for a minute."

They faced each other now, two big men. The journalist was taller, but Church was solid and looking at the other man gave him a momentary sense of his own robustness.

"I just wanted to ask you up front if you have a thing going with Eva. Because I don't want to butt in."

Church's head hurt. But not enough to keep him from speaking. "You listen to me, boy. Doctor von Reinsee's one of the best damned human beings you're ever going to meet. I respect the hell out of her. What's more, I'm a married man. I've got kids, and—"

"All right. O*kay*. So you don't have anything going. But you feel something for her. Right?"

"Christ, can't people even be *friends* anymore?" The world had begun to move in impermissible ways, making him feel dizzy. He had a sense that he was talking to a crazy man. It was terribly hard to speak normally. "Why does everybody feel compelled to rub shit all over everything?"

"Okay, okay. I *got* it. Calm down. I was only trying to do the right thing. I mean, she's a very attractive woman. And brave. And I just thought—is something the matter?"

"No. Just a headache. I need to sleep. So. What are you trying to do? Ask my permission to take Eva to the prom?"

The journalist's long, weathered face shone pale in the ambient light. With his hair and mustache undisciplined and terribly sad. Good luck, buddy, Church thought. *You*'re sure as hell not Eva's type.

"You don't think much of me, do you?" the journalist asked abruptly. "I mean, I suppose that's to be expected. . . ."

With his headache magically shrinking again, Church said:

"I try to judge each man on his merits, friend. I don't always do so well. But I try."

"I know that. I could sense that right away. You're a good man. And that brings me to my point. Think about—just think about—bending our agreement a little. This is a great story, John. Let me file it."

Church shook his head. "SOUTHCOM's involved now. The CINC's Public Affairs Office would have to clear anything I said."

"Take a chance. Do the right thing."

Church snorted. Stomach growing unruly again. "I've taken a lot of chances. Maybe too many. Anyway—"

The journalist grasped his upper arm. "John . . . people need heroes. And there aren't many these days. You're a hero. A real one. Just let me tell people—John? You know you're shaking?"

"I've got to go to the latrine," Church said. But he found he could barely speak. He broke free of the journalist's grip and staggered a few steps, but he could not remember the direction in which he wanted to go. His head exploded. Over and over again. He cried out once. Then a spectral dagger thrust into his abdomen and he collapsed. Twisting on the earth, he began to vomit blood.

CHRISTIAN RITTER VON Reinsee had nothing against traitors, as long as they did not betray him. He regarded Henry Vasquez as he would any other employee.

"I appreciate your coming all this way to see me on such short notice, Henry. Glass of wine?"

"No, sir. Thanks."

"None for me, either. Too early. This is actually my breakfast time, you know."

"Yes, sir."

Von Reinsee paced behind a chaise, skirting a fine pale table trimmed in black. "I miss the sunlight. But my eyes simply will not tolerate it any longer. Not this frightful southern sun.'' Sensing dust, he touched the meat of his thumb along the cape of a Bavarian wood carving of St. Christopher, suppressing a pulse of anger. He found slovenliness, of any kind, intolerable. Harder to bear than the sunlight. ''Of course, the darkness isn't so bad. A man can learn to accustom himself to nearly anything. Don't you think?''

''Yes, Mr. von Reinsee. I do.''

The older man nodded and resumed his slow pacing. ''We stand at the end of a century that has forced men to accustom themselves to a great many unpleasant things. Our 'enlightened twentieth century.' Perhaps I could offer you a cup of coffee?''

''That would be great. I've got to go back tonight and—''

''Coffee, then. And I'll join you, if I may.'' He rang for a servant and asked that coffee be brought in. When they were alone again, he said, ''I want to be very certain that we have an American or two along on this next raid. Not you, of course. I suspect you've already thought up your excuse for not going along. But there's no getting around it. If I am to make your people angry, I'm afraid I need to spill more of their blood. We need to kill gringos, Henry.''

''Mr. von Reinsee—''

Von Reinsee looked down at his guest. ''Oh, I know you need time to absorb the idea. You're still the prisoner of old instincts. But think it over calmly. I'm sure you'll understand. After all, there must be somebody back in the embassy you'd like to be rid of. Isn't there?''

Vasquez did not answer. He sat dejectedly, emotions transparent as those of a child.

''Come now, Henry. In for a penny, in for a pound. Besides, most of the casualties will be national police. Our glorious UMOPAR. But they're not in short supply. It's North Americans we're after. How was your last little adventure received by the way? Well, I take it?''

"Plymouth was thrilled," Vasquez said in a flat voice. "He likes cheap successes. From the cables, you'd think he led the raid himself."

Von Reinsee paced again. "Now there's a thought." But he quickly dismissed it. "No. Wouldn't do. Wouldn't do at all. I don't want anything to happen to Plymouth. He's a marvelous ambassador. Wonderfully predictable. With a great talent for wishful thinking. I would hate to see him replaced by someone competent."

The servant reappeared with a coffee service, pausing at the doorframe. Von Reinsee nodded his approval and the man quickly tabled the silver and china with its cargo of hidden liquid, steam, cookies, and bright fruits. After pouring the cups three-quarters full, the servant faded away.

"Now, Church," Von Reinsee resumed. "That man is a different matter. Shame my daughter's so fond of him."

"Church is turning into a celebrity," Vasquez said.

"Yes, Henry. That's it exactly. I want your compatriots angry. Not at me, of course. At our Columbian friends." He continued pacing while Vasquez took up a cup. "Now, don't you think your people would be rather upset if they thought the Colombians had murdered Colonel Church, their brand-new hero?"

"Church isn't a player."

"Oh, but he *is*. He has become a player. A famous one. An 'instant celebrity,' as your media likes to describe the phenomenon. His press is so good that I suspect even my fellow Bolivians would be angry with our friends from Cali and Bogotá over his passing." Von Reinsee tasted the coffee. For all the supposed glory of South American coffee, he found it lamentable and had his blend shipped in from Bremen. "A shame, really. He's not a bad sort. Family man and all." Von Reinsee stopped, put down his cup, and folded his arms over his tweed jacket. "I want him dead, Henry."

"Not my job."

"No. But you may have to help. Nothing physical on your part, of course. Information. Advice. A well-placed word. We'll see. But the unfortunate Colonel Church is destined to become a symbol of Colombian wantonness and savagery. Although I am genuinely sorry about the necessity of it."

"Is that all? Sir?"

"No. It is not all." Von Reinsee took up his cup of coffee again and walked behind a slope-backed divan covered in yellow-and-white striped satin. "Are you aware that approximately forty U.S. soldiers arrived in Mendoza this afternoon?"

Von Reinsee could see from Vasquez's face that the agent knew nothing about it. But he let the man answer.

"No, sir. No. Jesus. What does that do to the plan?"

Von Reinsee drank the sharp, almost mean-tasting liquid, letting its heat bring his insides back to life. "It complicates it. But only in the sense that it forces us to improve upon it. I was alarmed at first, until I thought about it. But this is obviously just a response—and a fine one—to all that publicity Colonel Church has received. A shame my own government doesn't have that sort of knack for public relations. Anyway, this is how I see things now, Henry. After the helicopter force goes in on the drug lab and our hired Colombians finish with them, I'm going to send the boys down to Mendoza. To finish the job."

Vasquez set his cup and saucer down on the edge of the table. "This is starting to sound like a goddamned war."

Von Reinsee turned to face him fully. "Oh, it *is* a war, Henry. And I expect your people to respond with fire and sword, so to speak." He made a dismissive gesture, tossing an imaginary object onto the floor. "This business of two drug labs. Or even three. Or ten. It's nothing. You and I know that. I'm trying to awaken your people. And if that means destroying a few helicopters and policemen and the odd U.S. Army colonel . . . or a few more soldiers, then I don't see it as a very high cost overall.'' He allowed himself another throat-shocking drink. ''I'm trying to *help* your country, Henry. To alert you to the threat posed to your national welfare by Colombian *narcotraficantes*.''

''Mr. von Reinsee, if they ever find out you're behind this, God help you.''

Von Reinsee smiled. ''Let me worry about that. I want you to worry about Henry Vasquez and his bright financial future. And there it is. The raid goes in. Ambush. Killed to a man. Then our 'Colombians' sweep down on Mendoza and make a crimson spectacle of those soldiers—really, they're a godsend. If Church is still there, he'll be the primary target. Should he be elsewhere, we'll find him and kill him in that place. I think that should be enough for a while. If all that doesn't excite your government, it may be beyond my power to do so. Do you like music, Henry?''

Vasquez had just poured himself another cup of coffee. With shaking hands.

''I guess.''

''What kind of music?''

Vasquez spilled a bit of coffee over his chin. Rattling his cup down on the table, he hurried a napkin over his face, his shirt. ''The usual stuff. You know. *Mu*sic.''

''Shostakovich?''

Vasquez rested his napkin on his knee. Von Reinsee hoped the man was not going to lose his nerve at the last minute. That would be awkward.

''He one of those classical guys?''

''Yes. In the common parlance. In my singular view, he was the greatest composer of our rather twisted century. Stravinsky thought too much; he was too clever by half. But Shostakovich had an unkillable heart. Musically speaking. Even Stalin could only nibble at his talent. I have a new recording of some of his string quartets. I plan to listen to a few of them tonight.'' Von Reinsee came closer, inspecting his hireling's discomfort. "A shame the poor man was Russian. That does leave me with ambivalent feelings toward him. Of course, so was Stravinsky. So many of the best. It's a phenomenon I cannot explain. The brilliance and the baseness of their kind." Von Reinsee sat down in a fine, hard chair quite close to his guest. "I suppose you have ambivalent feelings toward me, Henry?"

Vasquez broke under his stare and looked at the carpet. "We've got a deal," he said. "And I intend to honor my side."

"Yes," Von Reinsee said, reaching for a shortbread. "Honor is rather like virginity. Isn't it?"

ANNE HAD TO be persuaded to go out in public with her lover. Although Santa Cruz was far from the inbred diplomatic community up in La Paz, Bolivia was a small country socially. It often seemed to her that every Bolivian who owned a suit and tie knew every other Bolivian with a decent pair of shoes. And she did not want to become one of those plunging women who diminished themselves with scandal. Nor did she want to damage her husband's position. It was all he had left.

Yet, she knew she had already plunged deeply. She felt no remorse but suffered the common fear of being found out, of the private life turned meanly public, of looking like a tart and a fool. Rafael's looks and relative youth made it worse. She could see herself with the world's eyes, an aging woman gone dizzy and desperate, clawing after that which was already irretrievably lost. It would have been easier had he been older, perhaps with the bearable start of a paunch, or with thinning hair. But he sat beside her on the bed in their private twilight, like one of those laughably handsome Latins from the days of silent films. The ultimate Latin lover. Rafael recognized the situation clearly enough to mock himself and the collision of their backgrounds. He had a wonderful sense of humor Anne would never have expected

in a human being so beautiful. Sometimes, putting on
the voice of an old Havana gigolo, he would tell her,
"Weet ozzer weemens I mek dee sex . . . but weet joo,
I mek dee lahhhv. . . ."

And he made love to her as she had never known love
could be. She had been fond of sex since the first time
it had really worked for her, which had been a few years
after college, but she had always been judiciously terse
about it, impatient with the acrobatics suggested by in-
secure men. Now it was all different, and this man could
move her body any of the many ways he wanted, because he moved her inside as no one else had ever done.
As no one remotely had done. Sometimes, when they
lay together, him drained, her filled but slowly bleeding
his sap onto the bedclothes, she had to fight against
weepiness, against prayers of gratitude and further greed.
She thanked God and all the stars that she had been
blessed to know this true passion once in her life, and
it iced her heart to realize how easily, through any of a
hundred thousand accidents, she might have missed this
experience of love as it was meant to be.

"Come with me," he said to her, propped beside her,
just above her, with his cross of dark hair twisting with
his chest. "I promise there will be no problems. The
owner's a good friend. He won't let in any customers
who might not be safe. Really, it's just a restaurant for
locals."

"Why does this matter so much? Couldn't we just
order from room service and stay here? Aren't you
happy here?"

He lowered himself to kiss her on the cheek, brushing
his lips over the soft flesh just below the bone. He settled
closer and she could smell her traces on his mouth, with
the slight sourness of wine staling his breath. He was
the most perfect being she had ever seen.

"Yes. I'm happy here. My love. My heart. But I want
us to be free. For one night. I want to sit in a restaurant
and eat and drink with you. As if you were my wife."

The last word struck her like a bullet. She did not answer him. He strayed his hand down her side, over the roller coaster of flesh and bone.

"Please," he said. "Dress. And come with me to dinner. I will make you terribly drunk. Then we'll come back here and be lovers again."

She could tell that it was more than a whim, that it was a thing he truly wanted. And she did not want to lose him. Not yet.

Not ever. She did not ever want to lose him. And she knew the thought was stupid and useless and dangerous. If she wanted to hang on to any last shred of dignity. But it was true. It seemed to her now that he was the only truly good thing that had ever entered her life.

She reached up and kissed him once. The way she might have kissed a nice new boyfriend good night many years before.

"All right," she said. Before he could smile too much, she added, "I'll have to take a shower."

"Not for me."

She looked at him with the trademark smart-ass edge she had almost lost over the past few months.

"For the sake of mankind."

And the restaurant was lovely and festive, with strung lights in a walled garden and great outdoor grills that smelled unfashionably and gorgeously of meat and oil and charring wood. A hasty survey told Anne that none of her kind sat at the laden tables. The crowd through which the delighted owner led the way was a mix of eruptive families, laughing, scolding, laughing again, and young lovers sitting close, each couple certain of the unique quality of their experience. Anne wished she could warn them to cling to what was good in love at the expense of all else in life.

A little girl in a white dress ran between the tables, throwing herself against Rafael's leg before they could be seated, hugging another woman's man as if rehearsing for adulthood. Rafael smiled and picked her up just in time for her father to collect her with a rushed apology. Hoisted in her father's arms, the child giggled and reached back toward Rafael's face.

Everyone deferred to Rafael, greeting him, admiring him, sending them a bottle of dark wine from Argentina. It was a richer, warmer, far more human deference than was accorded an ambassador. The crowd treated Rafael as though he were a benevolent, beloved prince. Anne was shamelessly proud to be with him, glad she had taken the extra time to make herself as fine as fate and expensive cosmetics allowed.

A trio of musicians, guitar, violin, and accordion, sugared the night air for tips, and Rafael made them play songs she did not know, just for her, songs with Spanish lyrics too swift for her middling ability, words soft as a hand slipping under a dress. Rafael bent closer, smiling, telling her with each new song that this one was especially for her, although she was beautiful beyond any song, and that each next tune was old and based on some true and tragic affair in which a woman waited forever behind a shuttered window. It was all so well designed, so much the spinster tourist's dream, that it made Anne smile the wrong way even as she tried to think of ways to thank him, later, with her body.

Rafael raised his glass to her, and they drank the blooming wine together. The guitarist, plump and brown, softened his falsetto and Rafael put down his glass. He touched Anne's shoulder, drawing her closer to him. Lips against her hair, he whispered:

"Marry me, Anne. Leave him. Marry me."

She stood up, clutching the smallness of her purse with both hands, almost knocking her chair over backward. Her face tightened, helplessly, furiously, and she forced her eyes away from him. Pushing rudely past the musicians, she hurried inside, running for the lady's room, unable to find it, fighting back the tears, just wanting to hide and to do it quickly.

The toilets were around back. They were the least

attractive part of the restaurant. But she did not care. She locked herself inside and immediately began to choke with sobs, her tears explosive. She braced herself over the unclean sink, afraid she was going to vomit.

When her stomach calmed a little, she looked up. Into a cracked, chipped, heartless mirror.

"Bastard," she said. "Bastard, bastard, bastard."

IN THE RICH northern reaches of Bogotá, where the shopgirls in the boutiques slaughter passing males with bored glances and the bodyguard is the first one out of the Mercedes, there are many wonderful new apartment buildings. Creatively funded, they are monuments to man's longing for legitimacy. The smallest of the grand apartments has a room for a live-in maid in a country where becoming a maid is a step up the social ladder for most of the citizens. Many of the apartments are empty, and they will remain that way for years. It doesn't matter. The businessmen who build these highrises, with their marble hallways and smoked glass, can afford to lose a great deal of money so long as, after a few colorful presidential administrations, they or their children possess a clear title to something valuable and legal. Much of the money constructing these patrimonies was collected at a hideously destructive human cost in far less attractive urban settings north of the Rio Grande, but business is business.

On a rain-spoiled morning, the U.S. defense attaché to Colombia entered one of those apartment buildings. His hair was short and poorly cut, and he had wrapped himself in a trench coat his wife had bought at a factory outlet mall back home. Under the trench coat, with its large, poor stitches, the attaché wore a suit whose narrow lapels were out of place in this neighborhood, where even the armed chaffeurs wore gabardine that followed the body like a lover's hand. The attaché told the armed doorman that he was Mr. Smith and that he had come to look at the rental property on the eighth floor. The doorman handed him an envelope unevenly weighted with a key.

The attaché, who was alone and unarmed, was nervous, but he had been a soldier for a long time and it did not show unless you knew him. He took the glass-flanked elevator to the eighth floor, which held only two apartments, right or left. He opened the envelope with his thumb and turned to the door whose number matched the key. Straightening his back, he let himself in.

The apartment was empty and vast. Beyond a marble welcome, carpeting soft as cashmere lay dulled by rainy light soaking in through big windows. The last coat of paint still smelled of poison and a single shred of newspaper marred the floor. The attaché advanced slowly through a foyer large enough to hold a grand piano.

As he entered a room sized for extravagant parties, he sensed that he was not alone. He stopped. In a moment, a voice said:

"Considerate of you to come, Colonel Lamont."

The attaché did not answer. A man turned out of the shadows. He had silvering temples and wore a double-breasted suit with padded shoulders. Another man, a large shadow, waited along a hallway in the background, one hand held high under his jacket as if his heart pained him.

"I'm sorry I can't offer you a seat," the Colombian in the fine suit told the attaché.

"I can stand." The attaché's voice was stark and noncommittal. "What do you want?"

The Colombian frumped his chin and looked away. As if the attaché had asked a very good question. The man's profile looked heroic in the pearly light. But the attaché knew his host was not heroic. None of them were heroic. Although some of them were brave to the point of madness.

"I want," the Colombian said at last, "to tell you the truth."

The attaché waited.

"This business down in Bolivia. Your soldiers that were killed. My people want your government to understand . . . with absolute clarity . . . that we had nothing to do with that. We've tried everything we can think of, but you still don't believe us."

"Where did you go to school?" the attaché asked abruptly. It was a trick you picked up. Ask a sudden, unexpected question and you often got an honest answer that opened things up.

"University, you mean? Or law school? Stanford and Penn. Is there anything else you'd like to know about me?"

The attaché went quiet again.

"But back to Bolivia," the Colombian said. "We're at a loss. We've tried to help. Right now, we do not know what else we can do to convince you that we were not involved. We even identified the trigger man for you. Or trigger boy." His words took on a texture of metal. "A little piece of shit from the city dump. With one skill, like a circus performer or a whore. We even turned our own government loose on him, although they did their usual inept job. And now he's disappeared." The man turned his entire body to face the attaché, becoming a silhouette against a broad window, a dark face and shifting hands in ashen air. The attaché strolled across the room, as if pensive, so that the man would have to turn back into the light to follow him. "We should have killed the kid ourselves," the Colombian said, almost to himself. "After asking the little bastard a few questions."

"Every scrap of evidence we've seen," the attaché said, "makes it look like it was your people."

"Doesn't that tell you anything?" the Colombian

asked quickly. "Doesn't it seem as though there was too much evidence? And the laboratory your people raided down in the Chaparé. The newspapers claim it was a Colombian operation. Well, let me share something with you. That's partly true. It *was* one of our sites. Up until a few months ago. You know we always move." In the light, the man looked about forty, with the gray on his temples a September snow. "I will tell you something else. All the cocaine your people claim to have discovered there? Impossible. That lab was never that big an operation. Besides, we would never have warehoused so much at a lab. You should know better."

"If it wasn't your people," the attaché said, "who was it?"

The Colombian stepped closer. His shirt, solid blue from a distance, had fine blue-and-white stripes when he came within reach of a fist. His tie, thick as brocade, swirled lilac and cream.

"Have you ever considered the Brazilians?" the man asked. "You know they're moving in everywhere. Hasn't it occurred to you that the Brazilians might be playing with you, trying to get you to do their dirty work for them? The United States drives—or tries to drive— Colombian businessmen out of Bolivia. And who do you think is waiting just across the border to replace us?" The man made a face as if he had just fouled his shoe. "In fact, they're not even waiting. You should know that. The Brazilians have been buying into every imaginable industry in the Bolivian lowlands, legal and illegal. Even the politicians in Brasilia have an eye on eastern Bolivia. Look at the Brazilian investment in the Department of Santa Cruz. The place is almost a colony."

The attaché glanced through the big window, buying a few moments to think. Another high-rise looked back, its glass and granite darkened by rain. Huge clouds blew against the neighboring mountain, their wet froth exploding into mist, fog, air the color of pewter. Down in the street, a woman's quick white calves showed below a pink umbrella, and a taxi splashed uphill.

"All right," the attaché said, "if it was the Brazilians, give us names. Make the connections."

"We can't. That is, we don't know. We're as troubled by all this as you are."

The attaché snorted. "Unlikely. Now. Let me try a scenario on you. The Brazilians are getting too big for their britches, moving in on Cali's operations. What could be smarter than for your people to do exactly what you accuse the Brazilians of doing? Getting Uncle Sam into a pissing contest with the boys from Rio and São Paulo. So we do *your* dirty work for you."

The Colombian made a rejecting face. "Come on. If we were going to do that, would we use Colombians? A Colombian bum-kid hitman?" He flicked his fingers off his thumb, as if ridding them of some invisible filth. "We could buy all the Brazilian killers we wanted. Brazilians are cheap; they're surplus."

"If you've got something real, give it to us. But don't expect us to take your word on anything."

The Colombian's eyebrows climbed like dueling caterpillars. "No?" The very first syllable made it clear that his voice had hardened. "Well, perhaps you should come back to reality, Colonel. You know, if we wanted to, we could kill every man and woman you having working against us in this country. We know who they are, where they live, where they work, who they fuck, how often they shit." He smiled thinly. "Mostly they shit on each other, you know. But listen to me. How can we make it plainer to you that we don't want a fight with you gringos? Have cocaine sales been rising back in your Dallas or Boston? No. We have our North American market. And it's the market you give us. We do you a favor. We keep your blacks and your Mexicans and your dirty whites down for you. We keep them happy so they don't come out to where you live. We got your message. We don't market to *your* sons and daughters. Any of them who get mixed up in it, that's because they went looking for it.'' He lifted a hand toward a big window and the world beyond the glass. ''Look around you. We're global. Opportunities are everywhere. Maybe we'll do you a favor again and introduce ten or twenty million Russians to cocaine at a discount rate.'' Stepping even closer, he treated the attaché to a hint of his cologne. ''We do *not* want a war with Washington.'' He closed his lips tightly, then changed his mind and offered one last thought. ''That would be a war everyone would lose.''

''Except the Brazilians?'' the attaché said.

''Except the Brazilians.''

The attaché shook his head. ''I don't accept your premise. It stinks. The United States cares about every one of its citizens. And we're going to get you.''

''Don't be naive, Colonel. Do you really think a senator cares when one negro boy shoots another? Or if your welfare people make themselves happy with drugs?'' He raised his chin. ''You don't have one country. You have two. The one people like you live in, people with families and homes and cars and educations. And the other country that you all just wish would go away.''

''I don't have time for a philosophical debate.''

''And neither do I.'' Suddenly, the man reached out and took the attaché by the forearm. The attaché's first instinct was to hit him, but that was easily controlled. He looked hard at his host and the man slowly released his grip.

''Please,'' the Colombian said. ''This is going to end badly for all of us.'' The man seemed genuinely alarmed. Behind his wintery professionalism, the attaché had been listening carefully, observing, judging without committing. He was certain of one thing now—the Colombians were worried as hell.

''You'll have to show us some more leg,'' the attaché said. ''If it was the Brazilians, prove it to us. You've got the inside track, the resources. Finger the real bad guys for us.'' He looked at the Colombian with the no-nonsense expression a career in the Infantry had taught him. ''Now you tell me something I want to know. Why me? Why contact me? Why not the station chief? You know who he is. He's the one with the direct line to Washington.''

The Colombian made his just-stepped-in-the-shit-with-my-best-shoes face again. ''Your CIA. They're worthless. And your station chief is the most worthless of them all. If he did his job half as well as he talks, maybe you'd get somewhere. He only believes what he thinks his superiors want him to believe. He's like a bad priest.'' The man crossed his arms over his expensive jacket. ''Anyway, no one listens to your CIA in the present administration. We all know that. But your General Parnell. He's good. And he's connected. Better than people think. He'd make an excellent businessman in our world.''

''I'll pass on the compliment.''

''No. You pass on that we don't want a war. That we go out of our way not to hurt your people. That we're just trying to be good businessmen. We'll pass on anything we can discover about the Brazilians. If only your General Parnell will stop your government from doing anything rash.''

The attaché nodded. But there was no commitment in it.

''I'll pass on what you've told me. That's all I can promise.''

''Yes. Pass it on.''

Although his face suggested nothing of the kind, the attaché was delighted. It was a marvelous thing to see the drug scum at each other's throats.

The Colombian held out his hand, but the attaché pretended he did not see it. He nodded again and headed back toward the frivolously grand entryway.

On the threshold, he had a casual thought. He turned to his host a final time.

"Tell me something," the attaché said. "What does an apartment like this go for?"

Outlined against a big window, the Colombian said, "More than a colonel makes." His voice held a mean satisfaction, but it only lasted for five words. Swiftly, the man caught himself and added, "Of course, Colombia is a land of opportunity . . . an ambitious man . . ."

The attaché left without looking back.

ANGEL SAT UP on his cot, listening to his visitor. Beyond the cracked and broken panes of the glassed-in utility room, workers tended the countless roses, red, pink, yellow, and white, growing thickly under a glass heaven. The greenhouse was enormous and it was only one of many in the green landscape beyond Bogotá. Angel liked the place because it smelled good and his little room gave him good lines of sight, good lines of fire. Nobody was going to surprise him.

He liked the place, but he did not understand it. The workers cut the flowers and gathered them into cartons, then put them into trucks. Then, they said, the trucks took them to the airport, where the cartons were put on special airplanes that flew everywhere so people could have any flowers they wanted any time of the year. Angel thought flowers were okay, and he would have liked for his mother to have a house with a wall and flowers behind the wall, but he never understood why people cut them knowing that they would rot and stink after a couple of days. When you could have them longer just by letting them alone. Killing men made sense, because most of them deserved it, but killing flowers and carrying them around on airplanes seemed wasteful and stupid.

"This is the man," his visitor said, holding up a photograph. "You're going to kill his fucking ass."

Angel looked at the picture. Old guy with pushover eyes. Back home little girls had harder eyes than that.

"He looks like a priest or something," Angel said.

"He ain't no priest. He's a goddamned military officer, a gringo. A worthless turd like the rest of them." The visitor tossed a manila envelope onto the cot, then dropped the photograph on top of it. "There's four more pictures of him in there. From different angles. Just make sure you get the right guy."

"I always get the right guy," Angel said in a voice as calm as if he were naming his brand of cigarettes.

"There's other stuff in there, too. Information. Read it."

Coolly, careful not to give himself away, Angel took up the envelope and drew out the typed pages. He scrutinized them.

"The letters are too small," he said finally. "I can't read them right."

"What do you mean, the letters are too small?" The visitor took the papers out of Angel's hands and looked at the print. "Shit. They're regular letters."

"They're too small."

The visitor looked down at him. "You got bad eyes or something?" Then he got it. "Oh, Christ. You dumb shit. You can't even read."

Someday, Angel thought, I'm going to kill you. When the time is right.

"Big deal," Angel said. "You read them to me, if you're so smart."

The visitor shook his head. He wore jeans too tight for his belly and a soiled T-shirt too tight for his biceps. A discarded leather jacket lay on a broken chair, and whenever the man turned the right way, Angel saw the grip and hammer of the revolver tucked, painfully, into the back of the man's waistband. Angel wondered where a loser like that had learned to read.

Reading was something Angel was going to get around to some day. When he had time. And when he could pay somebody to teach him who would know how to keep his or her mouth shut.

In an impatient voice, the visitor read through the notes. Sitting his big behind on a board shelf where ants wandered crazily. Angel listened to the descriptions of his target's routines, his house and place of work, his family. He had a good memory and, when his visitor asked in a condescending voice if he should go over it again, Angel said:

"I got what I need." Then he added, "So it doesn't say anywhere that he's got a girlfriend or anything? No kind of deals going? No places he goes sneaking around alone?"

The visitor made the face of a man who knew how to live. "He's a gringo. Doesn't know how to have fun. Or what's good for him." He lifted his butt from the shelf and the wood recovered visibly. "So listen. Somebody's going to come for you. You'll know him right away. He's got red hair and his name's Adolfo. So don't go shooting him or something. He's going to get you out of here. You're going to take another trip. Until it's time to go to work."

"Where am I going?"

"Shit, how would I know? That's not my concern. The big boys decide." His mouth curled. "You're getting famous, kid. Lot of people looking for your skinny ass. And not because they want to kiss it."

"Then they're looking for trouble," Angel said matter-of-factly.

"Yeah. Everybody's looking for trouble these days. You sure you understand that stuff I read you?"

"Just leave me the pictures."

"You need anything else?"

Angel shook his head. He wanted to ask for medicine for his stomach. His night cramps were getting bad again and it was difficult to sleep. He felt as though something was eating him from the inside out. But he did not want this man, or any of them, to know anything about him that might sound like a weakness.

"All right," the visitor said, picking up his leather jacket. His gut rolled over the closure of his jeans and the sight made Angel despise him even more. "Anyway, they really want this guy dead. All of a sudden like. Wherever he is, wherever he goes. Dead."

"They want me to chop this one up like the others?"

His visitor thought about it for a moment, settling his jacket on his shoulders. Then he said:

"They didn't say nothing about that. Maybe they'll say later, when they get back to you with the setup for the hit." He looked at Angel. "Why? You like doing that or something?"

Angel looked at him scornfully. "I'm a professional. I do what I'm paid for."

His visitor started to reply, then changed his mind, and Angel sensed the man's ultimate fear. He was the kind of jerk who begged and cried and pissed all over himself when he realized he was going to get it.

The visitor opened the door and its glass shivered. The fragrance of roses, heavy as falling water, cascaded into the little room.

RUTH FINISHED PACKING another box of books and made a timeless gesture of weariness, wiping her forehead with her wrist. Sore-backed, she paused and sat on the arm of a sofa, looking across the room and out through the picture window. She could see the hills across the valley and the clear highland sky. It was a view John loved and that she liked well enough. Another thing to miss.

But there were other things that she would not miss. Uninterested in intrigue and not much interested in gossip, she had never been a good embassy wife. She had been feeling nostalgic about that, too, in her self-pity. But the morning had cured her.

A group of wives, acquaintances, and those who passed for friends, had organized a farewell breakfast for her, and she had gone gratefully, with a good heart. But she had not been there five minutes before she realized her foolishness. Some friends had not bothered to attend, now that John was on the outs. Others clearly had come to gloat and inspect her for signs of frailty. Even those closest to her had little charity in their eyes. Their words of support were jagged as scraps of tin. Then she had capped it all by making a fool of herself when the conversation turned to Anne Plymouth.

Anne was not well liked, because, as Ruth saw with the confidence of a well-loved woman, the ambassador's wife had remained attractive to an extent the other women found inappropriate to her age, to their ages, and therefore threatening. Anne Plymouth, with her good legs and good bones and the peaked upper lip of a French actress, was heartlessly, persistently attractive, and men liked her. She drew them like a TV football game on Thanksgiving afternoon. Worse, Anne was a loner. She did the things an ambassador's wife had to do, and did them well, but did no more. To Ruth, who relished her own closed world of family and music and books, Anne seemed interesting, separate the way a sensitive, imaginative child might be, and Ruth had often thought they might be friends if only one of them had really wanted it. To the others, Anne was a bitch.

"They say she's carrying on with some Bolivian playboy."

"That's disgusting," another wife judged, although Ruth knew the woman had slept with two of the embassy's Marine guards young enough to be her children.

"Who is it? Does anybody know?"

"I hear they're all diseased. And the way they smell."

"I always said she was a tramp," the wife of a repulsive USAID official said. Her husband was renowned for whoring during his frequent field trips. "The way she wags her ass whenever a man gets within fifty feet of her.''

''She should at least have some respect for her position.''

Ruth calmly positioned her china cup and saucer on the end table next to her and said:

''I've always rather liked Anne. I like her a lot better than I like rumors. Anyway, Anne takes care of herself, and more power to her.'' Ruth realized instantly how smarmy she sounded and tried to fix it with humor. ''If *I* woke up and found myself married to Ethan Plymouth, I'd have an affair every chance I got.''

But it was wrong. It changed no minds, only pushed them all rudely away. Even the wives who meant well. And she had made herself look a fool, since it was obvious that no man was going to rush to have an affair with her the way they would run after Anne Plymouth. She had even managed to insult John, in a slanting way.

One more disaster, she thought, turning from the view across the valley that was still the same in a changed world. Reaching for another handful of books from a high shelf, she just wanted to cry. But somebody had to be strong. The maid was upset at the thought of them leaving, and the kids, both of whom complained endlessly about all that Bolivia lacked, had suddenly discovered priceless friendships and crucial occasions that would be missed because of the family's unscheduled departure. Carla had even confided that she thought she was in love, sending a moment's graphic alarm through Ruth's imagination before her daughter's next moping declaration convinced her that some innocence remained in the world.

And she worried about John. She had heard nothing from him, and when she was not imagining him, Mr. Ten Thumbs, clumsily at war with building tools, her mind wandered to violence and death. She wished now that she had not let him go. Thinking that she should have argued with him, talked sense into him. The embassy snickers had a bothersome substance to them. John did have a touch of Don Quijote about him.

She wished he would call. Afraid that he was angry with her about the business with the newspapers. She had only wanted to help. To stand by her man. She carefully tucked a battered old half-leather edition of *Vanity Fair* into a box, thinking that Becky Sharp would have felt right at home with the embassy wives. She would have made mincemeat out of them. Then there was the shelf of poetry with John's beloved Wilfred Owen and Pablo Neruda, the first volume slender and brown, the other fittingly, flamingly red. John might have been a man in uniform, but he certainly wasn't uniform in his tastes. But then, side by side, she had ranked her Emily Dickinson with Anne Sexton. She decided, for the ten thousandth time in her life, that she and John really did belong together.

She startled herself when a small volume of erotic verse came out on the top layer of the box. She and John had enjoyed reading from it to one another, in bed. Then they had shelved it and forgotten it. Long enough for the children to age into some rudimentary awareness. She wondered if either of them had discovered it, decided not, and vowed to put it well away when next they unpacked their belongings.

That was a problem, too. Everything was out of kilter, off schedule. She figured it would be best if she took the kids to stay with her parents until John sorted things out with the military, until the renters were out and their house was ready. Her parents were game, but Ruth knew how wearing it would be on them and on the kids, and on her, too, after the first week. And the school year was going to be a mess. But she could not see any other option they could afford.

As long as they could all be together for Christmas, she bargained with herself, she would make the rest work.

A decomposing paperback of John O'Hara's short stories, as forgotten as the author himself, made Ruth think of Anne Plymouth in the instant before the phone rang.

It was Luther Darling calling from the embassy. He had called before, twice, to offer his help on any terms Ruth cared to make, but this time his voice was different.

He asked her not to get upset, then told her there was some bad news.

Ruth listened to him with an expression that shifted the way sand shifts when the undertow carves its retreat. She remained upright, one hand holding the phone hard against her ear and cheek, with the other hand frozen in midair. She listened and heard with ferocious clarity, then stopped really hearing, even though the voice continued. The little muscles that shaped her mouth struggled and quivered, and her eyelids quickened. Her chin, her full face, turned slightly from side to side. Suddenly, the hand that had stopped as though trying to halt time shot up to the side of her face, reaching an apogee in her hairline. Then the fingers streaked slowly floorward, scratching harshly as they wandered lower across her cheek, unable to still nerves gone independent, until the short, sharp nails cut into the side of her mouth and her hand made half a fist. She did not cry.

"HOW SICK IS he?" General Parnell asked.

His XO shook his head. "Lutoslawski says it's bad. He's treating him with everything he's got. But he doesn't have much of a diagnostic capability on-site."

Parnell sat back, pushing his chair back from his desk with his foot. His face was grim. "Jesus," he said. "Damn it."

"Lutoslawski says that, for all he knows, it might just be dysentery from hell. Or cholera with a mean streak. But, given that they've got some sort of mystery epidemic down there, he thinks the best bet is to evacuate Church." The XO focused on the tip of the general's shoe, which stuck up from the lip of his desk. "Quickly."

Parnell dropped his foot and closed on his desk again. "Well, make it happen."

"Sir, it's not that simple. Not in this case. Given that they've got an unidentified disease outbreak down there, there'll have to be special precautions. So we don't start an international epidemic."

"Well, take the precautions."

The XO shifted his weight. "We're already working on the problem, sir. But, to do it right, we're going to have to bring in a portable isolation unit from Atlanta. For the flight."

The CINC nodded impatiently. "Can we handle the case here? In Panama? I want to keep this in-house. Maintain control."

The XO nodded. "The hospital's isolation facility can handle it. CDC's sending down a couple of specialists, anyway. To scope out the epidemic. We're helping them expedite the official visas and customs clearance for their gear. They'll take a look at Church. In Bolivia, or en route. Wherever they link up."

Parnell made a face that warned the XO to choose his words with exceptional care. "This is turning into a circus. Just get the guy out of there. I don't want him dying because of some goddamned bureaucratic delay."

"Yes, sir."

The general shook his head again, shifting papers on his desk as though looking for something. But it was only a nervous habit. "How long will it take?"

"Sir, Rob Morino tells me he can tie it all together today and have a C-130 with the right gear on the ground in Bolivia tomorrow morning. Early."

Parnell nodded. "If Brother Church lives that long." He looked up. "Light a fire under Lutoslawski. Tell him I want Church to make it."

"Sir . . . he's doing all he can, but . . ."

"Tell him I want Church to make it. Can a C-21 land at Mendoza?"

The XO's mouth opened, but he did not speak.

"Don't give me that deer-in-the-headlights look, Tim. Can a C-21 land down there?"

"Sir . . . I doubt a little back-country field would have the data package. I mean, physically the airplane could land. But Air Force regs . . ."

"Yeah. Air Force regs." Parnell made his spare-me face. "Forget the damned C-21. Just tell Morino he's going to have a couple of other passengers on the C-130 manifest. And pack your gear."

The XO looked at him.

"Right," Parnell said. "We're going down there. You and me. Couple of security people. That's it."

"Press?"

"Later. After we cut the grass and sweep the sidewalk."

The XO remembered something. "Sir, you're scheduled to fly back to D.C. tomorrow. For the Chairman's roundtable. On roles and missions."

"He'll understand. The Chairman's been a soldier even longer than I have."

"Sir . . . this could be dangerous. Seriously. With this disease, and the narcos . . ."

Too active a man to be corralled behind a desk when there was a stampede on the horizon, Parnell shoved his chair back again and stretched out his legs. He made an arrowhead of his extended fingers, bouncing the point off his chin.

"You know, Tim . . . I've never had much time for Napoleon. The man was a butcher. And disloyal. And he lost. But he was good at Jaffa. His finest moment came when he went into that plague hospital where his soldiers were dying." Parnell budgeted a slight smile, but the intensity of his eyes did not lessen. "I'm not suggesting any comparisons with Napoleon. The point is just that an officer has to know when to lead from the front. And these days the front isn't always obvious.''

"Sir . . . we'll have to get country clearance. And the Bolivians—''

"Just stroke their chief of Defense. Tell him I'm really coming down to see him. To listen to his views on hemispheric security issues. And set something up with that other one, the general who's been muttering about a coup. I'm going to straighten his ass out once and for all. Make it sound like the Mendoza visit's incidental. A morale-builder, whistle-stop kind of thing.''

"Yes, sir. So . . . we'll just touch down in Mendoza, get Church loaded onto the 130 . . .''

"No. I'll stay there overnight. The airplane can get Church out, then come back. We've still got year-end flying hours. I want to get a feel for the place. Haven't slept on a cot in a while, anyway.''

"Yes, sir. Will that be all?''

Parnell had one final question, but his voice had already taken on a tone of dismissal:

"Anything new on that Colombian boy, the hit man?''

"No, sir.'' The XO was anxious to get back to his own office. He had a lot of phone calls to make, and he knew he would have to fight through a great many damned good reasons why this or that could not be done. At times, it seemed to him that slaying excuses was his principal mission in life. But one way or another, a properly equipped C-130 would touch down on the airstrip at Mendoza, Bolivia, the next morning. With an impatient, brilliant general on board. "No, sir,'' the XO reported, just before he turned to leave. "The two says everything's quiet on the drug front.''

CHURCH DREAMED OF green stairs. Multiplying beneath his feet as he descended, they plummeted into dark emptiness. He ran down faster, struggling to keep his balance. He did not want to go too fast, because then he would fall off into the void. But he had to keep pace with the expanding steps. Then he was floating in the darkness at a remove, watching the stairs sink without him. Racing downward. He did not know how he would ever get back to the top.

Briefly conscious, he wondered if this was dying.

Ruth was so old. Ruth was old and sad, so gray she barely looked like Ruth anymore. And he was a lieutenant again. Young. Alive. She could not understand that. His youth filled her with sorrow and he resented it. He sensed an obligation to love her, but there was someone else, whose love was contagion. The musky, terrible woman in the shadows. If he did not go with her now, the chance would never come again.

But if he left Ruth, there would be no going back. And he feared that. Because he did love her, after all, and the thought of losing her was a terrible thing. Withered Ruth, too real. His new love all darkness and devouring. He was afraid to go through a door where there was no door.

Unsure of his wakefulness, he struggled to breathe, gagging, choking, and dreamed of muffled voices. His body rolled like the sea, and his knees rose in waves as he struggled to submerge the pain in his abdomen. His insides flooded out of him and he was alert enough to feel shame, but his eyes would not open and his mouth filled with dirty water. He was drowning.

They were arguing about a little statue of a god, a gilded imitation of those old treasures from the highlands of Peru. Eva begged for it, but Ruth would not let her have it. Church wanted to tell Ruth that the figure was a worthless thing, that he would get her a replacement. But the discord existed in another place and he could not speak to them. He felt so sorry for Ruth, who was terribly afraid for no reason, and a surge of love for his wife overwhelmed him. But Eva was only a little girl, a child with hands like crab claws. It was wrong not to let her hold the statue.

The small golden figure sprouted in Ruth's hands, and she dropped it. The Buddha-like statue fell out of the sky, falling from an airplane, breaking apart even before it hit the ground. Church felt his intestines pump viciously.

He wanted his rucksack. There were Handi Wipes in one of the outside pockets and he could use them to clean himself before anybody noticed. He did not want anybody to see him like this.

But they were all looking at him, their uniforms black. He could not remember the Army changing the color of its uniforms. But every officer on the court-martial panel was dressed in black from neck to toe. Instead of neckties, they wore high-button collars. No one wore insignia and he could not tell their ranks. He was frightened. He wanted to tell them everything, because he had not done it, but they were convinced he had killed the men himself. He could not believe he had been accused, it was all a mistake. If he could not convince them of his innocence, they were going to send him to prison for the rest of his life, and Ruth would be embarrassed and he would never see his children.

One of the dead men, a soldier who looked like an Indian, showed him the newspapers. The papers were full of his guilt. But he was not a murderer. He had never wanted to hurt anyone. Then he realized they were secretly planning to kill him, and that he was guilty, after all. He lied to the board in panic, lying and lying, but he could not remember what he had said a moment later. Desperate, he suddenly realized that they could not try him in Bolivia, that it was against the regulations. He tried to explain their mistake, but they would not let him speak now. One of the men had a knife.

"Oh, God . . . please . . . hurt."

Hands set upon him and he struggled. Bloody corpses were dissecting him. Living dead men with stone eyes thrust their hands into his bowels and he screamed.

He did not know whether he had screamed or not. He

sensed wetness where there had been heat. Then the green stairs returned. Plummeting downward.

"*Not me,*" he cried, "*not me.*"

Writhing, he imagined that the pain would go away if he could curl up like a snake.

Uncertain to whom he was speaking, he imagined words for his voice:

"*I love you.*"

14

DREW MACCAULEY TOLD the young woman with the menus in her hand that he could find his own way, thank you. He was uncharacteristically late, but he knew Cadge would be waiting for him. Cadge was a friend, in a town where no man had many of them.

The usual Georgia Brown's lunchtime crowd downed last gulps of mineral water or hurried through coffee now that the eating and dealmaking were over and afternoon workloads loomed, all phones and faxes and fastidious memoranda. Only a few of the customers lingered over desserts or second coffees, most of them creatures of little consequence or out-of-towners who had caught wind of the restaurant's insider rep and had come to gobble and gawk.

A once-and-future mayor, a man confounded by his appetites, sat over cobbler with a trio of acquaintances: one of those Connecticut–New York axis types with other people's money to burn, a young, earnest acolyte with bits of colored cloth sewn over his lapels, and a chocolately young woman who smiled and said nothing. The mayoral candidate noticed MacCauley and nodded, eliciting a nod in return. You never knew who you might need.

MacCauley smiled mildly, noncommitally, at the other names with faces and faces with names as he strode to the back of the restaurant, feeling his size as he worked through the tightly placed tables and chairs spilling the first autumn coats over their backs. A notorious bankrupt, well placed in the Department of Commerce, twisted in his chair to shake hands as MacCauley passed.

Cadge gave a little wave, the gesture somehow calling attention to a glass nearly empty and clouded with the remains of tomato juice. And vodka, of course. Cadge was a drinker. But he wore it well, and his position allowed it.

MacCauley thrust out a quick, sportsman's hand and his friend half rose, taking the shake, then settled in again.

"Order?" MacCauley asked.

"Not yet. Not much of a lunch man these days. In any case."

A waiter appeared immediately, aware of whom he was serving. Without any menu fuss, MacCauley said, "The salad with the fried goat cheese."

"Very good, sir. And to drink?"

"Mineral water. Carbonated. No, on second thought, give me one of those." He pointed.

"And bring me another," Cadge said.

"Will you be eating as well, sir?"

"I'll have the chicken," Cadge said.

"Baked free-range, or the southern fried?"

"Nothing fried. And nothing too southern. Hell, just bring me the crab-cakes. Free-range chicken sounds so damned Republican somehow."

"Will there be anything else?"

"Just bring me another one of these."

"Yes, sir."

With the waiter prancing away, Cadge said, "Geez, though. This used to be a meat-and-potatoes town."

"Well, this *is* American cooking. And all that."

"It was a sad goddamned day when they invented this whole cholesterol thing."

At the next table, two women rose to leave. Mac-

Cauley did not recognize them and disregarded them. But one of the women—five-alarm lips—stared at him as she tortured her coat onto her shoulders.

"Cadge . . . I need your help."

"Looks to me like the whole damned party needs my help. Seen the latest polls? That little prick from Georgia."

"Old Ethan Plymouth has a problem down south."

Cadge made a dismissive face. "Ethan's always had problems. Second-rate mind feeding a first-rate ego."

"He's a friend."

"Yeah. Yes." The waiter brought the two drinks and a breadbasket. "To friendship."

"It's more than just Ethan, God bless him," Mac-Cauley said.

"Wife of his is a looker, though. I'll bet old Ethan doesn't know what to do with it."

"The military's absolutely out of control down there. *Our* military. And the press seems to think it's just dandy. I mean, am I missing something, Cadge?"

"That thing with the colonel? Makes good copy. Not our line, of course."

"The *Washington Times* had him front and center. In color."

Cadge munched a bit of bread that looked as though confetti had been baked into its crust. "They do good layout. Got to give them that. Not our style, of course."

"There's more to it. Parnell, the Pentagon's man down in Panama? The sonofabitch just sent in the Marines. Or the Army, anyway. He's got troops all over that clinic the guy was building. 'Doing good.' It's shameless publicity-seeking, Cadge."

"Sounds like a clever man. Can't you co-opt him?"

MacCauley picked up a wedge of gray bread. But he did not get it to his mouth. He fingered it, feeling the crust. "Well, he's queering up our policy down there. And making an ass out of Ethan."

"Ethan *is* an ass, Drew. It's no secret."

"For God's sake, Cadge. You're married to the man's sister."

"Perhaps not the wisest decision in my life. But that's another matter. So Ethan's getting the bum's rush?"

"Not yet. I mean, he's not exactly bound for bigger and better things, at the moment. But the local press down there is turning him into the diplomatic equivalent of Jack the Ripper. And our own press isn't much better."

"I spiked the worst of it."

"Not good enough, Cadge. And you know it. Your rag has to take a position. Against military involvement. Bonapartism and all that."

"I'd say 'Bonapartism' is stretching it a bit."

The crowd had thinned further, and in the background, MacCauley clearly heard the buttermilk voice of the impending mayor. Performing. They were all performers, of course. It was the one thing they were good at.

"Cadge, we can't let the military win this particular game. And not just because of Ethan. You know the department's under the gun. I have had to intervene personally, time and again, to salvage our Russia policy."

"It's your damned policy, Drew."

"The military has to be kept under control. Isn't that the lesson we all learned back when?"

"You know, I understand that I'm supposed to like the Russians now. But I do find it hard." He raised his near-empty glass, considering it. "Make damned fine vodka, though."

"This military headline-grabbing has to be exposed for what it is."

"Through a bit of State's own headline grabbing?"

"I don't want headlines."

"Headlines and deadlines. Story of my life. So what's the spin you've been thinking about all morning?"

The waiter appeared with a picturesque salad, lush as

summer in the Berkshires. The crabcakes looked like a fiesta for the Day of the Dead.

"Enjoy," the waiter commanded.

"Here's the deal," MacCauley said, leaning into the table, into his lunch, into a brilliant future. "Editorial page. Rationally pointing out that this colonel—Church—is no hero. Far from it. He's the man responsible for those dead soldiers down there. Trying to cover up his guilt with a cynical round of do-gooder theatrics."

"Was he? Responsible for those deaths? I thought Ethan was the ass who made that no-weapons rule."

"The colonel was his military adviser. He should have advised Ethan of the danger."

Cadge waved it away. "God, Drew. Ethan never takes advice. Until it's too late. He was like that in school."

"Cadge, I'm asking this as a personal favor. And it's the right thing. For the country. How are the crabcakes?"

"All right. I don't think I really taste food anymore. Used to like it well enough." He looked up, resting his knife and fork. "Let me think about it, Drew. God knows, I'm not a fan of the military. Nobody on the staff is. But there are limits. . . ."

"Would it help if I called Kate?"

Cadge smiled his after-two, third-drink smile. "Drew," he said admiringly, "you really are a bastard."

THE SODDEN FEEL of his pajamas woke von Reinsee. He had been dreaming, and he recalled that the last fragment had involved Eva, and that she had been in terrible danger, but the details receded from him like the memory of a caress. He sat up and switched on the bedside lamp, making light in his private darkness in the middle of other men's day.

The yellow glow coated the shoulders of the woman who slept beside him. She lay on her belly, her breath coming in small, steady sighs from a faintly opened mouth, and the sheet crested like a frozen wave just below her armpits. She had lovely skin, precise bones, and straight, well-cut hair so blond it was almost white. Her blue eyes hid in sleep.

The girl was Polish, one of the long succession of women sought out for him, kept on for six weeks if they were pleasing, then paid off generously before he could begin to feel anything toward them. He would miss this one, though. She possessed a bodily elegance that was terribly rare, and she was too decent for tawdry, premature theatrics. Yet she grew flatteringly aggressive, even a little frightening, as the excitement turned real. Her passion made him think of Heifetz playing the *Kreutzer.* She was intelligent, too, and well-read. Had her country not broken down, she would surely have had a better fate than that of the paid woman. But Marx had been right about one thing: economics were fundamental.

Suddenly, her eyes opened, then closed again, as she struggled with the light. She turned her torso, drawing the sheet behind her in a beautiful flowing motion, and raised herself on an elbow. A white breast swelled free.

"Pan?" she asked, offering a syllable's respect in her native tongue.

"It's nothing," he said, gladdened by the sight of her, by the stirred scent of her body. She was soft in repose, yet aristocratically austere, like the sound of a lone cello.

She moved a length of hair away from her eyes and looked at him a moment longer, and he wondered what life could possibly be like from her perspective. He always treated the women well, even allowing them the illusion of choice, but they seldom reached him beyond the excitement of a bodily response. This one was different, and he wondered now if he should not send her away ahead of schedule.

"Go back to sleep, my child," he said. "I'll turn out the light."

"It's all right," she said, her voice still broken with sleep, genuine and kind. The human ability to establish intimacy even under terrible circumstances was an endless source of wonder to him.

He made the room dark again. For his guest's sake. He was good in the dark, comfortable in it, and he found his way across the great bedroom to an armoire and selected a clean, dry pair of pajamas by feel. Then he left the room by the door that led to his private study.

He changed, folded up the sweated garments, then took down a volume of Schiller. But the book sat open on his lap, unread. So many things were in motion. It was important to keep exactly the proper tension on all of the reins, not too tight, not too loose. He thought again of Eva, wondering what on earth he was going to do about her; then he thought, angrily, of the men in La Paz. If they deserved to be called men. He had turned the screws and now they were jumping to send medical help to Mendoza. But they were so bureaucratic and incompetent and lost in the modern world that it would still be days before any aid of substance arrived. Every government south of the Rio Grande was a nineteenth-century monster confronted by twenty-first-century realities. Normally, it just made his business that much easier. At times like this, however, the inefficiencies were infuriating.

Thank God for the Yankees. They had gotten people on the ground, and that would help. Of course, they were going to die. In a day's time. But they were useful as a stopgap measure. It would be important to make sure that Eva was nowhere near them when the killing began. Rafael would have to see to that.

Rafael. Von Reinsee shook his head. The woman had made a scene in a restaurant, and people were talking. She was trouble. Too much horse for Rafael to ride. Now Rafael had followed her back to La Paz. It was an act of pathetic indiscipline, of weakness, but von Reinsee understood it. He would have preferred to take on any government in the world rather than attempt to combat the human heart.

Still, Rafael would have to do his duty. Eva would have to be removed from the Mendoza area. Before the next day dawned. Von Reinsee leaned far to his side, just reaching a telephone, and punched in three numbers.

"Benito. Find Mr. Gutiérrez in La Paz. I want to speak to him. I will expect his call at exactly six o'clock this evening. Yes. That's all."

He stood up to make it easier to return the receiver to its cradle, and he laid his book beside the telephone. He paced. He would have liked to listen to music, but he did not want to disturb the woman sleeping in the next room. It would have been ungentlemanly.

So many things were in motion. Even Rafael did not have the whole picture. Not that he could not be trusted. It was just not the proper way to do things. The survivor shared only the information he had to share, no more.

The business with the Brazilians, for example. As far as Rafael knew, they were the family's partners of the future. In fact, that remained an open question. The underlying objective was to set the Colombians and the Brazilians at each other's throats. With the Americans as the catalyst for the entire experiment. But only von Reinsee knew that. He had grown wary of the inroads both the Colombians and the Brazilians were making in Bolivia, and they had been slowly forcing him into an untenable position. Now, by the time they were done killing each other, whichever side emerged the stronger would still have been so weakened that von Reinsee, with all of his roots and means, would remain an indispensible ally for a very long time—and one whose bargaining position had been greatly strengthened. So let the thugs from Cali and São Paulo have at each other. Let them cover the landscape with each other's corpses. They would not be missed.

Von Reinsee poured himself a cordial glass of Zwack pear liqueur and took a bottle of Überkinger blue-label mineral water from the mini-refrigerator built into the bottom of one of the bookcases. The liqueur was to help him back to sleep, and the water was to prevent dehydration. It was important to think ahead.

Thirst quenched, he let himself back into the darkened bedroom with its air chilled to the crispness of a bottle of muscadet. He found his way to the bed and slipped under the sheet and light wool blanket, settling himself so that he got the fragrance and warmth of the Polish girl without coming too close.

"ANNE, I'M REALLY busy," Plymouth said. He glanced up from the cable he was reviewing just long enough to verify that it was, indeed, his wife who had interrupted his line of thought. Everything about him, the lack of connection in his eyes, the dismissive cant of the head, the tie that never hung quite right, summarized their wasted decades for Anne.

"This won't take long. Ethan, I'm leaving."

Her words had to filter down through more important matters.

"What?"

"I'm leaving Bolivia. And I'm leaving you."

He looked at her as though she had brought a dead animal into the room.

"Don't be silly, Anne."

"Don't condescend to me, you motherfucker."

He sat up straight at that. There were dark crumbs at one corner of his mouth. "*Anne.* For God's sake. Keep your voice down." He glanced at the wall behind which members of his staff were gathering for a meeting. Anne had plowed through them. Reassured by the wall's indifference, he brought an impatient expression to bear on his wife. "Now . . . what's this all about?"

With her husband paying attention at last, Anne lowered her voice. "It's not 'about' anything. I'm just sick of it all, Ethan. It's all nothing but a big lie, and I've had it.''

He was on time delay. She watched his eyes awaken. ''My God . . . it's not anyone in the embassy, is it? Not somebody in *my* embassy?''

''No, Ethan.''

''Or a Bolivian. Anne . . . for the love of God . . .''

''I'm not leaving you *for* anyone. I'm just leaving you. Is that so hard to understand?''

He was fully present at last. What there was of him. ''Anne . . . our lives together . . . we have a strong marriage. . . .''

She laughed.

Her husband reddened. ''Compared to our friends, I mean. You know what I mean.''

In a quiet voice condensed from polar decades, she said, ''We haven't had a marriage for years. You know that.''

He hushed his voice, as though they had entered a competition to see who could speak at the lowest volume and still be heard. ''If it's sex . . . you should've told me. . . .''

She laughed again, finding it impossible to keep the cruelty out of her tone. Remembering the night she had walked into the bathroom, late, to find him masturbating. In preference to making love to her. It had been, perhaps, the lowest point of her life.

''You're busy,'' she said. ''I don't want to waste any more of your time. You know, I almost just got on a plane. But I didn't want to be a coward about it, Ethan. I think we've both had about enough of that.''

''Now, wait a minute, Anne.''

''I've been waiting for years.''

''*Please*,'' he said suddenly. ''Anne, let's not make a scandal out of this.''

She dropped a single shard of laughter. And looked around his colorless office. Until she could stomach looking at him again.

"There won't be a scandal. I'll leave quietly. Tell them I'm sick. Tell them whatever you want. You're a superb liar, Ethan."

"Anne, I have never lied to you and I resent—"

"Save it. Good-bye, Ethan."

She turned to go, loathe to look at him for another moment. Now that the words had been spoken, a torrent of feelings began to wash over her. She wondered if she actually hated the man with whom she had shared almost half of her life.

His voice—ruptured—called her back:

"Anne. Annie. Please."

Closing her eyes, she turned around. When she felt strong enough, she opened them again. Like a child at a horror film.

"What?"

"Our daughter. What about little Robin?"

"Robin's fifteen. She'll turn it all into theater for her classmates."

Plymouth shook his head and raised a fan of stained fingertips. "You're hard, Anne."

"Yes. Thank God."

"Anne . . . the house. Our house in Potomac."

"It's yours." She almost spit. "A farewell present."

"You know I can't afford it. The upkeep . . . an ambassador's salary . . . you know my father lost everything. . . ."

She let him wait just one delicious slice of a moment. "I'll give you a settlement."

He got to his feet behind his desk. As if it were a thing he had forgotten to do. He was a tall man, but his shoulders were hammered down now. Reality had begun to sink in. Anne had never seen the man so openly distraught. It pleased her that she had reached him at least once in their lives together.

"Annie . . . we could put this back together. Think of all the good times."

She had to turn away before she could speak.
"The good times didn't last five minutes."

"NO. ABSOLUTELY NOT. I will not have it,"
Plymouth said. "I won't allow it."

The ambassador stood in front of a large window
whose thickness vagued the world. Bulletproof glass.
The thought made Sieger smile bitterly to himself. Over
the past few days it had been driven home to him that
there were more people inside the embassy who would
have liked to shoot Plymouth than outside. Even the ambassador's rich-bitch wife seemed to be one of them,
judging by the expression she had worn as she left.

"*Hen*ry," Plymouth said, turning to the DEA man,
"that's it. If you're too sick to go, I'm canceling the
mission. Postponing it, I mean. I want *you* to lead it. No
substitutes." He glanced at Sieger as if at a scabbed
beast.

Vasquez shivered. He truly did not look well. "Mr.
Ambassador . . . we can't cancel now. . . . I mean,
there's been a lot of work, preparations . . . and the Bolivians . . ." He looked across the table at Sieger.
"Kurt's been intimately involved. . . . He's an experienced leader. . . ."

Plymouth slapped a hand down on the conference table. But he was too tall and the angle was wrong. It
faded into an ineffectual gesture, angering him all the
more.

"It has been brought home to me—painfully—that I
cannot trust the military to do anything." He focused on
Sieger's chest. "In fact, I'm beginning to suspect col-
lusion with certain forces down here—wouldn't a drug-
financed dictatorship be just the thing for an
empire-builder like Parnell?" He turned his face away
as if to spit. "And to hell with the Bolivians. I'm tired
of their shenanigans." He gave the world beyond the
office windows a dismissive instant of attention.

"They're so corrupt they don't know the difference anymore. But they'll damned well do what I tell them." He
straightened his back. "*I* control the purse strings."

Henry Vasquez held out his hands. As if pleading with
a woman. "Sir . . . I *want* to lead this raid. But, like I
said . . . I got the shits so bad I can hardly sit here."

Plymouth folded his arms. "Well, take some Lomotil.
Take a lot of Lomotil. I don't care." He set his face.
"It's either or. You lead the mission. Or I cancel it."

Vasquez's torso shook. "Excuse me. Sorry, sir." He
got up hurriedly.

When the DEA agent had left the room, Plymouth
looked at his DCM and the station chief. The ambassador snorted, then turned to where Sieger stood beside
Luther Darling.

"You," the ambassador said. "You think I'm a fool.
But I know what you've been up to." He looked briefly
at Darling, then, shifting his expression to one of even
deeper disgust, turned back to Sieger. "You think I
don't know. All of you in it together. Trying to make a
fool of me. Well, let me tell you, mister. It won't fly.
There's going to be an investigation."

Sieger did not respond. He was very tired, having
slept little and with his body still not fully adjusted to
the altitude. He had been working harder than he had
ever worked in his life to learn, organize, coordinate—
to do all of the things an officer could do to prevent a
disaster. He still did not trust Vasquez's mode of operation, even if it had worked on the first drug lab raid.
Something felt terribly wrong about the whole business,
although he could not quite figure it out. All he knew
was that, if there was going to be a raid the next day,
he intended to do everything he could to make it more
competent than the last one. Given a choice, he would
have preferred to have Vasquez sidelined.

He did not believe he could trust anyone in the embassy except, perhaps, the captain sitting beside him.

"You," Plymouth said, addressing Luther Darling.

"Do you know why I ordered you to come to this meeting?"

Darling shook his head. "No, sir. I do not."

"Well, let me tell you why. I know what you are. You're a shitty little spy. And a traitor to the integrity of this embassy. And whoring around. When there's work to be done. Well, let me tell you, Captain. You're going out to the field. And you're going to stay there. You can try living in the bush with your Bolivian friends for a while. And you can start by holding their hands on this raid. I don't want to see you in La Paz. Period."

"Yes, sir," Darling said in a gray voice. "But I thought you were canceling the raid, sir. Or postponing it. Sir."

Plymouth opened his mouth to speak, but checked himself when the door opened. It was Henry Vasquez. Dragging back in. The agent came around the table and sat down again. His face dripped as though he had rinsed it, then had not found a towel.

"Sorry," Vasquez said.

"Henry," Plymouth said impatiently, "what's it going to be? Can you lead this operation? Or do we call it off?"

"Sir . . ."

"On or off?"

The DEA man looked sicker by the moment. He sat in his shirtsleeves, gut lopping over his belt, sweat everywhere. Sieger felt as though he had stumbled into one bad neighborhood.

"I'll go," Vasquez said, voice oddly slight for his husky frame. "I'll do what I can."

The ambassador smiled. Almost. "*That's* the stuff. *That's* right. Can do, Henry, can *do*."

"Sir," Sieger spoke up, "this is all wrong. Henry's too sick. Look at him. We can postpone this. Where's the harm?"

Vasquez looked up, white-faced. "*No*. No, postponement. Too much coordination."

Plymouth smirked. "Things too hot for a Pentagon staffer down here in the real world?"

"Sir," Sieger said, "I'm telling you straight—this is one half-assed operation. The plan's a joke. We couldn't design a better plan to get people killed. Landing straight on the objective. Twice in one week. It sets a pattern and—"

The ambassador held up his hand. "All right, Sieger. If you're that afraid, you don't have to go."

Sieger braked his reply at his teeth.

Plymouth smiled. "So. That's settled." He looked back at Henry Vasquez. "Well, Henry, you just get some rest. Big day tomorrow." He looked at his watch. "You're leaving when? Midnight? Thereabouts? You bring this one off, and the sky's the limit. We'll shove our eradication program down their throats and make 'em like the taste." He clapped his hands together and scanned the room. "Let's make it work, boys. Team spirit."

Back out in the lobby, Sieger closed in on the DEA agent.

"Henry . . . this is crazy. You said yourself you're too sick to lead the mission. Tell him to cancel."

The DEA man looked at him, and Sieger saw life-blown, fearing eyes.

"Not in your fucking lifetime," Vasquez said.

THE BIG AIRCRAFT with the Bolivian markings wheeled about on the side of the runway, readying itself to flee back into the sky as quickly as possible. The blast from the propellers created a storm of red dust that shut Eva's eyes and made her lower her face. Particles of earth scoured her skin and hair, and the groaning of the engines could have been the sound of a monstrous, suffering animal. The pitch changed and the dust storm eased, but the crew was not about to shut down. Word of the epidemic had spread widely now, just when the disease itself might have run out of ambition.

She had only one remaining patient, and he was the last one she would have chosen in this world.

She had left his bedside in the miraculous portable shelter his countrymen had brought with them, incapable of doing any more for him, yet unwilling to leave him, afraid to lose him in a moment's absence. But the trip to the airport had been necessary.

Shielding her eyes with a hand that radiated disinfectant, Eva watched a small door open near the front of the plane. Metal stairs lowered. A moment later a woman in jeans climbed down awkwardly, clutching the single railing and thrusting out a carry-all bag to keep her balance. She saw Eva at once and waved as soon as she was solidly on the earth. As the woman rounded the wing, the propeller draft hurricaned her hair.

Eva sensed that she should walk out to meet her, to help her, but she could not go any farther now. Behind the woman's back, the stairs retracted into the aircraft's belly, and a moment later, the engines angered and the big plane lurched away.

The woman closed the distance. She had the face of a strong person who had been weeping but who was determined not to cry in front of anyone else. Eva sensed that the other woman was bigger than her, in every way.

On a belated impulse, Eva stepped forward and reached to take the woman's bag.

"Let me help you, Ruth."

Ruth Church smiled. The smile of one condemned. "I've got it. How is he?"

Eva was not yet ready for that question. She had been working to formulate an answer that Ruth Church might be able to bear, but she had not managed to put together words that were at once tolerable and faintly accurate.

"He's waiting for you," Eva said.

"Is he conscious?" The other woman was already moving toward the jeep, unwilling to lose a second.

"He doesn't talk. But I think he sees. Part of the time."

Ruth Church nodded, biting into her lower lip. Her eyes shone. Eva reached to open the passenger door for her and Ruth suddenly closed a hand over her forearm.

"Is he dying?"

She looked into Eva's eyes, terrified of the answer.

The aircraft roused another storm of dust and grit. Both women turned their backs to the gale.

"I don't know," Eva said. But the engine noise had turned massive, overwhelming her words.

"What?" Ruth Church's eyes looked like slashes across her face. She bent closer to Eva, offering an ear, insisting on hearing the answer.

The plane began to roll down the runway.

"*I don't know*," Eva shouted. But the plane was quick and the volume of her voice ill-timed. Ruth Church recoiled at the shock to her ear. "I don't know," Eva said again, honestly and helplessly.

"My God," the other woman said. But she was speaking to herself now. A moment later, she bullied herself into the vehicle. Eva walked around the front to get behind the wheel, wishing the walk could last forever, or at least long enough for her to regain a bit of self-control.

As they drove through the dirt streets, the inhabitants scurried indoors at the sight of the white jeep. As though Eva were the plague carrier. There still had not been a single case of the mystery disease in Mendoza, and even the outbreak of cholera Eva had worried over just days before had not materialized. But the town's fear was as obvious as nudity.

Ruth Church found a handkerchief in her bag and held it to her forehead, then dried her cheeks. "I always forget how hot it is down here."

"It's the worst climate in Bolivia, I think."

"Thank you," Ruth said. "For coming to get me.

And for taking care of John. Mostly for taking care of John."

"It's nothing. It's the least I can do for him. I wish I could do more."

Unexpectedly, Ruth smiled. "You know, the pilots were so afraid—they didn't even want to come near *me*. As though I might have picked up this disease telepathically. Or over the telephone. Captain Darling had to do everything short of pointing a gun at them to get them to fly me down here. John would have been so disappointed in them. 'His pilots' he always calls them. I swear sometimes he thinks he's their father." Her voice had begun to break up and now she went serious again. "They say this disease is awful."

Yes, Eva thought bitterly, and how would they know? Who had been there to help her?

"Ruth," Eva said, testing the weight of the name, "John's symptoms aren't quite the same as what I saw out in the villages. At least, I don't think so. He's going to look very bad to you, but I've seen a lot worse over the last several days. I don't know. Maybe it's not even the same disease. Maybe it's just cholera with a little extra kick."

They passed an old woman carrying a load of hacked branches on her back.

" 'Just cholera,' " Ruth repeated. "That puts things in a certain perspective."

Eva gripped the steering wheel hard at the sight of an enormous gash in the roadway. "The gringos—I'm sorry—your people are sending a specially equipped aircraft down tomorrow morning. To take your husband to a hospital in Panama. They called us on their satellite system, it's a marvelous thing. They can do more for John there. All I want to do is keep him alive until they get here."

"Can you?"

Eva did not answer for a time. A dog trotted across the road, oblivious to the dangers of modernity. Eva

pounded the horn, using the opportunity to curse viciously in Spanish.

When Eva's outburst had ended and the air in the
vehicle had settled, Ruth asked again:

"Can you keep him alive?"

Eva opened her mouth, but there was no speech in
her. She felt the other woman's eyes lock onto her, demanding an answer. Eva moved her lips, her entire head,
but no sound would come. She thought again of how
utterly broken John Church had looked when she left
him. He fouled everything and they had been forced to
lay him on a plastic cover. Whenever the situation became unbearable, they lifted him up long enough to
scrub away the waste from beneath him. The sight of
him, of his discolored lips, made her want to squeeze
the IV bags, to force more liquid into his veins. To her
dismay, the U.S. Army doctor had brought no miracle
cures with him. Apart from a powerful dose of antibiotics that made no visible difference, he possessed nothing to offer Church beyond what Eva had given to the
poorest Indian.

"It could be dangerous for you," Eva said suddenly.
"He could be contagious."

"I'm his wife," Ruth said.

"Yes. John talks of you often. He loves you very
much."

The vehicle began the descent from the shack-covered
bluff down into the flood plain, where the clinic that had
started all this stood out on its hillock. Two figures
worked on its roof.

"And I love him," Ruth Church said abruptly. "Even
more than you do."

THE MILITARY DOCTOR made Ruth put on a
hooded outfit that looked like an economy-model space
suit. After warning her not to touch anything in the isolation shelter and telling her that her husband's appear-

ance might startle her, he led the way into the entry port of the inflatable shelter. Eva von Reinsee followed, a child playing dress up in her too-big protective garment, silent since the exchange in the jeep. Ruth was sorry about that now. But the woman's transparency, the public moping, had angered her and she wanted it stopped.

John looked better than she had expected. At least he was recognizable. Another hooded figure, presumably a nurse, wiped his behind with a gauzy rag that showed blood.

"John," Ruth said.

Wires connected his arms to machinery that meant nothing to her: shifting digits, green waves, and lines like a mountain range on the move. In comparison, John looked primitive. As though his skin had been rubbed with blue makeup spread thin. His hair was clotted and stained, and his eyes were closed. Veins snaked hugely along his temples. Chest heaving, he seemed to be preparing to lift a heavy weight at the gym. He looked much older.

Ruth had begun to feel relieved, had almost calibrated her response to her husband's misery, when his body began to jolt as if tortured with electric shocks. Quickly, the nurse and the doctor reached to turn him, guiding his head toward a bucket with a snap-open lid. His vomit looked like rice pudding streaked with strawberry preserves. A moment later, his bowels erupted, splashing. Instinctively, Ruth stepped back and was immediately ashamed of herself.

"Don't touch him," the doctor commanded. "We'll take care of him."

Eva von Reinsee, a tiny scarecrow, moved in to help. John's waste spattered her. The intimacy of it was almost unbearable to Ruth. But she kept herself under control. Wondering how they would know if John was dying.

The medical shelter was a miraculous thing, full of wonderful devices. Why couldn't they fix him? With so many tools at hand? What good was it all?

When she could not bear to watch any longer, Ruth focused on the IV bag, counting the drips. Soon she began to feel queasy herself and she climbed out of the half hypnosis. To her shock, she found John's eyes had opened.

She stepped in closer. Between the military doctor and Eva von Reinsee.

"Can he see?"

His eyes looked tormented. Watching distant demons. No one answered her question.

John quivered one last time, then settled. Terror pierced Ruth at the thought that he might be dying before her eyes, but his breathing resumed. It was steadier now, almost normal.

"Leave us alone," she said suddenly. In a voice loud enough to penetrate any mask.

The military doctor turned to her, raising a hand in protest.

"Leave us alone," Ruth commanded. "I want to be alone with my husband."

"Mrs. Church . . ."

"If there's anything you can do for John beyond wiping his behind, tell me. Otherwise, leave me alone with my husband."

She sensed the doctor's doubt through his mask and protective suit.

"Give me ten minutes with him," she said. "*Five* minutes. Please."

Eva von Reinsee spoke up, voice muffled by the space hood. "It won't hurt anything. Leave them alone for a few minutes."

Eva's voice had a tone of resignation Ruth found hideous. A wave of resentment came over her at the thought that the other woman might have had more of her husband's last hours of life than she would have.

The military doctor gestured to capture Ruth's atten-

tion. Then he pointed toward an object that looked like
a computer mouse.

"If he starts going into convulsions again, press this.
We'll be waiting just outside."

Ruth nodded. She could smell her own bitter sweat in
the prison of the space suit. She just wanted them all to
go.

And they went. On the way out, Eva von Reinsee
touched her elbow, but Ruth did not respond. She waited
in a private stillness, giving them time to clear off, then
giving them an extra few seconds before she turned
around to confirm that they had honored her wish.

Ruth dragged a stool close to the table-bed on which
John lay. For another minute she watched his breathing,
the small broken blood vessels where age and now this
sickness had spoiled the skin on his eyelids, his nose,
the shores of his cheeks. Something, perhaps blood,
pinked his sweat. As she watched, he turned his head
from side to side and his lips trembled, as if the dreamer
wished to speak.

She realized that she would miss the whisper of her
name if he called for her and she pawed clumsily with
her gloved hands to undo the hood of the protective suit.
When her fingers failed to find the seams and zippers,
she slowly drew off the gloves and undid the hood with
her bare hands. Her skin met cool, rancid air.

"Oh, John," she said, looking at him without the
plastic barrier.

She took his hand, surprised to find it limp and unknowing. Bloody filth welled slowly from beneath his
rump.

"You can't die," she said quietly. "John, you can't
do this to me." She did not care how selfish she
sounded. She was all selfishness now and unashamed of
it.

Her husband lay before her, obstinately unaware.

"You *can't* die. Not now. Not after I've waited for
you all these years." Her eyes blurred. "John, I *hated*

all those jungles. And I never gave a damn about the ruins. Or the churches. Or the stupid pottery.'' A bit of froth welled at the corner of his mouth and she wiped it away with a finger. ''All I wanted was *you*. Sometimes . . . sometimes I hoped you wouldn't get promoted. So you'd have to leave the Army. So I could have you all to myself. Safe at last.'' She turned her head slowly from side to side in immeasurable regret. ''And now we're finally there. We're going home, John. It's *my* turn now. And you had to go and do this.''

She tightened her grip on a hand that felt already dead, forcing her strength into him.

15

EVA WALKED DOWN the dirt road toward the river, away from the clinic and the town. Ruth Church was right. There was nothing she could do for the other woman's husband that others could not do as well or better. Her duty lay elsewhere.

It was unexpectedly hard to see herself so clearly. To discover such a taste for lies in herself. She wondered if she really had tried to take Church away from his wife. Perhaps that sort of meanness ran in the family.

The afternoon was hazy and luminous, the threatening rain postponed, time suspended. Eva's sense of loss had a vastness that spilled beyond her small body. People said they felt empty at times like this. But she felt swollen, as though she might fall to her knees and break open, infecting the world. And she was so terribly tired. Her legs felt stiff and unwilling, and her back hurt. She needed a long sleep. But her heart feared stillness. As though only the machine motion of her legs prevented a collapse of body and soul.

She was going to walk to the river. She needed simple goals now. Rehabilitation began with the smallest actions.

At a bend in the road, her feet stopped. A moment later, her eyes registered motion in the dust. A snake the length of a man's arm, brown and black, screwed toward her. It kept to the middle of the road, as she had done, as if they had made an appointment. Eva's heartbeat quickened, but she did not move. She watched the animal, registering its fluid, perfect motion. She had always been told that snakes would avoid you, if they could, but that water snakes were an exception. It was not far to the river.

Perhaps, she thought, the snake was unaware of her. Didn't snakes have poor eyesight? She could not remember. The animal did not hurry, but came on steadily, close enough for her to warn it with a stone.

Eva stood still.

She had made such a mess of things, had missed the obvious, had done harm. On this black, bright afternoon, it seemed to her as though she had done nothing but wrong to those around her. She had, perhaps, killed another woman's husband with her selfishness. Was there no decency left in the world?

The snake had a firm sense of direction. It closed the distance to a car length. She could see its dark lump eyes, the severity of its head and its searching tongue.

A bird with a rainbow wingspan dropped from a treetop, claws outstretched. With a precision Eva's hands had once possessed, it caught the snake and slapped down the air with its wings, rising again. Eva could feel the tendons hidden beneath the vanity of feathers. The bird appeared so large and strong it might have chosen her as prey instead of the snake.

Green-winged, yellow-breasted, casting a great, fluid shadow, the bird's ascent brought it close to Eva's head. She felt the artificial wind and saw the fine details on the snake's pale, twisting belly. At the last moment, she crouched to avoid being whipped by the serpent's tail.

Eva turned to follow the spectacle, to get at the wonder and meaning, and found the journalist standing just behind her.

She gasped. His face looked starved and beaked above the violent color of his clothing. Long fingers pointed toward her, as though he had been ready to clutch her from the bird's path.

He dropped his hands and smiled brown. Eva looked beyond him.

Together, they watched the bird sail into the trees, its claws bound by a living rope. Its wings made marvelous angles. With a screech like a snapped bone, the bird and its victim disappeared.

"Nature," the journalist said.

Eva did not reply. She believed she wanted to be alone and believed she resented his intrusion. She set off toward the river again, marching like a little hurt soldier, and he followed. His gait adjusted awkwardly to her smaller steps.

"Think you should check on the team that went out to the settlements?" he asked.

Eva walked. Waiting for the big river to appear through the trees. It seemed as though the only thing she wanted in life now was to see the water.

"I'd like to ride out there with you," the journalist continued. "If you don't mind."

"What about your shots?" Eva asked, a touch sharply.

He shrugged. "Guess I've been exposed already. With John and all." Their shadows preceded them in forward echelon, with the journalist's shadow markedly longer than Eva's, and the heat touched them like gauze. "Now that the Army's here, there'll be stateside interest." When she still did not answer, he added, "Publicity can be very helpful, you know."

Eva was certain she just wanted him to go away. But something left her unable to tell him. Perhaps, as they said up north, misery really did love company. And the journalist looked as though he had seen his share of misery. With his hepatitis eyes. He looked pathetic and earnest and chronically ill, and she did not want to do any more harm.

"The colonel's wife strikes me as a very strong

woman," he said. "There's a real force of nature under that hausfrau exterior."

"She loves her husband," Eva said flatly.

"Yeah. That certainly comes through." The shadow of his ponytail bounced with each step. "He going to make it, Eva?"

"God knows. I've lost my ability to judge."

"*I* think he's going to make it," the journalist said.

"Thank you, Doctor."

"Don't be hard. I just meant that I have one of those feelings you can't explain. That John Church is going to be around to bounce grandchildren on his knee."

Startling herself, Eva spoke her heart:

"I'd die in his place, if I could."

They walked through red dust. The river was near, and the ground water high, and the sky fat with the coming rains. But the road bloomed little clouds around their ankles.

Suddenly, Eva laughed. It sounded like an incidental cough against the symphony of insects. "Down here, you see, somebody always has to die. It's not like your country. Dying is our great solution. It's our ultimate mechanism for avoiding responsibility." She watched the journalist's dirty feet and worn sandals pacing her. "Dying is in our blood."

"Dying, my dear doctor, is in everybody's blood."

An obstinate woman, she shook her head. Still unable to see the shining brown muscle of the river. Waiting for it with a child's expectation. "It's different. In your country."

" 'My country.' "

They walked through veils of dead air.

"No more talk," Eva said. "It's too hot."

Then she caught a glimpse of the river through the foliage and quickened her steps. With her shirt wet on her back and her mouth dry.

There it was, a wonder the color of milk chocolate. Even with its mud flats naked and thirsty, the channel ran deep enough to take coastal vessels. But the nearest coast lay half a continent away and this stretch of the river was isolated by ferocious rapids upstream and falls where it bled down into a tributary of the Amazon. It was a world apart, one of nature's convents. Eva wanted to run to it, to splash into the water. But she was, in the end, a sensible, educated woman, and she knew that, if the creatures from the banks did not kill you, the invisible life in the river would fill you with poison.

They paused on a lip of earth. Coolness rose, and Brazil stretched dark green beyond the water. The air glistened. A mottled boat chugged. Fishing, smuggling, or both.

They stood for an immeasurable time. Finally, eyes glutted with beauty, Eva unclenched her scorched fists and looked up at her companion. The gray-shot ponytail was ludicrous, his dress the costume of a clown fallen on hard times. A single earring glinted, and it was the best detail of his wrecked face. The river breeze brought his tired smell to her. It was as if he willed his repulsiveness. He was a failed, near-useless creature, a false, self-selected saint who had made all the wrong choices. But Eva did not feel sorry for him. She felt repelled by the sight of herself.

WHEN ANNE GOT back to the residence, she found that Rafael had left seven messages for her. She told the maid not to take any further calls from the man, and she set to packing. In the conviction that it would make things easier, she limited herself to two suitcases. But the strictness only seemed to worsen the ordeal. She was not selfless, and there were lifelong possessions she could not bear to leave with Ethan. And then there were the sly little gifts from Rafael. She told herself at first that she would leave them all behind, but that was the first resolution she broke. She at least wanted these souvenirs of the best thing she had ever known.

The phone rang. She ignored it, then heard the maid take the call downstairs. It made her jealous even to share his voice with another woman. She wanted to grab the extension, to talk to him, and she rationalized that, if she had owed Ethan a proper farewell, she certainly owed one to Rafael. But she caught herself in time. Logic of that sort signposted the slippery slope to hell.

The phone rang again, and Anne packed furiously. She only had to make it through two more hours, then she could go to the airport. She already had her ticket, courtesy of the embassy's travel office. For the airport-closing nine o'clock flight to Lima, where she was holding a room at the Sheraton with her credit card. Tomorrow, she would be on her way to Washington by way of Bogotá and Miami. Then none of them would be able to touch her.

The maid knocked at the bedroom door.

"What?"

The girl sheeped into the room, staying close to the door. "Señora Plymouth, this man. He say to tell you he come here. You no talk to him, he come here."

"Fucker," Anne said.

"Please?"

"Nothing. That's all. *Todo. Gracias.*"

The maid disappeared as though tumbling back into lost centuries, leaving Anne alone. No, she did not want him coming to the residence. Because, even now, she had no interest in causing Ethan needless pain. Let him have his pathetic little world. Rafael knew she did not want him to show up at the door.

"Bastard," she said to herself.

It was indecent of him. Ungentlemanly. And she had thought he truly was a gentleman. She laughed. As if there were any left of that breed. Men were all monstrous children.

The thought of never seeing him again, of not feeling him against her and inside of her even one more time sent a cramp through her that made her sit down on the edge of the bed. Why had he needed to spoil it all? It had been good, grand, just fine as it was. Why did men have to spoil everything?

She knew that he had a bad side. His entire family was mixed up in every business going in Bolivia, and plenty of those businesses would not find favor with the chamber of commerce back home. But she had chosen to ignore all of that. As she had so long ignored Ethan's glad bullying of every powerless bureaucrat on his staff and the ministers of insolvent states. She had simply kept all of that at a remove. And she did not want it to come crashing through the door now.

And, she had to admit, she was ashamed. She did not want a scandal, either. She just wanted to close the door and get on the plane and go someplace where she could be lonely without the danger of running to a man who had already smashed her life, who would tire of her in weeks, if not months, and who would destroy what little pride and dignity she had left.

She loved him, and she had never known it would be possible to love like that. The love she felt for him was of the sort she had believed only existed in the books overweight women read on airplanes. Maybe, if it had been fifteen or twenty years earlier, she could have risked it, could have imagined it might last. But she had seen too much of the world to believe that any love could outlast the rental contract on an apartment.

She felt frightened in a way she had never felt frightened before. Sitting down on the bed, on Ethan's side, she picked up the phone. She knew the number by heart.

The line was busy. That jarred her.

She dialed again.

Still busy.

The bedside clock said five minutes after six. Anne stood up and closed her suitcases, her body a shell that did necessary things for her. She realized that she had forgotten to pack her makeup, and she had reached an age where she found makeup indispensable. She went into the bathroom, with its ceaseless Third-World gurgling, and swept her shelves clean.

She made one last attempt to call. The line was still engaged. Impatient now, she rang for the maid to help her with the suitcases. She intended to drive herself to the airport. Ethan could have someone fetch the car.

It was still too early for her flight, but she had decided to make one brief stop along the way.

"YES, UNCLE CHRISTIAN. Yes. He's here right now. In the other room. Or maybe in the toilet." Rafael smiled grimly, drumming his fingers on the console of the secure telephone. "The idiot ate a box of laxatives. To convince Plymouth he was sick. So he wouldn't have to go along on the raid tomorrow."

"But Plymouth ordered him to go anyway, am I not correct?" the distant voice asked.

"Yes. More or less. Anyway, Vasquez will lead the raid. If a bit unsteadily."

"Tell him to wear his red shirt."

Rafael stared at a painting of a winged saint in the costume of a seventeenth-century courtier. The saint shouldered a musket with a muzzle like the speaker on an old Victrola. "It's going to be hard to avoid hitting him. I'm not convinced every one of the boys is an expert marksman. And the ambush is set up to kill every man who goes in on the helicopters, and to do it fast. With all of the automatic weapons—"

"Rafael. What did I just tell you?"

Rafael paused, alerted by the brusque tone to answer carefully. "You said . . . 'Tell him to wear his red shirt.' "

"That's correct. And what else did I say?" The tiny voice was clipped and uncompromising.

Rafael did not get it. "Uncle Christian . . . maybe I didn't hear, but . . ."

''No. You heard correctly. I did not say another word.''

Slowly, as if thawing, Rafael's mouth opened. He understood now.

''Tell him to wear his red shirt,'' von Reinsee repeated. ''Reassure him. Then let him go. He knows much too much. Really, it's fortunate the cards have fallen this way. We would have needed to address the Henry Vasquez issue eventually.''

In the background, rooms away, a toilet flushed and pipes ached.

''There's more,'' Rafael said, wishing it were not so. He longed to call Anne again, to reach her before she did anything foolish. ''It's getting complicated. You knew Colonel Church is sick? Vasquez says they're going to fly him to Panama; the flights have already been cleared.''

''When?''

''In the morning. That means our people will probably miss him. First, they have to finish with the raiding party, then it takes time to drive down to Mendoza. And they'll have to walk in through the bush to surprise the gringos at the clinic.''

''All right,'' von Reinsee said. ''If we don't kill him here, we'll kill him in Panama. Have the boy do it.''

''Uncle Christian . . . maybe we don't have to kill Church. Vasquez has something even better. Their general, this Parnell. He's flying in. First to Mendoza, then to La Paz. We could take him at either place. If you want to land a big fish to make the gringos angry . . .''

''Fine. *Wonderful.*'' Von Reinsee's voice warmed. ''Rafael, I have always been blessed with remarkable fortune. It makes me wonder at times. Yes. Absolutely. Kill Parnell. God, yes.'' Rafael imagined that he actually heard a ghost of laughter at the other end of the phone. ''Have our 'Colombians' do it, of course. Really, this is a marvelous development. You're absolutely sure he's coming?''

"Uncle Christian?"

"Yes, my boy?"

"So we can forget about Church?"

There was no hesitation on the other end. "By no means. When you start something, you finish it."

"He's been good to Eva. He—"

The voice returned. With each word hacked out of stone. "When you start something, you finish it. Have the Colombian boy finish Church. Follow him to the moon, if you have to."

"Maybe he'll die anyway. He's very sick."

"Well, that would be inconvenient. It's far better if they think the Colombians killed him. Now—about Eva."

"It's all set, Uncle Christian. Just tell me to do it."

"Do it."

"She'll be fine. They'll hold her out in one of the settlements. Until the shooting's done."

"Good. Take care of her."

"You don't have to tell me that, Uncle Christian."

"Back to business, then. How many Americans will go along on the raid tomorrow?"

"Vasquez says four. Including himself. And an in-structor-pilot from Santa Cruz. The new lieutenant colonel's going. And Plymouth's sending a captain, a negro. Plymouth's mad at him."

"See that? We'll be doing the ambassador a favor. And how many of them at the clinic site?"

"Thirty-eight as of this afternoon, although some of the medical people could be working out in the settlements. Perhaps more will arrive tomorrow. With the evacuation flight and Parnell."

"What does Vasquez think?"

"He thinks maybe a few more will come. Bodyguards for the general. Maybe a press officer. That's all."

"Can your people handle so many?"

"If they can surprise them. It might be a real fight, though."

"It doesn't matter. Even if the gringos win the day, your people should be able to kill enough of them to make headlines around the world. I wouldn't be surprised if they were to retaliate directly against Colombia." The older man paused in satisfaction. "And you. I want you to stay in La Paz. Stay visible. Until all of this is over. You understand?"

"You don't want me to come back to Santa Cruz, then?"

"Just stay where you are. Go out. Visit people. Call on a government minister or two."

"Yes, Uncle."

"Do you have anything else for me?"

"No, Uncle."

"All right. Then it's my turn." Von Reinsee's voice turned northern, formidable. "Listen to me, Rafael. I want you to stop this nonsense with the woman. Today. No more of it. I've tried to be patient. But you've let it go out of control."

"Uncle Christian—"

"End it. Or I'll end it for you."

HENRY VASQUEZ DID not like any of it. He had tried to plan thoroughly, to bring all of his decades of expertise to bear, but now events had slipped from his control. And there was nothing he could do about it.

Gutiérrez, that smart-ass, pretty-boy rich kid, called the room in which he left Vasquez his "study," using the English word. Phony like everything else about him. Rafael Gutiérrez was just another greasy shit on the make. Vasquez knew the type. The only thing separating Gutiérrez from hundreds of thousands of others was his luck in being born into a family that had gotten into the criminal end of things early. Four and a half centuries early, when you could still pass it all off as your duty to Spain.

The "study" was cluttered with junk of the sort that

cost a lot and had nothing to do with Bolivia. Books in
classy leather covers that looked like nobody ever
touched them. And a computer the guy probably didn't
know how to turn on. It was all phony, a costume party
that never ended.

Vasquez's guts panged again, but it was only an early
warning this time. Christ. He hoped it would let up by
morning. Things were going to be bad enough.

He did not want to go on the raid. But he was into
things far enough to know that, if it got scratched, his
head would be on the line with von Reinsee. Who was
another shit. The biggest shit of all. The way Henry Vasquez saw it, if he went along on the raid, he at least had
a chance. If he screwed up old von Reinsee's plans, he
had no chance at all. It was a hell of a proposition.

His ass hurt and he stood up. He wandered around
the room, too nervous to give it a thorough going-over.
On the desk lay a number of travel guides in English:
Spain, Italy. Yeah. Everybody wanted to get away from
Bolivia. And he had wasted a decade of his life on the
place.

He had arrived with great hopes. Determined to put
things right. And back in the days of Operation Blast
Furnace, he had still been able to kid himself that his
work meant something. But over the years, recommen-
dations and programs he had put his heart and soul into
all just disappeared into faraway Washington offices,
and the programs that were implemented—halfheartedly—made no sense in the context of Bolivia. It had
taken him years to get the message that nobody up in *el
Norte* was serious about stopping the flow of drugs.

He had done good work. For nothing. Other men and
women who had possessed the good sense to stay closer
to the flagpole were promoted in his stead, and the only
thing that increased in his life was his waistline. Men
shot at him with impunity, and his hair began to gray
and thin out while the shooters bought fancy houses and
ran with women of the kind who had no time for him.

Eventually, he got the big picture. His side couldn't win. The bad guys were so far ahead of the game they were making the rules. They owned the governments, although they let the governments continue running the less profitable parts of their countries. And they brought home the bacon. The drug boys were the Robin Hoods of the Andean Ridge, turning the flow of wealth around, bringing back the silver that had been flowing outward for centuries. The slum kids didn't want to grow up to be policemen or even presidents. They wanted to be narcos. Because the narcos had it all. And up in Washington, and downrange in the little gringo islands called embassies, the bureaucrats still pretended that all the world's problems could be solved through talks and agreements and legal mechanisms. The world had left the diplomats behind. D.C. versus the druglords was a race between an oxcart and the space shuttle—and the narcos were the ones circling the planet. On top of everything else, the clowns in Washington really believed they could persuade the poor to stay poor because it was the right thing to do.

Henry Vasquez had been poor for a long time. Until he finally woke up to the future. He might die stupid, but he was not going to die broke.

This was it, though. When this round was over, he was going to throw in the towel. He had enough money. A paid-off house in the hill country outside of Austin. And the inside track on a state government job that did not involve taking a bullet because some United States congressman didn't like what crack cocaine was doing to property values in Washington, D.C.

The muscles in his abdomen quivered. But he had nothing left to give. He closed his eyes to let the pain pass. Then he idly chose one of the travel books from the desk top.

Photographs of paintings. And churches, the Vatican. Suntanned women on a beach stingy as their bikinis.

"Ever been there?"

Vasquez looked up in surprise. He had not heard any footsteps, had not sensed another presence. He was getting too old for this.

"What?"

"Have you ever been to Italy?" Rafael Gutiérrez asked.

Vasquez put down the book and shrugged. "Not my neck of the woods." He watched his host closely now, unhappy at having been surprised. Unhappy about many things.

"Too bad," Gutiérrez said. "It's a lovely country. A man could live there."

"A man can live lots of places."

"Yes."

"So what is it?" Vasquez asked. "What'd he say?"

Gutiérrez had eyelids that lifted very slowly. He always reminded Vasquez of a drowsy reptile. "He says you should wear your red shirt."

"Jesus, Rafael. It's going to be like Iwo Jima on fast forward down there. We're talking a lot of firepower."

"My uncle isn't worried. Hasn't he always taken care of you in the past?"

"This is different."

"Yes. It's more important." The younger man moved closer and Vasquez could smell his cologne. "Don't you think it's in our best interests to take care of you?"

Vasquez snorted. "You're damned right it's in your best interests. Henry Vasquez delivers."

"And we are grateful." Gutiérrez gestured for him to take a seat again. "And you are well paid."

Vasquez sat down on the softest-looking chair. "I never got a damned thing I didn't earn in this life. I just got to tell you, Rafael. This is going to be a bloody mess."

"That's the point."

"And I still haven't figured out how I'm going to explain my own survival." He looked at the handsome man intently. "Assuming I *do* survive."

''You doubt my uncle's word?''

''No, no. I didn't mean that. But accidents happen. Friendly fire. You know.''

''Afraid?''

''Damned right I'm afraid. And I don't mind admitting it. All that macho shit only goes so far.''

Gutiérrez smiled. ''Well, it's very brave of you to follow through on this. My uncle's very grateful. It would have been a terrible inconvenience had your ambassador canceled the raid. My uncle would have been . . . distraught.''

''Rafael, don't talk trash to me. I know the rules. And I'm going to do my part.'' He felt his guts quaking. ''All I ask is that you guys hold up your end.''

''Have we ever let you down?''

''This would be a hell of a time to start.''

''Henry? I know this has been a difficult day for you. But I have to raise one last point.''

Vasquez looked at him, thinking, The smooth little shit.

''You were very foolish to come here. You risked—''

''*Je*sus Christ,'' Vasquez said. He got to his feet. ''What the hell was I supposed to do? Send you a letter? Don't you want to know what's happening?''

Gutiérrez waved his hand in a manner Vasquez found effeminate. ''I know, I know. All the same, it's important to remain disciplined. How, for instance, would you explain it to your superiors if someone were to see you coming to visit me?''

''I'm trusted. They know I have to walk on the wild side now and then.''

''Yes.'' The younger man's expression hardened. ''Nonetheless, my uncle was extremely upset to learn that you had come here. He likes to do things in an orderly manner. German, you know.''

''All right. Got it.''

''He respects and admires you, Henry. But he wanted

me to tell you that, if you ever risk compromising our family like this again, you'll be killed." Gutiérrez smiled. "That does not include, of course, those occasions on which my uncle sends for you. He's confident of his own security measures."

Vasquez looked down at the floor, body and soul hurting. He believed he could smell his own fear.

"Just like that, huh?" Vasquez asked. "You can sit there and tell me just like that, with a smile no less, that you'd have me killed?"

"Business is business," the younger man said amicably.

As he stood up to leave, it occurred to Henry Vasquez that the threat was actually very reassuring. It meant that they expected him to live through the next day's events. It was only much later—when it was already too late—that he realized how artful his host had been.

SINCE RAFAEL DID not know she was coming, Anne had to park along the street. The dogs began barking as she walked up to the big wrought-iron gates and then she saw the vivid animals racing toward her through the wash of the floodlights. She was reaching to ring the bell, with muzzles snarling at her through black-painted arabesques, when the house door opened unbidden. A servant's voice called off the dogs and Anne assumed that Rafael or one of the staff who knew her had seen her approach on the closed-circuit television system. But she was wrong.

A dark figure hurried down the steps, anxious to leave the house behind. The man veered off the walkway onto the grass to avoid the floodlamps and Anne did not get a clear look at him until the gate buzzed, opening a fraction, and a hand reached to push it wide.

It was Henry Vasquez, the Drug Enforcement Agency rep from the embassy.

*   *   *

ANNE DID NOT mention encountering the agent to
Rafael. They never discussed anything beyond themselves, if they could help it, and in any case, Anne knew
she had seen something she had not been meant to see.
If Rafael wanted to talk about it, let him bring it up. She
had other things on her mind.

The meeting had shocked her, though. She had stood
helplessly, unnerved by the sight of a familiar face in
that setting. It had taken her a long moment to realize
that the DEA man, too, had been caught unawares. Vasquez mumbled something that could have been in English or Spanish, then quickly pushed past her, almost
making her lose her balance. He did not look back.

She just wanted to leave this country. Where everything was wrong. The truth was that she did not care
what Henry Vasquez was up to. It did not, could not,
matter. Not any more.

"My love," Rafael said. He moved to embrace her
without first dismissing the servants. But she backed
away from him.

"No. I only came . . . can we talk for a minute?"

"Of course. Certainly, Anne." He gestured toward
the stairs, the bedroom.

"No."

He smiled a terribly sad, childlike smile. "In there,
then." He stepped across the hallway and held open the
door to his study, a room she had visited only briefly.
The bedroom had been their world.

With the door shut behind them, he insisted on embracing her, but she broke free as soon as she decently
could. Unwilling to allow herself to feel anything now.

"You threatened me," she said. "That was
crummy."

"What do you mean?"

"That business about coming to the residence. I didn't
know you were such a bully."

He looked genuinely stricken. "Anne—"

"No. Listen to me." She found it painful to look at him, but in a very different way than it had troubled her to look at her husband earlier in the day. "What we had was beautiful. As beautiful as anything in my life has ever been. More beautiful than that. But it's over now. Done. I'm leaving Bolivia."

He reached out a hand, but she fled his touch. And he shook his head as if he had been struck and dazed.

"Anne . . . all right . . . we'll go together, then."

"*Stop it*. Don't you get it? It's *fin*ished. No more."

He dashed across the room as if seconds were precious and took up a stack of books and papers from his desk. He brought everything to her, an offering.

"Anne . . . I've been reading, studying. Looking for a place where we could go together. Milano, perhaps. We have an office there. A legal business. Or Madrid. Have you been to Madrid? We could be together always. You and I."

She reached up and slapped him. With all of her strength. Striking him so hard that he dropped the books and recoiled, lifting a hand to fend off a second blow.

"*Just stop it*," Anne cried. "You can't do this to me anymore. It's not a game. It's my *life*."

He shook his head. It was a gesture of terrible despair.

"Anne. Please. *Mi corazón*. This isn't a game for either of us."

"No," she said. "*No*. I don't care. Not even if you think you mean it. Because I will not stand for this."

"I love you, Anne."

"Be quiet. Don't ruin what's left, damn you. I will not stand for it. I will not run off with you like some middle-aged fool only to wake up and find you gone. Or to go through the fucking misery of watching you begin to watch younger women, of listening while the lies and excuses grow. *No*. I will not suffer your good intentions and your pity. Until the day comes when the thought of going to bed with an old woman makes you sick." She saw it all too clearly, and it was horrible. "It's over. It was great. And now it's done. I'm leaving."

But she did not go. She could not walk away just yet. She wanted to hold him in her eyes, her memory. The thought of never seeing him again, of never being touched by him again, seemed unspeakably wrong and unfair. It made her want to scream and keep on screaming.

"Anne . . . I'd give up everything for you."

"Romantic bullshit. Self-image. Get over it."

His face went sullen. And his voice changed. "I think you are making a great sin."

"Who are you to talk to me about sin? Mr. Dope Pusher."

"It's a sin to kill a beautiful living thing like this, such a rare thing."

"It was born dead."

"*Anne.*"

She turned to go. She could not bear any more of this. But he followed her quickly and grasped her by the shoulder before she could reach the door. An instant later, he had his arms around her, his lips on hers. At first she tried to break free. But he was much too strong. So she went cold, letting him invest his kiss for no return, deadening her body.

He gave up, even pushed her slightly away.

"You're *wrong*, Anne. You've made this all wrong."

"Good-bye, Rafael."

She went slowly at first, as though she had to fight the air to move through it. But when he did not follow, she picked up speed. By the time she reached the front door, she was running and weeping, and she did not even care about the dogs. She ran down the walkway, racing to escape, yet hoping against her will that other footsteps would follow. The dogs howled, enraged, but someone had restrained them. She rattled the gate, taking

out her anger on the cold iron, tormenting it, until someone had the decency to buzz her out.

She could barely see through her tears and she thought
she would be sick. The thin air left her gasping. She
walked and wept.

As she searched her purse for her car keys, a hand
grasped her arm. For an instant of animal joy, she
thought it was Rafael. Then a second hand closed over
her mouth.

HENRY VASQUEZ DROVE up through the old city
and on to the altiplano, where a new, dull city sprawled.
He hurried through the tollbooth and left the airport behind, with its crosses of runway lights and its concrete
prairies. Beyond the last huts and squatters, the high desert lay scorched under the moonlight, the far mountain
peaks vivid with snow. Now and then a thick Indian
shape appeared at the edge of the headlights, and a lone
dog sleepwalked across the road. Dark trucks, their beds
jagged with human cargo, rushed past. A late bus dirtied
the air. But with each minute, the world became an emp-
tier, lonelier place. He drove for over an hour, stopping
once to relieve himself, pistol ready in case Anne tried
anything inventive.

Before reaching Lake Titicaca, he turned off to the
right, driving through a village that had shut itself up
for the night then switching to four-wheel drive to follow a track through a series of washes and culverts. He
headed for a place he had used before, an abandoned
cluster of dwellings the locals avoided because of the
ghosts.

There was going to be one more ghost.

He drove the last few kilometers with the headlights
switched off. The moonlight silvered the track and odd
live things rushed and whirled at the periphery of his
vision. After cresting the last low ridge, he drove with

extra care, having once ruined an exhaust system on these rocks.

He parked by a roofless building whose faded walls shone blue. He yanked Anne from the floor of the passenger's side, still wary of her docility, standing her upright amid the stones and dried llama droppings. In her place, he would have been fighting like mad.

As if she didn't know what was coming. Or maybe she really didn't know. Maybe the stupid cunt thought her husband's position was going to save her ass even now.

He had gagged her with a cloth he used to check the oil, binding her wrists and ankles with duct tape, but she still could have fought. He had waited for her to attempt to twist and kick at his hand on the gear shift. But she had done nothing. As if her life didn't matter to her.

She was a good-looking woman and he had thought about having sex with her first, but he was afraid that someone might eventually find the body and run some kind of DNA test. No piece of ass was worth it. So he rammed the pistol into her back and said:

"I'm going to untape your legs so you can walk. You try to kick me or anything and you're dead meat."

She stood passively. He squatted and ripped off the heavy tape with a series of sharp motions, rougher than necessary, nearly toppling her. She had good legs. Wasted on Plymouth. Vasquez had known for weeks about her affair with Gutiérrez, but he had been holding the information back in case it ever came in handy. He would not have tipped Plymouth just to be a prick. He didn't have that kind of mean streak.

"Go," he said. "Walk straight ahead."

She obeyed him, slipping and stumbling in her city-woman shoes. In a space between two ruins, he reached out and stopped her with his hand. Her warmth shocked him, and he pulled his fingers away as if he had touched something dangerous.

It was her fault. The dumb bitch. She had just been

at the wrong place at the wrong time. Fate. The witches up in the market could have warned her. He knew she'd never have the sense to keep her mouth shut. And he had problems enough without her telling tales. He was too close to the big payoff to risk it. And in the end, what did she matter? What did anybody matter?

She made an anxious sound through her gag. But she did not sound afraid. She sounded as if she wanted to talk.

All right. Even if she screamed her lungs out, there was nobody to hear her.

Vasquez untied the knot at the base of her skull.

She gasped as the rag fell away.

"I just wanted to breathe," she said in a matter-of-fact voice.

"So breathe."

He stood behind her, watching the outline of her head and shoulders against the lucid sky. He closed his hand around the pistol grip, but could get no farther.

They stood for a long time in silence. Vasquez's guts cramped and gurgled. He knew what had to be done. But it was harder than he had expected. He even began to wonder if there might not be an alternative to this.

"I didn't want this," he said suddenly, startled at the sound of his own voice.

Anne's shoulders trembled. Then it passed. A moment later, she lowered herself to the earth. The movement was slow and awkward. Her hands were still tied behind her back, and the earth was broken and slippery with rocks.

On her knees, she raised her face to the sky. He could just see her white forehead and the tip of her nose from behind. She breathed once, so deeply he could hear her, then she said:

"Get it over with."

16

THE JOURNALIST WONDERED if this might not signify a new beginning. He still believed in new beginnings, although his experience in the human wilderness of Latin America had left him a witness mostly to endings. The endings left a gravel of bones in a village and, perhaps, one pared-down report on page ten of a newspaper in the United States, where accounts of massacre bordered ads for a sale on undergarments. The continent had its beginnings, of course, but they generally had to do with dreams and were mostly words, and their endings were predictable from the start.

He looked over at the small woman driving the jeep. The light from the instrument panel showed her in black silhouette with a few orange planes of flesh. The definite features and thin, shut lips sent a message of fortitude that refused to think too much. The journalist understood that.

"Do you believe in the soul?" he asked her suddenly, the words crossing the dark night between them on a bridge of engine noise.

Her eyebrows lowered as if she had been pestered by a child. The slight change in her expression moved the light over her face, whitening her cheekbone and deepening the hollow above her jaw.

"What an odd question," she said.

"I meant it seriously."

She shifted in her seat, small hands dutiful on the steering wheel. "Yes, of course. It's a very serious question. It's only . . . I suppose I find it rather personal." The light clung to her flesh, turning her eyes to porcelain. "Anyway, I haven't given it much thought lately. I couldn't speak meaningfully about it."

"But . . . you see so much death. You're sort of an attendant angel."

Her jaw drew in, shaping a defensive expression. He had learned, slowly, how to read men and women in interviews, and he realized that he had not yet penetrated the first layer of her defenses, of the shield that allowed her to survive in a world that killed giants.

"I'm far from angelic," she said, voice edged. "Besides, one of the things you learn early on in medical training is not to spend too much time on metaphysics. If you did, you'd be paralyzed. You wouldn't make the first incision. Or you'd make it badly."

"I believe in the soul."

He sensed her rising disdain. She had made herself very hard. He understood that, even respected it. But he did not want her to be hard with him.

"I believe in the soul," he repeated. "I don't know if it's immortal. And I'm not sure every animal that walks on two legs and has a command of language has one. But the best of us have souls." He looked at her in the oddly constant light. She was a fragile verity, with a dark world beyond the cabin of the vehicle. "John Church has a soul. And you have a soul, Eva."

"Well," she said, "my soul could use a shower. And a good night's sleep."

But her body would have neither. He could smell her, like meat gone a bit off, and he recalled the discoloration at the armpits of her shirt. Now they were on their way to a dying settlement whose name she could not remember.

"Sometimes," the journalist said, "I'm afraid that I'm nothing but a collection of appetites. Then, on the good days ... like today, by the river ... something beautiful washes over you and—"

"Beauty fools you," she said sharply.

He refused to be baited. "I know that. The California syndrome. Sun's shining on the beach and you think it's a fax from God." He looked at her uncompromising profile, thinking how horrible she would be if she were on the wrong side, how remorseless. "That's not what I'm talking about."

"I don't know what the soul is," she said. But her voice had shed its meanness and only sounded weary. "I don't want to be rude, but I don't know what the point of this is, Rick."

A bat or small bird teased across the fan of headlights.

He shrugged. "I just wonder about you. And the soul seemed as good a place to start as asking you about your favorite movies." He watched for a reaction from her, but she managed her expression with the discipline of a successful politician. "Anyway, I'd like to believe I have a soul. A flake of the divine." He smiled in the darkness, inviting her to smile, too. "God's dandruff."

She smiled. He saw it.

"That," she said, "sounds more realistic. But I'm not sure any of the world's churches would be prepared to accept it as doctrine." She glanced toward him. "I like it, though. 'God's dandruff.' I'll think of you that way now."

"I suppose ... I'm ridiculous to you."

Her smiled disappeared into the shadows and she swerved to avoid something feral in the road.

"That's harsh. There's enough harshness, don't you think?"

It did not take him long to think about that. "Yes. There's enough harshness."

She took an audible breath. "So. Changing the subject. You said you were finishing a novel?"

He answered slowly. "It's on my laptop. Technology's a wonderful thing."

"What's it about? The tribulations of an expat journalist in South America?"

"You're being harsh again."

She nursed a moment of silence. Face all shadows. Then she said:

"Sorry. I'm an ass sometimes."

"I'm an ass most of the time. I've made a career out of it."

"Isn't it odd, though, how we're hardest on the people who are most like us?"

"You think I'm like you?"

He read her look of surprise in the mechanical glow. "Oh, yes. Of course."

"I'm flattered."

"It's nothing to be flattered about. I just meant that neither of us have figured out how to fit in." She twitched as though a fly had come at her eyelid. "Tell me about the book."

He wanted very much to tell her about it. But it felt odd. He did not want to diminish himself in her eyes by describing it badly. Or by soiling himself with vanity, the way most writers did. Talking about writing was a feeble, spoiling thing, and the people who talked about it the most never wrote worth a damn.

"It's about . . . I suppose it's about recognition. Of the self. Of false belief. Of false beliefs that lead to fateful decisions."

She giggled. It horrified him for an instant. But a new familiarity in her voice retrieved his confidence for him.

"Not a book review," she said. "What's the story about?"

That was harder. Plot synopses were death. "Well, it's set in South America—I mean, that's what I know best—and it's about two brothers. From a good family."

"Which country is it set in?"

"It's not named. But it's mostly Argentina. With a bit of Colombia thrown in."

"Not Bolivia?"

He smiled an inward smile that tasted of failure. "Bolivia's where I ended up, not where I started. I washed up on the shore of a country without a coastline."

He felt her kinder smile before she glanced out at the black universe. "This really is the end of the world."

"It's about two brothers. It begins in the sixties, back when it seemed as if the whole world was about to change for the better. Although there were plenty of disagreements as to what 'better' meant. The older brother goes to the military academy. Like his father. But the younger brother goes to the university and falls in love with the idea of revolution. Social justice and all that."

"And all that."

"It's not trivialized in the book. It's just hard for me to talk about. Anyway, their lives take different paths. But eventually, slowly, they circle back toward each other. The upright military officer is drawn into the world of the government's secret police, the death squads. The revolutionary begins with high ideals, but finds himself forced to make excuses for the terror on the left. Until he ends up becoming part of it. As an urban guerrilla commander. Each brother elevates his cause above the personal and destroys any chance of happiness for themselves or the people they touch. They ruin women's lives, and rationalize that, too. It's a novel, so the paths of the two brothers have to cross. At a time when each of them has become disillusioned with the cause he's squandered his life on. They've each come to understand the other's position, almost to sympathize with it. But they're on a collision course they can't change. . . ."

"And what happens?"

"You'll have to read the book."

She thought for a moment. "It must end unhappily. If it's about South America. We find happy endings intolerable." The set of her profile told him she had taken his book seriously. She stared far down the road. "I suppose they kill each other. Or one of them kills the other. It's the only way. We need death. I told you. It's how we squirm out of things.''

"You'll just have to read it. I mean, maybe there's hope, after all."

She shook her head. "There's only activity." She looked ahead at the black world beyond the reach of the headlights. "The refusal to quit. Even if you don't make a damned bit of difference."

"The triumph," he said, "of the soul."

She looked down at the dashboard, then back at the night.

"Survival, maybe."

"Of the soul, Eva."

"Call it what you want."

"Want me to drive for a while? You seem pretty tired."

"I'm always tired," she said in her doctor's voice. "I know the way."

They drove on in a silence anxious to be broken.

"So. How long have you been working on it? Your novel?"

"Three years."

"Perhaps it will be an important book."

He smiled shyly in the darkness. "I'll be happy if it's a *good* book. That's all I want. To write a good book. Something of worth."

"You don't think journalism has worth?"

He thought about that. Briefly. "Not the same way. Not the way your work has worth. Journalists are hookers who want to be loved."

She began to speak, then held back the words. The night was endless and very dark. The journalist felt as though they were hurtling through the infinity of the universe.

"You can't see the stars tonight," he said.

She bent forward, looked up over the wheel. "No. The clouds have come in. Rain on the way. Maybe tomorrow morning."

He glanced to the side, away from his companion, and watched the vegetation pass by. Silver and black. Too swift for the eye to master, it gave him the feeling of falling in a dream. He wished he could hand this woman his book to read, to make her see him as a serious man, someone of merit.

"I wish you all the luck in the world," she said suddenly. "Truly. I think it must be a great thing to write a book. A great feeling, I mean. An accomplishment."

"It's not like what you do."

She snorted. Mannish. "What *I* do. Sometimes I wonder what I do. Generally, I feel as useless as a quack out of the Middle Ages."

He looked at her. A small woman, firm as stone.

"What you do," he said, "is noble."

She laughed. A girl's laugh. "We're very good at admiring one another. Aren't we?"

"Eva?"

She gave him a quick look, then turned her attention back to the road.

"Don't you ever . . ." He tried to make the words come right. "I mean, do you ever think about marriage, a family?"

She laughed again. But this laugh had a very complex architecture. Despair behind the delight.

"I'm a rag of a woman," she said. "Anyway, I've got my work. There's no time—"

"I think you're beautiful. I think you're an indescribably beautiful woman."

She did not laugh this time. And she did not speak. She drove. With night insects rushing against the windshield like snow.

He was sorry, afraid that he had gone too far too soon. Then he found his spine and decided he wasn't sorry at all. He was glad he had found the courage to say it. He had shut himself off from so much, found so many excuses. He could see that now. It was time for a new beginning. Whatever the cost.

When she spoke, her voice came weary and wistful.

"I suppose . . . I made a terrible fool out of myself. With Ruth Church. And with everybody else."

"No one noticed."

"She did. *You* did."

"John Church is a wonderful man."

He sensed her tightening. Small hands fierce on the steering wheel.

"I pray for him to be all right. He doesn't deserve this."

The journalist wanted to touch her, to stroke her arm. But he could not find that much courage.

"I'm just so *stu*pid," she went on. "How could I be so stupid?"

He did not want to think in the direction her thoughts were headed. So he tested a hypothesis out loud:

"I don't think you're in love with him, Eva. Not that way. Not the way his wife is. Or a lover would be."

"What is it then?" she demanded. Her voice was childlike and impatient. And suddenly defenseless.

"You're just lonely."

"I'm an ass."

"No. You just live in a world where women and men can't be friends. But you're not really of this world. And it all gets mixed up."

She made a face that tried to be hard and failed. "And what do you think I should do about it?"

He was ready to tell her when he saw the roadblock.

Two small pickup trucks parked sideways blocked the road.

Eva hit the brakes. She had been driving fast.

The jeep screamed like an animal, swinging its backside, and the journalist braced himself with both hands on the windshield. Eva shouted Spanish curses. She was furious. And, he realized instantly, she was afraid.

The jeep stopped at an angle and stalled. The abrupt silence seemed infinite and dark. Just as the journalist realized that there were no human beings in sight, a man stepped from the shadows. Carrying an automatic weapon.

Two more men followed him.

Eva cursed—screamed—and twisted the key in the ignition. The vehicle would not start.

The armed men began to run toward them, shouting.

"Eva—" the journalist said, wanting to help, afraid only for her.

The ignition sounded as though it were chewing bits of bone.

Another vehicle started up behind them.

"Eva," he told her, "go for it." And he leapt from the jeep. Into the oily night air. He had no idea how he was going to do it. But he intended to protect her, to buy time, to let her escape.

The jeep's engine turned over. The journalist did not know what to do at that turn of events, whether to jump back in or try to stop the approaching men. But his brief seconds of indecision did not matter, in the end. An unseen man hit him from behind, slamming him between the shoulder blades and knocking him to the asphalt.

As he lay on the ground, the dazzle of oncoming headlights seen from beneath Eva's jeep added to the shock of the blow.

His Spanish was good enough to understand all that was being said. Even thumped halfway to dreamland.

"Get her."

"Grab the bitch, goddamn it."

"Who's this fuck?"

"Get the cunt."

"No," the journalist shouted, trying to rise.

For an answer, he got a hard kick in the ribs.

Eva cursed like a warrior. He saw her feet and trouser legs appear on the other side of the vehicle, flanked by staggering calves in jeans, all of the limbs thinned by the glare from the headlights of the vehicle that had boxed them in.

A hand yanked him upward by the ponytail. The hurt was electric.

The men had bullied Eva into the flood of her jeep's headlamps, as if setting her up for an interrogation. She had gone silent and her eyes were huge, despite the harshness of the headlights.

"Eva," the journalist called.

He heard her voice, astonishingly self-possessed:

"Don't hurt him. He's not part of this."

"Bring him over here. Get the faggot over here beside this cunt."

Hands—fists—herded the journalist toward Eva.

"Only cowards hurt women," he said angrily in Spanish that had turned awkward on him.

The men laughed, and one of them said something in a dialect he could not quite get.

Eva seemed very small. He wanted to shield her. But there were so many of them. Five. No, seven. With guns.

He had been around plenty of men with guns. But he had always been in the position of the observer, even at the worst, bloodiest, most dangerous times.

"Look at them," a young man with a handsome, vicious face said. "Two fucking scarecrows." He stepped closer to Eva. "Who is this hippie fuck? You fuck scum like this? Is that what kind of whore you are?"

Someone laughed in the shadows and said, "She probably can't get anybody else to fuck her."

"You'd fuck her," another voice said.

"Maybe we should all fuck her, if she's not too dried up."

"They're all wet when they're scared."

The pretty boy moved closer still. "You scared, señorita von Reinsee?"

Eva didn't answer.

"Let her go," the journalist said. But his voice sounded weak and ridiculous even to him, and the others ignored him.

"Now," Pretty Boy said to Eva, "as an old acquaintance, I know you can follow orders. You were very good. You didn't go back up north after I told you not to."

"What do you want?" Eva asked in a voice thin as cellophane.

Pretty Boy looked at her, his expression arbitrary. "The rules have changed. Now you're not wanted down south, either." He came so close to her that they might have been dancing together. "But maybe—just maybe—if you behave yourself and do what you're told, everything will be okay."

Eva was quivering and she could not control her hands. The journalist had only seen one human being shake like that before. In Peru, the guerrillas with whom he had been traveling had taken a police captain alive. The man had shivered that way while he waited for the guerrillas to shoot him. Which they had done, after asking the man a few desultory questions.

"All right," Eva said. Her voice was the strongest thing about her now. And it was not terribly strong.

Suddenly, the journalist got the accents. Colombians. Absolutely. Lower-class Colombians. Not good news, considering that this was Bolivia.

He thought, bitterly, that there was probably a great story here.

"So," Pretty Boy said, "who's this bag of bones you picked up?"

The journalist did not hear Eva's answer, if there was one. He saw one of the men rooting through his backpack, bracing it against the side of the jeep. A moment later, the man had the laptop in his hand, holding it up in curiosity.

"*Careful*," the journalist called. "*Please*."

The man looked at him, startled by the urgency of the tone. All of the journalist's unexpected courage had disappeared now. The man held his life's work in his hand. *The novel*. And the irreplaceable computer.

"Please, don't hurt that. It's a—"

The man tossed the laptop sideward onto the road.

The journalist threw himself forward, desperate to catch it.

The plastic casing shattered on impact just as the first spray of bullets bit into the journalist's body. The bullets punched him down and rolled him over until he stopped against the tire of one of the pickups.

He felt as though he were swimming, although he could not explain why. His back was stiff, but his arms reached out, gathering the night like water.

"My book," he said. "My book."

Someone was screaming. Then there was more gunfire, but he felt nothing. It was like a celebration. *Fiesta.* The night had turned into a brilliant thing. A stream of air from a punctured tire cooled the wetness on his back.

Who was screaming? What was happening. Was that Eva's voice? Or were there other women? He wondered if the computer could be repaired. Perhaps someone who knew the technical side of computers could at least save his book, salvage the right parts of the machine. And he had the earlier chapters on a floppy.

"Motherfucker," a voice said in angry Spanish. Somebody stood over him with a gun. It was like watching a movie. The man stood over him with a gun and pointed it and fired. The muzzle blasts were stunning to the journalist's eyes and a succession of blows punched his body back against the sagging tire, but he felt nothing. Then his vision failed. His last coherent thought was not about the soul, nor of the woman who had let him fantasize briefly about a new beginning, but about his novel.

"JESUS CHRIST," PRETTY Boy shouted. His voice was vivid with horror. "What the fuck did you do that for? We weren't even supposed to hurt her."

He looked down at the tiny corpse in the stained blouse. The insects were already on her, attracted first by the headlights, then by the abundance of blood.

"That's fucking von Reinsee's daughter." The sight of the dead woman astonished him. He could not believe something so terrible had happened in his life, and he was already wondering where he could hide. Was there anyplace on the planet that would be safe? "We were supposed to fucking *protect* her, for the love of God. Keep her out of the shit. Scare her a little."

The man who had killed the doctor while the others fired at the journalist methodically loaded a fresh clip into his automatic rifle. He did not seem the least bit concerned about what had happened and it made the handsome young man wonder if the world had gone mad around him.

"Damn you," he swore, trying to drive home the gravity of the situation, "we just killed the big boss's *daugh*ter. Don't you think we should be a little bit concerned?"

The shooter, who had been an officer once, looked at him with calm brown eyes that glistened in the artificial light. Then the man raised his weapon and emptied the fresh clip into the handsome man's belly, driving him into the darkness. Behind his back, the two other men who knew the score killed off the remaining three men with whom they had lived and eaten for the past month.

"Depends on who your boss is," the shooter said belatedly.

HIS BOSS WAS Colombian, but he was not in Colombia. At the moment, he was in his favorite suite in the *Presidente* in Mexico City preparing for a night out with his wife. His favorite restaurants and his favorite people had little use for the morning, and the evening started at ten.

"You look splendid," he told his wife, coming up behind her as she argued with a contrary strand of hair. The mirror duplicated her struggle. She did look splendid, but much of it was the stuff of memories, and he would not have minded if his mistress had come along instead this time. But he was a loyal man, until you gave him a reason not to be.

"I've been thinking about Robert," she said, speaking of their youngest son, who had begun his first year away from the family at school in England. It was a very good, very old, extraordinarily exclusive school, but what the family lacked in heritage they more than made up in money. And the poor English were so threadbare, at the moment. Anyway, there was a precedent. Roberto's older brother, Huberto, had gone to the same school. He was at Princeton now.

"Robert's so shy," his wife said with a sigh. "I hope he'll be all right."

"Best thing for him. Force him out of his shell."

His wife finished with her hair and began fussing with her earrings. The boss, one of the great bosses, turned back to the enormity of the suite, then walked over to the window, stepping around the oversize bouquets his local colleagues had sent in his wife's honor. The view was peerless. Mexico City was absolutely brilliant, at its best like this, at night. On a clear day you could see Popocatepetl sleeping in the distance. But the clear days were rare, while the bright, close nights were dependable. And the boss liked dependability.

"I was shy like Roberto," he told the window, thinking of the faraway boy, of his inevitable loneliness. His wife did not hear him speak. The boss loved both of his boys, as well as the daughter wedged between them. Sylvia was at a convent school in the Loire. It was a good, progressive school, with high academic standards, but in the boss's view, its status as a convent school was its strongest selling point. Anyway, he loved his children and wanted the best for them. The gringos were making a rumpus about Huberto's student visa, but that would all work out. And then it would be Yale law. And Roberto . . . time would tell. Perhaps business. Like his father.

No. Not like his father. Real business. Respectable business.

The phone rang.

It was the concierge. Calling to inform him that his limousine was waiting.

Let it wait.

The Mexicans needed to wait a little. They had become very important, but not quite so important as they imagined. Still, the center of gravity was shifting. The affair with von Reinsee was a terrible annoyance. He was a shitlicking motherfucking bastard. But in the end, business was business. Now that the boss knew what was going on down there, everything could be turned to advantage.

Wouldn't want to kill von Reinsee, of course. Just the daughter. Then let the old man live a long time. On the whole, the German was a dependable business partner. This little folly of his was simply an aberration. The gringos would have to be pacified, but that was manageable. The boss was convinced that von Reinsee had read Washington wrong, in any case. He had decided to let the next day's massacre go ahead as planned. Since, far from raising the level of violence, the gringos would probably pull back into their shell. Whenever you killed enough of them, they got cold feet. Von Reinsee was too far removed from contemporary reality. With his opera shit. The boss, on the other hand, watched CNN every day. And the message was clear. Whether it was Beirut, or Mogadishu, or an obscure patch of jungle in Bolivia, when you killed enough of their soldiers, the Americans went home. Von Reinsee had it all wrong. Far from threatening the gentlemen of Cali, he was making Bolivia safer for them. Well, let the sorry old bastard find that out for himself.

It was important, of course, to keep things on a proper level with the gringos. Parnell, their man in Panama, was a little too good, too smart, to be taken lightly. So the boss was going to make them a gift. Of the little prick from the slums. Let the gringos kill him. On their turf. And let them be grateful.

Von Reinsee had done no lasting harm. Except to himself.

The boss had not taken the decision about von Reinsee's daughter lightly. But the old man had to pay some price for his duplicity. Of course, he would never know who had given the order. It was enough for the boss and his fellow Colombians to know that.

A shame. But life was cruel.

His wife rose and turned to face him, her figure not what it had been, but a woman still capable of announcing her wealth with grace. The boss was proud of her.

She crossed the room in a playfully sexy walk that was only slightly an embarrassment and came to him, haloed with perfume. Up close, though, she carried sorrow in her eyes. He wondered if she had learned something she did not need to know. But she only repeated:

"I'm concerned about Robert. He's such a sensitive boy. He doesn't have Hubert's social confidence."

The boss took his wife's arm and gave her a light kiss on the forehead, light enough neither to spoil nor taste her makeup.

"Roberto's got steel inside. You just spoil him. You can't go on treating him like a baby."

"I just want him to know how much we love him."

The boss smiled. "Well, tomorrow, when we fly up to Sonora to look at the horses . . . let's see if there isn't one for Roberto. For when he comes home at Christmas."

His wife drew back slightly. "Not a wild one."

The boss laughed lightly. "No. A fine one. A grand horse. Anyway, Roberto's got a good seat. He'll teach the English a thing or two about riding. Although, I have to say, I've always found all that foxhunting business cruel and more than a bit stupid. Polo's the thing for a man.''

His wife shook her head. The emeralds pendent from her ears and embracing her throat exploded with light. ''I worry.''

The boss put his arm around her shoulder. It was time to go. ''Well, don't. Someday Roberto's going to be president of Colombia.''

''YOU GOT SO many books,'' the woman said to Luther Darling in English. She was naked, as was her custom when they were alone. She was naked and pleasantly stained with lovemaking. ''When do you read all those books?''

''You're not always around,'' Luther said, slipping an emergency ration pack into an outer pocket of his rucksack. She had surprised and annoyed him by turning up. He had hoped to pack his gear in time to catch a few hours' sleep before meeting Sieger for a late-night flight down country to link up with the helicopters and the National Police. His mood had been bitter and unromantic. Of course, romance had not been required.

''A Bolivian officer wouldn't have so many books.''

He looked up from a recalcitrant strap. ''Then I suppose it's a good thing I'm not a Bolivian officer.''

She sulked on the damaged bedclothes, Cleopatra on her silks, Delilah bleeding lust on her divan. She reached to tilt his alarm clock toward her, made a disapproving noise, then cocked her head on her elbow.

''So this Colonel Sieger? You want to help him, right?''

Luther shrugged. ''He's got a full plate. You know what's going on at the embassy.''

''You like this guy?''

''Sieger?''

''Yeah. He's a handsome guy, you know?''

It was like dealing with a child. ''What you mean is,

he's not married and he's a gringo lieutenant colonel and that sounds pretty tasty. As to whether I like him or not, it's immaterial. He's a fellow officer. And what is this, anyway? You come over here for me to scratch your itch and you want to talk about Mr. Blue-Eyed Blond?''

She laughed. Her laugh was like a cheap trinket bought from a street stall. "You're jealous."

He set his pack on a chair across from the bed, thinking, This would be a better relationship if I were jealous.

"That's it."

He sat back down on the bed beside her and her face grew—tentatively—serious.

"Hey," she said. "Maybe you shouldn't go."

"What?"

"On this mission. This raid. Maybe you should stay here with me. Miss the plane."

He dismissed that with a combined breath and laugh, running his hand down her endless thigh without intent.

Her face went entirely serious. Just for an instant. And she touched the edge of his biceps.

"I mean it, Luther. Maybe you shouldn't go. Who knows what could happen?"

He woke. This was wrong. Her words, her voice, her timing.

"Esmeralda . . . are you trying to tell me something?"

She retreated, lolled back on the pillow, her breasts rolling, quivering, settling. Then she moved, a teenager's fantasy of a seductress.

"I just want you to stay here. That's all. I want more love."

His back straightened. "Do you *know* something?"

She giggled. "I know a lot about you. I know what you like."

"I'm serious."

"Show me how serious you are."

She had a blue spot on the outside of her thigh, like a tattoo to commemorate a beating.

"I've got to get something out of the bathroom," he

said, impatient with her endless, wiggling bullshit.

She became the curious child again. "Why you got to pack so much stuff for just a day?"

He glanced backward from the bathroom door. Her body lay long and golden, touched strategically with darkness.

"I've been trained to be prepared for anything."

From the bathroom, he heard her get up and move around. He could envision her nakedness perfectly. Had there been just a bit more to her, some casual decency beyond the disarming body, she would have been very hard to leave.

He surprised her by coming back out too soon. She was inspecting the contents of his rucksack.

She looked up, embarrassed only for an instant, before she regained the aggressive confidence of her nakedness.

"You got a gun," she said. "That's good."

KURT SIEGER FINISHED reassembling the 9mm and checked the action. Didn't have much stopping power, but it was better than nothing. Late in the day, when the embassy's attention had turned elsewhere, he had seen to it that Darling signed out two pistols and a couple of boxes of shells from the Marine-tended armory.

He did not like the mission. He did not like the country. He did not like the people, Bolivian or U.S., who were involved. And he did not like the feel of the future.

At first, he had believed that the ambassador had merely viewed him as expendable. Now he was convinced that he was being set up to be the scapegoat, should anything go wrong. And there was plenty that could go wrong.

Pistol in hand and uniformed in his battle dress, Sieger walked over to the floor-to-ceiling hotel room window. Straight down, the main avenue had a weary neon glow, a bygone feel. Small cars leaped down the alleys, duelling with headlights. Oddly, it seemed even more foreign to him than Rwanda had been.

He would have been glad to have McDonough and some of his boys along on this one. But they were back in Italy now, parachutes packed for the next crisis. God, it was all so much simpler and better when you had troops around you and a clear mission.

Sieger turned from the window and forced himself to drink more mineral water. He still had not gotten used to the altitude, and he worried about dehydrating. He had begun to worry about everything now, feeling his accustomed control of the world slipping. Over the past few days, he had worked in the embassy office until his eyes would no longer cooperate, trying to educate himself on the problem. And the more he read, the more disgusted he became. Church, damn him, had been right. Drug war. All they were doing was jerking off. When you looked at the statistics and then looked hard at the programs and their returns, it was clear that the embassy was losing ground. They were losing ground all over Latin America. And pretending desperately that the inconsequential measures civilized law allowed could make a difference. Looking at the narcos, Sieger felt for the first time in his life he could not win. Not until somebody changed the rules.

The raid in the morning, even if it turned out to be a spectacular success, would amount to trimming a hangnail from a cancer patient. It would take hundreds of raids to make a difference. And when you started making a difference, the bad guys would get serious. Then it would cost lives. And then it truly would be a war.

The numbers, the facts, were appalling. And they were there for all to read. Sieger could not understand how all of them, from Plymouth through the station chief and that DEA bugger Vasquez right up to the president, could fail to see that. The only place where they were making a difference was in the newspapers.

Sieger sat down on the bed and dialed the States

again. After a rush of intermediate noises and a dozen rings, he replaced the receiver, checked the international calling instructions, then redialed. But there was still no answer.

Sieger had never taken women too seriously. There had always been a woman around when needed, and the sex was generally satisfying. But what were you supposed to do with the body in the morning? Women liked to talk, and they liked to talk about things that did not interest him. Beyond the bedroom, their preferred activities bored him. And he was not the kind of man who cared to explain where he was going or why. He quietly despised his colleagues who, working late, whined excuses into the telephone to placate wives who were not fun any more. Women were like cars—you had to trade them in before the repair bills killed you.

And yet. This evening he had tried to call a woman he had been seeing for the better part of a year back in D.C. They had occasional fun together, and she did not push in too close. No promises. Still, when she did not answer, Sieger felt cheated. He needed to talk to someone. To somebody who had no hand in any of this and who could just listen with a modicum of decency. He was not even worried about security now. He was convinced that the embassy-sponsored operations had no security. All he wanted was a sympathetic ear. And a voice. A woman's voice.

He looked at his watch. Still half an hour before the embassy driver would come by. He laid back on the bed, crossing one boot over the other. He wasn't one for self-examination, all that useless poking at sores, but on this night he could not help pondering the course of his life.

It was a given that he liked soldiering. Yet, apart from a few intoxicating experiences, so much of it was drudgery, and so many of the jobs were unsatisfying, time spent waiting for something else. He knew, had long known, that he wanted to be a general officer. It was the goal he never shared with anyone, but which, over the years, others had come to suspect. He did not want to become a general by cheating or exploiting others. But he wanted to be a general. At least two stars. Division command. At least that. And yet, in this hotel room with its not-quite-square corners and its crippled pipes, he could not say *why* he wanted to be a general.

Was it purely the vanity of the thing? The outward form? Was it sheer ego, and nothing else? At any other time he could have found a dozen answers, from duty to the love of military life. Maybe it was the altitude sickness, the constant slight dizziness, but he could not quite believe any of the stock answers tonight. He was, he realized, habituated to military life. But that was not the same thing as love.

Or was it? The marriages he saw all around him seemed more habits than passions. Was a burst of excitement followed by lifelong habit all there was to it? His own experience had been of physical intoxication, followed by a cocksure decision and a slow, sloppy ending. He could not imagine himself as anything but a soldier anymore, and since he had been a lieutenant, he had assumed he was a good soldier. But now he wondered about that, too. He wondered if he had not been a bit too hard on the John Church types.

Maybe they were the real soldiers. The men who *could* imagine themselves doing something else but soldiered on anyway. Maybe they were the ones who understood what duty was all about.

He finished the opened bottle of mineral water and dialed the States again.

No answer.

Well, he hoped she was having a good time. Doing whatever she was doing.

It occurred to him that he had been alone for a very long time without noticing it.

He stood up to go to the bathroom when the phone rang. For an instant, he imagined it might be Tina, phoning from D.C.

But that was impossible. He had not tried to call her before tonight, had not even sent her a postcard. She would have no idea how to get in touch with him.

It was the front desk. The embassy vehicle had arrived.

Time to be a soldier.

THE AIRPORT SHOPS slept, with their treasures of drooping alpaca sweaters and postcards, green boxes of *mate de coca* tea bags and bars of traveler's chocolate. An Indian woman wrapped in a scourged apron mopped the floor and the overnight guards lazed in a corner. Rafael sat below a sign recommending Siemens electronics for a world-class office. His fingers threaded into his hair as though someone had tossed him his head and he had caught it open-handed. He watched the woman with the mop.

Half an hour after Anne left, he had panicked. He personally rang the airport and found her booked on a flight to Lima. With the least delay unbearable, he drove himself to the terminal and arrived to find her flight still on the ground, her seat as yet unfilled. He had waited by the gate, unsure of what could be done, but desperate to do it.

At first, she had been a stellar conquest and a boon to his uncle's craving for inside information. But there was justice in the world. Perhaps God's own justice. Against logic and expectation, he had fallen in love with her, with an older, married woman who seemed to want him only for sexual recreation. It maddened him in the first weeks as it maddened him now. He could not begin to say why he loved her and not another, but it was so. When he thought of her imperfections, they only made him want her more. The thought of other lovers from her past burned in him, but could not stop his loving. In the beginning, he worried that she would prove an embarrassment if he allowed himself to consider anything beyond an affair. But his heart, an unexpectedly powerful creature that had been hiding within him, was always a step, a dozen steps, ahead. Running toward her.

He had never experienced such a challenge in a woman. She was sarcastic to the point of bitterness, and wounded and lonely and kind. For the first time in his life, he had been forced to take a woman seriously, if only because she refused to take him seriously. Then it was love, without warning. Craving. Unreason. He wanted her ceaselessly, and would not take into account the endless practical reasons why he could not have her for his own.

He had waited by the gate until it closed and the aircraft thrust up into the sky, its beacons predatory. In a panic, he made the awed young woman with the passenger list check every name to be certain there had not been a mistake, in case Anne might have slipped aboard before he arrrived. The attendant assured him it was impossible. They had to check each passport.

It had been the last flight. But Rafael took a seat in the emptied lobby, with its hangover of a full day's cigarettes and irregularly washed bodies. He did not know what to do, where to look now. But at least she was still in La Paz. Or in Bolivia, somewhere. She could be found. In the morning, he could check with all the other airlines.

He sat on, feeling unreasonably closer to her here in the country's attempt at an international air terminal than he would have felt at home, where he had made love to her. It seemed to him that the future of the world depended upon finding her, and he remembered her with a vividness that left him in agony.

He dropped his hands and clasped the fingers together between his knees, a gesture imitating prayer. Then he raised his eyes to the spotted ceiling.

He would find her, he promised himself, no matter what it took. He would find her, and love her, and make her happy.

JOHN CHURCH WOKE in radiant happiness. He had
been dreaming about his wife. His consciousness remained toxic and confused, but he was alert enough to
grasp that he had been very ill. And he remained ill,
with a long sense of falling that was akin to a terrible
drunkenness. But the sickness in him was different now,
softened, although he still could not find the energy to
move his fingers. The world had called him back. His
dream of Ruth had pulsed with mortal beauty.

Nothing is so disorienting as happiness, and it took
him several minutes to be certain that he was awake,
since his surroundings were dark as the depths of a
dream. Slowly, as his eyes found the strength to wander,
he discovered colored points of light above his forehead.
That prompted shreds of memory. He did not know exactly where he was, but he thought it was some sort of
medical facility. There had been a great deal of commotion. Urgent hands upon him. The ghostly memory
of great pain nudged him, making him wince. Its weakened legacy still coursed in his belly.

A sense of rubbishy failure floated just beyond the
pain. His work, he saw, had come to nothing, and he
would have to leave it. Hardly mattered. A man mattered
so little, his efforts of transient consequence at best. He
thought, unaccountably, of a plump girl and her mother.
They had hitched a ride on his C-130 the year before,

heading up to La Paz for medical treatment. He recalled their embarrassed gratitude as they disembarked. He had bribed himself with the thankfulness of the poor, blackmailing himself into believing his random actions were achievements. Statistically, he had made no difference at all.

But he did not despair. The glassy clarity with which he saw himself brought with it a sense of freedom, of having risen from a swamp that had threatened to swallow him. He understood what truly mattered now.

Ruth. He had dreamed that Ruth was beside him, talking to him, touching him. He had been nearly devoured by visions, by images vivid and smeared, but the dream of Ruth had been fiercely real.

He drifted between wakefulness and the long drowse of disease. He felt his bowels quake, and his rectum burned, then cooled. He did not even have the strength to be ashamed. How sick am I? he wondered. Yet, he sensed that the worst was behind him, that he was going to live. It was amazing how the body could know a thing like that.

He had dreamed that Ruth was beside him. But there was no one beside him now. He felt terribly thirsty and tried to speak, to call out. But his lips remained frozen, crusted with his near death. Ruth had spoken to him. The words made no sense, but that had not mattered.

Bobbing on a tide of wakefulness, he thought of Eva. She seemed very far away now. His mind fastened with the unique acuity of sickness, and he saw that he had been playing a foolish game, unwilling to admit it to himself.

Poor Eva. Odd, how she held no appeal for him now. It was as if the fever had burned her out of his soul. Eva, with her withering child's body. What had he ever found appealing about her that way? Now that he had banished her, he could face his stupidity head-on. The clinic that had killed those men had been a deceit, not meant for the needy but intended to seduce. It was such an obvious thing. But he had lied to himself with the abandon of a little boy.

He had been playing with fire, toying unforgivably with Eva and cheating on Ruth even if he had never laid a finger on anybody else. Cheating was not only something you did with your body. In fact, the body was probably the least part of it, if the most obvious.

Eva, in the sorry, backcountry exile she had chosen for herself.

It was time to go home.

Bleeding shit, he began to fade back into unconsciousness. But he knew he was not going to die, and he did not have a sense of falling anymore. His heart was flying. Toward Ruth.

THEY CAME IN below the rain clouds and above a river with broad mud flats that stopped at a line of anemic jungle. The town's central grid began abruptly at a bluff, deceptively orderly from the air, tin roofs dreary. The airport lay red-earthed, gashed into the vegetation, with a small white tower that reminded Parnell of gunnery ranges. Showing off for the general, the aircrew came in combat steep and landed with one bounce. Engines howling, the C-130 rushed past the the fuselage of an old Douglas with washing spread on a broken-off wing. The aircraft calmed to a steady roll and turned tightly, nosing back into its own dust. From the ground, the sky showed a false horizon line, flannel gray below, with charcoal storm clouds above.

The pilots chattered, turning sunglassed profiles, and through the big windows and the dust Parnell saw two Army tactical vehicles, the rear one bearing a red cross on a white field. Before the lead vehicle, a man in battle dress stood beside a woman, while back by the compact ambulance, two figures wore the garments of cosmic beekeepers. The aircraft churned toward them.

It took Parnell a minute to realize what was different

about this airport: the absence of any crowd. Most Third
World airports, especially those at the world's end like
this, were centers of hand-to-hand business, of conversation and entertainment, or just idling spots for males
with nothing to do. But apart from the four figures waiting by the vehicles, this strip was deserted.

That would be the disease. Parnell wondered how bad
it was at this point. He did not trust the fragmentary and
contradictory reports that had made their way to him,
except to the extent that they painted a picture of a serious problem. Well, he would see for himself. Dead
soldiers and then disease. With the vultures back in D.C.
nonpartisan in their willingness to make politics of any
misery. Parnell found that diplomacy, which was nothing more than politics with a veneer of manners, was far
more difficult than combat had ever been. In combat you
generally knew who wanted to kill you. You even had
some idea as to why. But Washington was a town whose
cruelty congealed from a thousand acts of casual meanness. He was a strong man, with backbone, but his duty
trips to D.C. always left him feeling as though he had
awakened beside a prostitute.

Well, Washington was a long way off. Parnell
watched the figures out on the ground, sensing their anx-
iety, their desire to move, to act. He even knew who
they were. The lean man in the BDU's was Lutoslawski,
the medical honcho. He would be nervous for all the
wrong reasons. The woman would be Church's wife,
who would be nervous for all of the right reasons. With
her world hit by a hurricane. The aircraft made another
half turn, facing back into the runway, and Parnell lost
sight of the figures, the vehicles, and the stumpy tower.

"Let's go," he said loudly, standing up. Speaking
mostly to himself. His XO had already disappeared into
the hold to secure their rucks and to get the special
comms team and the military police bodyguards moving.
They had been snoozing in the back, sharing the aircraft's belly with a portable isolation unit used to trans-

port the exotically contagious. There were three doctors from CDC as well, and a military nurse. Two of the doctors would stay to investigate the epidemic, while the third and the nurse would ride shotgun on Church during the flight back to Panama.

Panama. Parnell had decided not to alert the local health officials about Church, since the docs assured him the isolation ward at the military hospital was tight. Given the chance, the local politicians and journalists would make an event like this into a circus, with the usual antigringo headlines and hands extended for compensatory aid. Perhaps there was danger for the Panamanians. Perhaps his choice had been wrong and was not a moral one. But Parnell got paid to make decisions. Church had done the right thing. Now he was going to do the right thing by Church. Sort out the bullshit later.

The engines lowered their pitch. A crew member leapt down the internal stairs and popped the door, dropping a short rack of steps onto the packed earth. Parnell followed right behind him, cap in hand. The air hung heavily, as though the clouds had packed it down, but it was a touch cooler than in Panama. The dust settled on his face, fine as talcum powder, and searched for a way into his mouth. Parnell marched straight for the brace of vehicles.

Lutoslawski, officer and doctor, saluted. Clear of the aircraft, Parnell aligned his cap, its front weighted with the four silver stars, and snapped a return salute. But he did not even look at the major. His eyes stayed on Church's wife.

He vaguely remembered an introduction to her. Some embassy function, most likely. Or an evening social at a mil-rep conference. He would have classified her as a typical member of the officers' wives club, except that her blouse was darkly stained and her khaki trousers had taken on a mottled camouflage all their own. As he closed the distance, he saw a worn face and eyes whose fire was running out of fuel. She looked as though she could pass out at any moment.

"Sir," the major said quickly, "you might want to stay back. We could be contagious."

Parnell ignored him. He thrust out a hand toward Mrs. Church, regretting that he had not had the XO track down her first name.

"Mrs. Church"—he felt the wet clay hand uncertain in his own—"I want you to know we're going to do every damned thing we can for your husband. No effort will be spared."

She began to open her mouth, and he sensed that she was reacting reflexively, conditioned by her long years as a military wife to respond with empty respect to the attentions of a four-star general.

Parnell closed a second hand, his bad hand, over her wrist. "Don't worry about anything but your husband. How's John doing?"

"There's hope," she said suddenly, as though the words had broken from her mouth against her will. "They told me this morning there's hope."

"You bet there's hope. Your husband's one tough customer." Parnell glanced back toward the wide, squat tactical vehicle, muscular grandchild of the jeeps with which he had grown up. "Have any luggage?"

The woman made a sleepwalker's gesture, then nudged to move toward the vehicle, attempting to break the handshake. But Parnell would not let her go. Not yet.

"Just get on board the aircraft, Mrs. Church. Go right up the back ramp. There'll be a doctor and a nurse waiting for you and your husband. I'll take care of the rest."

He released her then, heading for the vehicle to carry her scraps of luggage himself, although he rarely carried his own luggage anymore. He shouted to the beekeepers:

"Let's *go*. Load him up."

But as he fished back behind the passenger's seat of

the vehicle, he heard a noise from the past. At first it had been subsumed in the impatient grumbling of the C-130's engines, but now the sounds separated.

Helicopters. Old Hueys. The terrible sounds of his youth. Lawn mowers with rotors. The dark angels.

Parnell straightened his back and raised his face to the sky, bringing his good right hand instinctively to his hat brim, shielding his eyes against a hidden sun. A moment later, the slicks darted into view, flying echelon left in the middle distance, parallel to the runway. Two birds. Bay doors open, they were packed with tiny figures in buff uniforms. Heading north. He watched them until they disappeared over the scrub. Swallowed by a continent.

Parnell had good instincts. They had not kept him from bleeding, but they had kept him from dying, and they had propelled him to four-star rank. Without any further information, without the need for logic, those soldier's instincts told him now that there was trouble on the way. Maybe big trouble.

He felt an instant's twinge of fear, very deep. It was the fear that came from being on somebody else's turf, with inadequate intelligence and the feeling of being drawn into events shaped by other hands. The old ambush fear. Then he remembered who he was and where he was and how far he had come.

"Move *out*, damn it. Let's go," he shouted at the small crowd already moving crisply at the C-130's rump. They were loading a shiny metal stretcher encased inside its own transparent tent. With the propellers intervening, the crew and the medics did not hear a word Parnell said. But it did not matter. The act of speech was a challenge to the universe, a glove thrown down. Shoulders squared, Parnell carried Church's wife's luggage toward the aircraft, confident again, a shoot-first survivor ready for any trouble any tin-pot thug could bring to the party. Priority number one was to get Church and his wife in the air. Number two was to find out what kind of clusterfuck they had going on down here and bring some order to it. Changed wonderfully, Parnell began to hum to himself.

A large, cold raindrop struck him on the cheek.

THE PROBLEMS BEGAN before they left La Paz.
Gear stowed on the aircraft that would take them down-
country to link up with the helicopters and the National
Police, Sieger and Luther Darling waited an extra hour
on the apron of the runway. They closed their field jackets up to the neck against the chill of the highland night
and the stars above the black mountains looked unusu-
ally cold and distant. Everything was on hold for Henry
Vasquez, and when the DEA man finally appeared at the
rear end of midnight, bumping across the landscape and
steering his four-wheel-drive right onto the tarmac, his
haphazardness summed up the disorganization of the entire operation for Sieger.

There was something else, too. Something wrong. The
agent emerged from his vehicle with the shakes, talking
too loudly and underscoring his commands with exaggerated gestures. Worn by days of little sleep, Sieger
reduced the world to essential things the way he had
done half a lifetime before in Ranger school. And he
sensed something fundamental in the changes, large and
small, in Vasquez's behavior. The urgency with which
Vasquez, the late arrival, rushed everyone onto the C-
130 reminded Sieger of an emergency evacuation.

Sieger and Darling positioned themselves along the
troop seats in the fuselage, where they could lie down
and catch an hour or so of sleep. As they strapped them-

selves in under the cat's-eye darkness, with the propellers just beginning to clock and the engine noise rising, Darling leaned close to Sieger's ear and said:

"I wonder what's got Henry all wired. He's acting like he just held up the 7-Eleven."

Sieger shrugged in the darkness, thinking without any facts.

"Lot of pressure on his ass to get this one right." Then his voice became distinctly less charitable. "Let's damned well hope he does."

The aircraft took charge of their lives and lifted them skyward. As soon as the pilots leveled off, the two officers took a combat nap, rucks strapped down to serve as pillows and their rumps turned so that their holstered pistols would not bite into their hips. Sieger slept and dreamed turbulently, but when the changing pressure on his eardrums woke him and he opened his eyes to the paling light inside the cargo space, he could not remember the substance of the dreams. All that remained was a sense of loss, of the heart's incompetence. He let Luther Darling sleep on and sailor-walked across the deck, going forward, climbing the steep metal stairs to the cockpit.

They were flying directly into the dawn and the smoky-pink radiance above the clouds turned orange as it entered the aircraft, fleshing out the cockpit's metal skeleton with a luminous skin. The hangover of dreams clung to Sieger and a transient inability to master his thoughts opened him to the spectacle beyond the cockpit windows. A lucid, untouchable vastness waited.

There was privilege in the moment—vivid, fragile, piercing—and he knew it without being able to conquer the feeling with words. The glory on the horizon moved him, reminding the habituated soldier of countless bivouac sunrises met with a canteen cup of coffee clutched in both hands. He thought, with languageless sensing, of how memory transfigured the mundane, as though the past gained interest like a bank account until it threatened to grow richer than the present. Richer and, in moments such as this, more palpable. The sky, immediate and unknowable, glowed with a beauty no work of man would ever re-create, only to annihilate itself and incarnate a treasury of yesterdays. For one brilliant, languid moment, all of his being, the now and the remembered, merged. Into the sum of Kurt Sieger. Then it went.

He turned from the wonder, turning with the inevitability of a back turned to a lover, and saw Henry Vasquez nudged against the side of the commander's bench at the rear of the cockpit, pushing himself into the frame of the aircraft as if hiding.

It was probably a trick of that peculiar light just before the sun cracks the horizon, but the agent's eyes were ablaze in a way that shocked Sieger, who had never seen human eyes lit that way. They were the eyes of an animal, predator and prey, vicious, yet raw with fear, human only in their expression of encompassing regret. While Sieger watched, Vasquez slowly turned his head from side to side and a band of light climbed his face as the aircraft dropped toward its rendezvous.

One of the Bolivian pilots opened a thermos and poured coffee for himself. The scent filled the cockpit. Sieger wished he had a cup of hot black coffee now, although his kidneys wished him on the ground. Life's contradictory impulses. He turned away from Vasquez, unready to deal with the man himself or whatever trouble had taken a bite out of him. His instinct was to dismiss the DEA agent as just another windbag who loved to swagger in public. That would have made the nervous feeling in the air more bearable. Yet Sieger was not unfair, and Vasquez had been gutsy as all hell during the last raid. Too much of a good thing. This change just did not make sense.

Vasquez, usually so alert, did not even seem to see him.

Well, men were inconsistent when faced with danger. Brave one day, shit-scared the next. The agent would have to sort himself out. If he couldn't, Sieger was prepared to take charge. Maybe it would even be better that way. Fighting to wake fully, he tried to think on practical matters. With the sunrise turning the tawny face of the copilot to gold, the mask of a museumed god. And the heartbreaking coffee smell, reminiscent of better times than these.

Sloshed with emotions he could not understand, Sieger tried to review the plan of operations in his head, still discontented with it, irremediably angry at the mediocrity of it all. He would be glad to leave this godforsaken country and continent and the ambassador and Henry Vasquez behind. He wanted to erase them all from his life as soon as possible, to return to things he understood clearly and did well. He tried to concentrate.

But the agent's eyes followed him, ghastly. The man's expression was literally unforgettable, frightening in a way that was very difficult for Sieger to admit and impossible to understand. Back at the airport, Vasquez had been electricity on two legs. Now he was a refugee in his own private dreamland.

Something was fucked.

It was difficult for a man with a good chance of becoming a general to admit that another man's unease could bring a twist of nausea to his belly, and Sieger willed boldness upon himself. The mission was rolling and all a good soldier could do was to make the best of it.

"SO WHO ARE you?" Sieger asked the stranger with the sunglasses. Here on the ground, below the cloud bank, the morning was dark and brutally humid. The sunglasses felt affected and wrong. The stranger looked Anglo, from his careless posture to his alcohol-burned complexion. About fifty, the man had hair the color of winter slush and a big chest. Behind him, two old Hueys sat with their rotors sagging and the symbol of the *Diablos Rojos* painted on the pilots' doors.

Two helicopters. There should have been four.

"Rusty Haggerty," the man said, extending a hand rough as that of a lifelong mechanic or a bare-knuckles brawler.

Sieger was in no mood. He ignored the hand. "And what's your claim to fame, Mr. Haggerty?" In the background he could hear Vasquez, switched on once again, arguing in high-velocity Spanish with the officer in charge of the police detachment.

Haggerty folded his arms across his chest. Denim jacket over a T-shirt, bulge of a shoulder holster.

"I fly."

"You're an American. I mean, you're U.S."

"You got remarkable powers of observation, Colonel."

"So what are you doing here? The pilots—"

"Instructor-pilot. State payroll. I teach these boys how to keep from falling out of the sky. Mostly they do okay."

In the background, Vasquez shouted. Opaque words.

"Correct me if I'm wrong," Sieger said, "but you're not supposed to fly operational missions with them."

Haggerty sighed as though he had been through shit like this a thousand times in his career. "Colonel, I'm just here to check up on my boys. I'm authorized to randomly monitor their flying skills. And your buddy Henry Vasquez asked me to randomly monitor their skills today."

"Former military?"

Haggerty nodded.

"Warrant?"

"Yep."

"Vietnam?"

The man nodded again. "Two tours. Pretty country."

"And you washed up down here."

"Pay's good. The women are okay." He touched at

the bridge of his sunglasses, setting them closer to his eyes. "Listen, Colonel. I recommend you get down off your high horse and swallow whatever's eating you. We're going to be doing some dogshit flying today. Weather's going to hell, rainy season starting up. So you might just be glad to have somebody along who's flown through a monsoon or two." He gestured toward Vasquez. "Your bud's not one for listening to reason."

Sieger, realizing that he was shooting at the wrong target, returned to the point that had set him off in the first place:

"Okay, Rusty. I see two helicopters where I should be seeing four. What happened to the other two birds?"

The older man's eyebrows climbed above the rim of his sunglasses. "Jeez. Don't you guys talk to one another?"

"I ordered four helicopters for this mission. I had Captain Darling—"

"Yeah, well. Your bud Henry called down yesterday afternoon and said you only needed two slicks. Now who's right?"

Gone explosive, Sieger turned away. Sharply. Heading toward Vasquez, who, before exiting the C-130, had made an obscene display of changing out of his warm highland clothes into his mission uniform of combat boots, cutoff jeans, and the unforgettable red shirt. With a big old forty-five holstered on his belt. Sieger thought again that the red shirt was the stupidest thing he had ever seen. For a mission that could turn into a shooting match.

Vasquez stood bully-tall and close to the the National Police officer. Shouting at the smaller man, who stood his ground and shouted back. Off to the side, Luther Darling stood with his hands braced on the back of his hips.

"Henry?" Sieger barked before he had closed the distance. "Henry, what the hell's going on here?"

Behind the Bolivian officer, a platoon of sleepy boys

huddled on the edge of the runway. They looked like cows waiting to be herded. Uniforms mussed and weapons held as though they were unfamiliar and annoying.

Vasquez ignored him.

"Henry . . ." Sieger yelled, voice rising, and the weaker pitch making him angry with himself now, too. He strode toward the agent as if to strike him. "Damn it, why'd you call off the other helicopters?"

Finally, Vasquez turned, his meaty white thighs camouflaged with black hair, the cutoff jeans too tight and lumped heavily at the crotch under the candy-wrapped bigness of his gut.

"Piss off, Sieger. I got business."

"Tell me why you cut those two birds."

Vasquez shook his head in disgust. "Hell, man. We ain't got the flying hours. And we don't need four slicks for a kindergarten takedown like this. Two's already overkill."

"The plan calls for four."

The Bolivian officer watched them. He looked as though he understood as little of their speech as Sieger understood of his. But he heard the ugly music of the sounds. A small man, with an Indian face and unhappy eyes.

Vasquez shut a hand over his holster. But it was not a threat. Just a posture. "Sieger, I've about had enough. *I'm* in charge. The success of this mission's on *my* head. And I'm sick of my own military acting like a bunch of cunts. 'Can't do this, can't do that, might be dangerous.' What the hell you draw a paycheck for?"

"The plan calls for four birds. You agreed to it. The ambassador approved it."

Vasquez shook his head. Then he took a step toward Sieger, firmly excluding the Bolivian. In a lower voice, the agent said, "Come on, Kurt. Don't give me that. You know what a dickhead Plymouth is." He threw his head to the side, vaguely toward the north. "We got a mission to execute. Two birds, four birds, no big deal. We just got to get on with it.''

"The plan said four birds.''

Vasquez looked at him in disgust, eyes mean but otherwise unreadable.

"You coming, or not, Sieger? If you're scared, just say so, and no hard feelings. I'll do the mission myself.''

Sieger wanted to punch him. Hard. But nearly two decades of wearing a uniform had taught him just enough self-control to allow him to turn his back on the agent and walk off.

To take stock.

To decide.

To calm down just a little.

Count to ten, the way your dad told you a thousand years ago.

Never worked. Poor old Dad.

Sieger wished he could climb back into the sky and sink back into the dawn above the clouds.

But dawn was over.

He instinctively walked back toward the helicopters. But he did not want to deal with pilots, either. And there were more pressing matters. He did a left-face and marched for the vegetation crowding the edge of the aging concrete runway. In dry, knee-high grass, he unbuttoned the fly of his battle dress uniform, jerking his hips to raise the web belt weighed down with his pistol, canteen, and compass.

When he finished and turned back to the instant mess of the day, he found Luther Darling waiting.

"All right, Lu. What's going on? What's the argument about between my favorite DEA man and Che Guevara?''

Disgust washed over Darling's face. "The captain— the Bolivian—doesn't want to go. Says the rains are starting up, that it's too dangerous to fly.''

Sieger nodded. "Got a fellow gringo over there who seconds him. Heap bad weather.''

Darling looked down at the broken edge of the concrete. In the dull light, large red ants scurried inexhaust-
ably.

"Sir? I've been dealing with these guys for a while
now. And I don't think he's just worried about the
weather."

Sieger looked at him. A handsome man. Young. And
far from home.

"The Bolivians have their grapevine," Darling went
on. "We don't know half of what's going on down
here." He grimaced. "Truth be told, we don't know
one-tenth of what goes on. But the Bols are tuned in.
They know when an operation's headed for more than
one kind of bad weather. And this guy does *not* want to
go."

That makes two of us, Sieger thought.

BUT THEY WENT. The Bolivian officer remained
adamantly opposed to his own personal participation, but
he finally ordered a police sergeant and eight recruits to
board the helicopters. Vasquez rode with the Bolivian
NCO and four of his armed boys in the only bird that
had a spare headset for command and control, while Sieger, Darling, and the other four recruits strapped into the
Huey in which Haggerty occupied the copilot's seat.
They rode between the treetops and the sagging clouds,
bay doors open and the air ghosting rain. From his web
seat beside the door gunner, a seat that would allow him
to be the first man on the ground, Sieger could see Vasquez standing just behind the pilots of the trail bird,
instantly identifiable by his cherry-red shirt.

Sieger shook his head again, with the aircraft throbbing, shivering, roaring. He just wanted the whole business to be over so he could return to a world he
understood. And he did not want to waste any more
thoughts or energy on Henry Vasquez. Yet something
about Vasquez gnawed at him. The behavior change at

midnight, then the spooked look on his face in the cockpit at first light. Sieger felt as though there were answers right in front of his face, yet he could not even get to the right questions. At one point, the DEA man waved.

The policemen—policechildren—looked all of twelve or thirteen. Luther Darling had to explain to them how to hold their rifles with the muzzles pointed into the floor. Darling used gestures with them, since their native language was an Indian dialect and their Spanish seemed limited to the most fundamental commands. Their faces appeared identical and unknowing to Sieger, their eyes obscured by the surplus helmets made for much larger northern men. They should have been in the Boy Scouts, not in the para-military National Police on their way to raid a drug lab.

The helicopters lofted into ever darker skies. Down below, scrub farms hid in thickets and long fallow fields marked abandoned plantations. The hills lowered, grew sparse, disappeared. Then the dull earth produced mingling trees, an early warning of jungle up in the direction of the big rivers. Much of Sieger's anger had drained, leaving him thoughtful without clarity. He thought about women, about the pending release of the senior service college list, and about a force modernization project that would suck up months of his life when he returned to Washington. He thought about running on the Mall, with the young, vivid women jogging along the reflecting pool in their Barnard or Vassar T-shirts. Hair tied back, posture undefeated. Alive.

Maybe the raid would be another nonevent. Like the last one. You really could not trust your feelings. You just had to stay alert and avoid doing anything stupid.

The whole damned operation was stupid.

The helicopters followed a long, straight road for a time, then veered back out over the bush. A burned-out village and empty corrals sprawled amid copses of spreading trees, a few of them seared. The black ruins lay fresh and unweathered.

God only knew what that was all about.

Then there was another settlement, with most but not all of the low houses burned. Figures in orange space suits raised their masks toward the sky. The sight startled Sieger until he figured it out.

Those had to be the medics the CINC had sent down. For the epidemic. And that meant they were getting close to Mendoza, with the clinic and John Church.

With the damp heavy air washing over him, Sieger thought about Church with a feeling of embarrassment and shame. God, how he had misread that man. Church had known the score, had tried to give him fair warning. Sieger pictured the colonel as he had last seen him, a great, hurt bear, until he suddenly recalled the reports of the colonel's sickness and remembered the emergency evacuation flight-plan coordination that had occupied much of the embassy's military staff the day before. The CINC had decided to get Church out, no matter what.

It was a good decision. Church was worth saving.

Sieger had learned a great deal since he boarded his flight out of Washington. Things looked a lot different on the ground than they had back in the Pentagon, where the sweat and blood and fuckups of reality were reduced to the ice-cold Thursday morning four-screen briefings down in the watch center, with the Chief and his subordinate generals sitting in their blackened balcony and a horde of staffers crowding up behind them, ready to answer any questions the slides and briefing scripts had failed to anticipate. With a positive spin, of course. All Army deployments, worldwide, were captured in frigid charts, yellow letters on a black field, numbers not men, described, as necessary, by a disembodied voice. Thousands of soldiers, A-teams and full divisions, spread around the world. A Reserve veterinary team in sub-Saharan Africa. An armored battalion training in Kuwait. Special Forces in Thailand, National Guard engineers in Honduras. A medical team in Bolivia, gone to a place whose name did not matter in the great scheme of things. Sieger, of course, would not have figured on the chart, since this was an unscheduled deployment.

The aircraft tracked along the road again, with huge clouds smoking above the rotors. A smallish civilian jeep stood abandoned by the roadside.

Burned.

It was too small a matter to bear thinking about.

Suddenly, the helicopter banked, giving Sieger a straight look down at the ground. Treetops whirled just below him, making him faintly dizzy. When the fuselage leveled out, the aircraft left the road behind again. Looking forward past a boy's helmet and the half walls of the troop compartment, Sieger spotted a distant break in the vegetation. That would be the town. Mendoza. The target lay ten minutes' flight time to the northwest.

Beyond the town the horizon disappeared in darkness.

Rain.

Sieger's thoughts would not give him any peace. He had that occasional sense that he had missed or forgotten something that mattered greatly, but he could not grasp whatever it was. His world seemed to be slipping away from him. He looked at Luther Darling, whose face had gone inscrutable under the brim of his soft cap. The silver railroad tracks of his captaincy sat at a slight cant, with the camouflage fabric of the headgear crumpled forward like a forage cap from the Civil War. Darling was a good man. Honest, conscientious, and capable. Sieger had come to respect and like him in their miserable days of working together. He made a mental note to put in a good word for him with some of the high-powered Aviation boys back in the Building.

Darling looked ready. Very military. Even sitting, the man had good bearing. Yet, Sieger knew, they were not ready. Their pistols would not stop much of anything, if things went sour. They did not even have helmets. To an amateur, they might have looked the part, but they were not prepared for battle.

Sieger glanced back toward the trail chopper, which

was flying echelon left and closer than safety rules would have permitted in the U.S. Army.

Vasquez. In his sleazebag red shirt. A clown.

Well, if he and Darling were not dressed for battle, the DEA man sure as hell was a lot worse off.

Then Sieger had the greatest revelation of his life. It iced through him in a way the sodden rushing air did not, and he felt his mouth opening as if to shout. He watched the red-shirted man in the trail bird. Stunned. Hit between the eyes by the obvious.

In the middle distance, an airstrip opened up. Packed red earth. With a C-130 on the apron by the tower and two tactical vehicles parked near it, all with Uncle Sam's signature. Tiny figures. Moving. But that scene rushed through Sieger's eyes and skipped the conscious part of his brain. Horrified, he looked back at Vasquez. The agent noticed his attention and waved again, smiling now.

Sieger wanted to vomit. He bent forward in his seat, gasping for air. Beyond that, he could not move, and minutes slipped away.

What if he was wrong? What if he was just being paranoid? What if the goddamned country was getting to him, driving him off the deep end?

No.

It felt right.

And terribly, terribly wrong.

The aircraft followed another straight road, this one unpaved and pale under the charcoal clouds. Abruptly, Sieger unlatched his seat belt and, holding to the airframe, stepped past a boy with a rifle so he could speak into Luther Darling's ear. Raising his voice to beat the rotor noise, he leaned down and said:

"Luther? Tell me something." He felt his voice quiver. "Why would a guy wear a red shirt on a mission that could turn into the shoot-out at the OK Corral?"

Darling looked up at him uncomprehendingly. But his

face settled into an expression that said he was thinking about it.

Sieger waited. He wanted to hear it from someone else. He stared hard at the captain, demanding an answer.

After a minute or so, Darling motioned for him to bring his ear closer. And the loudened voice told Sieger:

"Beats me, sir. Nobody in their right mind would wear a red shirt into a potential firefight. You'd be the first thing everybody saw."

Sieger slammed his free hand down on the captain's shoulders. And he leaned back down, voice furious:

"Fucking *right*. You'd be the *first* thing everybody saw. Now tell me *why* you'd want to be the first thing everybody saw."

Darling did not get it for a moment. He made a What-on-earth-are-you-talking-about? face. But he was a good soldier, and smart.

The change that came over the younger man's face was remarkable. The muscles moved like flexed biceps. Cheeks rolling and stretching as the jaw opened. The inside of his speechless mouth showed pink, bright, and raw in the dark morning. His nostrils spread and his eyebrows tensed and closed. But the greatest change was in the eyes. They filled with shock . . . and, unmistakably, with the fear of one who has been taken by surprise.

"The bastard," Darling said finally, voice barely loud enough to be heard. "The goddamned sonofabitch."

Sieger nodded forcefully. "You got it. He *wants* to be seen. He's the guy they *don't* shoot. He's fucking set us up."

Just then the engine gunned and the helicopter nosed lower, swooping. The motion nearly threw Sieger off balance and he turned to see Haggerty, the ex-warrant officer, on the stick now, with the Bolivian pilot slacking off beside him. Then the aircraft jerked as if it had been hit by an enormous fist.

The fist was a wall of rain. It drenched the inside of the helicopter in seconds. As Sieger turned in desperation, he saw the door gunner cowering against the onslaught and the recruits huddling together as closely as their seat belts allowed. The airframe felt unstable, a carnival ride that teased the heart.

Clutching a ridge of steel to keep his feet, Sieger turned back to the cockpit. The rain had already soaked him from the waist down. Up front, the wipers jerked across the windscreen, but the world beyond had become invisible.

Haggerty, the old monsoon pilot, could see, though. He looked back at Sieger, only for an instant, and lifted one hand to communicate:

"Target in sight. We're going in."

Sieger stumbled forward, desperate to stop the action, to reverse time. But he slipped on the flooded metal floor and came down hard on his knees. Beyond the open bay doors and the torrent of rain, he could just make out the darkness of trees, their tips already above the rotors, as the helicopter came in fast.

Before Sieger could regain control of his life, the aircraft was settling on the ground.

"COME ON," SIEGER shouted against the noise of rotors and rain. He leapt into the downpour, pistol drawn, crouching, trying to get his bearings, to recall the layout from the overhead photographs. The rain had shocking force and weight, and Sieger felt it pounding him into the earth.

Vasquez was on the ground, too. Running. Away from his helicopter. Visible only because of his red shirt. Heading for a rank of dark buildings across the clearing.

Sieger turned, soaked through, and saw Luther Darling standing in the mud beside the chopper's bay door, streaming water off his shoulders and gesturing broadly at the recruits.

They did not want to get out of the aircraft.

The rotors slowed.

If it was a setup, Haggerty, the pilot, wasn't in on it. He was putting the engine to bed and throwing away his chance to escape.

Other things were thrown away, too. With time moving too swiftly to be managed, first one recruit, then another, threw his rifle out onto the earth, refusing to emerge from the imagined safety of the aircraft, frightened and unwilling to participate in gringo folly.

Sieger twisted his body again, shielding his eyes with his left hand. Vasquez was smaller, more distant, veiled by the storm.

Grabbing Darling by a sodden arm, Sieger screamed at him:

"Fuck them. Let's go. Stay on top of Vasquez."

But it was too late for that. Pops of light speckled the downpour, and the sharp noise of gunfire, a lot of gunfire, cut through the roar of the rain.

Sieger scooped up one of the rifles a boy had thrown down, ready to run for cover. But Darling stood upright and still, face raised as if to catch a scent. His splashed face had a startled look. As though he could not believe what was happening, could not understand it.

The firing came from multiple sides. Classic ambush. Presenting no good targets for the victims. The rain obscured the positions of the gunmen, welcome camouflage for killers.

Abruptly, Haggerty began to coax the chopper's engine, trying to reverse the slacking of the blades. But Sieger knew instinctively it was too late to get out that way. In confirmation, the chipping noise of rounds striking metal sounded close by and sparks flew above his head, just below the rotors. The door gunner struggled to free his weapon from its locked position. He had let the rain beat him out of doing his duty, and now he was paying for it.

With enough force to hurt, Sieger thrust the rifle across Darling's chest.

"Take it. Run. Get away from the helicopter."

Darling recoiled from the blow. But he grabbed the weapon, coming back to life. He crouched and began to run, mud sucking his boots. But he did not know where to go.

Sieger grabbed a second rifle from the edge of a puddle. Mud slimed the stock.

"Over there. Behind those mounds. *Move*, Luther."

Darling took off.

Before following him, Sieger grabbed one of the boys who was still strapped into his seat and frisked him until he felt a spare ammo clip in his pocket. Not caring if he broke the kid's leg, he yanked and tore until he had the good, hard metal in his hand. Terrified, the boy made no attempt to resist.

As Sieger's hand brushed away from the boy's knee, the recruit jolted as if he had been plugged into a socket. An instant later, wet of a different texture splashed Sieger's face as the kid's chest disintegrated like a broken egg.

Large-caliber round.

Sieger threw himself down into the mud, with more rounds striking metal just above him. Then the close, furious sound of an M-60 machine gun kicked in, chewing away at the invisible enemy. The door gunner had gotten down to work.

The result was only to draw more fire on the aircraft.

Across the field, the helicopter that had carried Vasquez exploded.

Using the blast as a distraction, Sieger rose and ran. Weighed down with mud, slopping through puddles, Sieger rushed, plodded and crawled away from the remaining aircraft as the wounded machine struggled to free itself from the earth. Sieger pictured the old ex-warrant gone desperate behind the controls, pulling pitch for the last time. He realized with a sick, cold clarity that the man could not be saved. Haggerty had made his choice. Each man looked for safety in what he knew.

The ambushers were no marksmen, but they had the range now. It sounded as though the aircraft had become the target for an entire battalion. Bullets on metal, like an orchestra of kids clanging knives and spoons on tin pots above the rhythm of the rain.

The nearby sound of the door-gunner's machine gun broke off, with Sieger running in slow motion as his feet sunk into the earth.

"*Over here*," a voice shouted, barely audible in the din of competing storms.

He saw Luther Darling, face dark, uniform rain-darkened, hands and rifle dark, sprawled behind a mound that could have been dirt or manure. As Sieger scrambled toward him, Darling fired to cover him. The captain had overcome his initial confusion and he stingily let off one round at a time, conserving the single clip of ammo in his weapon.

A spit of bullets threw mud into Sieger's face, into his eyes.

Terribly close.

At first, he thought someone had grabbed him by the ankle and tripped him. But, when he looked up from the ground, he was alone. The rain pounded his face, but he could just see the remaining helicopter climbing away from the ground, struggling, shivering. As Sieger watched, fireworks decorated its fuselage and the aircraft veered sharply to the side.

Sieger knew what was coming.

The tip of a rotor struck a tree. In an instant, the Huey canted sharply, and another rotor bit into the mud, cartwheeling the aircraft over and smashing the cockpit straight into the earth. The heat of the fireball seemed to dry the rain over Sieger's body and the air shrilled with flying scrap.

He twisted deeper into the mud, feeling the rush of air, the force of the blast, waiting in terror for the debris to strike him. But when there was no fresh pain, he rolled onto his belly, discovering a hurt that had been with him since he went down but that he had only vaguely perceived until now.

His leg. He twisted, looked down along his flank, stunned by the pain.

White bone gored the air. Blood spurted onto it, only to be washed away instantly by the rain.

"Fuck me," he said, realizing that he was going to die in this place. "Fuck me."

Then Luther Darling was beside him, saying:

"It's all right, man. It's okay."

But it was not all right. It would never be okay.

"Get the fuck back under cover. Get out of here."

Darling ignored him.

Helplessly, swarmed through by pain, Sieger screamed.

"Sorry, man," Darling said. "Sorry. Got to stop the bleeding."

Sieger felt a belt cinching around his leg, with Darling's hands driving it under him, through the mud.

Two doomed men squirming in the mud. Sieger saw it as clearly and definitely as a photograph in a magazine.

The air steamed with bullets. God only knew how many ambushers were out there. It sounded like thousands.

That was an illusion, of course. There would be a dozen, maybe two. Yes, a platoon's worth. They would have made sure the numbers were on their side.

"Oh, my God, my God," Sieger screamed. He could not help himself. The pain was irresistible.

Darling said nothing this time. He rose, and Sieger heard the younger man's deep breathing warm and gorgeously human against the roar of the rain.

Strong arms began lifting Sieger, and the pain, delayed only by a second, was so intense that he lost surface consciousness. Yet he could still see. In a way that was not healthy seeing:

The assaulting sky.

The sky falling to earth.

In bloody shreds.

This was what pain was like. Real pain. He did not think he could bear it. Then he went out truly, escaping into blackness.

When he awoke, the pain was enormous, but less. Almost bearable. He felt the slime of his body, of this place, this world. With the rain hitting his face so hard he could not understand why it did not tear the skin off. He was cold.

Cold in the jungle. His canteen had ridden up his back and its cap stabbed into a kidney. But he could not make up his mind to move.

Beside him, a rifle fired.

"I'm all right," Sieger said. The words came automatically. But he knew he was not all right. It was wishing.

He sensed another body moving closer, then he heard the associated sounds, and Luther Darling crowded alongside of him.

The firing was intermittent now. It had a bored sound.

"What's happening?" Sieger asked. "How long was I out? Where's my rifle?"

"Chill out, man," Darling said.

"How long was I out?"

"Five minutes. If that. You're going to be okay, sir."

"No."

"We're going to get out of here."

"No." Odd. Sieger listened to his own voice. There was no complaint in it. Just fact. Curious. He did not feel afraid at the moment. But the pain was mean. Shocking.

"Listen," Darling said. "I need you to do something for me. I need you to help out, sir. Can you help?"

"Yes," Sieger said. The pain was so vast. As vast as

the sunrise had been. And as impossible to grasp.

Darling panted. From exhaustion. Or fear. "All I want you to do is watch over that way." The younger man pointed across Sieger's chest. "Can you turn yourself just enough to watch our flank?"

"Yes," Sieger said. But he did not know if it was an honest answer.

"I'll cover the front and the right. You watch the left. It's jungle over there. Yell if you see any movement."

Darling sounded decisive. On the surface. But Sieger could hear the fear, too. And he was ashamed of himself. It was his fault that they were both here. Had he been a braver man, had he been willing to say fuck it to his career and do the right thing, they both would have lived. And Haggerty. And the Bolivian children in uniform. He sensed that he should feel even sorrier for them, but could not. The demarcation line for his emotions pretty much ended beyond himself and Darling.

A rip of bullets chewed into the low earthen barrier behind which they lay temporarily protected. The enemy knew exactly where they were. That made it only a matter of time.

Life was just a matter of time. And he had wasted so much of it.

"Give me a rifle," Sieger said. "You bring in my rifle?"

Instead of answering, Darling rolled farther away. To an angle from which he could return fire.

"No more ammo," the captain half shouted. "Last clip."

For a moment, Sieger felt triumphant. He had had the presence of mind to scarf up the extra clip from the recruit. He patted down his sodden uniform, finding his arms and hands intact and useful. But he did not find the clip. And then he remembered holding it in one hand as he ran. It was gone, lost, somewhere out there in the mud.

He felt for his pistol, brushing his hand over the

smaller holster that held the compass on his belt until the fingers reached the bigger, harder appendage. Yes. The pistol, at least. It had a good solid feel. Take out one or two of them if they got in close. He tugged the Velcro flap of the holster and began drawing the weapon when a particular motion electrified him with pain.

He shouted syllables without the integrity of words, and the sky poured into his open, gasping mouth.

He closed his eyes tightly and forced himself to continue. The pain made him want to release his bowels. It was immeasurable, endless, endless.

By the time he had freed the pistol, he felt as though he had run a long, hard race.

Exhausted.

Lungs on fire.

He held the weapon above his chest and primed it, fingers slipping and pinching. Then, unable to bring himself to look down at the wreckage of his leg, he rolled onto his side. He felt the awful, awkward shiftings along his lower body and worried briefly about infection from the mud before he regained his perspective. Infection was the least of his worries.

He peered at the jungle drooping behind the shifting walls of rain. It was within grenade range. But he had no grenades.

Maybe the men who were trying to kill him would have grenades.

The men who would kill him.

The men who already had killed him.

Why? What for?

Suddenly, the firing reerupted with the intensity of the initial attack. The steady thunder of the rain and the pocking and sizzle of the firearms seemed oddly mismatched, totally out of sequence with one another.

Sieger clutched the pistol dearly. What were they firing at?

Was it a rescue party? Maybe the whole thing had

been set up to be an ambush of an ambush?

No.

No. It didn't work that way.

Impacting rounds splashed mud from the top of the low parapet down onto his face.

A rifle sounded close by.

The captain. Darling. He was not alone. But Sieger could not bear to turn and look to confirm the continued presence of the other human being, could not face the pain of any more movement. The shot could have come from an enemy.

No. Bullshit. It was Darling. Had to be. The shot had been very close.

Then Sieger heard a new voice, crying out, in English: "Help me. Jesus, help me."

He knew the voice. But he could not place it.

"Help me, oh, Jesus."

The voice called endlessly. Pleading.

Darling rolled over beside him again.

"Sir? You okay."

No. Never again. Not okay.

"Yeah. What?"

"Just hang on. I'll be back."

Panic swept over Sieger and his courage disintegrated. He did not want to be left alone, to die alone. He realized immediately that the younger man had decided to run for it.

"I'm okay," Sieger said, his voice a broken thing. Like his leg. "Go. Just go."

"You're bleeding again. Belt must've come loose. When you moved. Hold on."

Darling yanked the belt tight, unleashing another nova of pain. Sieger cursed everything, tears searing his eyes.

Somewhere beyond their tiny barricade, the English-speaker cried out for Jesus and help, over and over again, piercing the barrage of rain.

Darling cinched the belt again, as they all learned to

do at the beginning of their military careers. The Army field belt had been designed to shut down veins and arteries.

A tourniquet done that tightly that high on the leg meant you would loose the limb if you didn't get prompt attention.

So it really was that bad. Darling had written off the leg. What fucking right did he have to do that?

All the right in the world.

"If we get through this . . . thank you. . . ."

"Save it, man. Just watch the trees for me."

"That was the kind of stuff . . ."

"Save it. Got to go."

And the younger man launched himself.

Should've said good-bye, Sieger thought. I would have liked someone to tell me good-bye.

He could not even hear the captain now. The huge sound of the rain swallowed everything. Perhaps he would drown in the mud. Before they closed in. His eyes ached. His eyelids had taken a pounding. And the rain would not quit. It was heavy, each drop metallic. Couldn't see much. Clutching his pistol, waiting for the end, Sieger thought:

This is what it feels like to be alone. Truly alone.

The firing picked up again. An epidemic of bullets.

Yeah. Probably saw Darling running for it. Still. It was the sensible thing to do. Nothing said you were obliged to stay and throw your life away.

For nothing.

Sieger heard an animal howl. A scream blended with a shout of fury. A war cry. From the most primitive place in the human soul.

He caught movement to the flank, the wrong flank. Something big.

Sieger twisted about, ready to shoot, determined to go out fighting, shooting, killing, hating.

He saw something towering and enormous. Falling toward him. A massive thing, purple as wine.

With a final roar of rage, Darling tumbled to earth with the thing he bore across his shoulders.

It was Henry Vasquez.

The rage in Sieger was far greater than the pain now. He tortured himself around until he faced the sack of human shit. In a red shirt soaked dark and stained. The agent was such a mess of blood and rain and mud it was impossible to count how many times he had been shot.

You bastard, Sieger thought. You *bas*tard.

Vasquez's eyes stared heavenward, blinking quickly at the torrent of rain.

"Jesus," he whispered. "Jesus . . . *Je*sus . . ."

Sieger shoved his pistol toward the man, wanting to jam the muzzle against the agent's temple, so Vasquez could feel it before he fired.

A stronger hand caught Sieger's wrist.

"Kill the fucker," Sieger said, although he did not know if his voice was audible any longer.

The firm hand on his wrist did not incite any further rage. On the contrary, the simple human touch seemed like a blessing. It was wonderful to feel another living human being's hand.

"We'll all be dead soon enough," Darling said. "Save the bullet."

"Sonofabitch," Sieger said. But it was more of a lament now.

Vasquez began to say the rosary, counting invisible beads. As he spoke, a thin snake of blood left the corner of his mouth only to be diluted to nothingness by the rain before it reached his jaw.

Despite the pain, Sieger dragged himself closer. Until he could sense the rank mortality of the man. Vasquez was unshaven, and at the back of his jaw, small red pimples clustered at the base of the black hairs. His skin, shining with rain, was veinous and ruined up close, and his nose was filthed. Examined too closely, at the wrong time, a man was a loathesome thing.

The firing slackened again, but it remained heavy

enough to keep their heads down, to hold them in place until somebody got around to maneuvering to take them from behind. Sieger tugged his already-dead leg behind him, tasting vomit at the back of his throat, closing on the agent in a rage that masked his own pain.

"Don't shoot him," Darling said. "It isn't right."

But Sieger was not going to shoot him. Not now. Not yet. Maybe never. He just had to know one thing. With his face close to the terrified face of the agent, Sieger asked, shouted:

"*Why?* For God's sake, *why*, you sonofabitch? *Why?*"

"Hail Mary, full of grace . . ."

With his free hand, Sieger grasped the red rag of a shirt, gathering the slimed fabric in his fist.

"You tell me *why*, you bastard."

Suddenly, Vasquez seemed to wake to the reality of the moment. Or perhaps to a parallel reality.

"Fucked me," he said in amazement. "The bastard fucked me."

"*Why?*"

"He fucked me."

"*Why'd you do it, Henry?*"

"He—"

"*Tell me why you did it.*" Sieger was crying without realizing it. "Before you die, you goddamned mother-fucker. Before I kill you."

"Too late now."

"Fucking right, it's too late."

But Darling came in close, restraining him again. Sieger imagined he had left his body. It was the second time that had happened to him. He could see the three of them lying there in the muck. With bullets sticking the air and the rain and all of nature's misery on display. He saw then that Darling, too, had been hit. The captain's cheek had been torn open as if a knife had slashed him. Pale meat showed under watered blood. All one, under the skin.

"Henry," Darling said, in a voice that was almost rational. "What do you mean? Too late for what?"

"Kill them all," Vasquez said. Then he wrenched himself up out of the mud a few inches. "Can't save them," he declared. He thumped back down into the mire, head sinking.

"Can't save who?" Darling insisted. "What's going to happen, Henry?"

The agent did not respond.

Darling brought his torn face in close and three breaths intermingled under the pounding rain. "You fucked us, Henry. You killed us. You owe us an answer."

"Jesus. Oh, Jesus, it hurts."

"Why is it too late? Who can't we save?"

Whenever he spoke, a flap of flesh jiggled on Darling's cheek. It looked like undercooked pork. Sieger noticed, belatedly, that the bottom half of the captain's ear had been shot away, as well.

Suddenly, Darling grabbed the agent by the hair. "Goddamn it, Henry. What's too late? Who's going to be killed?"

"Forgive me, Father, for I have sinned . . ."

"What's going on, you fuck?"

It looked as though a living creature had popped out of Vasquez's mouth. But it was only a clot, a pulp, of blood and waste. The agent bucked once, spewed into the sky, and struck Darling's face with crimson puke. Then he settled down and his eyes did not blink when the raindrops struck them.

"Shit," Darling said.

Sieger, inching closer, in ferocious pain, reached out a hand, reaching across the new corpse. It was his turn to make a human gesture. Shaking with the effort, he located Darling's elbow and traced down along the drenched forearm until he had taken the other man's hand in his own.

"It's all right," Sieger said, trying to make his voice

strong, to speak clearly through the downpour and the constant pain. The way a real soldier might. "I know what he's talking about."

It was a day of revelations, each one clearer than the last. He had entered a dreadful world. And he would not leave it alive.

Perfunctory bullets, pinning fire, sang overhead. Behind their last barricade, Darling raised his head until he and Sieger were looking directly into one another's eyes, blinking miserably under the beating rain. Each man gripped the other's hand fiercely.

"It's the clinic," Sieger said. "The soldiers. That's who they're going to kill. First us, then them. Kill the gringos. Lot of gringos."

Darling did not get it. "Why? Why, for God's—"

"Because somebody *wants* dead gringos. That's why Vasquez had us clustered on the same aircraft as that poor bugger pilot. The game is to take out gringos. Somebody wants to piss off Uncle Sam."

Spritzing rain like a dog, Darling shook his head. Not in disbelief. He just did not get it yet. A bullet hissed through the rain.

"But *why*?"

"Turf battle. Somebody wants the U.S. of A. to do their dirty work for them. One druglord against another. We're just the cost of doing business, Luther." He looked at the dead agent. "And that shitbird picked the wrong side."

The firing slackened further. Sieger tightened his grip on the younger man's hand, to the extent a further tightening was possible.

"The first raid," Sieger said, feeling his strength going and the pain beginning to overwhelm him. "You weren't there. It was a joke. Phony from jump street. I knew it was all wrong. But I couldn't get a grip on it. Couldn't . . ."

"The clinic," Darling said, as though the thought had

just penetrated him. "The CINC was coming in. On the evac flight."

"They're going to hit it, Luther. As soon as they're done with us."

The captain began shaking his head. With his ruined cheek. It was all too big. Sieger was afraid he was losing him. And everything depended on the younger man now.

"Luther. *Lis*ten to me. You've got to try to get word to them."

Darling shook his head in disbelief. Or surrender.

"You've *got* to do it, Luther. You've got to try."

"I can't . . . leave you here." The captain spoke slowly and flatly, a computer voice.

Sieger made a face. "That's bullshit. *Bull*shit. You stay, and all that means is you die, too. And so does everybody at the clinic." He looked hard at the younger man. Who, at a minimum, would take a variety of scars with him through life. "I'm fucking dead already. So what do you want on your conscience, Captain? The lives of everybody back at that clinic?"

"I can't just leave you, man."

More bullets hunted them. Rounds *thocked* into a hump of dirt just behind where they lay, splashing wet brown. It was the first time any rounds had struck at that angle. The narcos were very close.

"Moving up on the sides," Sieger said. "Fuck around and it'll be too late. You've got to go *now*."

Darling shook his head again, but less decisively this time.

"I don't even know where I am. I wouldn't know where to go."

Sieger lifted himself off his belly, waiting for a wave of pain that failed to come this time. He did not know if that was a good sign or a bad one.

Not that it mattered much.

Twisting himself so he could use both hands, he laid down his pistol and unlashed the compass from his belt. It was covered with mud.

"We came in from the southeast. We followed a road, a straight one, up from Mendoza. Then we veered left. If you just set an azimuth due northeast and stay on it, you'll hit the road. The dumbest lieutenant in the U.S. Army could do it." He looked at the younger man, hoping for a sign of spirit. But Darling's face remained still, ripped, dead except for the eyes. "Then . . . God knows. Steal a car, a truck. Whatever it takes."

"How far is it? To the road?"

Another spackle of bullets hunted the earth behind their position.

"Christ . . . I don't know. Five miles?"

There was a throbbing in his groin now. Like heat pumped through his lower organs. What would that be?

The younger man looked at him with sudden earnestness. But it was all defense, no offense. The rain splashed off the captain's face, running down both sides of his nose, mixing with blood in the depths of his torn cheek.

"Sir?"

"What?"

"I'm . . . afraid of the jungle . . . I—"

"Luther. For God's *sake*. Would you rather die here? Do you want everybody else to die?"

"I can't help it."

"Act like a fucking *soldier*."

"I . . . just don't know if I can."

The rain's fury increased. Unbelievable that the intensity could grow beyond what they had already endured.

"*Take the compass*. Take your pistol. And *go*. That's an order. You're a fucking soldier, and it's an order. Get out of here."

A shout in Spanish was distinctly audible. Despite the rain and the gunfire.

They were closing in.

"Luther . . . you've got to go. Wait any longer and you won't even make it to the trees."

The captain shook his head. A fine, earnest young

man. Afraid. So close to death. It was nothing to be ashamed of. Fifteen minutes before, Darling had been the bravest of men. Courage came and went.

Sieger truly did not want the younger man to die. For nothing.

"Sir . . . I can't leave you."

"I gave you a direct order."

"I—"

Sieger shouted. "*Listen* to me, goddamn it. *List*en. All my life I wanted to be a soldier. I even thought I was one. But I didn't know shit about what soldiering really means. And now I do. And I'm going to be a good soldier this one time in my life. And so are you, by God. Now get *out* of here." He looked at the younger man. "Later on . . . you can come back with Parnell and count the bodies. I intend to take a bunch of these fuckers with me. Now *go*."

There are times when you can see a decision happen in a man. Sieger saw it in Captain Luther Darling. His heart changed. It was visible, tangible. As real as life and death.

The younger man reached out and quickly grasped Sieger's closest hand, managing to hurt his distant, dying leg in the process.

"You're a great fucking soldier, sir."

Sieger tried to smile, but he was having difficulty with his facial muscles now. Still, his hands worked. The truth was that he was terrified, afraid of dying, afraid of what could happen before he died. But he could not let the younger man see it. He squeezed Darling's fingers then released them.

"These bozos are going to find out just how great."

Clutching his pistol, Luther Darling disappeared into the rain. A slightly delayed eruption of gunfire chased him, but, as nearly as Sieger could tell, his last friend made it safely into the trees.

Sieger was crying now. In raw fear. He did not want to die. The reality of the world struck him again and again, followed by tides of nausea. He had expected a better end, and a much-delayed one. In his dreams, he had always been the one to survive the trial, perhaps with a picturesque wound. Now it was here and real. A broken leg in the mud under a downpour. Surrounded by unworthy opponents. His death would not even win a battle. It all seemed such a terrible waste.

But Sieger was angry, too, with his last reserves of emotions all coming on at once, challenging one another, finally canceling each other out. He was hatefully angry, and he was ready to fight. With the rain slapping him into the mud and the foreign voices very near.

Suffering timelessly, he turned to the business of being a soldier.

19

DREW MACCAULEY WOKE early and pulled on a veteran flannel robe of which he was endlessly fond. Since there were guests in the house for the weekend, he shaved before going downstairs and brushed back his thinning hair. He disarmed the alarm system and brought in the *Washington Post*. The morning, a sharp early-October Saturday morning with the neighborhood still abed, had great promise. The weather would be fine, and he and his wife and an old friend from his news magazine days and the friend's far-smarter wife would drive in to Capitol Hill for breakfast at Eastern Market.

They would stand in line democratically in the food-scented air outside the market, an occasional practice that filled MacCauley with a buttery knowledge of his own superiority, and when they finally reached the Market Lunch counter inside the hall, he would order a stack of blues and a side order of scrapple from the black woman behind the register. After breakfast and a walk under the coloring leaves, his wife would drop him at his office for a few hours.

He had to fly to Geneva on Tuesday and he needed to do a couple of hours' work on a few little problems the Russian foreign minister had been unable to spike about Karabakh and the Partnership For Peace and pipelines and that sort of thing. One distraction after another. Some of the issues would have to be addressed at the

Rump Group session on Monday, and MacCauley wanted to be certain that he had the agenda stacked in favor of his policies. The DJ-5 was being especially obstinate on the partnership thing, and overall, none of the agencies in town could see the big picture. No one seemed to understand Russia but him. They simply didn't get it, didn't grasp that the Russians only did what seemed to be bad things out of absolute necessity, out of a historical imperative. You had to avoid making every little breach of manners an international crisis. The Russians were wonderful people, really, gifted, and in many ways far more attractive than the ignorant slovens of the American electorate. And Moscow needed help. The president understood that. Most of the time. But the others had no sense of the sweeping waves of history, no integrative understanding of the world. And the less said about the secretary, the better. With his corporate lawyer's mind and his little rat face.

But all that was for later. MacCauley went into the kitchen, ground a generous load of the coffee beans he had mailed in from Sweden, and snapped the rubber band off the newspaper. He separated the front section and turned immediately to the editorial page. And there it stood, right at the top. Cadge, God bless his alcoholic buns, had come through.

With the brilliant brown coffee smell rising, Mac-Cauley read. "Symptom of crisis." Good lead. Yes. Military out of control. Subverting the collective efforts of State and DEA and all of the other good little agencies. Why was the U.S. Army involved with the relatives of reputed drug lords? Why had U.S. taxpayers been funding the construction of a clinic in a town that already had one and where the resident physician was the daughter of one of the richest men in Bolivia? A following hint that the military might be subverting poor old Ethan's plan to eradicate coca in order to shield local generals who were in bed with the narcos was magnificently done. And when Cadge got to the colonel,

Church, he made him sound like Oliver North, only dirtier. The editorial wrapped with a suggestion that General Parnell, the CINC, was out of control down in the Andean Ridge, killing his own soldiers, by accident or design. Any discriminating reader would come away with the conviction that the war on drugs was not being won only because the U.S. military was subverting victory.

Oh, it was a bit heavy-handed. Certainly not going to win any prizes for journalistic excellence. But the military had to be brought back under control, and given the greater good achieved, a few blurred facts here and there were fully justified. MacCauley would not have written the piece just that way himself, of course. He prided himself on his style. But Cadge had done all right.

MacCauley stood up, took down his Renaissance Weekend souvenir mug, and poured his first cup of coffee. He had just taken the first searing sip when he heard footsteps on the stairs, too heavy to be his wife's.

It was Joel Rosen, his old friend, whom MacCauley had hoped would sleep another hour. Joel was, in fact, not terribly pleasant to be around, only necessary, and MacCauley valued his morning time alone. Now he would have to listen to more shit about Israel. Joel was losing all of his objectivity.

OCTAVIO KNEW THE trail and the landscape as well as he knew anything in his life and he had never seen such a disturbance here. The great black birds circled and called above the ruins as though a great feast waited down below, far more of them than attended the usual animal's death.

Descending the hillside, his llamas trotted, focused by two dogs. His younger brother threatened the trailing animals with a stick. In the distance, the mountains shone white and gray and Lake Titicaca drank the morning sun and glittered. The clear, dry air chilled the skin even as the sun warmed his back, and everything would have been fine and right except for the birds.

The ruins that had drawn the birds sat in a bowl. Octavio knew the story of the place. Devils had made the springs run dry. The trail the herders used skirted the decaying walls now, although a rough track that led deeper into the mountains occasionally showed the mark of a vehicle. Octavio was not afraid of the place by daylight, since he was strong and could read somewhat and he wore a very powerful charm concocted by his mother. But he would not have gone into the ruins at night. Even now, those birds could be the souls of demons, although they would remain imprisoned in their feathers until twilight in punishment for their evil deeds.

The sounds and smells of the approaching herd started a pack of wild dogs running. The dogs had been keeping the birds off the carrion, feasting first, and half a dozen of them bolted from their hiding place behind a roofless building, stretching out and yapping as they headed up the valley and away from man. Valiant, Octavio's lead herd dog, sprang after them, barking a belated warning. Octavio began to call him back, but his curiosity got the best of him. Hollering to his brother to keep the llamas on the trail, he cut down across the rocks and sparse grass, helping his footing with the long stick that was almost a natural extension of his body.

The herd dog went quiet as it disappeared into the ruins. Then, as Octavio approached the broken walls of the outbuilding, the dog skulked back into view, whining. It took up a position halfway to its master, tongue dangling, watching him, intent that he follow. Overhead, the birds complained, lowered, and climbed again.

Octavio expected to find a dead cow or llama. Itinerants rustled livestock at night, sometimes to sell, but usually to kill and eat. What they could not devour, or carve and carry, they abandoned. But Octavio did not get the heavy scents of slaughter or deadened campfires.

He saw the woman's body before he smelled her death. She lay to the side of what had been the settlement's central plaza back when his aunts and uncles had lived here, a time before his birth but alive in his family's told history. Although much of the corpse had been eaten or ravaged by the dogs, the city clothing, bloody and ragged, and the impractical shoe that remained by a gnawed foot, made the body female and white, as did its slightness and the shape of one leg that remained largely intact. Her face and torso had been chewed over, but the hair, clotted and stained, still had the look of a La Paz woman. Octavio stared at this death from a respectful distance, more fascinated than afraid, and without special pity. He was a country boy and he had seen a great deal of birth and death. And a woman such as this had no place, no reality, in the constellation of his life.

Realizing that his brother and the herd had already crested the far hill, he turned away. When his dog did not follow, he turned and found it nosing at the corpse. That angered Octavio and he shouted harshly at the animal, which responded with the quickness of deeply ingrained fear. After that, boy and dog walked quickly away, leaving the woman for the cawing birds.

He considered whether or not he should report his find, fearing implication. Awe and suspicion of the whites who lived in the city and drove out to eat fish on the shores of the lake had been with his people for centuries, and it was a sensible fear, similar to the fear his dog felt toward him. Still, Octavio was clever and he possessed the self-knowledge to see that he would not be able to keep such a thing secret. It demanded telling; it lived on the lips.

He decided that, initially, he would tell only his mother. She was the member of the family who went into the city to sell to the whites and she knew them best. And she was wise. Her knowledge of magic and charms was respected in all of the surrounding villages. She would know what to do.

Still trailing the family herd, he paused to look back

at the ruins. The dead woman lay out of sight again, but the settling, sparring birds marked her position clearly.

AMBASSADOR ETHAN RICE Plymouth sat at his desk in a rage that ached for an accessible target. Anne was a slut. An absolute slut. His mother had warned him against marrying an only child, but he had been too pigheaded to listen. And now this.

He had called on the station chief, a discreet man, to check the outgoing flight manifests. And Anne, the lying bitch, had not boarded any of them. She was just off whoring around with some sleazeball. In *his* country. The possibilities for humiliation were grave. Latins took that sort of thing seriously. It was just about the *only* thing they took seriously. If they found out that his wife was sleeping with some other member of the diplomatic community, or—God forbid—with a Bolivian, he, Ethan Rice Plymouth, would be a laughingstock. It was absolutely unacceptable behavior. And Anne knew it.

She had never been a good diplomat's wife, really. He saw that now. Too selfish. Self-absorbed. Unwilling to be the woman behind the man. When any other woman of her station would have been grateful. Thrilled. Amazed at her good fortune. Wife of an ambassador. Of a man with a splendid career that still had a long way to go. What Anne had done to him was unthinkable.

He wondered if she had given herself to any other affairs before this one, if he had not been the butt of secret jokes for years.

He hated. Her. His wife. Hated.

And that spick sonofabitch Vasquez. The DEA man had not called in the status of the lab raid on schedule. They were all lazy buggers, in the end, and could not be trusted. He had really believed Henry to be an exception. But it was already past noon and Plymouth had not heard a word. Vasquez was supposed to call in a message on relay if the satellite phone failed to connect.

An ambassador had to keep his finger on the pulse of an operation like this. Especially with the Bolivians becoming obstructionist—damn them, they were going to learn to dance to his tune and like it—and with that slick bastard Parnell worming his way into the country through the back door. On and off across the morning, Plymouth had been trying to think of a way to simply close down the U.S. Military Mission to La Paz in its entirety. Boot out the attaché, too. All of them. Gone.

The DCM called him on the intercom. He wanted to talk about the medical team coming in from Atlanta. One Bolivian ministry welcomed them, another was screaming about an infringement of nationalism. But Plymouth was in no mood for trivialities. He told the man he was busy.

It was a terrible mess. And, of course, Anne had planned it to fall on a Saturday, when nobody in Bolivia came to work. Well, he had damned well made sure that his embassy staff came to work on this particular Saturday. With a major counterdrug operation going down. Anyway, it was time to institute a regular Saturday work schedule. He had noticed all of them slacking off, even the station chief. It was time to get the embassy moving again, to come down like a ton of bricks on the Bols on the eradication issue. If they didn't get off their unwashed butts and start a serious eradication program down in the Chaparé, he was determined to decertify them. See how they liked that. When the money stopped flowing.

They were all corrupt, of course. Except for the rare European like von Reinsee. Corrupt and lazy. And that was the key to beating them. You worked Saturdays. You didn't take three- or four-hour lunches. That was why their sorry excuse for a civilization never got off the ground.

Plymouth shook his head, pushing back from his desk and looking out through his tinted, bulletproof windows.

The exteriors desperately needed washing. He had only a blurred view of the city beyond.

Anne, Anne. How could she do such a thing? He thought of her suddenly, unreasonably, on Mykonos, in her white two-piece bathing suit. They had been such a grand team in those days, the envy of all.

If she really had taken up with a local, he was going to hammer her, he decided. He did not know what he meant by that and, in fact, Anne held almost all of the cards. But it satisfied him to think it. Hammer her. Hammer the bitch.

His wife. His Anne. After all he had done for her, given her. An irresponsible, selfish slut.

And why in the hell didn't Vasquez call? Had the military types pulled some sort of stunt, hampering his operation? Everything *had* to happen as planned. The cable was already drafted, ready for release after a few verifying details had been typed in. It could be on Drew's desk Monday morning. And Drew would make sure it was one of the cables that actually made it to the Secretary.

God, how was he going to break the news to Drew about Anne?

She had embarrassed him profoundly, and he saw now that the repercussions would go on for a long time. But she was not going to damage his career. He would not stand for that. He'd hammer her if she so much as tried.

Plymouth sat at his desk, savoring his hatred for his wife and picking his nose until blood snaked down his fingers.

ANGEL TOOK AN instant dislike to Panama and the Panamanians. The room he had been given was filthy, without plumbing, and the lock on the door was not to be trusted. The ocean, a too-big, unsettling thing, was only a short walk away, but you could not smell it for the stink of people. His room was one of many in a four-

story tenement block populated mostly by blacks and
still scarred from the gringo invasion years before. He
had grown up combing refuse heaps and did not consider
himself a finicky person, but these Panamanians made
no effort to be clean. And to him, a proud highland
Colombian, blacks were on a par with jungle Indians.
His accommodations insulted him. And the food troubled his stomach, making the night cramps worse. The
human sounds that came to him were incredible and
foul.

The only good thing about his room was its proximity
to the U.S. military installation. First thing in the morning, he had walked part of the way up the hillside with
the big flag. Initially, he had a nameless guide who discreetly pointed out the entrances to the military hospital.
It was a clean location, good for a hit. The building
perched on the slope well below the security perimeter
of the American headquarters. Fitted to a bend in the
road, its facade lay beyond the line of sight of the gate
guards. On his own, Angel scouted the facility and the
approaches in detail, one more smiling Latin boy among
the throngs who haunted the bus stops and nearby park,
gauging the best firing angles and the swiftest routes of
escape.

His still-anonymous employers impressed him, although he refused to show it. The American he was to
kill, a man named Church, had not even arrived in Panama. But he was coming. Soon. Angel had arrived first,
because his people were the cleverest. He was gaining
more and more confidence in his employers, and he increasingly allowed himself to imagine a future of power,
wealth, and respect working for them.

The American was sick and might die. But if he lived,
Angel would be waiting for him. As he waited now, on
a clouding Saturday afternoon, with the air hot glue and
the rain getting ready to rush down out of the sky again.
He watched patiently for the ambulance that would bring
the sick colonel to the hospital sometime that day.

Frankly, Angel hoped the man would live. He very much wanted the opportunity to carry out such a complex mission, to prove his worth to the big men. It would be a waste if the gringo died of a sickness.

20

LUTHER DARLING STOOD, terrified, with the pistol in his right hand and the compass open in the trembling fingers of his left hand. He struggled to calm himself long enough to shoot a good azimuth. It did not have to be exact. But it had to take him toward the road and away from the narcos.

The rain tried to slap the instrument from his hand. The storm was less powerful here in the bush than it had been out in the clearing, but it still had the density and force of the summer storms that had grounded all aircraft back when he had served in an aviation battalion in Texas. Fat raindrops punched down through the imperfect cover of the trees or mashed big, thirsty leaves together, gathering into rivulets along sunken green spines, the water concentrating before it plunged into space again. The forest floor swamped under hundreds of thousands of miniature waterfalls. Still, here, in this partial shelter, a man could stand without feeling as if the downpour had the force to knock him to his knees.

Raindrops struck and smeared the lens of the compass and found their way into his eyes, making him blink until he could hardly see. He bent lower, closer, trying to set the metal ring, holding his body and the tool as steadily as he could manage.

The forest into which fate had driven him was not true jungle, only overgrown bush, but it was all the same to Darling. He imagined it as teeming with loathesome, malevolent animals and noxious plants capable of clutching him. The jungle, or anything remotely similar, was a nightmare to him. He was not by nature a timid soul, but the idea of jungle had always held an unreasonable horror for him, as if he had been born into the fear, and the experience of bushwhacking out of a crash site with Church earlier in the year had only worsened his reaction to such places.

Running, sick with fear and guilt, from the muddy living grave where he had abandoned Sieger, Darling's world had been a blur of panic. He had not known if the gunmen had seen him, could not tell if they were shooting at him. All he registered was the rain and the grasping mud trying to pull off his boots and trip him, and then he crashed into the undergrowth, where thorns and barbs slicked with rainwater tore at his uniform and his flesh as he ran, stumbled, fell, rose, and ran. Vines hung like snares, swaying in the rain, reaching out to snap an arm or leg. There was no path, only breaks here and there between tree trunks. He ran into the darkness of vegetation and rain, shocked to hyperlife by an inhuman terror that made his essential decisions for him, running until he suddenly decided he had come far enough to be safe for a moment and realizing that, if he didn't take a compass bearing, he was in danger of losing direction and ending up back where he had begun.

Its glass cover beaten by the rain, the compass needle would not settle. But he judged that he had been running due north. Had to correct that immediately. To reach the road.

He could not, did not, think about saving the others now. The clinic, to the extent it existed for him, was abstract, a fact relevant only in another universe. The threat of death and his fear of his surroundings struck him like a nervous disease, exaggerating his actions, making too much motion inevitable, while reducing the effectiveness of that motion. He tried one last time to set the ring on the compass.

A snake dropped in front of his face.

He almost fell over backward, then backed into a tree that made him leap forward again. Toward the swaying snake.

It wasn't a snake. Only another vine. Pried loose by the storm.

He gasped for breath, shivering, terribly cold without realizing it. Thistles and poisonous leaves made his limbs and hands burn, and the wet clutch of his uniform felt as though parasites had gotten to his skin. He lifted the compass again, using the hand that held the pistol to help steady it, wanting to be certain. Starting all over again. Fighting just to hold still.

And holding still was the most fortunate thing he had ever done in his life, because it let him see the gunmen before they saw him.

Dark shapes caught his attention. Moving. Moving trees. Or tall animals. The rain so reduced visibility that they had approached to within the length of a rotor blade before their motion tugged his eyes up from the compass.

Two men, moving close to one another as if they feared separation. Not native to this place any more than he was. They held short geometric weapons out in front of them and their path headed across his own at the angle of a half-closed scissors. Later, thinking back, replaying the action, with its discontinuous shreds of reality, Darling would realize that the gunmen were lost, that they had been trying to find a route to get in behind him and Sieger when the bush had sucked them in. He would think, too, that he had been fortunate to serve in a military that wore a dark camouflage pattern, and blessed by the rain that had darkened the fabric further, and touched by a miracle in being born black, or at least a soft brown, when the paler faces of his enemies showed foreign and out of place in the sliver of the world where they had come to die. He thought of all those things later, fighting his way through his jungle and grunting with pain as he drew knife-long thorns from his thigh or forearm. But in this instant of seeing, of pure, true seeing, he only saw and thought—or felt— the most essential things.

One of the narcos shook his head and cursed. Then he spotted Darling.

Too late.

At last, Darling faced a situation for which he had been trained. Far better trained than his enemies. He raised his pistol crisply and surely. He shot the man with the surprised face in the chest, then quickly shifted his aim. The second man tried to bolt and Darling's next shot struck him at the top of the arm. It spun the man around and Darling fired again, hitting him in the throat and making his neck snap. One of the narcos fired wildly, perhaps only a finger twitching on a trigger, but Darling flopped into the mud, clutching the precious compass as tightly as he held his pistol.

He heard coughing and moaning through the rain but saw or heard little motion. Nerves speeding, Darling rose, plunged forward, and fired repeatedly into the bodies at his feet. In seconds, they became the stillest objects in the world, with the rain erasing their blood as soon as it left their wounds.

Looking around, alert that there could be other gunmen, Darling stuffed the compass into a trouser pocket and grasped the nearest automatic weapon, a snug black machine all right angles. It was cold and slick with rain. It had not been the weapon that fired. The second corpse had discarded an identical weapon and Darling shoved his pistol clumsily into its holster, then took up the second weapon just long enough to eject its partially expended magazine, test its weight, and slip the mag into his pocket. He slung his new weapon around his neck, drew out the compass again, and scraped the mud from its lens, taking a very quick azimuth this time.

Changed by killing, Luther Darling pushed his way fervently through the undergrowth.

IN THE END there was only rage. After he had been shot again, this time by a bullet that struck and spun and tore a fistful of meat out of his ass cheek, Sieger's last fear went and the anger that remained had none of the bar fighter's stupidity. It was an empowering fury, something primitive and far beyond words, that heated his soul as it iced his nerves. An animal confidence returned to him and he almost felt as though he could fight his way out after all, operating purely on the strength of the hatred he felt for enemies whose faces he had never seen. He let them squander their ammunition, and when their firing slackened, he sent one stingy round toward them. To provoke them again. To keep them focused. To buy time for Darling.

He had to let them come to him, since he could not maneuver. All he could do was to scrape his body from side to side in the mud, as though he had fallen backward through time to a preman life form fighting for survival and that alone. He shoved Vasquez's carcass, rolling it, until the dead bulk with its sweat of rain shielded one of his flanks from grazing fire. Let the bastard serve some purpose.

As the narcos closed in, a voice shouted in punk English:

"Hey, you fuckers. You fuckers wanna die? Don't shoot no more."

Then the jabbering in Spanish picked up again, voices close enough for Sieger to distinguish each opaque syllable through the rain. They were on both of his flanks now, as well as to his front. But he still heard nothing, saw nothing behind him when he twisted his broken body to look. They had not completed the encirclement. That puzzled him. They couldn't be that stupid.

He did what the English-speaker wanted. He did not

shoot. Until, finally, a human shape rushed through the rain toward him.

Controlling his breathing, Sieger waited as long as he could, delaying until the man spotted him down in the mud and paused for a fateful second. Sieger put a round into the man's abdomen. The man clutched himself as though suffering a vicious cramp and dropped to his knees. Swaying and squeezing himself, shocked by what had happened to his body.

Sieger let him suffer. Saving the last bullets.

A hurricane of firing punched the mud and the nearest trees, sizzling through the rain. One of the stray rounds caught the man who knelt holding his belly and he fell face forward into the mud.

Sieger knew they would try to rush him. They had to. If he was right about the clinic. They would have to get on with it.

He wondered, briefly, if Darling had gotten away. But that was already a distant matter. His universe was a thing of all-consuming immediacy.

Shooting. Yelling. A few curses in English, meant to provoke. Sieger wanted to shout something valiant, a dare, but his throat was too dry, despite the rain. And his tongue and lips had no part in the game any more.

At last, they came running through the rain. Sloppily. Shouting and firing.

Shooting quickly but carefully, feeling no pain now, Sieger hit three of them before an unseen gunman ripped open his back with a burst of automatic weapons fire.

He had a few instants of life left, and he still saw the approaching figures, but Sieger's hands would not work anymore and he could not even tell if he still held a weapon. Someone else fired into his body, making a holiday of it, jerking him as if kicking him through the mud, and Sieger thought savagely that they were poor soldiers, with no discipline at all. Just scum.

They shot him again and again, and his last disconnected thought was that it was just a fucking shame.

*　　*　　*

WHEN THE AIRCRAFT touched down at Howard
Air Force Base in Panama, medics in hooded over-
garments rushed from an ambulance in the afternoon
rain, lugging a collapsible gurney with a bubblelike su-
perstructure. As they transferred her husband from the
isolation capsule that had been fitted into the fuselage,
Ruth Church got her first good look at him in hours. To
her surprise, his eyes were open. He did not see her,
though. She was too startled to move in closer, and the
medics worked quickly.

Apparently, no one had told them she was on board
and they focused on their work so thoroughly—scared
by the danger of infection, perhaps—that they were
about to drive off, leaving her behind with the doctor
who had flown down with the CINC to look after John.
The doctor had to run through the rain, shouting, to stop
the vehicle.

Ruth and the doctor rode in the back of the ambulance
with John. He was obscured again, this time by a milky
material that looked like bubble packing.

The ambulance howled and wove between the afternoon line of cars leaving the base, Ruth glanced wearily,
absently, at the orderly white buildings with their or-
ange-tiled roofs, a well-tended colonial outpost living on
borrowed time. Panama had been a good place for her
family, although better during the first tour than the second, with proper schools for the children and gypsy
bands of coatimundis migrating through the backyard.
John had worked behind a safe desk, and the greatest
threat had been a boa constrictor coiled around one of
the carport braces. The snake had delighted the children
considerably more than it had pleased her. Panama, with
its intermittent squalor and the silly Officers' Wives
Club. Golden days. Ruth turned away from the fogging
windows and wiped a hand over her wet hair, bending
closer to the doctor. He was a small man, with curly

gray-touched hair gone a bit out of control and designer eyeglass frames. He projected the arrogance of a provincial police chief.

"Am I being a fool?" she asked. "Or does John look better than he did?"

The doctor shook his head. But not in disagreement. His eyebrows tightened and Ruth noted that they wanted a trim.

"Frankly, Mrs. Church, this doesn't even strike me as life-threatening. I don't know what all the fuss is about. The special capsule and so forth. Everyone in the reporting chain seems to have panicked." He sat back as best he could in the crowded space and sighed. "I was diverted from an important field trip, you know."

"You should have seen him yesterday," Ruth told him. "They all thought he was dying, the doctors—"

"That was yesterday," the little doctor said. "And I wasn't there. All I can tell you is that, in my judgment, the lab results are going to show that this man had nothing but a potent case of cholera. Perhaps with a secondary infection of some sort that sent him into a coma. May never know exactly what put him under. But that sort of thing's routine, in my world. Pull 'em through with a couple bags of fluids. No need to overreact like this."

"Doctor—" Ruth was ready to give him a lecture he would never forget, when she saw that he had already forgotten her and had half forgotten her husband.

"I missed a trip to Central Africa for this," he muttered to himself.

LUTHER DARLING HAD feared the jungle because he feared the animals he imagined teeming through its vegetation. But he did not see a single beast. He fought his way through the brush and the sudden, seasonal swamps with any other living creatures cowering under the onslaught of the rain. He did not stop being afraid, but it was more manageable somehow now that he had killed. Killing other men had left him with an unexpected feeling of exhilaration, something nothing in his education had prepared him for, and not even the difficulty of following a compass azimuth through this dismal land could annihilate the thrill.

The vegetation had teeth all its own, and his uniform tore. The cargo pockets snagged, and long bladelike leaves sliced right through the wet, clinging fabric where his uniform had not been reinforced. Eventually, a thorn spiked right through a double-layered knee section, cutting and leaving a fiery itch behind. A vine stole his cap and it disappeared into the deluge and the thrashing swamp grass. Once, as he pushed a branch out of the way, he felt his cheek and it shocked him. He had not known that his flesh had been torn open, and he still did not realize that the lower curl of his ear had been shot away.

He did not think profoundly of family or lovers, nor did he ponder past events or future possibilities. His experience had nothing to do with the books and films he had digested about desperate men. In fact, he did not think at all in the way men who had never experienced true fear imagined such a man must feel. He existed from one brutal moment to the next, exhausted but largely unaware of that, too. As long as he struggled through the bush, his actions and reactions were determined by something deep, and savage, and distinctly unpoetic.

He could not tell if he had been fighting his way through this hellish world for an hour or an afternoon, and after a while, he began to grunt rhythmically to himself, settling into a pattern of movement he had never been taught but that his body understood, as if it had been remembered from long ago. Despite his weariness—a total, consuming thing—he moved more efficiently, relying on the compass less and less. But the language that had disappeared from his lips left his brain as well, returning only in monosyllabic words of hate and primitive desire. At that point, the closest he came to a recognizable human thought was a growing conviction that he was hopelessly lost and his ordeal would never end, that he would never find a way out of the bush. He was thinking something crudely along those lines when he crashed through a wall of fat, rain-flushed leaves and found himself standing at the edge of a paved road.

He walked to the center of it, fell to his knees, and vomited. He was so far removed from the routines of human experience that he did not hear the approaching truck and it almost hit him, old brakes screaming and the empty cargo bed fishtailing. The front fender came to rest the length of a baseball bat from his head.

Darling looked up, useless now, wondering if the faces barely visible up in the driver's cab were those of his enemies.

ETHAN PLYMOUTH COULD not reach anyone by telephone. As the hours passed with no word on the raid's success from Henry Vasquez, the ambassador's apprehension increased, aggravated by his inability to locate anyone who mattered in Bolivia on a Saturday afternoon. For that matter, he could not even locate anyone who didn't matter.

He tried the relevant ministries, but could not even reach a duty officer. They had closed down entirely. When he tried the National Police, he finally got a lieutenant who could only tell him that the general had been called out on a special task up in the altiplano. His secretary finally got an answer at the military airfield down in Santa Cruz where the State-paid contractors coached the *Diablos Rojos*, but the Bolivian on duty claimed to know nothing about the mission in question. Plymouth made a note to himself to tighten the reins on the contractors, who took a significant bite out of his counternarcotics budget without producing any noteworthy successes.

Then there was the issue of that bastard Parnell nosing around down in Mendoza. Running his own show. As if *he* were the ambassador. Plymouth had a mind to go down and take charge of things personally. But he did not like being away from his embassy, and the living conditions down in the Beni and in the Pando were horrid. And Anne might show up—he wanted to be on the spot, if that happened. Read her the riot act. Anyway, as the attaché had belatedly informed him, Parnell intended to fly up to La Paz for a meeting with the Bolivian defense minister on Monday.

None of it had been properly coordinated. The situation was intolerable.

But the critical issue was the lab raid. Couldn't lose sight of that. If that went well, everything else would fall into place. Plymouth had everything set to send the cable announcing the mission's success—he had done the semifinal wordsmithing himself—and he had quietly arranged for his public affairs officer to leak the right information to the international press. Had everything gone according to schedule, it might have hit the Sunday papers up north, almost guaranteeing that it would come to the president's attention. And, if he could get the eradication program going properly, perhaps he could even swing a presidential visit to Bolivia. That would put him a big one-up on Giles Manschette up in Bogotá. It would be the ultimate career accelerator. And the president would come with plenty of deliverables to reward Bolivian counternarcotics cooperation. It could mean a real takeoff for U.S.-Bolivian relations. And a big embassy for him, after a year or so back at the Department.

And some D.C. time would not be so bad just now. He would have to take care of the legal ramifications of Anne's unforgivable tawdriness. Robin would need him closer to hand, too, he decided, although he was not sure why. The last time he had seen his daughter she had

worn a small diamond pierced into a nostril, a lunacy
Plymouth laid to Anne's negligence as a mother.

Plymouth glanced at his watch and found the hour
discouragingly late. They were going to miss the sub-
mission deadlines for the Sunday editions. Henry Vasquez had to get off his fat butt and get on the horn. The
DEA man understood the criticality of timely reporting.
And he was throwing everything out of synch. You just
couldn't rely on those people, no matter how thoroughly
they seemed to have assimilated.

Plymouth had skipped lunch and he reached into a
desk drawer with his bloodstained fingers and drew an
Oreo from a half-empty bag. The Bols couldn't even
make proper cookies, not even with the help of German
bakers. Even the Germans went all to hell here. You had
to import anything worthwhile.

What in the name of God was the problem with Vasquez? Had those military sonsofbitches screwed the
whole business up? What was going on? Had Parnell
somehow gotten his finger into things?

The ambassador bit into the cookie, raining crumbs
on his desk pad and on the thighs of his trousers. He
found his mouth arid, and he rang out to his secretary
for a fresh cup of coffee.

A minute later, the door opened. But it wasn't Donna
with his coffee. The deputy chief of mission entered,
tentatively, followed by the station chief.

"Sir? May we come in for a moment?"

Plymouth grunted, swallowing cookie mush. "Looks
like you're already in. What's the problem?" His voice
was impatient, although nothing truly pressed upon his
time.

The two men approached his desk, faces glum, and
Plymouth thought, Oh, shit. The mission. What's happened now?

"Sir," the DCM said as he stood before the big desk,
"the director of the Bolivian National Police would like
to speak with you."

Plymouth shrugged. He wanted coffee. And to eat another cookie. But his supply was precious and he did not want to have to offer any of the Oreos to the other men.

"Well, I damned well need to talk to him. How soon can we set something up?"

The DCM's face did not change. "Sir, he needs to talk to you right now. He's waiting outside."

Plymouth's heart shriveled. His speech took a moment to find its form, then he said:

"Oh, God. Is it something with the mission? Has something gone wrong?"

The DCM and the station chief looked at each other, and finally, the CIA man stepped forward.

"No, sir. I mean . . . it's not about the drug mission. It's something else."

Plymouth felt a wave of relief. But his heart still raced. And his temper flared.

"What in the name of Christ could be so important that that corrupt bugger's got to come crashing in here on a Saturday afternoon? When he can't even answer his phone?"

The two visitors to the office looked down, or at the walls, or out of the windows. Anywhere but at the ambassador's face. After a terribly long time, during which a cavalcade of fears, one greater than the other, stood up and marched through Plymouth's consciousness, the DCM edged closer to the desk and said:

"It's a personal matter, Mr. Ambassador."

GARZA WANTED TO finish up and get out of the country. Back to Colombia, or at least across the border into Brazil, before von Reinsee and his people realized that they had not been in control of things after all. Before the old turd found out what happened to his daughter. It was time to kill the rest of the fucking gringos and go.

He worried. He was not a worrier by nature, but, so far, nothing had gone quite right. The helicopters had come in late, with their heart-stopping noises, and the rain had made it hard to see, hard to shoot accurately. Some of the gringos made it out of the aircraft. And the damned shoot-out with them took hours. And cost six men, two of whom disappeared into the bush and probably just ran away instead of circling around behind the *yanquis* the way they were supposed to do. They had begun the day with enough bullets to fight a war. Then they had fought one. They could not afford another drawn-out fight like the first. They had to hit the damned clinic, just do it to the fuckers, and get out.

His plan had called for a careful approach through the bush, with the jeeps and the truck hidden several kilometers away. But now the day was dying, and the rain darkened everything prematurely anyway, and it took three times as long to move through the muck and the shit as it should have taken. If you didn't get lost.

But the job had to be done. His bosses did not understand explanations for why a man failed.

Garza decided that the best thing to do was to drive in closer, leaving the vehicles just out of sight, and move fast. With the rain, the gringos would not be able to see much. Until it was too late. And it was not absolutely essential to kill them all. They just had to kill enough of them to make a big smell.

On the top of the bluffs where the town ended, Garza stopped his little convoy and got out in the rain, not liking it much, weary of the miserableness of this country in all its shapes. He went forward to make certain that his vehicles would not be visible from the clinic if they pushed closer. Working his way behind a crumbling shack, he stood in sagging mud atop an embankment and scanned the horizon in the direction where the clinic lay.

Nothing. A gray wall of rain. He could only see the

first line of trees down in the flood plain. Then the world ended.

He was tempted to drive right up on them. Just drive up and get out shooting. But that would be too sloppy. Given the force of the rain, the vehicles might get stuck down in the low ground. And Garza wanted to be able to leave the place quickly.

He returned to his train of jeeps and the tarped-over truck full of gunmen and led the procession part way down the road that descended from the town. They parked in a grove where the bluff formed a little shelf and got out into a deserted world, with all of the town's residents in their houses or shacks or shelters, waiting out the storm.

When the force of the rain hit them again, the men grumbled and cursed. They were a sour bunch now, with friends and partners dead and little to show for the losses. Garza barely trusted half of them.

"Come on. Quick," he said. "We got no time to screw off. Let's go."

He led the way down into the vegetation, heading for the remembered clinic, knowing that all he had to do from this spot was to keep the road on his left and the high ground to his right.

But it was not as easy as he had hoped. As soon as the cluster of men hit the low ground, the going slowed, with the water up to their knees much of the time and once coming up to their waists. The marsh stank and pulled off shoes and even boots, and Garza's confidence in his ability to navigate disintegrated. The rain made it impossible to see twenty meters ahead and the undergrowth repeatedly reduced even that distance. Then one of his men screamed and kept screaming, and Garza turned to see him waving a long thin snake. The serpent had dug its fangs so deeply into his wrist that he could not separate it from his body.

Another man grabbed the snake behind the head and

snapped its neck. But all movement had stopped. The bitten man clutched his wrist and cursed.

Garza waded over to him and looked at the dead, twitching snake where it lay looped over the rushes. He did not recognize its markings. None of the snakes he knew from the cocaine labs in southern Colombia looked quite the same and he could not tell if this one was deadly or relatively harmless.

"Go back to the truck," he told the man.

The man only stared at him. Eyes vast.

"Hey, motherfucker. I said go back to the truck and wait for us."

But the man only looked from side to side. In fear. "Boss, I don't know where the truck is. You can't see shit in this."

"Fuck." But, as Garza looked away, he realized that he did not know where he was going. The marsh had become a closed world. Like that fucking Moses, he thought. Dick around in here for forty years.

"Come on," Garza told his men in his most decisive voice. "This is shit. We'll take the goddamn road. Anybody comes along, just cut their fucking heads off. But no guns. Until we get to the gringos."

It took them half an hour to find their way back to the ribbon of packed mud that passed for a road.

Garza made them move quickly then. It was still a good fifteen-minute walk to the clinic site, and the world turned an ever deeper shade of gray. With the rain hitting them all hard, making even Garza want to take cover.

Filthy shit you got to do, he thought. Living like a fucking animal. And for what?

For money. He knew that very well.

Garza had been a lieutenant in the Colombian army before he realized that the future did not belong to the Bogotá government, and now he made his men space out and move in two long, not quite orderly columns on either side of the road. He walked down the middle.

Hoping no vehicles would happen along. Because that would mean shooting, not knives, and the gunfire would destroy any chance they had of surprising the gringos. But what could you do? When even nature started screwing with you.

After they had almost closed on the clinic site, he raised his hand for his men to stop. Some of them did not understand the signal, but he got them to halt with a subsequent gesture. Then he waved them closer.

"Listen," he said, in a whisper just loud enough to reach their ears above the drumming of the rain, "it's good. It's okay. The fucking gringos are just up ahead, just around the bend. We're going to move fast now. As soon as you see the building and their tents and shit, run straight for them and kill anything that moves. Go right through the place. Through everything. When we come out the other side, we all turn around and go back through again. Fast. Kill anybody left alive. And then we get out of this shit hole. And don't bunch up. Keep some space between your dirty asses, okay?"

But tired, nervous men do not instinctively keep space between themselves. Unless they have been well trained, they bunch up. And as they closed on the clinic, the gunmen clustered together in twos, threes, fours, eighteen men in all. Only Garza kept his distance. Anxious, he led and did not look back.

They saw the clinic's white firmness when they were about forty meters away. One man, nervous, shouted, and they all began to run forward. Firing at the building.

Unexpectedly, the fire was returned. From the front, from the sides. Flashes of silvered gold, with small red ghosts at the core. Piercing the rain. Garza stopped in shock, only to see two of his men crumple in front of him. And there was a barrier of wire.

He turned, and his men were falling everywhere, tumbling crazily, as if hit from several weapons at once. In seconds, a blow knocked him onto his back in the mud and he cursed, with the rain trying to hold him down.

"Shoot back," he screamed as he struggled to rise, slipping on the stewed earth. *"Shoot back, you bastards."*

From one knee, he put a burst into the vegetation where he believed he had seen the brilliance of a muzzle. Then he rose, knowing he had been shot but not knowing where, caring only that he could still move. The pain was still buried under shock.

His men were running. Those who could run. He saw five backs heading down the road they had traveled. One of the men turned to fire behind himself and a burst of gunfire lifted him into the air for an instant, jiggling him like a baby. He dropped in a confusion of limbs, weapon still spitting.

Garza ran, too. Shooting behind himself without looking back, trying to force the ambushers' aim off, to drive their heads down. He ran hard, fighting the mud.

A foreign lethargy passed over him in long waves and made him want to sit down. He could not keep up with the other men; something besides the mud weighted his body, slowing his limbs. He almost called out to them, to ask for help, but he caught himself. If he was going to die, he was not going to die begging like some cunt.

Staggering, running a few steps, then staggering again, Garza watched the last of his men blur into the rain, leaving him behind. They had bunched into a terrified thing with eight legs and waving arms, spitting unaimed bullets.

The human knot came undone. Light pierced the storm in sharp bursts from the side of the road, and the men fell, each death taking its own shape. One man splashed down immediately and heavily, but another blundered on, stripped of his bearings, until a second burst cut away his legs. A small man, little more than a boy, crawled forward, puking blood. Inexplicably, the last of the four sat down slowly, almost gently, one arm dangling by a shred of tissue and the shoulder pumping blood, and he turned his weapon on himself, exploding his brains skyward in a challenge to the rain.

Garza saw it all. Eyes heightened by fear, it was only the task of a second or two to register and understand. The gringos had watched them go by, guns tracking them all the while. It had been a trap, a perfect ambush. Nobody was getting out alive.

Except him. With the explosive energy of fear, Garza bolted sideward, heading into the marsh, abandoning his own useless weapon. He had heard that the gringos would not shoot a man without a weapon.

He was trying to climb the slimed side of an irrigation ditch when a blow, a huge flat thing, smashed him into the mud.

Not a bullet. A man was on top of him. Pounding him, shoving his face down into the mud, making him taste the wet earth.

Garza wanted to fight back. But he had nothing left. He tried to speak, to tell his attacker not to kill him, that he was unarmed. But the man's blows left no air in his lungs.

"Fucking maggot," the human beast on his back cried. The assailant struck a blow into what must have been a wound because the pain was so enormous it wrenched Garza from the grip of the earth and almost let him throw the man off. But the attacker was too big, too heavy. And another blow sent him into unconsciousness.

"STOP IT," A voice said. "It's all right, son. He's not going anywhere."

PFC Cragg looked up. The sight of the gray-haired man with the four wet stars took him by surprise. The amphetamine of combat still pulsed through him and Cragg tightened his grip on his weapon, as if the general were another enemy. Seconds before, he had been smashing the rifle's butt down between his captive's shoulder blades.

"Maggot," Cragg said one last time to his prisoner's bloodstained back. He had spoken without thinking. The world was going by very quickly.

"I want him alive," the general said. "I want to have a little talk with this guy."

"Yes, sir." Cragg remembered himself and saluted, clutching his weapon awkwardly. His hands shook. That surprised him.

The presence of the general was anything but calming. Cragg had only recently deployed to Panama from his Basic Training and Advanced Individual Training at Fort Leonard Wood, and before he could get his feet on the ground, they had sent his platoon down to Bolivia, which seemed to be an even worse pit than the Zone. He had never been close to a general until today. He had not even known who General Parnell was until his squad leader told him. The Commander in Chief. That was confusing, but Cragg was too embarrassed by his ignorance to ask any further questions. He had always thought that the President was the Commander in Chief.

The realization that he had just been in combat swept over PFC Cragg afresh.

Combat.

He was a veteran.

This counted, didn't it?

His impressions tumbled over one another, and he seemed to remember things vividly and hardly to remember them at all. He had hesitated to shoot, unable to fix on a target, then he had shot wildly. He hoped nobody had been keeping tabs on him. Then he had been running after this guy as if his body had a will of its own. Screaming at the top of his lungs. He was still surprised by what he had done.

Combat was kind of like white-water rafting. It all just came rushing toward you. You almost lost it. But somehow you did the right thing. Then the rapids were behind you. Like they never existed. It was weird.

The general smiled and returned his salute. He looked like a general out of the movies and seemed okay. He had made decisions like lightning after the captain showed up with his face all ripped open. Like he'd really been through a war. The general had pitched right in, helping them select their fighting positions and dig them and camouflage them. With the sky raining cats and dogs. The old guy seemed like he really enjoyed it. And he understood fields of fire, almost as sharp as a drill sergeant. Nobody was going to get away by the time they finished setting up the ambush. They had prepared to fight in any direction, although Cragg had heard the general tell one of the officers, "Ten to one they just come right up that road. They won't be organized enough to do anything else in this weather."

"That was a hell of a tackle," the general said, with the rain whacking them both. "You play football in high school, PFC?"

"Yes, sir."

"What position?"

"Halfback. Sir."

"What's your first name, son?"

"Dan." Then, remembering, he quickly added, "Sir."

The general nodded, smile dissolving, as though the rain were washing it away. He didn't look mean, exactly. Only like he couldn't smile for very long.

"Well, Dan," the general said, "you just baby-sit this guy until I can get some medics down here." Then he changed and his face went very dark for a second. "Christ, I'm sorry, soldier. I'm teaching you bad habits. Let's check this joker for weapons."

The general stood in a trough of brown water, pistol trained on the unconscious man as though he really meant business. Cragg patted his prisoner down then rolled him over to check his waistband. The guy was coated with mud, but you could still see that his left shoulder had been ripped to shreds in the front. Sure enough, he had a pistol tucked away. Cragg removed it with a hand that was almost under control. He still felt a wild, almost uncontrollable energy inside.

"Christ," the general said. "Looks like he caught a round with some spin on it."

The wounded man groaned without opening his eyes. But if the general felt a twinge of mercy, Cragg didn't share it. The guy was a maggot. *The enemy.*

"Well, sir," the private lectured the general, "that's what he gets for messing with the Combat Engineers."

ANGEL DESPISED THE men and women who surrounded him in Panama. Listless by day and loud by night, they proved to him the Colombian highlander's article of faith that coastal people, lowlanders, were dirty and without morals. Women who reminded him of diseased monkeys tapped at the door of his room, smiled pointedly, and offered their company. Angel ignored them and waited patiently for the afternoon cloudbursts to wash humanity back inside its cages. At night, he slept badly, with the cramps in his stomach driving him to the bucket in the corner of the room. Sometimes there was blood.

He worried about his sister. He would not see her for a long time now, and he would not see his mother. He had entered a different world and all he could do was to send them money while watching through the eyes of other men to know if they were safe. His long days alone, first in the hothouse and now in this hole, left him time to think. Too much time. He concluded that mankind was a filthy creation, a mistake on the part of God, and that each man was condemned from birth. Sort of the way the priest said it. Less spooky, but uglier in practical ways. The best a man could do was to maintain his honor. Honor was the only possession of value.

At least once a day, he got a visit from a Panamanian in a white shirt cut to be worn out over the trousers to disguise the size of the belly. Gold chains flashing around a damp neck, the Panamanian brought food and rationed Angel's pocket money, as if fearing he would disappear or go on a drunk. It was clear to Angel that the guy had no understanding of men beyond the scope of his own appetites.

The Panamanian had other sorts of knowledge, though. He knew what went on inside the gringo hospital. He knew the exact status of the target, who was regaining his health by the day.

With the morning sun burning, brown children played a game of screams on the courtyard garbage heap. The Panamanian appeared again at the flimsy door. Tapping like one of the whores. The man wore sunglasses even though he stood in the shade and he smelled of syrupy cologne. Sweat bled from his temples.

"Today's the day," he said. "You got to move. They're doing the paperwork to release the mother-fucker."

When Angel didn't answer him, the man continued:

"Get your things. I'll give you a ride to the foot of the hill."

Angel had few possessions and he moved methodically. But he was not quick enough to suit his visitor, who rolled his shoulders like a boxer and paced. This gringo was obviously a very important hit. And the Panamanian had no faith that the business would come off right. He was a weak man, Angel decided, the sort that was easy to kill.

As they went down the railless concrete stairs, the Panamanian's gold chains glinted and he asked Angel:

"How old are you, anyway?"

Angel looked straight ahead, concerned with more important matters than a fat half-breed's worries.

"Old enough to kill anybody who needs killing," he said. And he stroked the pistol hidden under the jacket he had bought in an oriental shop. It had dragons on the back and it was very beautiful. Panama was miserably hot and he had needed something lighter than his leather jacket. To cover the pistol in his waistband. The pistol that was true as the voice of God. A pistol was better than any priest.

The Panamanian barked at a pack of children who had surrounded his car, a green Mercedes with rust eating at the wheel wells. Angel, remembering his own childhood, called the children back. He offered them an opened bag of candies he had brought from his room as he wiped out all traces of his presence.

The bravest kid was a girl like a palm leaf. She edged up toward him and suddenly snatched the bag from Angel's outstretched hand. Then she and her playmates ran off, shrieking in triumph.

"Nothing but scum," the Panamanian said.

"Yeah," Angel said, thinking of the man's entire country.

The Panamanian put Angel's single bag into the trunk amid a litter of plastic oil containers, tools, and dirt-browned tires.

"You remember where you got to go afterwards, right? Get there quick."

Angel nodded. He found the man's nervousness insulting and unworthy.

The interior of the car steamed and the lowered windows barely helped. As they drove, the city air greased over them. The packed buses, so lovely by night, spewed poison from their rumps. With the old Mercedes clanking and burping, the driver headed for the hill with the huge Panamanian flag at the summit. The traffic was so thick that Angel might have made better time walking. But the Panamanian clearly wanted to be able to tell his bosses that he had done everything in his power to guarantee results.

The Panamanian's nervousness spiked as they approached the hillside where the U.S. facilities began, and, just before the plaza where the locals massed to wait for their buses, he pulled over, brushing the curb, and told Angel to get out. As soon as the door closed, the man drove off.

Angel walked calmly uphill, past the brown and black faces of those who could not afford cars of their own. Some of them were dressed neatly, with a scrubbed look, while others had the unclean appearance of his recent neighbors. A young woman with sunglasses and abundant hair falling over a white blouse made him look back, but then he remembered all that he had learned about women and their difficulty, and he walked on, concentrating on the job.

There weren't many gringos. He had heard they were leaving. But the buildings that still belonged to them looked better than anything downtown. Locals in jeans worked on the lawns and shrubbery. The Yankees at least had some pride in themselves, and that was something. Angel considered that he could have been a pretty good gringo, maybe as good as any of them, had he been born up north.

The only problem with the hospital's location was that there was no good excuse for loitering. It was very different from the slutty downtown. Nobody just hung around here. The gringos were always on the move. The best Angel could do was to sit on a bench down the sidewalk from the hospital's main entrance, facing the line of cars parked curbside as if waiting to be picked up. It meant he had to sit with his back to the building.

At least it was a quiet street. He would hear any commotion. And he could beat any emerging party to the spot where the hospital walkway joined the sidewalk. Then there was a good line of escape down between the buildings that would let him put obstacles between himself and any pursuers in a matter of seconds. The Panamanian had assured him that Church would have no special protection, no guards. All in all, it seemed a less dangerous operation than most of the jobs Angel had carried out.

He pulled a paperback from his back pocket. He could

not read it, not even the title, but he had selected it based on the picture of a bare-chested warrior on the cover. The man had tremendous muscles and he wore crossed bandoliers for the machine gun he held at his hip. He looked like a real man. Angel had given serious thought to beginning a bodybuilding program as soon as his business situation permitted, and the cover illustration was exemplary and inspirational.

The book was a tool, an excuse to be sitting on a bench. But just holding it in his hands made Angel feel empowered. Anyone who passed by would think he was a man who read books. He held the book proudly, extended slightly, so that any passerby would be certain to see it.

There were few passersby, and they ignored him. Now and then individuals or small groups left the hospital, but the correct face never appeared. The takeoff of an ambulance startled him. But its howls fled down the hill and turned toward the great bridge over the canal.

The heat gathered around him like a pile of blankets. The coast, the sea, was nothing like the pictures you saw. It was uncomfortable and mean. He sweated in his new jacket, wishing he could take it off. Maybe, he thought, he should have bought one of those shirts like the Panamanian wore. That would have let him hide the pistol. Or maybe not. He was too thin, the pistol would probably show. You had to have a gut.

A blond girl, clearly a gringa, walked down the opposite sidewalk and he could not help looking at her. Her cotton dress was somehow different from those worn by the downtown women and it flowed with her, as if she made her own breeze. Her hair was light and it looked very clean. She reminded Angel of a woman from the movies.

Maybe it would be different with a girl like that, he thought. Maybe they had brains enough to respect a man for the right reasons. He could not help imagining ways to bring her into his life. She strolled down the hill, trailing the beauty of another world, and Angel dreamed of situations in which he might come to her rescue, winning her respect and love.

A heavy door slammed. Behind his back. Angel lowered his book and looked over his shoulder with enforced calm.

It was him. The gringo.

Church walked with the help of a woman Angel recognized from the photographs as the gringo's wife. Then there was a man in uniform on the far side, but he did not look like he had a weapon. Not a bodyguard. Church smiled and seemed to be insisting that he was capable of walking without assistance. But he wobbled on the short flight of steps and the others gripped his arms.

This was going to be easy.

Angel calmly stuffed the paperback into a back pocket and stood up, stretching as though his back had begun to hurt him. Timing his movements carefully, he began to stroll up toward the intersection of walkway and pavement.

The Americans did not even notice him. All of their attention focused on helping Church walk toward the line of parked cars.

Angel felt the pistol hard against his body. But it was too early to draw it. That had to happen very quickly, in close.

He put one foot in front of the other, pausing once to glance back down the hill, as if watching for a bus or a car. Making the timing work perfectly.

Seconds. Just seconds.

Church tried to shake off his helpers. With an exasperated smile. For a moment, Angel looked into the man's eyes, but Church chose to disregard him.

Yes, Angel thought. That's right. Just like that.

In the end, he quickened his pace toward the trio, drawing his pistol with one perfect motion and raising the barrel.

The woman saw him. And she was quick. Quicker

than any man would have been. Wordlessly, she thrust herself in front of her husband.

Angel didn't have a clear shot. He hesitated for a sliver of a second, a man of honor to the last, ever reluctant to shoot a woman. Before he could overcome that reluctance, a Special Forces sniper positioned on the roof of a neighboring building shot him in the head.

AN ACCURATELY DRESSED old man cantered along a tree line on a horse the color of bitter chocolate. His days and nights had become matters of even stricter routine than they had been in the past, and he occupied himself as fully as he could with work or physical activity. He kept no woman now, although he occasionally thought of the last one, a fine Polish girl whom he had hastened to send away, and he had even discarded his beloved hobby of listening to music. The music brought memories, or tricked him into thinking about things he could not bear to ponder. There was nothing left that mattered to him now, with his daughter dead and his nephew disappeared and probably dead as well.

He had gambled and lost.

Business, on the other hand, was going well. He had mended his fences with the Colombians, gaining advantageous terms, and he was still dealing discreetly and effectively with his newer partners from São Paulo. There was, in the end, wealth enough for all, given the world's remarkable appetite for the fruit of the coca plant. They were even exporting to Russia, which amused him as well as promising profits that increased with that country's hopelessness. That was the marvelous thing about narcotics. Depressions, crises, disasters only increased humanity's appetite for escape.

The horse clopped along the familiar route, a bit awkward on the damp soil, too well-bred for an imperfect world. The rains had ceased, but the earth had yet to dry. Then the long southern summer would slowly turn the mud to dust, and the cycle would begin again.

How many more of these cycles would he have to endure?

The tree line turned sharply and the old man turned with it. They were approaching an exposed trail that dried faster than the rest, and there would be an opportunity to gallop, to push the animal, to test it. And himself. The first edge of the sun chipped the perfection of the horizon.

Before von Reinsee could spur his horse into a run, a figure stepped from the trees.

It was his nephew. Unshaven. And holding an automatic weapon. Looking like a thug from the gutter.

Von Reinsee reigned in his horse and the animal reared a little, full of spirit.

"For God's sake, Rafael. Where have you been? I thought we'd lost you."

Face dead, his nephew stepped closer and raised the weapon.

"You killed her," he half spoke, half shouted. His facial muscles were dead, but his eyes were mad. "You had her killed, Uncle Christian. Didn't you?"

Von Reinsee did not understand.

"Rafael. Stop it. I don't know what on earth you're talking about. I'm just glad you're back."

The horse would not settle. It sensed danger.

"You killed her," the dead face said. The mad eyes began to trickle.

With a shock, von Reinsee decided he knew what his nephew was talking about.

"Lord, Rafael. You think *I* had my own daughter killed? Eva?"

The younger man fired. But he only aimed at the horse, at its head and neck. The magnificent animal jerked, climbed the air, and the far side of its skull split. It twisted and fell, taking the old man down with it. His thighbone snapped like a crust as the big animal landed on top of it.

Von Reinsee gasped and a sound like a growl pained from his throat. He had fallen hard and his shoulder blade had broken as well, although he did not realize it.

His nephew stepped in close, standing over him as though he were going to urinate on him. But his hands kept their grip on the automatic weapon as he waited for the older man to regain a sense of things.

"Why?" von Reinsee said at last. "*Why*, Rafael?" He did not understand any of this. The death of a fine horse. The smaller death of his leg, and the requirement to master the shock and pain, to not let his guard down in front of anyone.

"You killed her," the younger man repeated, with conviction now. And he emptied the weapon's magazine into his uncle.

The old man was tough, and his nephew was more accustomed to mobile phones than to handling guns. He did not control the weapon and only three of the bullets, the first three, found their target. They entered the abdomen a bit below the heart. The wounding was mortal, but the old man lived long enough to anguish over what had just happened. Tasting his own blood, he whispered:

"*Family.*"

EPILOGUE

"**BUT I** *NEVER* get less than a B," the young woman pleaded.

John Church looked at her with more sympathy than he could allow himself to reveal. She was the sort of earnest undergraduate for whom ideas were brittle things to be memorized and whose hair would never quite obey her. She sat in his office in the April light and looked for all the world like a subject from Vermeer. *A Woman Weighing Her Grade Point Average.*

"When you do B-level work," Church said, "I'll be delighted to give you a B."

"I usually get As."

"When you do A work, I'll be even happier to give you an A."

She looked at him with a face preparing to weep over the dead. "But what's *wrong* with my paper?"

With all the passion of a lonely undergraduate, she had written two and one-half double-spaced pages on "The Plight of Women in Peru," and he had written almost as much in red in his critique. She had done no research and had not even proofread her effort before turning it in.

Even so, had he been charged to grade on intentions, Church might have given her an A-plus. The young woman sitting before him in the wash of lemon light wanted to redeem a world she had not yet experienced, and her longing to make distant things vaguely better burned the air between them. But his task now was to teach as much as his students could absorb while exposing them to at least a hint of reality. His employer was a small, cash-strapped college drowsing in Ohio, its undergraduates the sort of young men and women who had not bothered to apply to better schools. They would work out their lives close to home, pay their taxes, and make their communities go.

"First of all," Church began, "you cite only one source. And that's a television report. Remember when we talked about sources in class?" He looked at the young woman and saw that she was thinking ahead and not really listening. But he pressed on with his duty. "You haven't substantiated any of the claims you make. Nor have you developed the logic of your argument." He leaned forward, wanting her to learn to pay attention. "What I see in your paper is a great deal of honorable but uninformed emotion. And . . . to be honest, Miss MacKinnon . . . you need to work hard on your grammar."

"But I used Spellcheck."

Church opened his mouth, then chose not to respond. He wondered what sort of grading systems the other faculty members used. He had already eased his standards considerably to avoid failing those students who at least came to class and did what they were told.

Mistaking his silence for weakness, the student pressed on:

"*And* I turned the assignment in on time."

Church nodded in agreement. "That's one of the reasons you didn't get a D."

He had thought her on the edge of tears, but now she grew sullen.

"You just don't understand," she told him.

She looked plain and sad and beautifully human, with her fingers curled upward on the paper in her lap, an unconscious supplication.

"What is it that I don't understand?" Church asked in a patient voice he might have used back in Bolivia.

The student chased a strand of colorless hair from the corner of an eye. "As a male, you can't, like, understand how women are all suffering in Latin America. What all they go through and stuff." She looked at him fiercely. *"You're not qualified."*

But Church could see that she instantly regretted the tone she had taken. Her militancy was a tentative, fragile thing with which she remained uncomfortable, something about which she had read in a magazine or that had been espoused by a friend. She looked as though she expected to be punished now.

Sitting in the comfort of his homeland, where his family thrived and all things seemed so simple, John Church almost launched into a story. About flesh-and-blood suffering and a woman doctor, about good intentions and needless deaths and ambassadors who performed so badly they could only be promoted. About child assassins, election years, and a backwater clinic that had been finished only to be abandoned for lack of operating funds. And about the relentless splendor of the world.

But he said nothing. He did not want to become one of those fogeys who annihilate the interest of the young with their reminiscences. And there were, of course, things you could not get into words. In the end, he simply took a moment to look out of his window at the freshening lawn and its constant ballet of squirrels.

"By the time we're qualified," he told the young woman, "it's too late. In the meantime, that's still a C paper."

AUTHOR'S NOTE

THIS IS A SUSPENSE novel. Such novels need villains. One of the villains in this book is a Drug Enforcement Agency (DEA) agent. Following my experiences in the Andean Ridge, I later had the privilege of working with DEA agents within U.S. borders. Those agents were uniformly dedicated and quietly heroic, and I admire their skills as I do their courage. On its home turf, the DEA is an expert and indispensible agency, executing a difficult mission in very difficult times. I owe the men and women of that agency a book with a DEA hero.